Gone with the Win

GONE WITH THE WIN

A Bed-and-Breakfast Mystery

Mary Daheim

WILLIAM MORROW
An Imprint of HarperCollins*Publishers*

GONE WITH THE WIN. Copyright © 2013 by Mary Daheim. All rights reserved. Printed in the United States of America. No part of this book may be used or reproduced in any manner whatsoever without written permission except in the case of brief quotations embodied in critical articles and reviews. For information address HarperCollins Publishers, 10 East 53rd Street, New York, NY 10022.

HarperCollins books may be purchased for educational, business, or sales promotional use. For information please write: Special Markets Department, HarperCollins Publishers, 10 East 53rd Street, New York, NY 10022.

FIRST EDITION

Designed by Dana Mendelson

Library of Congress Cataloging-in-Publication Data has been applied for.

ISBN 978-0-06-208984-7

13 14 15 16 17   OV/RRD   10 9 8 7 6 5 4 3 2 1

Author's Note

The story takes place in November 2005.

Gone with the Win

Chapter 1

Judith McMonigle Flynn pulled her aging Subaru into the driveway, smiled at the sight of her husband's classic MG, and glanced up at the squirrel on the garage roof. "Ha ha," she said out loud, "you can't get me. No scampering around inside the walls, no taunting the resident cat, no digging up my flower beds will faze me. I'm a liberated B&B innkeeper, free of outside interferences. I'm focusing on my family and my livelihood. And no more sleuthing for me! The only dead body I'm interested in will be yours if you steal any more of my tulip bulbs. Take that, my furry little fiend!"

She got out of the car and started unloading her Falstaff Market grocery bags. The first day of November was off to a good start in every way. Not even the garden's unfinished cleanup of fallen leaves, drooping dahlias, and faded chrysanthemums made her feel guilty. After saying good-bye to her Monday-night guests at Hillside Manor, she'd gone to St. Bruno's noon All Saints' Day Mass at the bottom of Heraldsgate Hill and then back up to the business district to restock the larder. Best of all, Judith had heard from her son, Mike, about his new posting with the U.S. Forest Service. Instead of being transferred to some far-flung outpost in Alaska or Florida, he and his wife and two sons would be at nearby Mount Tahoma, less than two hours away.

"Hold it!" Joe Flynn called from the back porch steps. "You shouldn't do that!"

Judith smiled at her husband. "These bags aren't heavy except for . . ." She stopped, realizing that Joe wasn't talking to her, but to Gertrude Grover, who was racing her wheelchair after Sweetums the cat.

"Brakes!" Joe yelled at his mother-in-law. "Whoa . . . !"

Gertrude slammed into the birdbath and let out a yelp. Joe rushed across the yard. Judith set the three grocery bags on the edge of the driveway and hurried to see if her mother was seriously injured. Sweetums arched his yellow-and-white furry body before stalking off toward the Rankerses' enormous hedge.

The old lady had landed facedown in the birdbath. Joe grabbed the back of her heavy cardigan and tugged. Gertrude lifted her head and turned this way and that, sputtering a bit. "I can't see!" she cried. "I'm blind!"

Judith put a hand to her breast. "I'll call 911," she said to Joe in a strangled voice, and hurried to where she'd left her purse by the groceries. Her fingers seemed to have a will of their own as she watched Joe trying to get Gertrude into a comfortable position in the wheelchair.

"Now what?" the 911 operator said in a too-familiar voice. "You got another stiff?"

"No!" Judith shouted. "It's my mother. She's had an accident."

"Okay," the voice said in a jaded tone. "Hang on, the EMTs are nearby." The fire station was only a few blocks from Hillside Manor. "Is Mrs. Grover still alive?"

"Uh . . ." Judith saw her mother take a swing at Joe. "Yes. But she can't see. Maybe she has a concussion."

"Any broken bones?"

Gertrude kicked Joe in the shins. "No," Judith said, "unless it's her ribs. She may've punctured a lung."

Just as the first sirens sounded in the distance, Gertrude got her motorized wheelchair in gear, shook her fist at Joe, and began cussing. "Move it, noodlehead," she shouted. "I'll bet you tampered with my brakes, you no-good excuse for a son-in-law!"

"I never . . ." Joe yelled back, but stopped when he heard a crunching sound. "You just ran over your glasses, you crazy old bat!"

Judith winced. "Maybe," she said into the phone, "you should tell the EMTs not to . . ." She paused, realizing they were already pulling into the cul-de-sac. "Never mind. I'll ring off now. Thanks."

Gertrude was sailing up the ramp into the converted toolshed that served as her apartment.

"Dammit," Joe said under his breath, going past Judith to meet the emergency crew, "I'll bet your ghastly mother did that on purpose!"

"I still want her checked out," Judith called over her shoulder. "Don't be so mean!"

Gertrude was already arranging herself at the card table. "Well?" she said to Judith. "Get my spare pair of glasses so I can see the jumble puzzle in the newspaper."

"Wait," Judith cautioned. "Here come the medics."

"The . . ." Gertrude peered at the two men who were entering into the toolshed. "Hey, I didn't invite you! If you expect refreshments, forget it!"

For once, Judith didn't recognize the male and female EMTs. "Hi," she said feebly, edging toward the door. "It's kind of cramped in here. I'll get out of your way. My mother crashed her wheelchair into the birdbath. She may have broken ribs or a concussion."

"Concussion?" Gertrude rasped, gesturing at Judith. "That one must've had a concussion when she married Lunkhead."

The medics chuckled obligingly. "Let's check you out first, ma'am," the fair-haired young man said. "We'll start with your name, okay?"

"It's Joan Crawford," Gertrude replied. "But don't call me

Mommy Dearest. My dim-bulb daughter's still trying to learn to spell before she can write the book."

Judith escaped without enduring any more insults from Gertrude. To her dismay, Cousin Renie was rushing up to Joe. "Now what?" she yelled. "If you've got another corpse, I won't give you any geoducks!"

"Calm down," Joe said in his mellow voice. "The old bat crashed her wheelchair. The good news is that she doesn't seem to be hurt. The bad news is that she doesn't seem—"

"Skip it," Renie snapped. "You want the geoducks or what?"

"No, we don't want them," Joe declared. "They're the only clam that's like eating an inner tube. Where did you get geoducks?"

"Auntie Vance and Uncle Vince brought them down from the island," Renie replied. "You think Bill and I will eat them? They're gruesome. How about the EMTs?"

Judith shook her head. "If they do, we'll have to call more EMTs."

Renie scowled. "Who do I hate this week?"

"How about some of your graphic design clients?" Joe suggested.

Renie wrinkled her pug nose. "I don't hate them. They pay the bills. Besides, they're too dumb to know a geoduck from Daffy Duck. Damn!" She glanced at her watch. "It's garbage pickup day. If I hurry, maybe I can dump the vile stuff in the can. Give Aunt Gert my love. See you." She practically ran down the driveway.

Joe leaned to one side to peer after Renie. "No cops? No firefighters? How come your mother doesn't rate the rest of the emergency crew? Could it be that they're tired of coming here?"

Judith glared at her husband. "Could it be now that you've finished your independent investigation of the city's police department, somebody put a skull and crossbones by our address?"

"Hardly," Joe said. "Woody Price wouldn't let that happen. My old pal's our precinct captain now, in case you've forgotten."

"I have not. In fact, I was thinking about asking them to dinner this weekend. We haven't seen Woody and Sondra socially for months. Maybe I should tell Renie to save those geoducks and we'll invite the mayor separately. Has he seen your report yet? If he criticizes you for the lapses you uncovered in the ranks, I'll make him eat geoduck fritters for his dinner. The smell alone would knock him out."

"Good idea," Joe murmured. "About Woody and Sondra, that is."

"I'll call Sondra this afternoon," Judith said, casting a worried glance at the toolshed. "What's taking the EMTs so long? Do you suppose Mother did break something?"

"Like what? The medics' spirits?" Joe picked up the groceries. "You work it out. I'm putting this stuff away before the ice cream melts." He started picking up the bags while Judith trudged back to the toolshed.

"Okay," Gertrude was saying to the EMTs as she sorted out a hand of cards. "You're in, Emily. Your bid, Jake. I usually start at two-fifty in three-handed pinochle. Have we got three quarters in the pot?"

Shaking her head, Judith retreated into the backyard.

Just before two-thirty, the EMTs apparently had another call. They had already reported to Joe that Mrs. Grover was in excellent shape for her age and that she was now four dollars and fifty cents richer after waxing them at pinochle. Judith listened to her husband's news with gritted teeth. "Did they also find her charming company?" she inquired.

"Yes," Joe replied with a stony face. "Do you think she actually has a split personality?"

"No," Judith said sadly. "But she's canny. She knows how to behave when she has to and she knows how to drive us nuts. The Rankerses like spending time with her." She gave a start. "Where *are* the Rankerses? They didn't show up when the EMTs arrived."

Joe glanced out through the window above the kitchen sink.

"They're home now. Oh, Carl told me this morning they were going to a parish school event for one of their grandkids."

"Just as well they missed Mother's crash," Judith said, taking frozen puff pastry sheets from the fridge. "Hey—I didn't call Sondra yet. Would you call Woody instead? He'll know more about his work schedule than she will. I'm a veteran cop wife. We're always the last to know."

"Sure. I'll go up to my office to do that," Joe said, heading down the hallway to the back stairs.

Judith checked her guest register. Four of the six rooms were full—not too bad for the first week in November. The Sutcliffes from Houston, the Epsteins from Los Angeles, the Porcinis from Basking Ridge, New Jersey—Judith hoped she didn't call them the Porcines—and a Mary Smith from New York City. Renie had teased her about taking a reservation from anyone named Mary Smith, especially one living in a heavily populated area. Judith had laughed. Surely there really were dozens of Mary Smiths in the New York area.

Arlene Rankers showed up via the back door shortly after four. "New neighbors," she announced. "Our Cathy finally sold the house on the corner. The family moving in is originally from India. Or Indiana. Or maybe Indianapolis. Or maybe all three."

"That's . . . good," Judith said, opening a container of shrimp for the pastry puffs she was making for her guests' social hour. "Children?"

"Only the younger ones," Arlene replied, admiring the plump pink shrimp. "The parents are adults."

Judith never knew when her neighbor was joking. "How soon are they moving in?"

"Immediately," Arlene replied, still ogling the shrimp. "They wanted to be settled by today, but the closing was held up over the weekend. Their last name is Bhatt. With an *h*. Carl and I are going to take them a welcome basket. I wonder if the other neighbors would like to join us."

"Count me in," Judith said. "I bet the Steins, the Porters, the

Ericsons, and the Dooleys will contribute, too. I don't know about Herself's current occupants. They're standoffish," she added, referring to the house owned by Joe's first wife. Vivian rented the property while spending most of her time basking and boozing in the Florida sun.

"*Very* standoffish," Arlene agreed. "I've hardly talked to them. Frosch is their last name. He's Herbert and she's Elma. One son—Brick—who lives in Idaho. Herbert works for the Boring Aerospace Company. Elma is a cook at one of the public schools over by Teal Lake. They're car-racing fans and she shops at Target and GutBusters. I don't think they always pay their bills on time. Elma had gallbladder surgery last month. They're a complete mystery to me."

As ever, Judith was astonished by how much her neighbor knew about people she didn't know. ABS—better known as Arlene's Broadcasting System—was ever efficient. "Have you been looking at their mail?" she asked with a sly glance.

Arlene gasped. "What a naughty idea! But you know how Newton gets things confused in the cul-de-sac since he took over our route."

That much was true, as Judith had learned from frustrating experience. "Come to think of it, I did get the Steins' *Smithsonian* magazine last week. Joe read three articles before he took it over to their house. Oh—and the Porters' light bill."

"Newton has poor eyesight," Arlene remarked. "I must go home and fix those geoducks Serena left. Very generous of your cousin. I wish Carl didn't loathe them so much." She started for the back door, but stopped. "How much was it?"

"What?" Judith asked.

Arlene frowned. "The Porters' light bill, of course."

"I don't know. I didn't open it."

"Didn't you want to compare? I always do."

Judith shrugged. "I know ours is high. The guests, of course."

"Of course." Arlene left.

Twenty minutes later the first guests arrived. Alan and Deirdre

Sutcliffe might be from Houston, but they weren't wearing cowboy hats and boots. In fact, they were bundled up like Eskimos.

"When will the snow start?" Alan asked, struggling with the hood on his fur-lined parka.

"I've no idea," Judith replied. "Some years we don't get snow."

Deirdre's green eyes widened in shock. "But how do you have the dogsled races?"

"We don't have dogsleds," Judith said. "Maybe you're thinking of Alaska. Are you heading that way from here?"

The Sutcliffes exchanged glances. "We could," Alan said. "Would we get back in time for dinner tomorrow if we left early in the morning? We've got a reservation someplace downtown."

"Ah . . . no." Judith kept a straight face. The newcomers weren't her first geography-challenged guests. Recently at least two couples had insisted they could visit the White House between breakfast and lunch. A pair of retired schoolteachers had wondered why they hadn't gone through customs since they were now in Canada. "Even Ketchikan in southeastern Alaska is almost seven hundred air miles from here," Judith said.

"Oh my!" Deirdre exclaimed. "Are you sure? It looks so close on our globe in the study."

Judith refrained from suggesting they buy a bigger globe. Calling upon her well-honed tact, she further enlightened the visitors with the usual brochures, maps, and other local information including the five-day weather forecast. By the time the Sutcliffes headed for Room Three, they had gotten over being upset because they'd forgotten their earmuffs.

The Epsteins had no illusions, being from the West Coast and having once lived in the city during their college days. The Porcinis didn't arrive until almost six, due to an unexpected layover in Minneapolis. Judith was setting out the hors d'oeuvres on the living room buffet when she realized that Mary Smith hadn't yet arrived. Apparently she hadn't flown out of Newark as the Porcinis had done, but had left New York via JFK. Late arrivals were not unusual, especially via plane—or train for that matter.

Judith dished up beef stew and dumplings to take out to Gertrude, who preferred her "supper" at five, but waited until the guests had dispersed. It was usually after six-thirty before the Flynns sat down to eat, but it gave them time for a cocktail. As Judith entered the toolshed, she was prepared for her mother's habitual complaints about the tardy arrival of her meal. Surprisingly, the old lady was all smiles.

"Arlene stopped in," Gertrude said. "She knows how to treat an old lady. We sure had fun while you were gone to Little Bulgaria."

"Little Bavaria," Judith murmured, setting Gertrude's tray on the card table.

"Bavaria, Bulgaria, Bulimia—those foreign countries are all the same to me." Gertrude stared at her plate. "What are those white things? Golf balls? Where's the meat? Is that a carrot or did you whack off one of your fingers?"

"It's beef stew and dumplings," Judith said wearily. "One of your favorites. I suppose Arlene makes it better than I do."

Gertrude stabbed at a dumpling. "Hunh. Not as tough as it looks. But then neither are you."

"You, however, are," Judith declared, sitting on the arm of the sofa. "Are you sure you don't have any aches and pains from your crash?"

Her mother shrugged. "No more than I usually have, which is plenty. But unlike you, I still have my own hips."

"You're lucky," Judith said, smiling. "Renie and I didn't get such sturdy original parts like you and Aunt Deb. She has to be careful with her virtual shoulder replacement, just like I do with my hip."

"You and Serena got shortchanged in the smarts department, too," Gertrude said before taking a big bite of beef. "Mmm. Not bad."

Judith stood up and leaned down to kiss her mother's wrinkled cheek. "I'm smart enough to make good stew."

Gertrude patted her daughter's hand. "You are at that. Dumplings are fluffy, too. Gravy's not bad. And those *are* carrots after all. Hey—I found a spud!"

"Go for it," Judith said. "Oh—I forgot the banana cream pie. And no, I didn't make it. I bought it at Falstaff's. On special."

Gertrude shot her daughter a flinty look. "Even so, I'll bet you paid more than two ninety-nine for it."

Judith was at the door. "A bit. It *is* the twenty-first century."

The old lady looked surprised. "It is? When did that happen?"

"When you weren't looking," Judith said. She blew her mother a kiss and went back to the house.

No Mary Smith yet?" Judith asked Joe, who was making their drinks on the kitchen counter.

"Mary Smith?" Joe frowned. "Oh—the missing guest? Not unless she sneaked in while I was still upstairs. Everybody else is yukking it up in the living room. What's with the snowshoes in the entry hall?"

Judith sighed. "Probably the Texans who thought this was Alaska. They must have brought them in from the front porch. I missed those."

Joe chuckled. "Why don't you send your guests a map before they come here? While you were out of town, a couple of honeymooners from Wichita wondered why Japan looked so close. They thought we were on the ocean, not the Sound."

"A lot of people confuse the Sound and the ocean," Judith said, accepting her Scotch from Joe. "Why don't we take our drinks into the front parlor. That way I'll be closer to the door when Ms. Smith arrives."

The Flynns went through the dining room, into the entry hall, and passed the living room, where they could hear the guests visiting amicably. Before going into the parlor, Judith glanced through the front door's peephole, but there was no sign of a car or taxi in front of Hillside Manor. Joe asked if she wanted him to build a fire, but she said no. They wouldn't have time to enjoy it before dinner. Later, they'd adjourn to the vacated living room.

The domestic exchange between husband and wife centered on Mike's new posting. "They'll be able to come for Thanksgiving," Judith said with a big smile. "And Christmas, too."

Joe frowned. "I thought Kristin and Renie were having some kind of disagreement. As in wanting to knock out each other's lights."

"Oh, they'll get over it," Judith said with her usual optimism. "Renie doesn't think Kristin shows me enough respect. You know our daughter-in-law likes to deliver a lecture now and then."

"She shouldn't deliver it to you," Joe declared. "How did I miss it?"

"It was a year ago," Judith said, her smile fading. "It didn't bother me, but somehow it annoyed Renie, who told her if she ever did it again, she'd . . . react more strongly."

"Not physically, I hope. Kristin's built like an Amazon. Renie's a squirt. She wouldn't stand a chance."

"But she's cunning," Judith pointed out. "Anyway, Kristin stated that she'd never attend any event under the same roof with Renie."

Joe took a deep drink and gazed at the ceiling. "Great. How are you going to sort out that one?"

"I'm sure it's already blown over," Judith said. "No doubt they've both forgotten about it."

"Are you nuts? Neither of those women would forget something like that. Dammit, Jude-girl, you've got your head in the sand—again. Do you want me to intervene?"

"No! I'll handle it," Judith asserted. "Yes, Kristin can be overbearing and Renie is feisty, but they're adults."

"Adult warriors—the worst kind. Oh," he said suddenly, "I talked to Woody. He and Sondra can come for dinner Friday."

"Great," Judith said. "Maybe I'll ask Renie and Bill, too. They like the Prices." She cocked an ear in the direction of the entry hall. "Some of the guests are leaving. I think the first two are the Porcinis."

A comfortable silence fell between Judith and Joe as they shared the parlor's cushioned window seat. Raindrops tapped at the glass behind them, a gentle reminder that autumn was well entrenched.

"You know," Judith said at last, putting her hand on Joe's shoulder, "there was a time when I never dreamed we'd spend our lives together. All those wasted years with Dan and Vivian. But Fate was kind. Maybe that long dry spell made what we have now even better."

Joe stared at her face, the gold flecks dancing in his green eyes. " 'Dry' isn't the right word, given that both our exes drank so much."

"Sad, but true," Judith agreed. "If Herself hadn't gotten you drunk and hijacked you to Vegas to get married, I wouldn't have been left at the altar with your baby on the way. I do owe Dan a debt of gratitude for taking on Mike and me."

"Dumbest thing I ever did," Joe murmured. "At least I got Caitlin out of that mess," he added, referring to his daughter by his first wife.

Judith smiled. "I've been thinking about how happy I am. It's such a relief to have Ingrid Heffelman off my back since I helped her in Little Bavaria. She doesn't have to worry anymore about me besmirching her precious state B&B association's reputation with my penchant for finding dead bodies. I'm getting too old to risk my neck tracking down killers. I just wish I could figure out a way to make my so-called admirers take down their site about my alleged adventures. I hate it when people get mixed up and think the acronym for Female Amateur Sleuth Tracking Offenders isn't FASTO, but FATSO."

Joe grinned at Judith. "You're too sensitive about gaining weight. With your height, you could put on ten, even fifteen pounds and I probably wouldn't notice. As for the dangers involved in your years of sleuthing, you can't say I never warned you along the way."

"I know." Judith lowered her gaze. "It isn't as if I went around looking for trouble." She paused, hearing the other two couples leave. "I suppose we should head for the kitchen. I'll have to reheat the stew."

"What's the rush?" Joe asked, his hand caressing Judith's thigh. "We're alone at last. Why not do something else?"

Judith put her arms around Joe. "Why not? We haven't been impulsive for at least two weeks."

"That's too long," he said softly, his face almost touching hers.

"Hmm," Judith murmured—just as the doorbell chimed.

"Damn!" Joe cried. "Did one of the guests forget their key?"

Judith edged away from her husband. "I'll get it. It might be the tardy Mary Smith."

Joe pulled Judith back on the window seat. "Stay put. I know how to check in a guest. I'll interrogate her and send her to her room. Then we can take up where we left off."

Glimpsing the gold flecks in what Judith called his magic eyes, she shrugged. "Why not? I'll stay out of sight."

Settling back against the cushions, she heard Joe greet the newcomer. It was a woman, undoubtedly Mary Smith. Idly, Judith wondered if the stew had dried up. If necessary, she'd make fresh dumplings. Maybe she should have let Joe start a fire after all. That would make the parlor even more cozy and romantic. This would be a perfect ending to a very good day. Except, of course, for Gertrude's collision with the birdbath. But even that, Judith consoled herself, was only a minor irritation.

Her reverie was interrupted by the exchange in the entry hall. Joe's mellow tone had sharpened; the woman sounded angry.

"So what?" she said. "I've got my ID. What more do you need?"

Judith recognized the voice, but couldn't quite place it.

"How about a credit card?" Joe said, obviously irked. "You didn't give one on this reservation."

"That's because I'm paying cash," the woman said.

Judith leaned closer, hearing what sounded like rummaging.

"Here," the newcomer said. "Two hundred bucks. Does that cover it? Or do you want to call the cops?"

"I *am* a cop," Joe said a bit wearily. "Retired. Okay. Fine. But most people don't use an alias."

"I had to," the woman replied, sounding petulant. "I was afraid Judith wouldn't want to see me again after Little Bavaria. Fact is, I wouldn't blame her."

Judith got off the window seat and hurried out of the parlor. "Ruby Tooms," she said, offering her hand. "I had no idea it was you!"

Sheepishly, Ruby took her hostess's hand. "Like I told Mr. Flynn, I figured you might not want to run into me. But I have to talk to you." She brushed back a strand of pale blond hair and grimaced. "I need your help. I want you to find my mother's killer."

Chapter 2

Judith knew Joe was staring at her and not at Ruby. "Excuse me," he said, keeping his voice level and low. "Am I missing something here?"

"Not really," Judith replied, avoiding her husband's gaze. "But I should speak to Ruby privately. Do you mind? Dinner's on the stove."

"Hey," Ruby said, "if Mr. Flynn's a cop, why can't he listen in?"

"*Retired* cop," Joe repeated. "Mrs. Flynn's retired, too. From sleuthing, that is." He grabbed Judith's arm. "Isn't that right, my darling?"

"Yes," Judith replied with a lift of her chin. "That's true. But the least we can do—both having had experience with homicides—is hear her story. Then we can advise her how to proceed. She has, after all, paid two hundred bucks for the privilege, which is more than her room costs. Unless you'd rather make change or refund the money."

Joe frowned. "Okay, come into the kitchen," he said to Ruby. "You've paid for dinner, too. That includes a drink, if you want one."

"I sure do," Ruby said. "I took the bus from Little Bavaria. It stopped at every little dumpy place along the way. That highway through the mountains is a bitch. There was a big wreck, so we had to wait until the mess was cleared off the road. It was raining like hell until we got close to the city. Make mine Scotch rocks—just like your wife's."

Joe glanced at Judith. "Sounds like you do know her."

"We met when Ruby was working two jobs as a waitress and bartender during Oktoberfest. It turned out that her father used to patronize Dan's café—or at least the bar."

Joe looked askance. "Anybody who hung out at The Meat & Mingle must have an interesting résumé—or should I say 'police record'?" Seeing Judith's dark eyes snap, he shrugged and led the way toward the kitchen. "You two sit and talk," he said, opening the swinging half doors leading from the dining room. "I know my way around a stove."

Ruby sat down across from Judith. "Have all your husbands been able to cook?"

"I've only had two," Judith replied. "Dan's cooking was a vocation. Joe's is an avocation."

"Dan," Ruby echoed. "He owned The Meat & Mingle, right?" She saw Judith nod. "Big guy? *Really* big guy?"

"Yes," Judith said. "I thought you told me you were too young to go into the bar to haul out your father."

"I was. I had to go into the restaurant part. I saw Dan—I guessed he was Dan—behind the serving area giving orders."

As Joe handed Ruby her drink and topped off his wife's, a flood of bittersweet memories rushed over Judith. To Dan's credit, he had been a good cook and a fine bartender. But he'd had no head for business, letting his employees rob him blind. Misplaced loyalty, Judith had called it at the time. Later, after The Meat & Mingle had gone broke, she called it something else.

Ruby raised her glass. "To the bad old days," she said.

They clinked glasses. "Although I've quit sleuthing," Judith began, "and Joe's retired from the police force, he does some private investigating." Seeing a sharp glance of reproach from her husband, she quickly backtracked. "He doesn't handle homicide cases, but he could recommend investigators who do."

Ruby didn't look overly upset. Judith suspected that she was used to rejection and disappointment. Though probably far from forty, the Little Bavaria waitress and barmaid seemed to have spent twice that many years in the school of hard knocks.

"Okay." Ruby shrugged her narrow shoulders. "I'll give you the short version. Not long after Dad got fingered for stealing your wallet in the bar, Mom divorced him. He didn't do time for that caper, but a year or so later—I was still in high school—he held up a convenience store. No gun—he had a knife, but got busted and served three years of a five-year stretch. Mom got a boyfriend a couple of notches up the social ladder from Dad. I mean," she went on with a droll expression, "he could spell and he had a steady job in construction. They were talking marriage when about a month later, a neighbor found her strangled in our house six blocks from The Meat & Mingle. I don't know if you were still living in the area at the time."

Judith frowned. "Maybe not. Dan died a couple of years after the café and bar shut down. By then, I may've moved back here with my son, Mike. If I'd still been out in the Thurlow District, I'd probably remember her murder. But offhand, I don't."

Joe had turned the stew on to simmer. After topping off his drink, he sat down next to Judith. "Was your mother early forties, currently working at a nearby nursing home, and the neighbor found her when she noticed the mail hadn't been picked up for a couple of days?"

Even as Ruby nodded, Judith turned to stare at her husband. "You remember the case? Were you on it?"

"No, but I recall it was never solved." He gave Judith a quirky look. "I remember the case because I knew it happened near Dan's café. I may've married somebody else the first time around, but I never forgot about you. I assumed you still lived in the area. I didn't know Dan was dead, and my first reaction was it could have been *you*. I panicked. Then the victim was ID'd, but I dreamed about you for a week after that."

Judith put her hand on Joe's. "That's so sweet."

"Hey," Ruby said, "break it up, folks. Or so I tell my lovey-dovey couples in the bar before they start coupling on the bar-room floor."

Judith removed her hand and sat up straight. "Suspects?"

Ruby leaned back in the chair. "Not bad old Dad. He and his buddy who hung out with him at The Meat & Mingle were both in the slammer. Mom was working as an aide at a nursing home. Peebles Place, closer to the Sound. Everybody called it Feebles Place. You remember it?"

"Vaguely," Judith replied.

"It wasn't top-of-the-line," Ruby continued, "but it survived the occasional violation. There was one old patient, Hector Sparks, who had the hots for Mom—her first name was Opal, by the way. Not that Hector could put any moves on her, being partially paralyzed and about ninety. Face it, Mom could be a bit of a flirt. She liked men, men liked her. But she was no floozy. In fact, she insisted Hector teased all the women—at least the pretty ones—who worked at Peebles. Anyway, Hector talked about leaving Mom all his money. He didn't—he outlived her, but his daughter and her family got wind of it, and pitched a five-star fit." She paused to sip from her drink. "They almost got Mom fired, but before that happened, she was killed."

"So," Judith said, "the Sparks family became prime suspects?"

"I made sure of that," Ruby replied grimly. "But they had solid alibis and there was no proof."

"No DNA back then," Joe noted. "How was your mother strangled?"

Ruby's gaze became steely. "With a strap—the kind they used at Peebles Place to lift patients who can't move on their own. What do you two sleuths make of that?"

"Suggestive," Judith remarked.

Joe, however, demurred. "Would your mother have had one of those at home for any reason?"

Ruby sighed. "She could have. Mom knitted. She always carried her knitting with her, and sometimes she'd absentmindedly put something from the nursing home in the bag. One time I found a coffee mug, another time a thermometer. She didn't steal stuff, she was just kind of ditzy."

Joe nodded. "What about her current boyfriend?"

Ruby shrugged. "Duke—real first name Darrell—Swisher was okay. He hung out a lot at the racetrack. Dad knew him before Mom did. Dad knew everybody at the track. Whatever he didn't spend on booze, he spent on the ponies. Anyway, for some reason Duke liked my father, and when he found out Dad was in jail, he stopped by our house to ask if he could do anything for Mom. Turned out there were quite a few things he could do, Dad not exactly being a handyman. One of the things he did for Mom was to sleep with her. After her divorce was final, he proposed. She even had a ring. That was more than she had from Dad. I mean she'd *had* one, but he'd pawned it a long time ago."

Judith finished her drink. "Had Duke ever been married? I ask that in case there was a jealous ex lurking in the background."

"Yes," Ruby replied, "but he'd been divorced for a long time. The ex-wife remarried and moved away. Montana, maybe."

Joe left the table to dish up dinner. Judith asked if Duke had children.

Ruby nodded. "A couple, I think. I never met them. I don't know if Mom did or not. They may've been grown or gone with their mother."

"Was Duke ever a suspect?" Joe asked, handing Judith her food.

"He was questioned," Ruby replied, "but he was cleared."

Joe pressed on. "What was approximate time of death?"

"It was June sixth—D-day. I always remember that because Grandpa Stone—Mom's dad—had been at Omaha Beach. Mrs. Crabbe from next door was the one who found Mom two days after she'd been killed. She'd noticed how much mail there was, including a package. I opened it later. It was a dress Mom had ordered from some catalog company. When nobody came to the door, Mrs. Crabbe turned the knob and it was unlocked. She found

Mom on the floor by the sofa and almost passed out, but she had sense enough to call 911. The EMTs came, along with the cops and the firefighters. They had to treat Mrs. Crabbe for shock. As for what time Mom was killed, the medical examiner figured somewhere between noon and five o'clock Wednesday afternoon."

Judith swallowed a bite of beef before posing a question. "Where were you during this time period?"

Ruby laughed. "I was wondering when you'd ask that. It was senior week. All sorts of hoo-ha going on. Class trip to Wild Waves, parties, commencement rehearsal. I often spent a lot of time with my best bud, Freddy Mae. I started doing that back in junior high. Mom sometimes worked nights, and frankly, I liked hanging out with Freddy Mae's family. By the time Mom was killed, my brother, Ozzie, was in the navy. He joined up right out of high school, two years ahead of me."

Judith nodded. "Your only sibling?"

"Right. Dad knocked Mom up with Ozzie. They were really young when they got married. Big mistake. Getting married, I mean. Ozzie's okay, but I haven't seen him in over a year. He decided to make the navy his career. He's currently stationed in San Diego. Ozzie can retire in another three, four years. Lucky guy." Ruby's expression was rueful.

Joe, who had seemed focused on his food, put down his fork and moved a few inches away from the table. "Okay. Let's get down to basics. No sign of a break-in?"

Ruby shook her head.

"Any sign of robbery, other injuries to your mother, evidence of a struggle or sexual assault?"

Ruby shook her head again.

"No serious suspects other than the boyfriend, Duke, or the relatives of the old guy in the nursing home?"

"No." Ruby smiled sheepishly. "Not much to go on, huh?"

Joe grimaced. "No wonder it's a cold case. I'm guessing—but whoever investigates this for you will have to check it out—there was no evidence at the scene?"

"Not that I heard about," Ruby replied.

Joe drummed his fingers on the table. "One possibility—it was a mistake. Somebody goes to the wrong house, broad daylight or not. Let's say it was a man if only because I assume your mother wasn't frail, being fairly young and able to do some heavy lifting at the retirement home. Mom pitches a five-star fit at the sight of the intruder, who panics. It sounds far-fetched, but it happens. I had a case like that early on in my homicide career. Maybe the killer is drunk or on drugs, assumes the house is empty, and then your mother finds him—or her—and the guy goes wacko. That happens, too. Again, a case of panic."

"Yeah," Ruby said, holding a piece of dumpling on her fork. "I guess. But I'd like to know for sure."

Judith had also finished her dinner. "Is there anything more you can tell us? Sometimes it's minor things that are important."

Joe turned to his wife. "Let's not play trivia, okay?"

"I'm not," she declared. "It's the way I work a . . . I mean, how I figure things out. Like around the house. And garden."

To Judith's surprise, Joe merely shrugged and turned his gaze back to Ruby.

"Gosh," she said, a hand to her head, "I don't remember after all these years. The only weird memory I have about that whole time is that Duke mentioned a horse running the day Mom was killed. The name reminded me of my favorite book. I asked him to put a six-buck combo on it and it won, going off at nine to one. The horse's name was Gone With The Win. At Mom's funeral, Duke gave me the forty bucks I'd won."

Judith smiled. "Did you often send bets to the track?"

"Hardly ever." Ruby put down her fork. "I worked part-time after school at the old supermarket across from the gas station. Dad was a dud when it came to child support—especially when he was in jail. Besides, I'd turned eighteen, and that ended his noncontribution anyway. Retirement and nursing homes charge big bucks, but they don't pay them to their employees. Money was tight for Mom and me."

Joe stood up and began clearing the table. "I'll check my file and find somebody to take on your case." He looked at Judith and patted his slight paunch. "No dessert for me. I'm really trying to lose a few pounds."

"Uh-huh," Judith said, smiling despite not believing him. After being married to the obese Dan, she didn't care if Joe had a minor tummy bulge. At least he didn't look like the Goodyear Blimp.

"I forgot to take Mother's dessert to her," she said, wincing. "Joe, would you mind? It's the last of the banana cream pie."

Joe looked put-upon, but murmured he'd do it—when he'd finished his other chores.

"My mother has her own apartment out back," Judith explained to Ruby. "She actually owns this house, but prefers her privacy." The truth was that Gertrude had refused to live under the same roof as Joe Flynn, but there was no need to offer details. "It's very cozy," she went on, seeing the faintly bewildered look in Ruby's blue eyes. "Besides, she isn't bothered by the B&B guests coming in and out."

"She must be kind of old," Ruby remarked.

"Yes, Mother is getting up there." *Way* up there, Judith thought, and immediately felt guilty. "She seems . . . ageless." *As in immortal, eternal, everlasting, and probably will outlive the rest of us.* "She likes her independence."

Ruby made a face. "My mom didn't like being independent. That's why she stuck by my dad for so long. She had trouble getting along without a man. Of course, she had trouble getting along with Dad, too."

Joe had finished loading the dishwasher and was heading for the back stairs. Judith rose from her chair. "I have ice cream if you'd like dessert. Or maybe an after-dinner drink?"

"I'll skip the ice cream, but thanks," Ruby said, also standing up. "Mr. Flynn should've let me bus the table. I'm used to it."

"You're a paying guest," Judith said, going to the liquor cupboard. "Brandy, Drambuie, Galliano, or . . . I guess that's it unless there's something else in the dining room's guest liquor cabinet."

"Galliano sounds good," Ruby replied.

Judith poured a measure into matching Isle of Murano glasses purchased when she and Renie visited Venice in their halcyon single years. "Let's go in the living room and be comfortable," she said, handing Ruby her drink.

"I feel sort of dumb," Ruby blurted on their way through the dining room. "I'm probably on a fool's errand. I feel like a pest. But I heard you had a big rep for crime solving."

"Don't believe everything you hear," Judith said, indicating that Ruby should sit on one of the two matching blue sofas flanking the fireplace. "My expertise is overrated. But it's natural for you to want to know who killed your mother. In fact, I'm surprised you haven't done this sooner. Or," she continued, seating herself across from her guest, "is this your first serious attempt at solving the mystery of her death?"

Ruby paused after a sip of the golden liqueur. "Good stuff. I haven't tasted this since the last time I had a Harvey Wallbanger." She licked her lips before speaking again. "I moved away after Mom died. Ozzie and I sold the house and split the profits, which weren't all that much after we paid off Mom's bills. First, I went to a community college over in the eastern part of the state, but studying wasn't for me. Then I headed for Sun Valley. Don't know why, just thought maybe I'd like it. I met a guy there and we moved in together for a couple of years, but that didn't work out. Hell, you don't want to hear all this. Cut to the chase. Never did marry any of the guys I met along the way, and three years ago I finally ended up in Little Bavaria, where I got dumped by a ski bum. I liked it there. Last spring I saw a couple of stories on the news about old murders that hadn't been solved until DNA came along. I got to wondering about Mom. Then you showed up and I heard you were a hotshot sleuth. I liked you. I even kind of liked your lippy cousin." She shrugged. "That's it. Here I am. But you're retired. Sorry 'bout that."

Judith smiled weakly. "I never intended to be any kind of sleuth. I just seemed to get mixed up in murders. The first one happened right here at the B&B in the dining room. How could I *not* get involved? And then . . . well, some other situations arose, and being curious by nature, I just couldn't help myself. But I promised Joe I'd quit. Sleuthing can be a dangerous . . . hobby."

Ruby gazed in the direction of the big bay window, where the lights of the city glittered in the distance. "Yeah, I suppose it could be risky. Just my luck." She sipped her drink before speaking again. "That's okay. Your hubby will probably come up with somebody good."

"I'm sure he will," Judith said. "If it'll help, your room is vacant for the next two nights. I won't charge you. It's not your fault I'm on the inactive list."

"Oh . . ." Ruby looked uncertain. "You sure?"

"Yes," Judith asserted. "I gather you haven't lived in the city for a long time. It's changed and grown. The least I can do is help you navigate it. Besides, I know from living way out south in the Thurlow District that it's almost like being cut off from the city itself."

Ruby nodded. "I never did know my way around even when I was growing up. I don't think I went downtown more than six, seven times."

"Understandable," Judith agreed as Joe entered the living room.

"Galliano?" he remarked, leaning against the sofa and looking over Judith's shoulder.

"You want some?" Judith asked, craning her neck to look at him.

"No, thanks. I need more than that after facing off with your mother." He turned to Ruby. "I've got three names for you, including a woman investigator. Good people." He moved around to come between the sofas and hand over his list. "Two are downtown and one is over on the Bluff. No fee from anyone to hear you out. I haven't called any of them yet, but I'll do that tomorrow first thing when they're on the job."

Ruby's face lighted up. "Thanks, Mr. Flynn. You're a doll."

He patted his paunch with one hand and ran the other through his graying red hair. "A kewpie doll, maybe."

They all laughed. But Judith knew murder was never a laughing matter.

Chapter 3

Ruby Tooms decided to take advantage of Judith's offer to stay on at Hillside Manor. It had been years since she'd spent time in the city and decided to do some exploring.

"I might even head out to the Thurlow District," she told Judith Wednesday morning. "You got a bus schedule?"

Judith said she had one in her visitor information. "You'll have to transfer downtown," she added. "I haven't been there since . . . well, since I moved here. The café's gone, and probably so are many of the other businesses. Believe it or not, I've heard the neighborhood has improved."

Ruby shrugged. "It didn't have any other direction to go unless it slid into the Sound." Getting up from the kitchen table, she poured herself another mug of coffee. "I've lost touch with my old pals from the bad old days. Maybe there's no point in going there. But I'd like to see if our house is still standing. Say," she went on before sitting down again, "do you think I should make a list of all those people who might've been mixed up in my mother's murder? I could give it to the private eye who takes on my case."

"That's a good idea," Judith replied, opening the dishwasher to empty it. "When will you start contacting the PIs Joe recommended?"

"Tomorrow, I guess," Ruby said without enthusiasm. "I wish your hubby did this kind of work."

"He did it for years as a cop. He's sort of burned out."

Ruby nodded as she sat down. "I get it. Darn."

Judith paused in the act of putting silverware away. "You're not guilt-tripping Joe, you're doing it to me. Honestly, I can't get involved. I made a promise to my husband. I never, ever intended to get involved in murder. I just happened to be in the wrong place at the wrong time and I let my curiosity run away with me. Besides, it's dangerous. I'm emphasizing this because I don't want you to start snooping around and try to figure out things for yourself. Leave it to a pro."

"Okay, okay," Ruby said wearily. "I get it. But I still want a look around the old hood."

"That's fine," Judith declared, softening her tone. "But don't go near any of the people involved—if in fact they're still there."

Ruby took a last gulp of coffee and stood up. "I won't. Honest. Now give me that bus schedule so I can at least *look* at the scene of the crime. I need to do that. What do they call it? Closure?"

"Yes." Judith smiled. "Just make sure that nobody tries to close *you*—permanently."

I hate bicycles!" Renie screamed into Judith's ear. "Wait—I don't mean bicycles as a mode of transport, I mean the dinks who ride them. If they're going to hog the roads, why can't they obey the rules? Are they all suicidal? I just saw some bozo ignore the four-way stop at the top of the hill and almost crash into a woman with a baby in a stroller. The baby slugged him. Ha ha."

"There are lanes for bikes," Judith pointed out reasonably.

"On the sidewalk?" Renie snapped. "That's where this idiot ended up. If I hadn't been in a hurry, I'd have run over him. I've no patience for people who break rules."

"And you don't?" Judith retorted.

"Only when I'm forced to." Renie had lowered her voice. "But that's not what I'm calling about."

"Which is?" Judith asked, putting down the recipe book she'd been leafing through to get some new appetizer ideas.

"Uh . . . I forget. I got so upset about the . . . oh! Can I bring something for dinner with the Prices Friday night?"

"No, I'm fine. I'm serving a pork loin. I'll get a dessert at Falstaff's."

"I could make Chocolate Glop," Renie suggested. "It's Bill's favorite. My sister-in-law, Bippy, makes it for everybody's birthdays."

"Is that what it's really called?"

"It's what I call it. I don't think Bippy has an actual name for it. It just . . . *is*."

"No thanks, I'll rely on Falstaff's. They have real names for their desserts. At least I'll know what we're eating."

"And take all of the fun out of it? Okay, it's your dinner. Think I'll go out and run over a bicyclist." Renie hung up.

Shaking her head, Judith set the phone down and went back to her recipe book. A few minutes later, a frowning Joe entered the kitchen to get a fresh diet soda.

"What's wrong?" Judith asked, looking up from a list of ingredients for smoked salmon latkes.

"I just talked to Woody," he said, leaning against the refrigerator. "The mayor is grudgingly going along with some of my suggestions to improve relations with people who aren't related to the police."

"That's good news," Judith said, "assuming I know what you're talking about. Or that the mayor does. Why do you look disturbed?"

Joe opened the fridge and removed a can of Diet 7UP. "I mentioned Ruby's cold case, just to see if Woody remembered it. Turns out it was his first homicide assignment."

Judith's dark eyes widened. "No! I mean . . . what did he say?"

Joe popped the top on the soda can and sighed. "Woody's

always felt it was a real blot on his résumé. It isn't, of course. Every tec has a few of those after a long career. But you know Woody—he's got a lot of pride. It still bothers him. He told me he'd like to meet Ruby. He remembers her as a teenage kid."

Judith's expression was sympathetic. "I suppose he does. Woody's very kindhearted. Does he feel as if he failed her?"

"Right." Joe sipped his soda. "When we were partners and had cases we couldn't close for various reasons, I urged Woody to let go. If he ever had spare time and wanted to do some further checking, go ahead. But never let an unsolved murder become a millstone that would distract him from the current job. And he didn't. But it still bothers him."

Judith moved closer to her husband and looked him in the eye. "Joe, are you trying to tell me something?"

His frown turned into a full-fledged scowl. "Hell, no! I just wish I'd never stirred up Woody's sensitive conscience."

"Oh." Judith backed away and shrugged. "I thought maybe you were reconsidering taking on Ruby's problem."

Joe vigorously shook his head. "I don't give a damn about Ruby. I mean, other than that she's on a mission that probably has a dead end." He grinned sheepishly. "Sorry. It's Woody that bothers me. I don't want to spend Friday night listening to him beat himself up over a cold case."

"Okay." Judith glanced at her recipe. "Sondra can console him. She's used to it. Do we have any crème fraîche? I need it for the smoked salmon latkes."

Joe opened the fridge. "I don't see any. We've got smoked salmon in the pantry from the last fishing trip Bill and I took."

"Check the freezer," Judith said.

Joe complied. After some mild cussing and haphazard rummaging, he produced a container of the desired item. "Here. It was behind a bunch of your mother's pig hocks and her cigarettes. Why does she have to put her smokes in the freezer?"

"Because she doesn't have a freezer in the toolshed. She thinks the cigarettes stay fresher if they're frozen."

"How about taking out the cigarettes and putting your mother in the freezer?"

Judith uttered an impatient sigh. "Just be thankful that Mother doesn't like you. Otherwise, she'd never have insisted on having her own apartment. Would you really want her living in this house?"

"I really don't want her living, period." Joe suddenly looked chagrined. "Sorry, I didn't quite mean that."

Judith couldn't help but smile, if wryly. "Skip it. Can you get me a can of that smoked salmon?"

Joe wordlessly went down the hall to the pantry. Judith started peeling potatoes. Looking out the window over the sink, she noticed that it had begun to rain, light drops bouncing off the Rankerses' monster laurel hedge. Typical November, she thought, with temperatures in the high forties and probably some wind by nightfall.

Joe returned with the smoked salmon. After setting the can on the counter, he kissed his wife's cheek. "Maybe you *have* reformed," he murmured.

Judith gazed at him with innocent eyes. "I gave you my word. When have I ever lied to you?"

Joe looked dubious. "You lie to everybody else when it suits you."

"I do not lie. I tell fibs only when absolutely necessary."

Joe's green eyes danced. "Some of those fibs are real whoppers. You're very good at it."

Her dark-eyed gaze met his. "I repeat, have I ever lied—or fibbed—to you?"

Joe didn't answer immediately. "How," he finally asked, "would I know if you did?"

Shortly after the current group of guests left on their appointed evening rounds, Judith began to worry about Ruby. It was almost seven-thirty and she had not yet returned to Hillside Manor.

"Maybe," Joe suggested when he and Judith were finished

cleaning up the kitchen, "she ran into some old pals. Not every-body flees the Thurlow neighborhood like you did."

"It's possible," Judith conceded. "If she hasn't eaten, I saved enough of the spare ribs and the rest of dinner for her because I assumed she'd eat with us."

"Ruby's a free spirit," Joe said. "Sounds as if she likes to keep on the move. Never married?"

"No," Judith said, turning on the dishwasher. "She had some guy with her at an event in Little Bavaria, but he was kind of a drip. I figure she dumped him about the time Renie and I left town."

"There can't be a lot of eligible men in a little place like—"

Joe was interrupted by the phone, which happened to be sit-ting behind him on the counter. "Flynn here," he said, never breaking the habit after thirty years as a cop.

Judith assumed it was for her, so she paused in the kitchen, watching Joe. His ruddy face darkened. "Okay, I'll be right over. Thanks." He hurried off. "That was Carl Rankers," he said, head-ing down the back hall to grab his jacket. "They've got Ruby and she's a mess. Mistook their house for ours. Drunk, he figures. It's raining hard, so I'll go get her."

"Wait!" Judith cried. "I'm going with you!"

"Stay put," Joe called, already at the back door.

But there was no stopping Judith. By the time she caught up with Joe, he was already on the Rankerses' front porch. Carl opened the door.

"We've never had one of your guests come here before," Carl said in his droll manner. "Kind of exciting, at least for Arlene. She's making coffee. Want some?"

"No thanks," Joe replied, leading the way in through the dining room and the adjacent living room. "Save it to sober up my wife's latest guest." He shot Judith a reproachful glance. "She likes to take in the occasional stray."

Arlene poked her head out from the kitchen. "Five minutes," she announced. "Booby, are you alive?"

The object of her question was flopped on the beige sofa, eyes closed, mouth agape. Judith moved closer, noting that Ruby's face was dirty—or bruised. "Ruby," she said softly, "are you awake?"

The other woman's closed eyes flickered open—and shut. "Unf." She shifted her body with obvious painful effort. "Oof."

Judith sat down next to Ruby and looked up at Joe's disgruntled face. "Go home. This is going to take a while. If I need help, Carl's here."

The two men exchanged wordless male glances. "No," Joe said. "Carl's got a bad back. I've only got flat feet."

Carl put a hand on Joe's shoulder. "Come on, let's go watch whichever overpaid NBA teams are on TV. This is women's work."

Joe took one last look at Ruby, whose eyes were still closed. "Oh, hell, why not? Call when you need me," he said, following Carl back out to the hallway and presumably to the family room downstairs.

Arlene stepped into the living room. "Thank goodness they're gone. Men are so helpless except for heavy lifting. Though Carl isn't very good at that with his bad back. I *told* him not to lift our SUV by himself. Men aren't very good at listening either. Is Booby dead?"

"It's Ruby," Judith said. "Just passed out. Is the coffee ready?"

"Almost," Arlene replied, tapping her fingernails against the kitchen doorframe. "Maybe she needs smelling salts. I don't have any."

"Neither do I," Judith said, gently trying to arrange her unconscious guest into a more comfortable position. "But we can't leave her here to sleep it off. How on earth did Ruby get this far?"

Arlene moved across the room to help Judith. "Well," she went on as she handed Judith some throw pillows to put under the head of their patient, "I'm not sure. Carl heard something out on the front porch, but he thought it was your cat, flinging himself at the storm door. He does that sometimes if we're serving fish. But we weren't. I'd made lasagna instead. Finally, Carl opened the door and Ruby fell into his arms. We never got a sensible word out of her. Of course, that's not unusual around here, especially when our children visit."

"That happened how long ago?" Judith asked.

Arlene's pretty face puckered in recollection. "Ten minutes before Carl called? She mumbled your name, so we thought she must be a guest who'd confused our houses, given that they're similar in style and it's such a dark, rainy night. But night often is . . . dark, I mean."

Judith nodded. "I wonder if she took the bus, but I don't see how she could have walked the two blocks from the bus stop. She would've had to cross Heraldsgate Avenue and that's not easy, being so busy and so steep. Maybe she took a cab. Or got a ride," she murmured, frowning "It looks as if her face is bruised."

"Maybe she fell down," Arlene suggested. "You're right—she wasn't in very good shape to walk. And she does reek like a distillery. Not that I've ever been to a distillery. Why would I do that? Carl took a tour once of a brewery and said it smelled awful. Goodness, your guests usually aren't drunk. When Carl and I have taken over the B&B for you, I don't recall anyone being more than a tad tiddly."

"That's true," Judith replied, noting that Ruby had begun to stir. "While I can't control how much liquor guests consume when they're off the premises—or if they bring their own supply with them—I clearly state that excessive use of alcohol or any other harmful substance is grounds for being ejected. Is the coffee ready?"

"It must be," Arlene said. She hurried off to the kitchen.

Ruby was groaning and had flung a hand over her eyes. "Oooh . . . what . . . ?"

"It's me . . . Judith. You're at our neighbors' house. You'll be fine."

"Huh?" Ruby removed her arm and blinked several times. "That light . . . can you turn it down?"

"Sure." Judith reached around to click off the lamp on the end table. "Coffee's coming."

"Coffee." Ruby uttered the word as if it were foreign to her.

"Can you sit up if I help you?"

"Not sure." Ruby licked her dry lips. "What happened? I feel like I was run over by a truck."

"You're lucky you weren't," Judith said, but immediately felt repentant. "I mean, how did you get here?"

Ruby had raised her head and her bloodshot eyes were wide open. "I'm not sure. Where did you say we are?"

Arlene appeared with a tray, three mugs, cream, sugar, and artificial sweetener. "You're at our house," she said, setting the tray on the end table. "I'm Arlene. Carl is downstairs with Joe watching tall men in long shorts with names like Dako and Manu and Nazr and Beno and Radoslav and Tim. Wouldn't you think Tim would feel out of place? And Tony, too." She shook her head.

Ruby looked justifiably confused. She stared at Judith. "Are you sure you know where we are?"

Judith nodded. "Yes."

"Does it matter?" Arlene asked. "*We* know where you are. Have some coffee. It's Sully's. Carl and I like it very much. For all I know, Tim and Tony do, too." She poured coffee into a mug. "Sugar? Cream?"

"Black," Ruby answered, still looking dazed as she turned from Arlene to Judith. "Do you know what happened to me?"

"No," Judith replied. "Do you mean you don't remember anything?"

Ruby inched her way up on the throw pillows and took the coffee mug from Arlene. "I'm not sure. I took the bus downtown and transferred to the one that went out to the Thurlow District. I found our old house, but I almost didn't recognize the place. It's been updated." She blew on the coffee before taking a sip. "Then I walked around the block. No vacant lots, condos instead. Most of the houses looked like they'd been fixed up. At least one had been torn down and a real modern glass thing had been built in its place. Kind of ugly." She put a hand to her head. "Anybody got aspirin?"

"I'll get some," Arlene volunteered. "And water." She dashed back to the kitchen.

Judith helped Ruby sit up straighter. "Did you walk through the business district?"

Ruby nodded. "It's only three blocks from where I grew up at the end of the bus line. Man, but it's grown! I had lunch at a real nice café not far from where The Meat & Mingle used to be. That's where I met . . ." Her face scrunched up in confusion. "Who was it?"

Arlene had returned with the aspirin and water. "Nazr? Manu? Tim?" She made a self-deprecating gesture. "I'm just throwing out names. You never know when one will hit home."

"None of the above," Ruby replied glumly, swallowing the aspirin with a gulp of water. "Damn! I can't remember anything!"

Judith pointed to Ruby's cheek. "Somehow you got a bruise. Did you fall? Or . . . ?" She left the query unfinished.

Ruby scowled. "Did somebody slug me? I'm blank. Could I have a concussion?"

Judith grimaced. "You might. Maybe we should go to the ER."

But Ruby emphatically shook her head. "Forget it. All I want to do is sleep. If I've got a headache, it's from a hangover. I ought to know—I've done it before."

Judith hesitated, but decided not to argue. "Okay. Finish your coffee while I get Joe."

"I'll do that," Arlene said, already heading toward the hall. "I'd like to see if Tony and Tim have adjusted to playing with those people who have such peculiar names. And why are those shorts so long? They aren't at all short. They look like *frocks* to me."

Ruby turned to Judith. "Is she for real?"

Judith smiled. "Arlene is one of the most real people on the planet. She's the best neighbor and a very good friend. She just has a different way of making people think about things."

"If you say so," Ruby remarked doubtfully before she took

another swig from her mug. "She makes damned good coffee, I'll say that."

Joe and Carl reappeared with Arlene. "Let's take Ruby to our house," Joe said. "It's still raining hard."

Ruby offered Joe a weak smile. "Thanks. You guys are great. I'm not used to people looking out for me."

Five minutes later, Joe, Judith, and Ruby arrived at Hillside Manor's back door. "Go ahead," Joe said to Judith. "I've got Ruby."

As usual, the back door was unlocked until ten o'clock. Judith stepped inside and thought the hallway seemed strangely cool. After hanging her jacket on a peg, she entered the kitchen. The usually pristine floor was tracked with dark patches.

"Joe?" she said, turning around to see him helping Ruby down the hall. "Did you come back over here?"

"No," he said. "Has your mother vandalized the place?"

"It's not Mother . . . her wheelchair would leave long tracks. Look."

Joe kept his arm around Ruby. "Jesus!" he said under his breath. "Did a guest . . ." He steered Ruby into a kitchen chair. "Stay here. Both of you," he ordered, suddenly the brisk, controlled policeman that Judith remembered from their first meeting forty years earlier. She stood motionless as he brushed past her, through the swinging half doors, and presumably into the front hall.

Ruby propped her head up on one hand. "What's going on?"

"I don't know," Judith said, but jumped when she heard Joe swear again. "Something's not quite right."

"One of your guests?" Ruby inquired.

Judith shook her head. She couldn't hear any further sound from Joe. Growing more anxious by the second, she was about to head for the front of the house when he returned to the kitchen, cell phone at her ear. "That's right. The cul-de-sac. You make one smart-ass comment about 911 being called to this address and I'll give you the address of the unemployment office." He clicked off.

"What is it?" Judith asked.

Joe grimaced. "Lippy 911 operator," he muttered, putting the cell back in his shirt pocket. "Okay," he finally said, leaning on the back of an empty kitchen chair. "We probably had an intruder. Whoever it was came in through the back door but didn't go out that way. Instead—I don't know this for sure—whoever it was probably went to another part of the house because the wet marks end in the front hall."

Judith shivered. "Is the intruder still here?"

Joe shook his head. "No, because the front door was open. I suspect whoever it was left when he—or she—heard us coming through the back. Until the cops get here, we don't leave the kitchen." He gave both Judith and Ruby a dour look. "Relax, ladies. Pretend you can enjoy yourselves. For now, Hillside Manor is a crime scene. What else is new?"

Chapter 4

The patrol officers who arrived within five minutes were known to the Flynns. They were also known to each other as an old and tired joke. The tall, lanky female was Smith; her short, stocky male partner was Wesson. After two years on the Heraldsgate Hill beat, Smith and Wesson had heard it all and laughed at none of it.

Judith remained in the kitchen with Ruby, but recognized the voices of the officers talking to Joe in the entry hall. "These cops are rather young, but they know what they're doing," she assured her bleary-eyed guest. "I'm glad they didn't use their siren. Are you sure I can't get you something to drink?"

"I feel like I've had plenty to drink," Ruby replied, "but I don't remember doing it. If I'm hungover, I'd like to know if I had fun."

"Don't push yourself," Judith cautioned. "You may be in shock. After a good night's sleep, things may start coming back to you." She paused, hearing the voices of the trio grow fainter. "Joe must be going around the house with them. I wonder if they went into the living room or upstairs."

Ruby looked up at the kitchen's high ceiling. "Can you hear them walking around up there?"

Judith shook her head. "Not unless they tromp. As you may've noticed, the hall is carpeted." She paused again. "Yes, they have gone upstairs. If they'd stayed on this floor, we could still hear them. I imagine Joe checked out the parlor and the living and dining rooms while he was waiting, so I assume nothing was amiss. I wonder if I should check on Mother. Do you mind if I run out to make sure she's okay?"

Ruby shrugged. "Go ahead."

Judith grabbed her jacket to ward off the rain. To her relief, Gertrude was at the card table, playing solitaire. "Well?" the old lady said. "To what do I owe this dubious pleasure?"

"I just thought I'd see if you were all right," Judith explained. "Sometimes an accident like yours has a delayed reaction."

Gertrude narrowed her faded blue eyes. "Like death?"

Judith expelled an exasperated sigh. "No, Mother. You know I worry about you."

"Okay, Toots, I'll give you credit for that much." She slapped an ace on a deuce and palmed a string of clubs. "Gotcha! I win this game."

"Good for you. It's been quiet around here tonight, right? I mean, so you could focus on the cards."

Gertrude scowled. "I can always focus on the cards. It's your aunt Deb who drives me nuts when we play bridge. She likes to gab, and then we get into it when she's my partner. I'm not there to visit, I'm there to . . ." Her eyes narrowed. "What's going on? You find another stiff on the front porch?"

"Of course not!" Judith winced. Gertrude was the only person who could see through her daughter's so-called fibs. "Okay, okay. Someone apparently came in the back door and walked through the house. It could've been a guest, but they usually use the front door because they have a key and know we don't lock up until ten."

"Did you call the cops or is Lunkhead pretending he remembers how to figure out how his pants got stolen while he was wearing them?"

"Two patrol officers are going through the house now."

"So Dim Bulb doesn't remember," Gertrude said, putting the

deck into her card shuffler. "I hope he's not running around in his BVDs."

"He's not." Judith remained patient. "Just make sure you're locked in, and if you hear anything unusual, let me know."

"Like your so-called better half's brain working? If that happens, I won't call you, I'll call the *Times* and the TV stations. That's *news*."

Judith leaned down to kiss her mother's cheek. "Fine. Just be careful." She hurried out of the toolshed, but made sure that the door was securely locked behind her.

When she returned to the kitchen, Joe was coming through the half doors from the dining room. "I used your master key so Smith and Wesson could check all the rooms," he said, looking grim. "Only one was disturbed." His gaze turned to Ruby. "You're in Room Two, right?" He didn't wait for a response. "It's been trashed. What have you got that somebody wants?"

Ruby looked startled. "Nothing. I travel light. Besides, I don't have anything worth stealing. Not even over-the-counter meds."

Joe nodded once. "Okay, you can check to see if anything's missing as soon as the cops finish processing the room. They don't expect to find much, but you never know. I'm making sure they vacuum."

"Vacuum?" Ruby was obviously puzzled.

"For hair, fibers, whatever," Joe said . . . and grinned. "Don't you watch crime shows on TV?"

Ruby shook her head. "I've seen enough crime in real life."

Joe leaned against the fridge. "It's how they collect samples for DNA. That's what piqued your interest in your mother's case, isn't it?"

"Yes," Ruby agreed, "but I don't know how it works. I mean, I don't know how they find the stuff they use to figure out that somebody was the wrong perp or the real one wasn't caught in the first place."

"Technology moves fast these days," Joe said, his head cocked in the direction of the entry hall. "The patrol officers aren't equipped to do a thorough job, so they've called in the forensics specialists. It may take a while before you can go up to your room, but can you tell me what you left behind here?"

Ruby looked askance. "You're lucky I can tell you my name right now." She put her elbows on the table and cradled her head in her hands. "One travel bag with nightgown, underwear, a sweater, a couple of pairs of socks, jeans, a sweatshirt . . . oh, travel slippers. Some makeup. A toothbrush and tooth-paste, deodorant, birth control pills . . ." She paused, appar-ently expecting some kind of reaction from the Flynns. There was none. Ruby continued with her recital. "Travel alarm clock, heavy-duty nail file, and Fermin the Vermin, my stuffed ham-ster. He's my good-luck charm. Oh—my journal. I started keeping one after I moved to Little Bavaria. It helped me get over the ski bum who dumped me."

Joe's expression hadn't change. "Okay. No camera?"

"No. I've got one on my cell."

"Is that in your purse?" Joe asked.

"Yes." Ruby looked around. "Where *is* my purse?"

Judith also gave the kitchen a quick check. "I don't think you had it with you. It must be at the Rankerses' house. I'll call them." She stood up to get the phone from the counter. Joe left the kitchen, presumably to check on Smith and Wesson.

Arlene answered. "Goodness," she said in response to the question, "I don't think Ruby had a purse with her. Or maybe Carl put it somewhere after he helped her get inside. Let me ask him. He's still downstairs watching the tall shorts people with the peculiar names."

Hearing a door open, Judith realized that Arlene was taking the phone with her. Soft footsteps followed, then the faint voice of a sportscaster saying, "Duncan grabs the rebound, passes off to Barry . . ." Arlene spoke to Carl, but Judith couldn't quite make out what she said or what he responded.

Arlene was back upstairs. "Ruby didn't have a purse," she said.

"She must've lost it. Carl checked the porch and the walk. No luck, I'm afraid. Was she mugged?"

"I don't know," Judith answered slowly, her back turned to Ruby. *Drugged,* she thought, *might be more like it.* "Thanks, Ar——"

"Exactly. Are they making a social call or . . . you know."

"Uh——know what?"

"What I was going to ask. Are the police just in the neighborhood and happened to drop by or did you find another . . . how should I put it? Future obituary?"

"No!" Judith winced, but kept her back turned. "We may have had a prowler."

"Oh." Arlene sounded disappointed. "Here comes Carl. The game must be over. I'm glad. I feel embarrassed for those poor young men who have to wear frocks on TV. Maybe their names are so odd because they use aliases. I would. Or would I? I do wear a frock for the right occasion, but basketball isn't one of them." She rang off.

Judith finally sat back down and looked at Ruby. "You didn't have a purse with you."

The bald statement clearly stunned the other woman. "Damn! You mean it got snatched?"

"Maybe," Judith allowed. "Or you dropped it somewhere."

Ruby held her head again. "What the hell is going on?"

Judith didn't respond. She heard the front door open and Joe speak to a woman . . . and then a man. The voices were swallowed up in the stairwell as they moved to the second floor.

"The forensics specialists," Judith murmured. "They'll collect the specimens. If there are any."

"I wish they could find my money, my credit cards, my cell phone, my ID, my . . ." Ruby's bloodshot eyes welled up with tears. "Why do I always have such rotten luck?"

Judith reached across the table to put her hand on Ruby's arm. "Hey—don't make yourself sick. You're here with us. We'll get this sorted out somehow. You need to rest. As soon as they finish in your room, I'm going to put you to bed. Unless you're hungry. Are you?"

Ruby wiped away her tears with the back of her hand. "I'm empty, but I'm not hungry."

"I saved you some spare ribs."

Ruby looked surprised. "You did? That was real nice of you. But maybe I'll just have some toast."

"Sure." Judith got up. A glance at the old schoolhouse clock told her it was going on nine. Some of the guests would be returning soon. She grimaced, wondering how to explain the cruiser and a police department van parked by the B&B. "Maybe," she said, after putting a slice of bread in the toaster, "you'll remember some of what happened to you in the morning. Trauma often causes temporary amnesia."

"Do I want to remember?" Ruby asked grimly.

"It might not be pleasant, but it *is* important, especially if a crime has been committed."

Ruby looked jarred. "You mean maybe I was raped?"

"No," Judith said quietly, "but somebody may have stolen your purse. How much money did you have in it?"

"A little over two hundred bucks," Ruby replied. "Hey, wouldn't somebody at that café know something? It's the last thing I do remember." She made a face. "Damn. I don't recall the name . . . something about a cat, maybe."

"That won't be hard to find if it's near the site of The Meat & Mingle." She removed the toast and buttered it. "Jam? Jelly?"

"Why not?"

"Raspberry, strawberry, or blackberry?"

Ruby smiled. "Blackberry. If I didn't feel so crappy, this would be kind of fun. Somebody's waiting on me for a change instead of the other way around."

Judith spread a thick layer of jelly on the toast, set it on a plate, and handed it to Ruby. "You may think of me as a sleuth or a tourist or a business owner, but basically, I'm just a glorified waitress and housekeeper. Oh—and a bartender when Dan and I owned The Meat & Mingle. But my real career used to be as a librarian. Let me check the computer for that restaurant."

Ruby hadn't eaten half the toast before Judith came up with a name. "The Persian Cat?"

"That's right," Ruby said, grinning. "The guy who seemed to be running it wore a turban. Maybe he's Persian. Or would that be Indian? All those countries over there confuse me."

"For all I know, he may've been born in the Thurlow District," Judith said, jotting down the phone number. "That might explain his confusion about headgear. They could be closing about now. I think I'll let Joe call the restaurant when he's done with the police work. Assuming, of course, they'll answer if it's after hours. It's best to get information as soon as possible from witnesses."

"You sound like a cop."

Judith shrugged. "I've lived with one for fifteen years."

"That's great. You guys seem happy."

"We are." She sat down. "We both had unhappy first marriages. We'd been engaged before we . . . got offtrack." She grew silent, hearing voices in the entry hall. "The police may be leaving," she said softly.

Judith was right. Joe came back into the kitchen. "All clear. Feeling better, Ruby?"

"A little. Your wife is great."

Joe moved behind Judith's chair and put his hands on her shoulders. "I know that. She comes from great stock. Just like her mother."

"Joe . . ." Judith made a face. "Don't listen to him. He and my mother don't get along." She craned her neck to give Joe a dirty look.

He squeezed Judith's shoulders, but ignored her reaction. "Can you describe your journal?"

Ruby frowned. "Nothing fancy. Dark green cover, drawing of trees and mountains with the word 'Musings.' "

Joe shook his head. "I'm afraid we didn't see it. Did you have anything else in the room with personal information?"

Ruby reflected briefly. "No. But my purse is missing. My ID and credit cards and my cell are in it."

Joe nodded. "Right."

Judith and Ruby waited for Joe to elaborate, but he didn't. Instead, he removed his hands from his wife's shoulders and started down the back hall. "I'm going up to my office for a few minutes."

Ruby frowned at Judith. "What does that mean?"

"He wants to think," Judith said. "Did you tell anybody what you planned to do while you were in the city? About your mom, I mean."

"No. It was none of their business. I told my boss at the restaurant that I wanted to get away for a few days. I had the time coming, so it wasn't a big deal."

It was Judith's turn to mull. "Did you talk to anyone in the old neighborhood? Before you got to The Persian Cat, I mean?"

"I didn't run into anybody I knew. I planned to check out a couple of old pals, but I never got around to it. Are you going to ask Mr. Flynn to call the restaurant?"

"Maybe I should do that," Judith said, noting that the schoolhouse clock was ticking its way toward 9:20. "I don't know how long Joe's going to be upstairs. And please call us by our first names. You're not a stranger."

Ruby's smile lighted up her tired face. "I doubt you've ever met a stranger."

Judith smiled back, though a bit ruefully. "That's what my first husband's mother said about me. It was grudging—and about the only nice thing she ever did say to me."

"She must've been a bitch," Ruby remarked.

"She was a very unhappy woman." Judith got up from the chair to pick up the phone. "What does your purse look like? I forget."

"It's faux brown leather with a big faux gold clasp and a couple of pockets on the outside. They're not faux, they're real, but I hardly ever use them."

Judith nodded and dialed the restaurant. Unfortunately, she reached a recording, giving The Persian Cat's hours and that reservations were necessary only for dinner. She could call back during business hours to make a reservation. "I wonder . . ."

she murmured, trying an old trick of redialing the number but changing the last digit by one. A deep male voice answered on the second ring.

"I'm sorry to bother you," she said, "but my niece lost her purse today when she was at your restaurant. Did you find it by any chance?"

"No purse," the accented voice answered. "She must've lost it 'nother place. Sorry."

"Oh, dear," Judith said in a woeful voice, quickly offering a concise description of Ruby. "I wonder if the man who approached her took it. Did you notice him with her? He acted rather oddly."

"Then how did she pay?" the man responded. "She must've lost it after she was here."

"Maybe the man paid her bill," Judith said.

"He steals purse and pays for her meal? That's craziness. We're closed. I'm busy." He hung up.

Judith sighed. "I should've let Joe call. That was a washout. I'm not at the top of my game tonight."

Ruby shrugged. "Don't worry about it. They were busy. Maybe he wouldn't remember the guy who talked to me. I sure don't."

Judith heard the front door open. Judging from the voices, it was the Porcinis from New Jersey. They headed upstairs to Room Five.

"Don't worry about it anymore tonight," Judith said. "You should get to bed. I'll come up with you. The guests can let themselves in after we lock up at ten."

"You don't have to—" Ruby was interrupted by the doorbell. "Guess somebody forgot their key."

"No," Judith said. "It's not yet ten. Stay put. I'll be right back."

A quick look through the peephole revealed Corinne Dooley, who lived on the other side of the fence from the Flynns' double garage.

"Hi," Judith said, opening the door and noticing that Corinne was holding a brown purse. "Come in. You're all wet."

Corinne crossed the threshold, running a hand through her

disheveled graying blond locks. Never quite sure how many children the prolific Dooleys had, Judith was amazed that her neighbor's hair hadn't fallen out in clumps by now. But Corinne was always an amazing sea of calm amid utter chaos. Grandchildren as well as nieces and nephews added to the lively mix.

"Tyler found this in our garbage can," Corinne said, handing over the purse. "It had one of your brochures inside. Do you think it belongs to a guest?"

"It just might," Judith said, gingerly holding the purse. "It was in your garbage can? How did he happen to find it?"

Corinne waved a hand. "One of the other kids threw out Tyler's trumpet. They get tired of hearing him practice. Being the baby of the family, sometimes they pick on him. He found the purse just now when he was looking for the trumpet."

"Thanks, Corinne," Judith said. "I'm not sure I know which one Tyler is—unless he's our paper boy."

"He is," Corinne replied. "He has been, since a year ago last summer. You probably never see him. He does the route around five-thirty and starts in the cul-de-sac." She smiled conspiratorially and lowered her voice. "I don't suppose you have any mysteries you'd like solved. He's taking after his older brothers when it comes to playing detective. Tyler thought he saw a cop car in your driveway earlier."

"Ah . . . well, it had to do with the loss of this purse," Judith said, unwilling to reveal too much. "My guest thought it might've been stolen. Maybe she dropped it coming from . . . the bus."

"In our garbage can?" Corinne laughed. "What did she do, climb over the fence? We aren't exactly on the route from the bus stop to your house unless she was out for an evening stroll."

"It's a long story," Judith said. "Tell Tyler that if I ever have a mystery—even a small mystery—I'll let him know. His brothers were always a big help in my former sleuthing days."

Corinne's blue eyes widened. "You quit?"

"Yes," Judith said, ruing the lack of conviction in her voice. "I'm getting too old for that sort of thing."

"But you're so good at it," Corinne asserted. "And it does make the neighborhood more interesting. Not that I enjoy murders, but the mystery part is a good topic of dinnertime conversation. At least when we can hear each other over all the noise and breaking of crockery."

"Hard on the nerves, though," Judith said. "The murders, I mean."

"So's dinnertime," Corinne said, her hand on the doorknob. "But I go with the flow. Glad Tyler found the purse. Good night, Judith."

Judith closed the door behind her neighbor. When she turned around, she saw Ruby leaning out of the dining room doorway.

"My purse?" she said in relief. "Wow!"

"I didn't open it. I wondered about fingerprints, but I suspect if there are any, they'd be smudged after going through various Dooley hands." Judith handed the purse to Ruby. "Go ahead, open it in the living room, where we can be more comfortable."

They sat down opposite each other on the matching sofas. "Sorry there's no fire," Judith said. "Joe never got around to making one."

Ruby's gaze roamed around the long living room with its plate rail, bay window, bookshelves, comfortable furniture, and grandfather clock. Her gaze rested on the baby grand piano at the far end of the room by the French doors. "Do you play?"

"Not very well," Judith admitted. "Somebody gave that piano to my grandparents. This was originally their home. The house was built a hundred years ago. They raised six children in it, including my father."

"I took piano lessons," Ruby said wistfully. "They were free if Ozzie and I did chores around the teacher's house. She was a widow."

"A nice arrangement for everyone." Judith pointed at Ruby's purse. "Aren't you going to open that?"

"I'm almost afraid to. It feels lighter."

"There's only one way to find out."

"Right." Ruby slowly opened the purse. "My wallet's here! But I'll bet the . . . no, they didn't take my money. Or my credit cards. Wow!" Excitedly, she rummaged through the rest of the contents—and finally her expression sobered. "My cell's gone."

Judith wasn't surprised. "Whoever took your cell—and your journal—is looking for something. I wonder if it pertains to your mother's murder." Her expression turned bleak. "Let's hope it's not her killer."

Chapter 5

Judging from Ruby's obvious alarm, Judith wished she could take back her words. "Look," she said, "I may be crazy. I don't see how anyone could know you were on a mission. Maybe whoever took your purse and then came here is an old boyfriend. In the morning you may remember what happened. Meanwhile, let's go upstairs so you can get some rest."

Ruby didn't argue. If the return of her purse had elated her, Judith's comment deflated her. When they reached Room Two, Ruby insisted on straightening up everything before she collapsed and fell into a vegetable-like state.

"I understand," Judith said before heading downstairs, "but if you want anything, feel free to let me know. I'll be up until at least eleven."

Coming into the entry hall, she almost collided with the Epsteins from L.A., who had just returned from dinner on the ship canal. They seemed most intrigued by the opening and closing of a nearby bridge to allow ships to make their passage through the city. The pair had headed upstairs when the Sutcliffes arrived, musing over why they hadn't seen any igloos or Eskimos in fur-lined parkas. Judith left them to their confusion and went into the living room, where Joe was on the sofa reading a spy novel.

"Well?" he said, looking up.

Judith sat down next to him. "I'll fill you in on what you missed."

Joe listened without interruption. "Okay, that's about what I figured. Except for the purse getting returned. That's puzzling."

"I agree. Somebody breaks into our house but gets rid of a stolen purse less than fifty yards away?"

Joe shook his head. "Maybe the purse was put in the Dooleys' garbage before whoever it was came here. But if it was stolen in the Thurlow District—and we don't know that for sure— why haul it to Heraldsgate Hill? Apparently the alleged thief only wanted the cell phone . . . and the journal. Damn, this is bizarre. Maybe I should go to The Persian Cat tomorrow and see if I can get more out of the staff."

Judith stared at Joe. "You're taking on the case?"

He winced. "It's getting personal, given the intruder."

Judith was briefly speechless. "I thought you were starting another assignment."

Joe shook his head. "Turns out the subject—another one of those damned insurance frauds—is in the hospital. He broke his leg in three places skateboarding. That should prove he's not help-lessly crippled, but the SANECO people are hedging their bets until he's released."

"So you've got some free time," Judith remarked, gazing across the room and keeping her tone casual.

Joe wasn't making eye contact either. "I feel duty-bound to follow through with our home being broken into by some weirdo."

"Yes, of course. It makes perfect sense."

But Judith wondered about Joe's real intentions. He might not own up to it, but she knew he'd caught a cold case of homicide.

The rain had let up by Thursday morning. Ruby was the last of the guests to come down for breakfast a little before ten-thirty. She'd used the back stairs and looked more clear-eyed, but claimed she still felt fuzzy-headed.

"I had some really wacko dreams," she said, sitting down at the kitchen table. "Dancing dudes in turbans, cats in garbage cans, old folks racing wheelchairs, and a trumpet that played like a piano. Or was it a piano that . . ." She shook her head. "Never mind. My head's still woolly."

"Does it ache?" Judith asked, having just finished clearing away the other guests' breakfast dishes.

"Not really. It just feels foggy."

Judith poured coffee for Ruby. "Nothing's come back to you yet?"

"Not exactly." Ruby grimaced. "I hear a man's voice. He's saying something like, 'Hi, there. New in town?' Weird, huh? I mean, that's not exactly a twenty-first-century come-on."

"That doesn't mean he didn't say it."

Ruby laughed. "I guess not. But it's dumb." She gazed around the kitchen. "Where is everybody?"

"Mother's gone off to play bridge, Joe had some errands to run, and all the guests have checked out. Only the Porcinis are staying over. It looks like I'll have at least one vacancy tonight, but the weekend's full."

Ruby looked alarmed. "Including my room?"

"Yes, but if you want to stay, we have a spare room in the family quarters on the third floor."

"Oh, I shouldn't," Ruby said in a wan voice. "I have to be back Monday anyway."

Judith leaned on the table. "You're welcome here. We haven't even begun to scratch the surface of what happened to your mother."

" 'We'?" Ruby repeated. "I thought you and Mr. Flynn weren't getting involved."

"That's *Joe* to you. He feels obligated to find out who broke into our house. Besides, he's got some free time right now."

Ruby put her hand on Judith's. "I can't believe you guys are so nice. I mean, I—"

The sound of a siren interrupted. Both women listened as it

came closer to the cul-de-sac. "Now what?" Judith murmured, heading for the entry hall.

Ruby followed her. "Maybe it's a fire."

Judith opened the front door, looking out into the overcast morning. A moment later a fire engine pulled into the cul-de-sac and stopped in front of Herself's rental. More sirens could be heard close by. The EMTs and the police—Judith knew the drill all too well.

"I don't see any smoke," Ruby said.

Judith shook her head. "I don't either. But here comes Arlene. And Naomi Stein, from the house on the other corner. I'm guessing a medical emergency."

Ruby made a face. "Do you know the people who live there?"

"Only by sight," Judith said. "The Frosches aren't very friendly." She gave a start as a young man met the firefighters on the porch. "I've never seen him before. I think they have a son, but he lives . . . I forget."

"In Idaho," Arlene called from the middle of the cul-de-sac. "His name is Brick. I saw him once this summer."

Naomi had joined Arlene. "I didn't know they had a son," she said.

Judith and Ruby left the porch to watch with the other women. "Arlene, I thought you told me Mr. and Mrs. Frosch both worked."

"They do," Arlene said. "But they can't work if they're dying."

"True," Judith agreed under her breath.

The police and the EMTs pulled in. Judith glanced at the Porters' house between the Rankerses' and the Steins'. Both Gabe and Rochelle Porter worked, too, so they were probably gone for the day, as were the Ericsons, who lived on the other side of the rental.

The firefighters and the young man had gone back inside. Ruby grabbed Judith's arm. "I recognize . . . no, I must be wrong," she said, shaking herself and letting her hand fall away.

"What?" Judith asked.

"Never mind," Ruby replied. "I'm still fuzzy."

Judith didn't recognize the two patrol officers. They were

male, one black, one Hispanic, and both very young. Rookies, Judith figured. She did know the lead EMT—Kinsella, who had been an all-too-frequent visitor over the years. He glanced at the B&B, but quickly turned away as if reliving a bad dream. Judith felt like making an obscene gesture, but decided that would be a really bad idea.

Naomi had turned to Arlene. "Have you met the new people who live in the corner house next to the rental?"

"Only once," Arlene replied. "Bhumi Bhatt works for a national investment firm. Bhandra Bhatt tutors children in math, shops exclusively at Nordquist's, and reads only nonfiction. Two children, nine-year-old boy, Bhupa, and six-year-old girl, Bhopad. They go to Pastoral Day School on the other side of the hill. The family has moved three times in the past seven years, living most recently in Denver. Oh—their cat died last week. He was fourteen, and didn't want to leave Colorado. His name was Rocky. For the mountains, I suppose."

Naomi's expression was blasé, accustomed as she was to Arlene's knowledge about people she claimed to be utter strangers. "I've only seen the Bhatts from across the cul-de-sac. Very good-looking people." She gestured at the rental. "If that was the Frosches' son, the sick person must be . . . ?"

"Elma or Herbert," Arlene said. "He prefers being called Herb."

"Working for Boring," Judith suggested. "Herb may be on the night shift. If Elma cooks at the public schools, she's probably at work."

Arlene gestured at the vehicles in front of the Frosch house. "Elma's VW is there and the midsize sedan belongs to Herb. He does work odd hours." She took a few steps forward, studying the rear of a black Ford Explorer Sport Trac. "Idaho plates," she said. "The son," she added ominously.

"Dare I ask," Judith began, "if you know anything about him—" She broke off as a gurney was rolled out of the rental.

"Nothing to see here," Medic Kinsella shouted at the four women. "Not one of yours," he added, looking directly at Judith.

"Fine," Judith murmured, but was startled to see the young man and an older version of him she vaguely recognized. "It must be Elma."

"There go the firefighters," Naomi said. "And police." She turned to Judith. "Why don't you ask those officers. You must know them."

"I don't," Judith replied through taut lips. "They're new."

The younger and the older Frosches got into the Ford Explorer.

Arlene threw up her hands. "That's disgusting! Nobody lingered long enough to answer any questions. What's wrong with people? Don't they think we care about our neighbors?"

Naomi patted Arlene's arm. "Don't fuss. You'll find out soon enough. Bad news travels fast."

"Not fast enough." Arlene took a few steps across the cul-de-sac. "But maybe sooner than I expected. The front door isn't closed shut."

"Arlene!" Naomi cried. "You wouldn't!"

Arlene scowled at Naomi. "We can't leave their door open." Her blue-eyed gaze veered to Judith. "Especially with burglars breaking into houses around here. Isn't that what the block watch and neighbors are for? I'll make sure everything is secure." As if marching to a regimental drumbeat, she headed for the rental.

Naomi laughed and shook her head, but followed Arlene. Ruby stared at Judith. "Are you going with them?"

"No." Resolutely, Judith turned her back on the rental and led the way to the B&B. "They're harmless. Really," she said after they got inside. "Naomi might protest, but she's curious, too. It's . . . ah . . . natural. The Frosches aren't neighborly and . . . um . . . well . . . I've got a key."

Ruby was wide-eyed. "You do? How come?"

"My husband's ex-wife owns that house. She lives in Florida, so we keep a key if any problems come up. Until now, the rental agency has handled everything, but Herself—I mean, Vivian—feels better if Joe and I have access in case . . . just in case."

"That's . . . good of you. No hard feelings between you and his ex?"

"Not anymore," Judith said, heading for the kitchen. "It's all in the past." She picked up the pace as the phone rang. To her dismay, it was her cleaning woman, Phyliss Rackley. "Where are you?" Judith asked, trying to hide her irritation. "You were supposed to be here by ten."

"The good Lord had other plans for me," Phyliss said in a sulky voice. "My dentist had an emergency he had to take first. Then the bus broke down. I'm standing on a corner waiting for the next one. In fact, I'm outside of a little grocery store and . . . oh, no! The bus went by without stopping! The Lord must have it in for me today. I can't think why. I haven't sinned that much except for being annoyed by having to wait so long for the dentist. Evil thoughts—that'll do it every time."

"The Lord probably doesn't have it in for you, Phyliss, but I will if you don't get over here in half an hour. The morning is almost gone."

"Don't worry, I'll be there. I'll pray on it. It's starting to rain again. Oh, no! I left my bumbershoot at the dentist's! Satan's ruining my life. He's tempting me to anger."

Judith ignored the remark. "I keep an extra umbrella here," she said, also trying to keep her temper. "Stay under the store overhang and don't miss the next bus." She hung up before Phyliss could say another exasperating word.

Ruby had taken it upon herself to clean the dining room coffee urn. "Just trying to be useful. You got a Bible-thumper working for you?"

Judith nodded once. "My cleaning woman. She's very good, but very . . . pious. Or something like that. She also has a lot of health and dental problems. Fortunately, none of them are serious."

"Want me to start in on some of her chores?" Ruby offered. "She won't be able to catch up."

Judith was surprised. "You're not going to continue your quest?"

Ruby slumped into a kitchen chair. "I feel like a dork. I make one crummy try at it and end up losing my purse and getting amnesia. Maybe it's not worth it. What can I really do on my own?"

"It's probably just as well you don't overtax yourself," Judith said. "Did you think you recognized someone in the cul-de-sac?"

Ruby shook her head, but didn't meet Judith's gaze. "Not really. You know how some people are a type. I mean, they're the same height, build, coloring, age group." She shrugged. "They look familiar until you get up close."

"True," Judith agreed as Joe entered through the back door.

"I've got some news," he announced, hanging up his jacket in the hallway. "It's raining."

Judith made a face at her husband as he came into the kitchen. "Funny Joe. That's not news around here."

"No," he responded, taking a diet soda out of the fridge, "but I stopped to see Woody at the precinct station. He's going to pull his old files." Joe sat down next to Judith and looked at Ruby. "He's intrigued, of course. Being a captain, he may not get to it until tomorrow, but he'll bring them when he comes to dinner. You're sticking around, right?"

Ruby looked surprised. "Yeah, well, I guess I better. I was about to give it up. I feel guilty for causing everybody so much trouble."

Joe shook his head. "Don't. Look, I'm doing this for my old partner as much as for you. This case has bothered him for years." He nudged Judith. "So what was that 911 call to Herself's house about? It came in while I was talking to Woody, but I had to leave before I could find out."

Judith looked into his curious green eyes. "Believe it or not, I have no idea. We think it was for Mrs. Frosch. Somebody left on a gurney and it wasn't Mr. Frosch or the young man I assume is their son."

Joe took a quick swallow of soda. "You mean it could be a mere medical emergency?"

Judith shrugged. "It happens."

"No, it doesn't," Arlene called out from the hallway. "Naomi and I found out why the front door was left open." She entered the kitchen and sat down by Ruby. "A young woman was in the living room. We hadn't even started to look at . . . I mean, *look around* to make sure everything was in order—the stove and faucets not on, the pilot light—"

"Stop!" Judith cried. "Who was it?"

"How do I know?" Arlene shot back. "Apparently she's either the wife or the girlfriend of their son, Brick. Her name is Elaine, but she prefers Lainie, with an *i* and *e* at the end. Of her name, I mean."

"So," Judith asked when Arlene had stopped for breath, "what happened to Elma? It *was* Elma, right?"

"Yes," Arlene replied. "Elma was suffering from an overdose of antacids. No gallbladder, as you may recall."

Joe looked bemused. "Arlene, that's bull. Nobody ODs on antacids. You'd throw up before you could do that."

Arlene grimaced. "I wanted to throw up hearing about it, but that's what Lainie told us. You don't think Naomi and I aren't suspicious? Are you going to notify Vivian about what happened to her tenant?"

"Ah . . ." Joe glanced at Judith. "I doubt it. Maybe I'll find out what *really* happened first. There's no need to bother my ex about it yet."

"Right," Judith muttered. "She might take to drink. More than usual, that is."

Joe looked askance, but kept his mouth shut.

Arlene, however, wasn't finished. "Naomi and I think Brick has spent some time in jail."

"Why is that?" Joe asked calmly.

"Because of Lainie's tattoos." Arlene pointed to her forearm. "She had several tattoos with slashes through them like days crossed out inside of hearts. I asked her what they meant. I wasn't being nosy, I wanted to show her I was a kind neighbor. She said

they marked off the *time* Brick was *away*. Doesn't that sound as if
he'd been in prison?"

"Maybe," Judith suggested, "he was in the military."

Arlene bristled. "Then why didn't she have an American flag or
an anchor or an army patch as a tattoo?"

Ruby finally spoke up. "You could be right. Mom knew a
woman at work who marked off the months on the fridge while
her guy was in the slammer. Vehicular assault. She wondered
what that fridge would look like when he got out, but the woman
divorced him before he was sprung."

Joe put his arm around Judith. "I can't believe you lived in the
Thurlow District all those years. Why didn't you ask me to liber-
ate you?"

Judith glared at him. "You know damned well why I didn't.
I thought you were wildly happy with Herself. How did I know
you'd tried to call me after she hijacked you, but Mother kept
hanging up after telling you I was dead?"

"But you weren't," Arlene pointed out. "That was very naughty
of your mother to tell such a lie."

"Skip it," Judith snapped, darting dirty looks at Arlene and Joe.

"I know when I'm not wanted," Joe murmured. "I'm taking my
soda and going upstairs. Let me know when lunch is ready."

Arlene was right behind him. "Check Brick Frosch's criminal
record, Joe. Carl needs to know as the block watch captain."

"I like her," Ruby said as soon as Arlene made her exit.

"How can you not?" Judith said, smiling. She paused, hearing
an exchange between the Porcinis as they left for the day. "It's
going on noon. I'd better start lunch."

"I can help," Ruby volunteered. "I'd like to meet your mother."

"You would?" Judith grimaced. "I mean, sure, why not? I was
thinking of something you might do about your own mother.
I don't suppose you kept any of the newspaper accounts of her
murder?"

"No," Ruby said, getting up from the table. "It was too awful."

"You might check out the media archives on my computer.

Some detail could trigger a memory that might be meaningful in retrospect."

"I suppose." Ruby moved aimlessly around the kitchen. "Is Mr. . . . I mean, Joe really taking on my case? What does he charge?"

"If," Judith said, removing a loaf of light rye from the bread box, "he's doing this for Woody Price, he won't charge you anything. Consider your own interest a throw-in."

"That sounds wrong," Ruby declared. "If I hadn't come here, Joe wouldn't be doing this."

"Joe and Woody would probably revisit the case eventually. Besides, you'll get to meet the Prices. They're wonderful people."

Ruby looked wistful. "Wonderful people . . . funny, but I didn't think there were any of those left. Until I met you, I mean."

Judith didn't know whether to laugh or cry.

Chapter 6

The rest of Thursday passed uneventfully. Phyliss showed up shortly after noon, full of complaints, but praising the Lord for her deliverance from the metro transit system, which she likened to the Babylonian Captivity.

Judith made a trip to Falstaff's and Holliday's Drug Store. Joe had an afternoon meeting with a prospective client across the lake. Ruby spent all afternoon going through the local newspaper files and taking notes. Gertrude threatened to kill Aunt Deb after they'd gone set doubled and redoubled at their Holy Childhood bridge club. Emmy O'Flapdoodle—not her real name, but that's what Judith's mother always called her—and Marie Goetzenheimer had to separate the Grover sisters-in-law to keep their hostess, Agatha Dunze, from calling the police. In other words, it had been a normal day at Hillside Manor.

"Gosh," Renie said over the phone that evening, "Mom was actually *mad* at Aunt Gert. Usually, she just laughs her off and tells her to stop taking the game so seriously."

"You know how Mother prefers to focus on her card games," Judith replied. "She plays to win. And Aunt Deb does go on."

"So what? Mom likes the social part. She doesn't give a hoot who wins. Speaking of hoots, I ran into Arlene at the hardware store this afternoon. I hear you had some excitement this morning. Any news on the rental occupants?"

"Joe checked the 911 call and found it apparently wasn't serious. I relayed the message to Arlene."

"Oh? Then how come Margo Holliday told me at the drugstore that she heard it was life-threatening?"

"She did?" Judith was surprised. "I was at Holliday's this afternoon, too. I must've missed you and Margo. I didn't go back to the pharmacy section. Was Margo breaking customer confidentiality?"

"Hardly," Renie replied. "She heard it from that woman who lives in the corner house. What's her name? Band-Aid or something like that?"

"Bhandra," Judith said thoughtfully. "They just moved in. The rest of us are putting together a welcome basket for them."

Renie laughed. "With a copy of your sleuthing résumé?"

"Not funny," Judith snapped. And hung up on her cousin.

Judith didn't have time to go over Ruby's notes on the cold case until after the departing guests had checked out at eleven. She and Ruby sat in the living room while Phyliss Rackley scrubbed the kitchen floor. Ruby had jotted down a copious amount of information, but none of it struck Judith as helpful.

"The most important part," she said to Ruby, "are the names of witnesses and persons of interest." She scanned the list:

Myrna Grissom, manager of Peebles Place

Erma Schram, aide at Peebles

Luella Crabbe, next-door neighbor

Freddy Mae Morris, friend

Frank & Dorothy Morris, parents of Freddy Mae

Darrell (Duke) Swisher, Opal Tooms's fiancé, construction worker

Jorge Gonzales, racetrack trainer

Jimmy Tooms, Opal's ex-husband

Hector Sparks, nursing home patient

Marla & Lee Watkins, daughter and son-in-law of Hector Sparks

Ruby and Ozzie Tooms, victim's children

"Did your brother come home when your mother was killed?"

Ruby nodded. "Ozzie stuck around for over a week to help with Mom's funeral. The cops asked if he knew anybody who might have it in for her. He didn't, any more than I did, except for Mr. and Mrs. Watkins. While he was on leave, he proposed to Freddy Mae."

"Your girlfriend?"

"Yeah." Ruby laughed. "She accepted, but they didn't get married for another year or so. He had to go overseas. They're still together. I'm surprised." Her amused expression faded. "Heck, I'm surprised anybody sticks together these days."

"Do they have children?"

Ruby shook her head. "Turned out Freddy Mae couldn't have kids. They thought about adopting, but being in the service, they moved a lot. I guess they figured maybe it was just as well not to have a family."

Judith studied the names again. "I don't see anything that jumps out at me. Duke had an alibi. Your dad was in jail. The rest . . ." She swept a hand over the tablet. "Just coworkers, neighbors, and the nursing home's hired help. Oh—what about Hector's daughter and her husband? What cleared them of suspicion?"

"They were both at work," Ruby said. "Lee was a bus driver and Marla worked at a nursery—The Garden of Eden. You remember it?"

Judith wrinkled her nose. "Yes. It wasn't much of a nursery and the florist part had a poor selection. Is it still around?"

"I don't know. Mom always called it The Garden of Weedin' because the plants she bought there often had weeds in them. You couldn't tell until you got the plants out of the containers. She liked to work in the yard. Thought it was good exercise."

"I like to garden," Judith said. "When I have time." She sighed.

"I'm not much help. How many of these people are still around?"

"Gosh—I don't really know. Hector Sparks is probably long gone. He was questioned, but only had good things to say about Mom."

"Where's The Persian Cat located?"

"The Lockjaw Tavern's old site. Maybe you remember it."

"Vaguely," Judith replied. "It made The Meat & Mingle look good. So did another old dive just down the street—Spooner's Schooners."

"I never was inside either of those places." Ruby frowned. "When they were still there, you could look through the windows and . . ." She pressed her fist against her lips. "You can see inside the café now, too," she continued after a long pause. "What *did* I see?"

"Yesterday?" Judith prompted. "Or a long time ago?"

Ruby held her head. "I'm not sure. It was a man with kind of a hooked nose and a jutting chin." Her hands fell away and she stared helplessly at Judith. "Why do I remember seeing him? Am I nuts?"

Judith shook her head. "No. I think you're starting to remember things. Don't push it. It's a good sign. By the way, if you need to have any clothes washed, just put them in the hamper inside the armoire in the hall between Rooms One and Three."

Ruby nodded. "Thanks. I still feel as if I'm imposing."

Judith smiled. "I often let guests who stay a few nights do that. It's an uphill climb and a long walk to the nearest Laundromat. Besides, you don't need distractions. Just focus on what you remember."

But Ruby had no more memories that night. And Judith had no insight into that list of names that rang no bells, sounded no whistles, and yet somehow set off an alarm at the back of her brain.

Where," Joe asked the next morning while Judith was dishing up scrambled eggs for the guests, "did Ruby go so early?"

"She took breakfast out to Mother, who'll be glad of the company."

Joe cocked his head to one side. "She will?"

"You know Mother can be quite charming when she meets new people," Judith said, putting a cover on the pewter chafing dish. "It's almost as if she turns into a different person."

"You mean somebody I might like?"

"Joe . . ." Judith heard the first of the guests entering the dining room. "Never mind. Help me with the French toast and the muffins. Oh—bring some ketchup and the syrup."

Twenty minutes later, all of the guests had come downstairs. Joe was putting more toast on a plate. "Is Ruby still with your allegedly charming mother?"

Judith nodded. "It's been almost an hour, but no doubt Mother is exuding the charm she so cleverly hides from us."

"Too incredible to contemplate," he murmured. "I thought I'd go over the case files with Ruby this afternoon. I should take another look before Woody and Sondra get here this evening."

"Good idea. Maybe I should sit in on that."

"Fine," Joe said, before taking the toast out to the dining room just as Phyliss appeared from the basement.

"Hallelujah!" the cleaning woman exclaimed, carrying a full laundry hamper through the back hall. "The Lord showed me where to find that new bottle of bleach. Otherwise, I'd never get those brown stains out of Mr. Flynn's handkerchief."

Judith turned sharply to stare at Phyliss. "What stains?"

"I told you, the white one in the wash. Coffee or tea, maybe. Hard to get out sometimes. It's Mr. Flynn's right? It's got the initial *F* on it."

"Joe doesn't have any initialed handkerchiefs," Judith said.

Phyliss set the hamper down under the open end of the kitchen counter. "Then it must be a guest's. You want to see it? It's not ironed yet." She leaned down, her white sausage curls flopping every which way. "Got it. Clean as a repented sinner's soul."

Judith took the rumpled handkerchief from Phyliss. It was a bit frayed around the edges, but the stamped initial was still visible. "Where did you find it? I mean, was it in one of the rooms?"

Phyliss's plain, lean face looked blank. "I'm not sure. Could be. I didn't have time to do all the laundry yesterday, only your own stuff and your mother's. This is mostly from the guest rooms. When I strip the beds, I don't pay attention to what's between the sheets. It might give me sinful thoughts."

Joe returned from the dining room. "Heading for the barber to get my hair cut," he said, trying to edge around Judith and Phyliss. "Anything you need on top of the hill?"

"Nothing I can think of," Judith replied. "Is this yours?" She held out the handkerchief.

"No," Joe said. "You know I don't have initials on mine." He kissed Judith's cheek. "Got to go. Barber appointment's at nine-thirty."

Phyliss looked worried. "Satan's at work here," she declared.

"I doubt it," Judith said, seeing Joe almost collide with Ruby at the back door. "Maybe our guest knows something about it."

Phyliss turned to look behind her. "A man's hankie? She doesn't look like a man to me. Satan's in our midst. One of those change-lings, maybe." She shuddered, the sausage curls dancing along her furrowed brow. "I'm going back to the basement."

"What's with her?" Ruby asked as Phyllis raced down the hall.

"I told you yesterday, she's . . . a bit different. Very religious." Judith presented the handkerchief. "Is this yours?"

Ruby shot Judith a puzzled look. "No. Why would it be?"

"It was in the laundry."

Ruby looked Judith in the eye. "I've never seen it before."

Judith shrugged. "A careless guest, probably." A quick recollection of the current and previous guest lists contained no one with a first or last name beginning with F. But she carefully placed the handkerchief in a drawer. "How was Mother?"

Ruby beamed. "Awesome! She's so full of life. You're lucky to have her."

"I am," Judith admitted with a pang of guilt. Opal Tooms hadn't reached half of Gertrude's age.

"A little forgetful," Ruby said, pouring herself some coffee. "She insisted she didn't remember your old neighborhood."

"She never saw it," Judith said, after glancing into the dining room to make sure her guests didn't need attention. "Dan cut me off from my family during the years we lived there."

"Jeez, you really did have a bad time!" Ruby shook her head. "To think I feel sorry for myself. After all the sad stories I've heard in bars, I should know better."

"You expect sad stories in bars," Judith said. "I heard my share of them while I was living out on my own."

The phone rang. Judith picked it up off the counter. It was a reservation request from an Oregon couple for the Thanksgiving weekend. Luckily, Judith had one room left. She jotted down the information, thanked the female caller, and hung up.

The rest of the morning moved along swiftly. Joe returned from the barber, his hair noticeably shorter—and, Judith realized with a pang, more of his forehead was bared. By eleven, all the departing guests had checked out. The rain had stopped, so Ruby had gone for a walk, hoping to clear her head and retrieve her memory. Phyliss was upstairs cleaning the guest rooms. After Judith had taken lunch to Gertrude, she checked e-mail for reservations and found two more requests, both for early December. By two o'clock, Ruby had returned, her memory not improved, but her spirits lifted by the views from Heraldsgate Hill.

"Time to talk about the case," Joe announced from the kitchen doorway. "Living room, ladies."

Ruby was just finishing lunch while Judith was contemplating how long to cook the pork loin she was serving her dinner guests. "Start without me," she said. "I have to figure out what to do with the entrée. It might take me a few minutes."

She had made her decision ten minutes later when Renie stomped through the back door. "I had to run errands at the bottom of the hill," she said, flopping into a kitchen chair. "Halfway up the Counterbalance, I decided you might need some help. What can I do?"

"Nothing, really," Judith said. "I chose a fairly easy recipe."

"Ha! There's no such thing." Renie lifted the lid of the sheep-shaped cookie jar. "What's in here? Dog biscuits?"

Judith grimaced. "I haven't baked recently. They're macaroons. I think."

Renie cocked an ear in the direction of the living room. "I haven't talked to you much lately. That design for Nordquist's spring catalog has kept me busy. They want a theme and they can't decide whether it should be inspired by Monet, Manet, or Mandalay. Do I hear Joe?"

"Yes," Judith said, crushing garlic with rosemary. "Oh! Remember Ruby from Little Bavaria?"

"Ruby?" Renie's round face looked momentarily puzzled. "Was she one of the people I got into a fight with during Oktoberfest?"

"She was the bartender and waitress we got to know whose dad was a Meat & Mingle customer."

"Right." Renie grinned. "I actually liked her. Why do you ask?"

"I forgot to tell you she's a guest."

Renie didn't respond. She merely stared at her cousin until Judith felt compelled to speak again. "Okay, okay," she said, putting aside the garlic-and-rosemary paste. "I didn't mean to hold out on you. It's a long story." She sat down across from Renie. "I'll keep it short."

"No, you won't," Renie retorted. "I knew damned well something was going on besides Mrs. Frosch getting a gut ache. Dish."

Judith did—for at least five minutes, with only a couple of interruptions from Renie. "So," she said in conclusion, "the subject will come up tonight. You probably should warn Bill. He might get bored."

"Not necessarily," Renie responded. "He'll have something different to discuss with Oscar. I get tired of hearing them yakking about soccer."

"I didn't think Bill liked soccer," Judith said—and could have bitten her tongue for encouraging accounts of her cousin's husband's conversations with a stuffed animal. "I mean—"

"He doesn't," Renie interrupted. "But Oscar insists he played soccer in The Village. In The Jungle, actually. I think they swung on vines instead of just kicking the ball around on the ground. Snakes, you know. Kind of dangerous."

"Stop. Please. Do you want to say hello to Ruby or do you want to go home to your own cozy insane asylum?"

"I'll wait," Renie said, looking wistfully at the cookie jar. "I really do want to help you. Can I peel potatoes or something? You can tell me more about the long-ago murder you're not trying to solve."

Judith stood up. "Okay, you do the potatoes. I think I've filled you in about the cold case. I just wish Ruby would start remembering what happened to her before she blacked out in the old neighborhood. Say," she said suddenly, "being a psychologist, could Bill figure out a way for her to get her memory back?"

Renie shrugged. "I suppose he could always hit her over the head with a hammer."

"I'm serious," Judith said, hauling a bag of potatoes out of a bin under the counter.

"I'll ask him," Renie said. "I take it you don't want to go out to your old hood to help rekindle her memory?"

"I really don't," Judith admitted. "It holds too many dreary memories of my own. Though Ruby says it's changed a lot for the better."

"Short of becoming a nuclear waste dump, it had nowhere else to go," Renie remarked, getting a peeler out of a drawer. "Did you say the old folks' home was called Peebles?"

"Yes." Judith looked up from her recipe. "Why?"

"They got taken over years ago by AEGISGOOD, a national nursing-home chain. Do you remember a brochure I did for them back then?"

"No," Judith replied. "You do so many different projects that I can't keep up. Did you go out there?"

Renie cast a gimlet eye at her cousin. "No. Do you think I wanted to see my future unfold before me?"

Judith laughed. "I can't imagine you living in a nursing home. Opal Tooms wouldn't be the only one to meet an untimely end."

"I'd be too weak to do any damage. But I did meet some of the staff." Renie made a face in an apparent effort at recalling names. "A woman who ran the place . . . I want to say 'Gruesome,' but that was only the way she looked."

"Grissom?" Judith suggested.

"Right. Myrna Grissom. Talk about a hatchet face. She could've cut petrified wood with it."

"Did she strike you as honest?"

Renie recoiled in her chair. "Strike me? Hey, I didn't hit her first!"

"Don't be an idiot. You know what I mean."

"Well . . ." Renie leaned forward, elbows on the table. "Honest, as in straightforward? Yes. Honest as in integrity? Probably not. We weren't discussing ethics. I wanted her to ooze compassion. She tried, but flunked. I recall thinking that Myrna saw her patients as dollar signs, not people."

"Anything about her employees?"

Renie sat up straight and tapped her long fingernails on the table. "Hmm. Chattel. That's the word that comes to mind, but it was more attitude than what she actually said. Frankly, we didn't go into much detail about staff. I was aiming for the concept. Color, too—purple or mauve? I ended up with puce."

Judith scowled at her cousin. "What does *that* mean?"

"Seriously? Now that I'm beginning to remember more about that project, if you want to know the truth, it meant I was only lukewarm about Peebles. Purple would have made a strong statement and mauve would have been more soothing. My choice of puce indicated I didn't care much for the setup or for Myrna. It means flea in French, going back to bloodstained sheets left by flea bites. Somehow it fit with what I perceived as Myrna's attitude toward her patients."

Judith grimaced. "As well as I know you, sometimes the way your mind works is . . . a bit strange."

"At least it still works," Renie said. "Is Ms. Gruesome a suspect?"

Judith shook her head. "I doubt it. There are other more likely people involved. But apparently all of them were eliminated because . . ." She stopped and bit her lip. "Hey, coz, I'm really not trying to solve this thing. Joe is, because of Woody's involvement. I'm only helping Ruby put things down on paper to help get her memory back."

"Of course," Renie deadpanned.

Judith's dark eyes snapped. "I mean it."

"I know you do." Renie's expression didn't change.

"You'd better."

"Sure. So what do we do now? Make a sentimental journey out to the Thurlow District?"

"Coz . . ." Judith said, exasperated. "Please. Yes, the case will be discussed tonight at dinner, but that's it as far as I'm concerned. Joe and Ruby are going over Woody's files in the living room. I'm in the kitchen getting dinner prepared. That's it."

"Got it," Renie said, standing up. She headed for the swinging half doors that led to the dining room.

"Hey," Judith called after her, "where are you going?"

"To have a sit-down with Joe and Ruby," Renie called out. "Hurry up. You'll miss something."

Judith dug her heels into the floor. She refused to be sucked in by Renie. Of course, she'd told Joe she'd join him and Ruby. But domestic duties had intervened. In retirement, running the house and the business was her priority. On the other hand, she'd promised to help Ruby. And she owed Woody, if only for friendship's sake. The pork loin didn't have to go into the oven for another three hours. She couldn't let Ruby, Woody, or Joe down.

Judith got up from the chair. She headed for the living room and hoped she hadn't left retirement from sleuthing behind her.

Chapter 7

To sum up," Joe said to Judith when she sat down beside him on the sofa, "according to Woody's case file, there were some shaky alibis. Suspicion isn't enough to nail anyone down with the two-day gap before the body was found and the five-hour window for time of death."

"True," Judith murmured. "Whose alibis were iffy?"

"Several," Joe replied, picking up the single sheet of paper. "These people are witnesses, not suspects. Woody eliminated Mrs. Crabbe, who found the body. She was in her late sixties then and died in 1994."

"Besides," Ruby put in, "she had arthritis and probably couldn't have managed to strangle Mom, even by surprise. Nice old girl. I can't imagine her doing such a thing. I'm part of the alibi for Freddy Mae and her parents and vice versa because I was staying at their house. They hardly knew Mom. They're retired in Arizona and later on became Ozzie's in-laws, but that happened after Mom was killed. Dad was in the slammer and now he's dead, too. Hector Sparks must be long gone, but he was so crippled that he couldn't get out of bed by himself."

"And the rest?" Judith asked.

Joe put the list on the coffee table. "We'll save that for Woody this evening. With the big window for time of death, it's hard for anybody to have an ironclad alibi, especially if they were in the vicinity."

Renie pointed to a name on the list. "This trainer, Gonzales. I wonder if Uncle Al knows him from the track. He's pals with everybody who hangs out there." She turned to Ruby. "Did your mother know him?"

"I doubt it," Ruby replied. "He was Duke's alibi."

Joe nodded. "Woody's last check on these people was 1998. Gonzales was at the new track by then." He stood up. "We're done here. To be continued tonight during the cocktail hour. Seven o'clock," he said, looking at Renie.

"Bill likes to eat at six," she said, also getting up.

"Bill will have to wait," Judith said. "Why can't he have a late-afternoon snack?"

"Can't do that. His snacks are precisely timed. My best bet is to drug him so he takes a longer nap. See you later." She made her exit.

Judith headed for the kitchen, Joe went upstairs, and Ruby disappeared into the powder room off the entry hall.

Three minutes later, Renie returned via the back door. "Action at the Frosch place," she announced. "Better check it out."

Judith put aside the recipe book she'd been studying and followed Renie outside to the Camry that was parked in the driveway. "Pretend we're just . . . chatting," she suggested, casting a curious glance at Herb and Lainie, who were talking to a pudgy, dark-haired middle-aged man whose back was turned to the cousins.

Renie nodded before mouthing unspoken words. Judith smiled agreeably. She managed to catch a few snatches of the conversation between Lainie and the stranger.

" . . . not a thin dime . . ." Brick's girlfriend said heatedly.

" . . . crazy old coot," the pudgy man said. " . . . not that Tooms tart?"

Judith and Renie exchanged curious glances.

Herb spoke up in a loud, belligerent voice. "Why would we be living in a rental if we were rich?"

"You're lying!" the stranger shouted. "You must've blown the money! I'll fix your wagon!" Head down, shoulders hunched, he stalked away to a blue sedan and roared out of the cul-de-sac. Lainie whirled around and stomped back into the house, leaving Herb on the sidewalk.

Judith couldn't resist. "Let's comfort Mr. Frosch. He *is* our default tenant." She hurried from the driveway, calling his name. Renie was right behind her. "Is there a problem?" Judith asked just as Herb started back toward the house.

"Awww . . ." Herb waved his arm in a disgusted gesture. "Damned jailbird. Got prison pallor all over him. No big deal." He paused, peering closely at Judith. "You're . . . ?"

"Judith Flynn, Vivian's—your landlady's—on-site stand-in along with my husband, Joe. She sends her best wishes for your wife's recovery. I hope that man didn't harass you."

"Oh. Thanks. That's nice." He ran a hand through what was left of his fair hair. "No big deal. That guy—Beaker Schram—was my wife's ex. Years ago, Elma and a coworker got into it. I hardly remember what it was all about, except it had to do with some old goat who kept telling every good-looking woman he met that he was leaving her his fortune. For all I know, he was on welfare. Now this jackass gets sprung and comes around making trouble. Guess he thought Elma had inherited a big wad. Schram's nuts. Probably spent all his time in the slammer brooding about losing Elma and a pile of money. To hell with him." He started moving toward the house.

"The Tombs?" Renie asked. "Schram was in a New York City jail?"

Herb turned to scowl at her. "No. Why are you talking about tombs in New York? Schram did time somewhere in this state."

Renie looked ingenuous. "But he mentioned something that sounded like tombs. My mistake."

Briefly, Herb looked puzzled. "Ah! Think it was another gal's name at Elma's work. Speaking of work, I gotta run." He went into the house.

"So," Judith murmured, "we have a real connection between the Frosches and Opal. What a coincidence."

"Not really," Renie said as they walked back to the Camry. "Bear in mind that as a native, there aren't that many residents who go back as far as we do. When we had the city's sesquicentennial celebration of its founding several years ago, there were only a thousand people who had ancestors prestatehood in 1889. You and I and all our relatives made up a big chunk of those people. Everybody who has come here since is a virtual newcomer. For all we know, you and I are related to the Frosch and Tooms families."

Judith shuddered. "I hope not."

Room Two had been taken by a visiting botany professor from Indiana, so Ruby had moved her belongings up to the guest bedroom on the third floor. She was coming down the front staircase when Judith went back inside.

"Let's sit in the living room," she suggested to Ruby. "I need to take a few deep breaths."

"How come?" Ruby asked, looking wary. "Is something wrong?"

"No, no," Judith assured her, indicating her guest should sit on the opposite sofa by the hearth. "I have a question about someone your mom worked with. What do you remember about Erma Schram, the aide on Woody's list?"

"Erma." Ruby frowned. "Mom didn't talk much about her job unless it was something funny or unusual. But she mentioned Erma a couple of times. Mom didn't like her. She said Erma could get nasty. In fact, at one point she thought Erma was trying to get her fired, but I don't remember why. Maybe Erma was in a bad place. She was going through a divorce with a guy who was in prison."

Judith dropped her bombshell. "I think Erma is Elma Frosch."

Ruby's reaction puzzled Judith. "Elma Frosch?"

"The sick woman from the rental house."

"No!" Ruby held her head. "How can that be?"

"Her ex showed up a little while ago and was giving Mr. Frosch and Lainie—Brick's girlfriend—a bad time. He mentioned your mother's name, but I don't know why. After Beaker Schram drove off, Herb told Renie and me Elma's ex had been in prison."

Ruby turned pale. "B-B-Beaker S-S-Schram?"

"Do you know him?"

"No." Ruby looked puzzled. "But that name . . . Mom must've mentioned him when she was bitching about Erma. Oh, damn! Why can't I remember stuff?"

"What kind of stuff?" Judith asked gently.

Ruby sighed, though her color was coming back. "I don't know. His name creeps me out. I couldn't know him from a long time ago, could I?"

"Maybe. I suppose he and Elma lived in the Thurlow District. Mr. Frosch said Beaker had spent some time in prison. Would your dad have known him?"

"I've no idea." She suddenly brightened. "You saw him. Was he a Meat & Mingle customer?"

Judith made a face. "I didn't get a good look at him. His back was turned and he charged off with his head down like an angry bull."

"Ohmigod! Do you think he killed Mom?"

Judith thought back to the brief and fragmentary conversation between the two men. "I got the impression he might've been in prison when your mother was killed. But I can't be sure about that. Joe should be able to check that out—or Woody could. Schram's name isn't on the witness list, though Erma's is—even if she's changed her first name. Maybe she did that in an effort to get a new start in life after divorcing and remarrying."

"That kind of makes sense," Ruby allowed.

Judith stood up. "It may not mean anything, except it verifies a connection between your mother and the Frosches. That may not mean anything either. The link to the Frosches being here is via Joe's ex-wife. Vivian left a trail of people, including husbands, behind her in this city."

Ruby was also on her feet. "No wonder she moved to Florida. That must be a relief to you . . . and Joe."

Judith didn't argue.

By five-fifteen, the new arrivals had checked in. They would all stay until Monday morning except for a California couple who were heading to Canada the next day, but had stopped over to visit relatives in one of the city's eastside suburbs.

Shortly after six, Judith put the pork loin in the oven. At 6:10, Gertrude wheeled her way into the kitchen and demanded to know why her supper was so late.

"I told you," Judith said, trying to be patient, "the Prices and Renie and Bill are coming to dinner. You're welcome to eat with us. You do want some of the roast pork, don't you?"

"Are you wrecking it with fancy foreign stuff?" the old lady demanded. "I like my pork to taste like *pork,* not goofy spices and weeds you pull out of the garden. What's wrong with a pig hock now and then? A boiled dinner—when was the last time you made one of those?"

Judith juggled four acorn squashes she'd taken out of the fridge. "It's not easy to find pig hocks, Mother. Falstaff's rarely carries them."

Gertrude glared at the squashes. "What are you going to do with those? Bounce them off of Dumb Cluck's head?"

"I'm baking them with brown sugar and butter."

"I hate acorn squash."

"I have beans for you."

Gertrude looked wary. "What kind? I'm hungry for lima beans."

"That's fine," Judith said. "I have some in the pantry."

"They won't get done in there."

Judith took a deep breath. "I know that. It takes five minutes to warm them up. Why not eat dinner with us? The Prices are like family."

"That's the problem," Gertrude grumbled. "Who says I want to eat with family? What's worse, my nutty niece and her screwball husband *are* family. Forget it. I like my own company better than yours."

"Fine. Are you going to wait here until it's ready?"

Gertrude nodded in the direction of the living room. "Not with that gaggle of geese you call guests out there. It's a good thing I'm deaf." She reversed the wheelchair and headed for the door, narrowly missing Ruby, who was about to set foot in the hall from the back stairs.

"You ought to ticket your mother for speeding," Ruby said with a laugh when she entered the kitchen. "Guess what? I took a nap. I haven't done that in ages. It's so relaxing here. Can I help?"

"Yes," Judith replied. "Find a small can of lima beans in the pantry for the speeding geezer. Then make a drink and keep me company."

It took Ruby only a couple of minutes to find the lima beans. "Any news on the neighbor who got hauled off in the ambulance?" she asked.

"No," Judith replied, putting a baking dish of new potatoes into the oven next to the pork loin. The squashes were already on the top rack. "Just the usual neighborhood gossip about what was wrong with her."

Ruby had gotten out a glass. "Want me to fix you a drink?"

"Thanks, but not yet," Judith said. "I'll wait until the Prices and the Joneses get here. The trouble with company is that the living room's in use most nights until seven. I can host another couple in the parlor, but I need more room for a bigger party."

Ruby shrugged. "Most people don't mind eating later."

"Unless they're Mother and Renic's husband," Judith said.

Ruby was making herself a vodka martini when Joe arrived in the kitchen. "Woody and Sondra are on their way. The former fifteen-minute drive from their house on the other side of the lake now is forty-five minutes with all the newcomers. Too bad he can't take a squad car."

But to the Flynns' surprise, the Prices arrived at exactly seven. They looked unchanged from when Judith and Joe had seen them six months earlier. If they were aging, they were doing it well. Sondra's raven pageboy bob was untouched by gray and Woody's salt-and-pepper hair hadn't receded noticeably since then. The lines in his ebony face were a bit more deeply etched, but his wife's pecan skin was scarcely marked by time. Judith commented on her youthful looks, but Sondra laughed.

"You should see my insides," she said as Joe helped her out of a forest-green leather jacket. "They must look like a jumble of writhing snakes. Being a police captain's wife will give me an ulcer yet."

Woody gave her a flinty look. "She's waiting for her widow's pension. I think she liked it better when I spent more time chasing bad guys than sitting in an office. Frankly, I liked it better, too."

Joe faked a playful punch at his former partner. "You're saying that because you finally outrank me. Hey, you have to meet . . ." He looked around the entry hall and peered into the living room. "Where's Ruby?"

Judith nodded in the direction of the kitchen. "She's playing barmaid. She's had more recent experience than I've had."

"Ruby," Woody said in his soft, deep voice. "She was a teenager when I last saw her. My Lord, where did all those years go?"

Sondra made a face. "Oh, that's right, we're rehashing that Thurlow District murder. I hope you guys can help. My better half here still wakes me up with an occasional nightmare over that case."

Before Judith could lead the Prices into the living room, the Joneses arrived. Renie hugged Woody and kissed him soundly on the cheek. *"Rigoletto!"* she cried. "Second opera this season. You going? We are, despite the 1930s Chicago setting with an Al Capone theme."

"At least," Woody said, reaching around Renie to shake Bill's hand, "Capone was Italian."

"But the real Duke of Mantua wasn't," Renie said, letting go of Woody. "He was French. I mean, he wasn't even the Duke of Mantua. He was King Francis the First. Or would that be Roi François le Premier?"

"It could be Hitler for all I care," Bill growled, trying to get Renie out of her faux lynx coat. "Have you got this thing on backward again?"

"I don't know," Renie snapped. "Where are its eyes? If they're looking at you, then maybe I screwed up. So what?"

Judith intervened. "Why don't we adjourn to the . . ." she began, but stopped as Ruby appeared with the beverage tray.

"Sorry," Ruby said, smiling. "I can't shake hands until I put this on the buffet."

The others followed her into the living room. Introductions were made, with Woody looking less than his usual stoic self as he shook Ruby's hand. "My, my—you were still in high school the last time we met. You and your mother have been on my conscience ever since."

Ruby's expression was ironic. "Do you think her killer *has* a conscience?"

Woody's dark eyes glittered. "*Had* might be the key word. I've often wondered if the perp is dead, too."

"Could be," Ruby murmured. "What'll you have? I'm serving. Mr. Flynn—I mean, *Joe*—has probably told you I ended up in a bar. But I'm a waitress, too. I've tried to be respectable."

"That's commendable," Woody said, smiling. "You didn't get off to a very good start. A lot of people who've been through what you have go off the rails and never get back on track." He nodded at the buffet. "I'll have some of that Canadian Club with soda. Make that two—Sondra will have the same. We've been married so long that we're starting to look alike."

Ruby smiled wistfully, glancing beyond the Prices to the Flynns—and finally to the Joneses, who had stopped berating each other and sat down on the sofa next to Judith. "Happy couples," she said softly. "I'm not used to that. I mean, I *hope* you're all happy."

To prove the point, Bill kissed Renie. "Who says we're not happy?" she asked. "We work really hard at not being dull."

"You got that right," Bill shot back. "We even argue about how happy we are. Unless we're mad."

Renie wrinkled her pug nose. "Are we mad now?"

Bill shook his head. "I don't think so." He looked at Ruby. "Make mine bourbon. Same for my ornery wife."

"Two Scotch rocks," Joe chimed in from his place across the hearth from Judith. "Sounds like we've all been married too long."

"Joe . . ." Judith said. "We haven't been married nearly as long as . . ."

Her husband waved a hand. "No, but it seems like it. I mean," he said quickly, "we were supposed to have been married longer than anybody else here has been. We just got . . . to borrow a phrase from Woody, *derailed*. But we got back on track. Finally."

Ruby filled the drink orders and sat in a side chair Joe had pulled up for her by the coffee table. "I feel like I'm at a meeting," she said.

"You are," Judith said. "You're meeting your past."

Joe raised his glass. "Then here's to the future. And justice."

With solemn expressions, the others echoed his toast. Woody's first statement acknowledged that some of the people on the list were dead. "Luella Crabbe and Hector Sparks, both deceased, neither ever under suspicion. Jimmy Tooms was in prison," he went on with a swift look at Ruby, "but that doesn't mean he couldn't have had an accomplice. You told us at the time of your mother's murder that you didn't think your father had a motive."

Ruby fingered her chin. "He wasn't all that upset about the divorce. He was supposed to pay Mom child support, but that didn't happen very often, especially when he was in jail. Mom didn't play around on him, so it wasn't like he was jealous. And he wouldn't have made any money off her death because all she had was the house and a small life insurance policy that went to Ozzie and me."

Woody nodded. "So you told us at the time. I never seriously considered your dad as a suspect."

Judith couldn't keep from asking the question that had been on her mind all afternoon. "Do you remember much about Erma Schram?"

Woody looked thoughtful. "The aide? Fairly young, sort of defensive. I interviewed her because she was working the day shift that Opal often had. Usually, they both had the same schedule, so I thought maybe Erma might know something about Opal's private life. She didn't."

"Did she mention anything about her own?" Judith asked.

Woody frowned and sipped from his drink. "No. Mrs. Grissom—the manager—told me she was in the process of getting a divorce."

Judith briefly related the coincidental connection between her Frosch neighbors and Opal. Joe, who hadn't yet heard about the revelation, looked fit to spit. "How," he demanded as his wife finished her tale, "could my ex-wife rent to somebody who was mixed up in a murder case that's landed in the lap of my present wife? Vivian never lived in the Thurlow District."

Judith took umbrage. "She lived right next door to the neighborhood with Johnny Agra, probably less than two miles from where Dan and I lived."

"Just my luck," Joe muttered. "Why didn't I stay single?"

"Hey!" Judith cried. "Watch it!" She saw the sheepish expression on her husband's face and calmed down before turning back to Woody. "I'd like to know where this Beaker Schram was at the time of Opal's murder. He may've been in jail. Can you check?"

Woody assured her he could. "His name never came up while I was—" The sound of a siren interrupted him. "Is it coming this way?"

Everyone sat motionless, ears pricked up as the sound grew closer, followed by other sirens. But they stopped well short of the cul-de-sac.

"Hunh," Joe said. "It must be an accident on the Avenue. Too many drivers run the arterials to beat the north–south stream of cars."

"It could be a pedestrian," Bill said. "Some of them just *have* to wear all black at night so they can't be seen against a dark background."

"They're burglars," Renie asserted. "You can tell from the black bag marked 'SWAG.' They should put those letters in fluorescent caps and instead of ski masks they could wear baseball caps with—"

"I hear the doorbell," Judith broke in. "Excuse me."

An out-of-breath Naomi Stein was on the porch with her big Labrador retriever straining at the leash. "Oh, Judith," she said, "I just saw a terrible hit-and-run on the hill! I called 911 on my cell, but I thought I should tell you in case you thought . . . well, I mean . . . you have . . . that is . . ."

"Did you wait for the police?" Judith asked, ushering Naomi and the dog into the hall.

"No," Naomi replied, shaking rain off her yellow slicker. "Uzi got scared and started for home. I couldn't stop him. He's a load."

Joe had come into the hall. "Did you say a hit-and-run?"

"That's right," Naomi said, getting her breath. "The guy was right in the middle of a crosswalk at the corner. "I swear the car sped up and deliberately hit him." She winced. "I was just as glad Uzi took off. I didn't want to see . . . whatever happened to him."

"You're a witness," Joe said quietly. "You'll have to give a statement. By chance, the precinct captain is here."

Naomi's jaw dropped, but she quickly recovered herself and glanced at Judith. "Of course he is," she said under her breath. "Does he always bring accident forms when he visits?"

"No," Joe said with a straight face, "but he can contact the on-duty officers and they can come here to take your account of the incident. In fact," he went on, stepping closer to the still-open front door, "it sounds like the ambulance is leaving, siren on. Maybe the victim's still alive."

Naomi put a hand to her breast. "I hope so."

"Come into the living room," Judith said. "Would you like a drink?"

Joe held up a hand. "Hold it. Wait until Naomi gives her statement. We don't want anybody to think she was under the influence if this ends up in court."

Naomi nodded. "Of course. But I wouldn't mind a glass of water."

"I'll get it while Joe brings you a chair," Judith volunteered as she headed for the kitchen.

By the time she was putting ice into a glass, Arlene came through the back door. "I missed something," she announced. "Carl said he heard sirens a few minutes ago when I was downstairs on the phone. I wish my children wouldn't *shout* when they're talking to me. My hearing is fine."

Judith poured water into the glass and quickly explained what Naomi had seen on the main thoroughfare. Arlene was agog.

"How," she asked when she and Judith entered the living room, "could I miss a horrible tragedy like that? I must be slowing down!"

"Arlene," Naomi said with a hint of reproach, "you're a ghoul."

"Nonsense!" Arlene retorted with a wave of her hand. "I wouldn't have left the scene of the crime. I know my civic duty. And Tulip would never have tried to run off on me."

"Tulip," Naomi declared, "is a six-pound Boston terrier."

"Eight," Arlene said. "You should have gotten a smaller dog."

"Ladies," Joe intervened as he pulled up two more chairs, "sit down. We aren't here to discuss pet pooches. In fact, let's be quiet. Woody is trying to contact the patrol officers."

Arlene stared at Woody, who was standing at the other end of the room by the French doors. "Goodness," she said to Sondra, "I haven't seen you two in ages! You should come by when we don't have a crime in the neighborhood."

"We thought we had," Sondra murmured.

Arlene shrugged and sat down. "Timing is everything. But I don't know why. When you stop to think about it, what does it really mean?" She looked at the grandfather clock in the corner. "It's seven thirty-four. What difference would it make if it was seven-fourteen or seven fifty-six?"

Renie snorted. "Last week it would've been eight thirty-four because we were still on that stupid daylight saving time. Would somebody please tell me what we're saving it *for*? It's a waste of time and furthermore it costs more money to set and reset—"

Bill put a hand over Renie's mouth. "That's it." With his free hand, he held out his glass to Joe. "I could use a half inch more if we aren't going to eat until freaking midnight. If my ulcer hasn't already come back, it's on its way now. Boppin'!"

Joe took the glass—along with his own—and headed for the buffet. The doorbell rang again. Woody was halfway across the living room. "It's Smith and Wesson," he announced. "They pulled up as I rang off."

Naomi shot Judith a puzzled look. "Are these people guests or gunrunners?"

"They're the new evening patrol cops," Judith said. "They're a bit sensitive about their names."

Naomi shook herself. "I should think so. Why not Arm and Hammer?"

"They're the daytime police," Arlene said, reaching out to pat Uzi.

"She's kidding," Judith said, standing up as Woody led the ill-named female and male officers into the living room.

Woody beckoned to Naomi. "We should probably do this in the front parlor, Mrs. Stein."

"Please," she said, getting up. "Call me Naomi. We've met before."

"So we have," Woody murmured. "I know this neighborhood better than I know my own."

Arlene also stood up. "Do you need a witness for the witness? I volunteer."

Woody's smile was forced. "No, Arlene, but thanks. I'll be the witness." He moved on into the entry hall.

Arlene sat down again. "Judith, do you think I might have a glass of white wine while I'm waiting for the results?"

"The results?" Judith asked. "Of what?"

"Of whatever happened to that poor pedestrian." Arlene seemed puzzled. "You're the sleuth. If that person was crossing the street only a block away, we probably know him."

Judith had started for the makeshift bar on the buffet. "With all the condos and apartment houses around here, we probably don't."

"Speak for yourself," Arlene said, before turning to Joe, who was walking toward the parlor door by the grandfather clock. "You need a witness to the witness's witnesses? Really!"

"For old times' sake," Joe said without looking at Arlene—and closed the door behind him.

"Where's Carl?" Bill asked. "I'm the only man here."

"Hey," Renie said, "maybe Smith and Wesson could tell you their image problems with those names. Then you could give them some advice about self-esteem."

"Like what?" Bill shot back. "Tell them to change their names to Humpty and Dumpty? To hell with it. I don't give advice. I just listen and nod in a sage sort of way. I'm half asleep most of the time. Nobody takes advice anyway. They might as well throw their money down a manhole."

Renie frowned. "Then we couldn't pay our bills."

Bill frowned right back. "Are you sure we're paying them now? Why does my reading lamp keep blinking?"

"Bills!" Ruby suddenly exclaimed. "I just remembered!"

All eyes swerved to Ruby. "What bills?" Judith asked, handing Arlene a glass of wine.

"The light bill at our house," Ruby replied, her own eyes shut. "A couple of days before Mom was killed, we'd gotten a shutoff notice. Mom didn't get paid for another week and she was fussing about how to pay it. But she never did, and the lights weren't shut off."

Judith sat down on the sofa. "Did you call to ask about it?"

"No." Ruby had opened her eyes and was staring at Judith. "I never even thought about it at the time. Not with Mom getting killed and everything else going on. When the next bill came, Ozzie was still on leave and he opened it. It was just a regular bill, with the payment posted the day after Mom died. I guess she must've paid it after all. But now it seems strange. I mean, she'd said we only had thirty-six dollars in the checking account, and that was right. Ozzie and I had to go through all that stuff."

Questions leaped to Judith's lips, but she reined in her curiosity. Ruby and her brother had been teenagers, virtual orphans in a broken, dysfunctional family. It was probably all they could do to get through the days that followed their tragedy. And then Ozzie would have had to return to duty while Ruby moved in with Freddy Mae's family.

Renie, however, wasn't so reticent. "You must've had someone to help you sell the house and get everything in order. How did you and your brother handle that?"

"Legal Aid," Ruby replied. "It was all we could afford. Ozzie thought maybe because he was in the navy, he could get a naval lawyer, but that was too much hassle. We lucked out, though. The house sold pretty fast. I suppose we got screwed, but we just wanted to be done."

"You should have had our Cathy sell it," Arlene said. "She's a real estate whiz. Of course she was still in high school back then." She paused, scowling. "Or was she? Goodness, how time flies!"

Judith heard voices in the entry hall, indicating that the patrol officers were leaving. Naomi entered the living room from the door by the grandfather clock. "That wasn't much fun," she declared. "Mind if I make myself a martini?"

"Go for it," Judith said.

"Hey," Renie called to Naomi, "make one for Uzi. I really like seeing drunk dogs make fools of themselves. It makes me almost like them."

"Not funny, Serena," Naomi shot back. "Have you ever gotten your bunny gassed?"

Renie looked puzzled. "Do you mean Clarence or Bill?"

"Knock it off," Bill said under his breath.

Renie jumped off the sofa. "That's it! I need a refill." She stomped off to the buffet, almost stepping on Uzi. "What about you, Sondra?"

"Why not?" the other woman murmured. "Excuse me, Judith, but do I smell something burning?"

"The pork!" Judith struggled up from the sofa. A swift look at the grandfather clock told her it was ten to eight. According to the directions, the loin shouldn't be done for another ten minutes. Hurrying as fast as she dared with her artificial hip, she nipped past a startled Joe and Woody on their way back to the living room. Smoke was pouring into the dining room. She pushed through the half doors, barely able to see her mother sitting by the stove in her wheelchair. The fire alarm went off before Judith could say a word.

Gertrude looked more annoyed than startled. "Turn that thing off!" she yelled. "I'm not *that* deaf!"

"What . . . ?" Judith coughed as she tried to wave away the smoke that was coming from what was left of the pork loin. Backpedaling to the sink, she filled a kettle and dumped it into the baking dish. The water splashed up, shattering the oven light. Glass scattered all over the acorn squash and the new potatoes. But the smoke immediately began to disperse as the loin sizzled and sputtered in its death rattle. The heat, however, was still intense. Judith reached to turn off the oven and noticed it was set at five hundred degrees. "Mother!" she screamed. "Did you turn this up?"

"You bet," Gertrude said, wiping her watery eyes with a hankie. "It's almost eight. I like to eat supper at five. You want me to starve or should I go outside and graze on what's left of the dahlias? I hear some fancy restaurants serve flowers nowadays."

Joe, Bill, and Woody had charged into the kitchen. Judging from how fast the smoke was dissipating, someone had opened the front door.

And the back door, Judith realized as all the women entered

via the hall. "Hey," Renie said, "I think dinner's over. We must've missed it when we went outside to catch a breath of fresh air. When do the firefighters show up? We haven't heard a siren in almost an hour."

"Get some pizzas," Bill said. "It's two hours past my dinner-time. Pizza hoppin'!" He rubbed his hands in a familiar mock gesture of glee.

Gertrude sneered at Judith. "How come my squirrel-bait niece married a semisensible man? Why didn't you do the same?"

Judith ignored her mother. The squash was ruined and so were the potatoes. "It's a total loss," she lamented. "I'm so sorry."

"Cheer up," Renie said, phone in hand. "I'm calling Punchinello's. They're only two blocks away and they owe me. They left off my mushrooms the last time. I'll get salads, too, and French bread and . . . Hi, I'd like three large pizzas with the works, three with pepperoni, three with Canadian bacon and *mushrooms*—got that?—three with . . ."

"Make mine kosher," Naomi said, holding up her martini glass.

"Your gin isn't kosher," Arlene pointed out. "Or is it?"

"Who cares?" Naomi retorted. "I made a double. Hey, Serena," she called to Renie, who had just clicked off the phone, "let's get Carl and Hamish and the Porters and the Ericsons over here and have a real neighborhood party!"

"Don't forget the Bhatts," Arlene said. "It can be a housewarming party for them as newcomers, even if it isn't at their house. But it's certainly *warm*."

Judith started to protest but stopped. The evening had already gone as far downhill as it could go—unless Hillside Manor suddenly slid off its moorings and landed at the bottom of Heraldsgate Hill. Murder case be damned—she was retired from sleuthing. It was time to party. "Don't forget the Dooleys!" she cried. "We can't leave them out."

And party they did. But Judith had no inkling that part of the solution to the cold case was in a comment her mother made about the too-hot oven.

Chapter 8

Judith had no idea how many people had congregated all over the main floor of Hillside Manor that November evening. She counted at least eleven Dooleys, and along with the Bhatts and the rest of the longtime cul-de-sac residents, she estimated at least forty people. Renie had ordered more food and Arlene had pitched in with her usual efficient energy. When the grandfather clock struck the quarter hour before ten, Judith realized she'd better disperse her company before the paying guests returned from their own revels.

It was no wonder that she awoke the next morning with a headache. "Did I really drink that much?" she asked Joe as he came out of the bathroom.

"I don't think so," he replied. "I didn't notice anybody who was really gassed. But I do need to replenish the liquor cabinet."

"I guess it was all the noise and so many people at once," Judith said, getting out of bed. "I'll admit I've never seen Mother dance the polka with Woody. Especially when she stayed in her wheelchair. Or did she?"

"I missed that. I was too caught up watching Bill do his Clint Eastwood imitation while Gabe Porter juggled some of your English bone china on top of the piano."

"Was that when Corinne Dooley was trying to find one of her grandchildren under the piano?"

"That wasn't her grandkid," Joe said, putting on his pants. "That was Mr. Dooley. In all these years, I've never known his first name. Does he have one?"

"I guess so," Judith said vaguely, heading for the bathroom. "He's always kept a low profile."

"Maybe that's why he was under the piano," Joe suggested.

"Could be." Judith closed the bathroom door and looked in the mirror. She practically scared herself. *If I didn't drink too much, I sure did something to look this awful,* she thought. *Maybe I should stick to sleuthing. It's less stressful.*

But after taking two Excedrin, she was feeling somewhat revived by seven o'clock. Joe was already in the kitchen, having offered to make his own version of the original Joe's Special egg dish for the B&B guests. By the time Judith took breakfast to her mother just before eight, the old lady was all smiles.

"That was some whoop-de-do you had last night," she said. "Why don't you do that more often? It's a good thing I wrecked that bunch of stuff you had in the oven."

"You practically wrecked the oven," Judith retorted. "And could've burned down the house. We've already had one fire here in the past few years. It's a good thing no serious damage was done."

Gertrude shrugged. "You got something against having fun?"

Judith didn't feel like arguing. "It was great to have Woody and Sondra here. Yes, it was good to get together with the neighbors, too. Running an inn makes it hard to entertain anybody but family."

Gertrude nodded absently while she forked up Joe's Special. "Mmmm. Not bad. Is this Gloria McDonough's recipe from the parish cookbook?"

"It's the one you like so much," Judith replied. She'd always fibbed about Joe's recipe, knowing her mother wouldn't touch anything he'd cooked with a ten-foot two-by-four. "Got to feed the real guests," she said, and hurried back to the house.

By the time Phyliss Rackley arrived at nine, all of the guests had come down for breakfast. Although Joe, Arlene, and Carl had done an adequate job of helping Judith clean up from the party, the living room and parlor still required more work than usual.

"We had some neighbors in last night," Judith informed her cleaning woman. "You might want to start in the living room. I wasn't able to tidy up everything. Some of the neighbors brought their children."

Phyliss shrugged her narrow shoulders. "Youngsters need to be in a wholesome family get-together now and then. Our new pastor has some kiddies of his own and he often preaches about enclosure."

"Enclosure?" Judith echoed. "I don't get it."

Phyliss looked a trifle perplexed. "Maybe that's the wrong word. Pastor Smugsworth meant they needed inclusure—to be included in picnics and barbecues and swimming in the lake. But not go off the deep end—of the lake, that is. They can get baptized there, too."

"Oh. Inclusion. Yes, that's . . . all good." Judith nodded once for emphasis.

Phyliss went off on her rounds while Judith checked to make sure her guests were enjoying their breakfast. They were a fairly subdued, almost complacent group, but seemed more than satisfied, especially with Joe's contribution.

By eleven, they had all dispersed to check out or start their day's activities. Luckily, none of them were still around when Phyliss stalked into the kitchen with an empty wine bottle and two cigarette butts.

"What kind of debauchery did your neighbors have last night?" she demanded. "This looks like a godless orgy to me! And don't tell me they're all some of you wanton Catholics!"

"They're not," Judith responded with fervor. "They're not only *good* Catholics, but equally *good* Lutherans, Methodists, Jews, Presbyterians, and Hindus."

"An unholy polyglot!" Phyliss cried. "Where were the Muslims and the Buddhists and the Baptists and the dreaded Episcopalians?"

"The dreaded . . . ?" Judith felt her headache coming back. "Never mind," she said quickly. "Yes, we had some adult beverages and maybe a couple of people smoked cigarettes. Satan, however, was not invited."

"He might as well have been," Phyliss grumbled, throwing the offending items into the garbage under the sink before self-righteously heading for the guest rooms.

Ruby came downstairs shortly before noon. "Ohmigod!" she groaned, holding her head. "Did I tie one on last night or what?"

Judith, who was an old hand at calculating when people had drunk too much liquor, smiled. "You had four drinks. I suspect you usually can handle that, but you've been on an emotional roller coaster. Your defenses were down last night."

Ruby's hand fell away. "I guess. I had some weird dreams, too, but I don't remember them." She slumped into a kitchen chair and looked at the schoolhouse clock. "It's almost lunchtime!"

"You can still have breakfast," Judith said. "I saved some of Joe's Special. I'll warm it up for you. I have to get Mother's lunch anyway."

"Where *is* Joe?" Ruby asked.

"He went to the liquor store to replenish our supplies," Judith replied. "That reminds me—I never did go over Naomi's statement last night. Joe made a copy for himself. I forgot to ask him why."

"Does he do insurance investigations?" Ruby asked.

"Yes, fairly often," Judith replied, putting the last of Joe's egg dish into the microwave. "Would you like some toast?"

"Sure," Ruby said. "I can take your mother's lunch out to her when it's ready. She was a hoot last night."

"She can be many things," Judith murmured. There was no need to inform Ruby that a "hoot" usually wasn't one of them as far as her daughter was concerned.

While waiting for the toast to pop up, Judith scanned the e-mail printouts from guests. A file folder was under the last two she'd received that morning. She glanced inside to find Joe's copy of the accident report and Naomi's statement marked with an FYI Post-it note.

"I didn't notice this earlier," she said after removing the egg dish from the microwave and taking out the toast. "I'll go over it before I start Mother's lunch."

Her jaw dropped as she saw the victim's name: *Bernard Frosch, 31, Caldwell, ID.* "My God!" she cried. "It's the neighbors' son!"

"Which neighbor?" Ruby asked.

"The ones in the rental—the only neighbors who weren't here last night. Not only is the mother in the hospital, but now the son must be there, too. How horrible." She quickly read through the rest of the information. "He was taken to Norway General with multiple contusions and possible broken bones."

Ruby leaned forward, staring at the report. "Are you sure it's the same guy? I thought his first name was something else."

"It was," Judith said, turning to Naomi's statement. "He had an odd name, like . . . I forget. Arlene would know. Whatever it was, it sounded like a nickname." She summed up the eyewitness information for Ruby. "Male pedestrian crossing Heraldsgate Avenue in legal but unmarked crosswalk. Northbound car on Heraldsgate Avenue suddenly sped up. Dark-color medium sedan, state license plate, not vanity type, but no recollection of numbers or letters. Driver may have been male and alone. After hitting pedestrian, car picked up speed and disappeared after reaching the top of the hill."

Judith paused, checking out the notes that had apparently been made by Smith or Wesson. "Visibility impaired due to darkness and rainy conditions. Victim wearing dark clothing. No other eyewitness except for above." There was also a diagram of where the accident had occurred.

"It *could* be an accident," she said. "People go faster when they get halfway up the hill because the top part isn't as steep as the bottom. Once they reach the flat, drivers often run the four-way arterial."

"It's sure steep," Ruby said. "I'd never been on what you call the Counterbalance until I came here. There's a terrific view of the bay from there between the tall buildings."

Judith nodded. "Some Midwestern visitors are scared to drive on that street. They zigzag all over the place to get to the bottom."

"Good thing I'm used to living in a mountain town," Ruby remarked. "Maybe it really was an accident."

"Maybe." Judith knew she didn't sound convincing. "It's ironic that the son was hit soon after Mrs. Frosch was taken to the hospital. The driver kept going, which is suspicious, though maybe out of shock . . ." A knock on the back door interrupted her. "Who could that be?" she said, getting up. "Family and friends usually just walk in."

Judith opened the door, saw the dark-haired teenager, and immediately guessed his identity. "You're Tyler Dooley, right?"

"Yes," he said. "I missed the party last night. I had choir practice. But I wanted to say hi. Mom told me you didn't have any mysteries to solve because you've retired, but I think I solved one for you anyway."

"Come in," Judith said, wishing she hadn't left the accident report and Naomi's statement on the kitchen table. "Meet a friend of ours from Little Bavaria, Ruby Tooms. Ruby, this is one of the Dooleys—Tyler."

Ruby got halfway out of her chair to shake hands. "Hi, Tyler. I met some of your family last night. Quite a crew, enough for a football team."

Tyler grinned. "We could fill a small stadium." His gaze traveled to the paperwork on the table. "You reviewing some old cases, Mrs. Flynn?"

"Ah—no, Mrs. Stein witnessed an accident on the Avenue last night," Judith replied. "Did you hear the sirens?"

Tyler shook his head. "Darn—I missed that. I hear them fairly often around here." The comment was made matter-of-factly. "Any injuries?"

If Judith wasn't candid, she knew Arlene would get the word out soon enough. "Here," she said, handing over both sheets of paper. "Have a seat. But first, what's the mystery you solved?"

"I know who put that purse in our garbage can," Tyler said, looking at Ruby. "It belongs to you, right? Mom met you last night and your name's on the driver's license. It was the lady who lives in the house next to the Ericsons."

"Mrs. Frosch?" Judith said in surprise. "How do you know that?"

"Because," Tyler said, very seriously, "when I left for band practice that night, I saw her driving by in the Ford Explorer with Idaho plates parked at their house." He ran a hand through his dark hair. "I like to observe stuff. A lady was driving and I saw the Explorer when I delivered the newspapers the next morning. A piece of my sheet music was stuck to a tire. I must've dropped it after I left home because I didn't have it when I got to practice. It couldn't have gone further than the curb. The wind had died down, though it was still raining. I figured she must've pulled over and stopped after I kept walking."

Judith was impressed, despite having a quibble. "You're sure it was Mrs. Frosch? She was the one who had to be taken to the hospital."

Tyler grimaced. "Could I pick her out of a lineup? No. It was too dark."

"The Explorer belongs to the Frosches' son," Judith said. "It might have been his wife or girlfriend visiting from Idaho. The son was the one who got hit by a car last night."

"Whoa!" Tyler cried. "They're in a world of hurt. What's with them?"

"Maybe nothing except bad luck," Judith said. "But I wonder how one of them got hold of Ruby's purse in the first place."

Ruby lifted her hands in a helpless gesture. "Don't ask me. I never heard of anybody by that name. Is there any way we can find out?"

Judith fingered her chin. "Well . . . there may be. Let me think on it."

Tyler's expression was eager. "Should I do surveillance on their house? That telescope my brothers used is still in place."

"Go ahead," Judith replied. "You might see . . . something."

Tyler saluted. "Keep me posted. I have to walk my dog, Barkley, now that it's stopped raining. If you see me with him in the cul-de-sac, pretend you don't know me. I should probably keep a low profile, right?"

"First, you should be careful," Judith warned. "As for your low profile, you *are* the neighborhood paper boy."

"Right," Tyler said, heading for the door, "but how many people notice me that early in the morning? That means I'm sort of anonymous. I think of myself as a kind of phantom."

Judith laughed. "I've only seen you once or twice. Thanks, Tyler."

"I've just begun to sleuth," he said over his shoulder before heading out the back door.

Ruby had finished eating and stood up. "Is he reliable?"

"The other Dooley boys certainly were," Judith replied, taking out a loaf of bread to make Gertrude's sandwich. "Tyler seems bright, just like most of his family. But I doubt it was Mrs. Frosch driving the Explorer. She may've already been ill. More likely, it was the younger woman."

"Could it tie in with Mom?" Ruby asked, putting her plate and silverware into the dishwasher. "It's weird that Mrs. Frosch knew her."

Judith put lettuce and two slices of baloney on Gertrude's sandwich. "True, but sometimes I truly believe that the six-degrees-of-separation theory is a couple of degrees too many. Renie and Bill unknowingly bought their house just around the corner from where her great-uncle and his wife had lived before she was born. You still want to deliver Mother's lunch?" she asked, adding a dill pickle, chips, and a slice of blueberry pie to the plate.

"Sure," Ruby replied. "I'll bet she's got more stories about her flaming youth. I liked the one about the guy with the biplane who made a pass at her while they were in the air upside down."

"Ah—yes, he got *fresh,* as she always puts it. But he didn't get *far* before she grounded him."

Chuckling, Ruby headed for the toolshed while Judith went to check the mail. Overhead, the noonday sun was trying to peek through the clouds. After retrieving the mail that was mostly advertising, she gazed thoughtfully at the rental. It occurred to her that as a good neighbor she should show her concern for Mrs. Frosch and the injured son. Putting the mail on the small desk in the entry hall, she crossed the cul-de-sac and rang the doorbell.

The young woman with curly black hair who opened the door was Lainie, Brick's girlfriend or wife.

"Yeah?" she said, dark eyes suspicious.

Judith introduced herself, pointing to the B&B. "I wanted to ask how Mrs. Frosch and her son are doing. I hear they're in the hospital."

"Not anymore," Lainie replied, her jaw tightening. "Mrs. Frosch is in the morgue. She died this morning."

Lainie slammed the door in Judith's face.

Chapter 9

Judith was so upset—and annoyed—that she almost walked in front of Renie's Camry as her cousin raced into the cul-de-sac. Renie applied the brakes before rolling down the window.

"Are you sleepwalking?" she demanded. "You want to be Hit-and-Run Victim Number Two from this neighborhood?"

"No, of course not," Judith said, trying to collect herself and make sure all her body parts were still in place. "Mrs. Frosch died this morning."

"No kidding," Renie said drily. "What a shock. 'Death Comes to Mrs. Flynn's Neighbors, Chapter Nineteen.' What else is new?"

"Don't be so callous," Judith said. "Pull into the driveway and come in the house." She noticed a large floral display in the passenger seat. "Where did you get that big bouquet?"

"At the florist's, where else? You think I stole them out of somebody's greenhouse?"

"You might. What are you doing with them?"

"They looked bored in the florist's cooler. I thought I'd take them for a spin."

"Seriously . . ." Judith began.

Renie waved an impatient hand. "They're for the O'Connor-Braun wedding this afternoon at Our Lady, Star of the Sea. I designed the invitations and other stuff for Meg O'Connor. Thus, I also got stuck choosing the flowers."

Inspiration struck Judith. "Can you get more just like them?"

Renie recoiled in the driver's seat. The cousins were more like sisters, both being only children and raised two blocks away from each other. They could often read each other's mind. "Why? What are you talking . . . oh! No, I can't. Instead of yakking it up with you, I'm turning around and going right up to SOTS," she declared, using the parish's nickname.

"Coz," Judith said in a piteous tone, "please?"

Renie sat up and drummed her fingernails on the steering wheel. "I'll have to pretend I lost the sympathy card. Is the son about to join Elke or whatever her name is? Or was?"

"That's what you're going to find out," Judith replied, darting a look to make sure there was no sign of Lainie spying on them.

"Got it. Take cover." Renie closed the window and reversed to the rental, narrowly missing the Ford Explorer.

Judith hurried inside Hillside Manor. There was no sign of Ruby. Apparently, she was listening to yet another tale of Gertrude's flapper-era adventures. Five minutes later, Joe entered through the back door carrying a carton of what looked like liquor bottles. "Why is Renie's Camry parked in Rankerses' driveway? Did she run out of gas?"

Judith winced. "She's doing research. Mrs. Frosch died last night. The wife or girlfriend slammed the door in my face. I was only trying to offer condolences."

"Right. Maybe natural causes, maybe not." Joe looked askance as he set the carton on the counter. "I've got more boxes still in the car."

Judith gritted her teeth at the thought of the bill. The only consolation was that part of it was a tax write-off. By the time Joe had brought in the third carton, he was out of breath, but recovered quickly. "So what is Renie doing?"

"I told you—I flunked," Judith replied. "I assume Brick is still alive and in the hospital. I'm sorry about Mrs. Frosch's death.

I wonder if Arlene knows. In fact, all the neighbors should be informed."

Joe was foraging in the fridge. "Let's see—one dead, one hospitalized, Renie trying to act sympathetic and hauling a big bouquet through the front door, a hostile Lainie confronting your ornery cousin . . . what could possibly go wrong?"

"Renie will be fine. She was in a good mood—for Renie."

"That means no weaponry?" Joe said, putting pastrami on a slice of Russian rye.

"No unless you consider chrysanthemums dangerous," Judith replied as Ruby came in through the back door.

"Wow! Your mother had some real stories!" she exclaimed. "Bathtub gin and all."

"Oh," Judith said. "Yes, the one where her priggish boss came in while they were taking inventory—of how much gin they could make in the office sink. They heard him coming, so they threw the gin *and* the sink out into the alley three floors down."

Ruby nodded. "And a bum who was hanging out down there licked the sink dry."

"Right," Judith said, putting the last of the liquor bottles away. "Mother told her boss that a baby alligator had come up through the drain and that was the only way they could get rid of it. The guy was dumb enough to believe her. Later he became a U.S. congressman. Mother never voted for him because he was a Republican."

Joe had sat down at the kitchen table with his lunch. Ruby took a bottle of Evian water from the fridge and wandered off into the dining room. Phyliss called out from the top of the basement stairs to announce that Beelzebub's familiar had eaten a pair of Joe's socks.

"Damn that Sweetums," Judith said under her breath as she heard Phyliss continue on to the upstairs. "Weren't those your good socks?"

"I don't have any good socks," Joe replied. "Why don't you women darn socks like my mother used to do?"

"Why don't you stop wearing them out?" Judith demanded. "I've never darned a sock in my life. Go buy some new ones." She looked inside the fridge for the pastrami, but couldn't find it. "Did you eat all the pastrami or did you hide it from me?"

"There wasn't much left," Joe said. "Isn't there baloney in there?"

Judith glared at her husband. "I gave the last of that to Mother. How about you doing a grocery run for a change? I'll make a list. We got wiped out on food last night, despite Renie's gargantuan order from Punchinello's. There wasn't a bit of pizza left."

"Sure," Joe said. "Maybe I can find some socks on top of the hill at Bartleby's Drug Store."

"Good idea," Judith muttered, getting a frying pan out of the cupboard. "I'm stuck with a fried egg sandwich."

"I thought you liked a fried egg sandwich," Joe said. "By the way, what's Ruby up to today? Has she given up on her mother's case?"

"I'm beginning to feel as if we should adopt her," Judith said. "But she does have to go back to work Monday in . . ." She paused to answer the phone that was sitting on the counter.

"I need rescuing," Renie yipped into her cousin's ear. "I'm stuck in the Rankerses' monster hedge."

"What?" Judith hurried to the kitchen window. She could see the imposing profusion of shiny laurel leaves, but no sign of Renie. "Never mind. How did you end up in the hedge?"

"I couldn't park Cammy in your driveway where Lainie could see it, so I put the car in Arlene and Carl's driveway. They're not home. Then I decided I should crawl through the hedge into your yard, where I couldn't be spotted. I'm somewhere in the vicinity of the birdbath. Hurry up. There's a bunch of bugs in here with me."

Joe had already gotten up. "I can practically hear Renie without the phone. I'll rescue her. Stay put."

"Joe's coming," Judith informed her cousin.

"Good. I'll keep talking so he knows where I am. I was brilliant, by the way. At least right up until I got stuck in the hedge."

"What did you find out about Brick?"

"Brick? Ouch! Something just poked me. Damned branch . . . I thought his name was Bernard. Oh, hi, Joe. Glad you're here. I'm hanging up now, coz. See you soon."

Shaking her head, Judith disconnected the phone. Maybe Joe would have to hose down Renie before she could come in the house. Phyliss had already cleaned the kitchen floor.

But only a couple of minutes passed before her husband and her cousin came through the back hall. Renie didn't look much worse than she usually did except for some dirt smudges on her jeans, a few dried leaves sticking to her car coat, and a twig dangling from the front of her Notre Dame sweatshirt.

"Got any Pepsi?" she asked, plopping down in a kitchen chair.

"No," Judith said. "We're out. I'm about to make a grocery list for Joe, who is heading for the store any minute." She paused to fix her husband with a hard stare before turning back to her cousin. "Can't you drink a Coke instead?"

Renie brushed herself off. "If I have to."

"Get it yourself," Judith said, breaking an egg into the frying pan. "I haven't had lunch yet."

Renie had disappeared behind the fridge door. "Hey—you've only got diet pop! You know I won't drink that stuff."

"It's not my fault you never gain an ounce while I have to check the scale every day," Judith declared. "Go ahead, suffer. Why don't you get a glass of water, you little pig?"

"No." Renie shut the fridge and stomped back to the kitchen table. "I'd rather suffer. Hurry up, make that list. I'm not telling you what I found out until I've got some Pepsi. Ha ha."

Judith nodded at Joe. "Start writing."

"I haven't had dessert," Joe protested.

"You don't need dessert at lunch," Judith snapped. "And don't give me a dirty look. I noticed you'd moved your belt down a notch the other day. Do you really want to look like the late Dan McMonigle?"

"Gee," Joe mumbled, "somebody's crabby today." But he got up and fetched a tablet from the counter. "Go ahead. I'm set."

Judith flipped the egg before she started rattling off items. She was still adding to the list by the time she sat down across from Joe. He was halfway through the tablet's second page before she finished.

"I'm off," he said. "I'll get caught up later on what Renie was doing before she ended up in the hedge."

As Joe left the kitchen from one direction, Ruby entered from the other. "Hi, Serena," she said, sitting in the chair Joe had vacated. "It sounds like a busy place in here. I've been in the living room starting my new journal. Did your cousin tell you my other one got snatched?"

"I think that was mentioned in the recap," Renie said. "But why? Did you have a lot of lurid secrets in it?"

Ruby snorted. "I should be so lucky. I didn't write in it every day. I only put down stuff like . . . what do you call it? Musings, maybe, about my life and whatever was bothering me at the moment."

Renie scowled. "Like not having any Pepsi?"

Ruby laughed. "No. Usually it was my love life—or lack of it. Sometimes I wrote about whatever job I had. No really important stuff."

Judith swallowed a bite of her sandwich. "How far back did the missing journal go?"

Ruby thought for a minute. "A year, maybe two?"

"Did you ever write about your mother's murder?" Renie asked.

"Not until recently," Ruby replied, then looked at Judith. "I jotted down some stuff about how you'd fingered the killer in Little Bavaria and maybe you could take on my mom's murder. No names, though."

Judith nodded. "But the killer—if he or she is still around—wouldn't know that. Nobody would, until they read it."

Ruby looked alarmed. "You really think the killer took my

purse? Does that mean one of the Frosches could have murdered my mom? That's just too crazy!"

"I won't say that," Judith said. "I'm not dismissing Tyler Dooley's account about your purse, but we don't have all the facts."

"Fine, I'll talk," Renie grumbled. "If Joe's like Bill when it comes to grocery shopping, he won't be back until after dinner. Do we ask men to read all the labels on every package and can?"

Judith shook her head. "I don't know that Joe does—"

"Never mind," Renie broke in. "First of all, Brick or Bernard or whatever is recovering, listed in still-alive condition. Elma went into a diabetic coma and died. She's had the disease for years. Heart failure, they think. No autopsy requested. Apparently, she wasn't very careful about her diet or her injections. Lainie didn't seem overcome with grief, though she wasn't blatantly callous. I got the impression she didn't know the senior Frosches very well. No wedding ring, so she probably isn't Mrs. Frosch the Younger. This is her first visit here. End of report."

"Hmm," Judith murmured. "Not bad. Nothing about the purse?"

Renie scowled. "Jeez, how much did you expect me to get out of her in five minutes?"

"Okay, okay," Judith said, trying to keep her temper. "Who did you say the bouquet had come from?"

"The neighbors," Renie replied.

Judith finished her sandwich. "Can I fix you something?" she asked her cousin.

"Are you kidding?" Renie retorted. "I didn't eat breakfast until almost eleven. You know I don't wake up until ten if I can help it."

"Right," Judith said. "I thought you might have had an off-day."

"Nope." Renie stood up. "Now, how am I going to get back through the hedge to retrieve Cammy? I've got to go down to the florist's and get the blasted bouquet for the wedding." She paused. "To hell with it. I'll tell them to make up another bouquet and deliver it with the rest of the floral decorations. See you later." She headed for the back door.

Ruby's mobile face showed concern after Renie left. "What if she gets stuck again?"

"Then we'll have to rescue her," Judith said. "I suspect she'll brazen it out and just walk around the end of the hedge and hope Lainie isn't posted at the window. I wonder if Mr. Frosch is working or if he's making funeral arrangements. I didn't see his car when I made my aborted neighborly call."

"You know," Ruby said, her hands propping up her chin, "I think we should abort this whole deal. I mean, all I've done is cause you guys a lot of trouble. I feel like one big cloud of gloom and doom. I come to this neighborhood and the next thing I know people are getting killed and run over and stuck in hedges. You wanted to retire, and I screwed that up, too. Maybe I should head back home today instead of tomorrow."

Judith held up her hands in protest. "No. Look what your arrival in the Thurlow District did. You stirred things up. Who snatches a purse and doesn't take the money? You lost your memory, which leads me to believe someone deliberately drugged you. We can't stop now. There's a connection between your mom and the Frosches. Yes, it's possible that Mrs. Frosch died of natural causes and that their son wasn't run down deliberately, but I have my doubts, at least about Brick's accident. In fact," Judith said, standing up, "let's drive out to the Thurlow District. I should go down memory lane, painful as it might be."

To Judith's surprise, Ruby emphatically shook her head. "No. I don't want to do that. My trip was a disaster. Is there anything I can do here? I mean, like check records or something on the computer?"

"Well . . ." Judith considered the idea. "Yes. Some vital statistics are free. Why not start with the Frosches? If you come across a site that requires a fee, I'll give you my credit card number to pay for it."

Ruby's blue eyes widened. "You'd trust me to do that?"

"Yes, of course."

Ruby smiled wanly. "I'm not used to people who trust other people. Or maybe I was a gullible kid and learned the hard way."

"The Thurlow District wasn't an ideal locale for trustworthiness," Judith said ruefully, thinking back to her own experiences. "We never really got into Woody's case notes last night. I'll take a set with me and make some other notes about your own recollections." She picked up the tablet that Joe had used for the grocery list, but the phone rang before she could start writing.

"Tyler D, as in Detective here," the teenager said in a hushed voice. "The telescope can take in the rental and the yard. But the bare branches of the cherry trees out back block some of the view."

"Oh!" Judith said. "I forgot about those." The last time she'd thought about the cherry trees, a dead body had been deposited under one of them. "Have you seen anything interesting?" she inquired.

"Not yet, but I'm on the case. Or will be until I have to play in the band at the high school football game tonight."

"Okay, keep me posted," Judith said. "I'm going out for a while, but Ruby's standing by."

"Got it," Tyler responded. "Over and out."

Judith relayed the information to Ruby, who seemed amused. "He's serious," she remarked.

"Yes," Judith agreed, starting to write down the names of the Frosches. "His brothers took sleuthing very seriously, too."

"Are you going to the Thurlow District by yourself?" Ruby asked.

"Well . . ." Judith glanced at the schoolhouse clock. It was a quarter after one. "Maybe Renie will go with me. She should be home soon. I'll give her a call. Joe never mentioned trying to get hold of The Persian Cat's owner." She paused, tapping a finger against her cheek. "That's my first stop." She dialed her cousin's number.

A breathless Renie answered on the fourth ring. "I just got home. Now what?"

"Want to go for a ride with me?"

"Hoo boy, that's a loaded question. Where?"

Judith grimaced before replying. "My old neighborhood."

"Ha! Either you're kidding or you're nuts. No thanks. Think I'll go chew on some aluminum foil instead."

"Hey, the Thurlow District has gone upscale. Well . . . semi-upscale."

"That wouldn't be hard to do. You mean they no longer have the nightly rolling of the drunks down the main street and they did away with weekend rodent patrol?"

"Coz, really—it's not like it used to be," Judith asserted. "Yes, I haven't been out there since I moved back home, but you know that most of this city has been going through gentrification in the past couple of decades, including the Thurlow District. Please?"

"You need a guard, right? Should I arm myself? Bill's Desert Eagle would probably come in handy."

"Oh, for heaven's . . . are you coming or not?"

"Yeah, I'll come if only because I don't want you going alone. I gather Ruby isn't accompanying you?"

"No. She's doing some research."

"I hope it doesn't include the really dangerous parts of the Thurlow District. You'll have to pick me up. Bill needs the car. He's taking Oscar to check out the new firing range across the lake. Maybe Oscar will shoot off a few rounds with the Desert Eagle."

"Stop. I'll collect you in ten minutes. I have to change first."

"Into what? A prison uniform so you'll fit right into the old hood?"

Judith hung up.

I'm not armed," Renie announced when she got into Judith's Subaru. "Unless you count my nail scissors."

"I do," Judith said, pulling out onto the steep hill in front of the Jones residence. "I remember when you and Bill went to see some arty French movie and the jerk next to you grabbed your leg. Bill was so caught up in the film that you didn't want to bother him, so you stabbed the guy with those scissors."

"Bill understood that movie and I didn't," Renie said. "I knew he'd be upset if I distracted him, so I decided to handle the situation myself. Turned out that though Bill understood the concept, he thought the movie sucked scissors. Not *my* scissors, but in a metaphorical—"

"Skip it," Judith said, heading for the major thoroughfare that would take them south to the Thurlow District. "I know the story. I mean the one about the jerk."

"Right. The movie didn't seem to have a story. It was all nuance and symbolism about the human condition. Or maybe it was about prune farming. Hey, what's our plan and why isn't Ruby part of it?"

"She got spooked by her earlier foray," Judith replied. "I don't blame her. She really had a bad time and still doesn't remember anything more about what happened."

"Do you suppose she was hypnotized?"

Judith paused at the arterial. "Drugged sounds more like it. She does recall being at The Persian Cat. I'd like to talk to her brother, Ozzie, but I haven't asked her about contacting him. He wasn't around when Mrs. Tooms was killed, but being a bit older, he might fill in some gaps. Ozzie's stationed in San Diego."

"He's married to her old pal Freddy Mae, right?"

Judith nodded as she finally managed to join the parade of southbound traffic. "Freddy Mae might help, too. I tend to think that whoever killed Opal Tooms was known to her and was probably from the neighborhood. The family doesn't sound like they left their home turf very often. Ruby seldom got as far as downtown."

"Typical of people who live on the fringes," Renie remarked.

"I rarely left the neighborhood," Judith said as they approached the viaduct along the bay. "Dan let me visit Mother twice a month, but I never saw you or the rest of my family. I had to wait until

Dan was asleep—or passed out—to phone you. I felt like a prisoner, working days at the library and nights at the café."

"I never understood how you put up with that lifestyle," Renie said. "After the first few years, Dan wouldn't let any of us visit you."

"It was just as well," Judith admitted. "I didn't want you to see the squalor we lived in." She shook her head as they passed the football and baseball stadiums. "Dan had such a violent temper. I never knew what he might do if I rebelled."

"I didn't blame Aunt Gertrude for despising Dan," Renie said, "but I never understood why she was opposed to you finally marrying Joe. That didn't make sense, given that Joe is Mike's father."

"You expect Mother to be reasonable? She blamed Joe for deserting me in the first place." Judith stopped at a traffic light to take the turnoff to the Thurlow District. "Let's hope the bridge isn't up over the waterway. Since they built the new one, it takes forever for it to go up and down."

"All our bridges take forever," Renie said. "Living on the other side of the hill, I always get stuck waiting for boat traffic in the ship canal."

To Judith's relief the bridge was in place. "It's such a short drive to our old so-called home, but a world away from Heraldsgate Hill."

"It is," Renie said quietly. "And it wasn't a home. It was a prison."

But on the outskirts of the much-maligned neighborhood, the cousins saw changes. New businesses had sprung up and strip malls had been replaced with shopping centers. Supermarkets, restaurants, and home furnishing stores stood in place of the seedy hangouts and shuck-and-jive used-car lots that had lined the main thoroughfare.

"Okay," Renie said, "it does look different around here. But we're still a couple of miles from your old neighborhood."

Judith didn't respond. She was too busy keeping her eye on traffic while also taking in the young families strolling on the sidewalks. They were well dressed and looked as if they might even know where they were going. She felt as if she was entering foreign territory.

But Judith got her bearings when she saw a sign pointing to the Thurlow Public Library. Although she could only see part of the grounds off the main street, it was obvious that the library had undergone a face-lift. Instead of the half-dozen broken stone steps that led up to the entrance, colorful oversize books served as the staircase.

"Good grief," she exclaimed, "even my old workplace has changed. I wonder who runs the library these days."

"Are you disoriented?" Renie asked in an amused tone.

"Yes! What happened to the shabby Laundromat and the drug-dealing mom-and-pop grocery store and the bail bondsman where Home Depot is now on our left?"

"Don't ask me," Renie said. "Where was The Meat & Mingle?"

"In the middle of the next block on your left," Judith replied.

Renie was silent until they approached the site. "You mean your old dump morphed into Oriana's Spa de Beauté?"

"Good Lord!" Judith cried. "So it did!"

"Unless you want a mani and a pedi, we might as well skip that one," Renie said.

"Right. Now, where do I find a parking place?"

"Can't you do what you always did and just pull up onto the sidewalk?"

Judith shot Renie a dirty look. "I never did that. I might've run over some of our customers who were lying there."

"There's a parking sign in the next block on the right," Renie said.

After waiting for a half-dozen pedestrians to cross at the corner, Judith pulled into the lot and found an empty space. "Where do I pay?"

"I don't think you do," Renie replied. "I glimpsed a sign that said something to the effect that this is free parking for local merchants."

"What a concept," Judith murmured. "We don't have that on Heraldsgate Hill except at the grocery stores and the bank."

"That's because everybody except us is rich," Renie said. "Gosh, none of these vehicles look as if they've been in a bumper-car marathon. On the other hand, I don't feel so inferior because we won't have to park between a Rolls and a Lamborghini like I do at Falstaff's. If you want to drop in at The Persian Cat, I spotted it a couple of doors down."

Judith turned off the ignition and set the hand brake. "I wonder if that would do us much good. The owner wasn't very helpful on the phone. We might have better luck with one of his servers, though."

The early morning clouds had lifted, though there was a slight chill in the autumn air as the cousins walked to the café. At almost two-thirty in the afternoon, only about a dozen patrons were seated at tables covered by colorful cloths depicting mullahs, horses, angels, and warriors. Persian carpets hung from the walls, and the floor was made up of colorful tiles.

A pretty redhead welcomed the cousins and led them to a corner table. Judith glanced into the kitchen, but didn't see anyone who looked like the turbaned owner Ruby had described. Before the waitress could present menus, Renie asked if they had any small lamb shish kebabs.

"We do, as appetizers," the waitress replied. "They're very good. My name is Crissy. Can I get you each a serving and a beverage?"

"Yes," Renie replied. "Tea sounds good with that."

Judith agreed. Crissy headed for the kitchen. As soon as she was out of earshot, Renie posed a question. "While they're grilling the lamb, when you do you start grilling Crissy?"

"As soon she brings our order. Did you expect me to leap up and nail her to the service counter?"

Renie shrugged. "Why not? It'd save time."

"You already saved time by ordering without a menu," Judith said. "I assume your late breakfast didn't fill you up."

"It sure didn't. I had to run those errands and I only had a bowl of Cheerios. In a way, this *is* breakfast, if a bit later than usual."

Two older women had just vacated a table, but suddenly stopped to stare at the cousins. "Judith?" the stouter of the pair said.

"Yes. Oh! Jane Bradford, one of my library patrons! How nice to see you." Judith held out her hand before introducing Renie.

Jane, in turn, introduced her companion, who turned out to be her sister-in-law, Ida, visiting from Oregon. "It's so lovely to see you again, Judith," Jane said. "You were always so helpful. What brings you back to this part of the world?"

"Well . . ." Catching a warning glance from Renie, Judith paused. "A trip down memory lane. A friend who'd been in the neighborhood this week told me how much it had changed. I decided to see for myself."

Jane laughed and poked her sister in-law in the shoulder. "That's what Ida told me. She hasn't been up here in over ten years."

"Fifteen," Ida said, her lean face grim. "The last time Harold and I visited Jane and Jonathan, the power went out, their plumbing backed up, and the woman who lived behind them was killed. I told Jane if she and Harold wanted to see us, they could come to Tigard, where life is much quieter and there aren't so many disruptions."

Jane patted Ida's arm. "I'll admit it was unfortunate, though you've noticed vast improvements since then."

Judith didn't recall where Jane lived. "Was that when Opal— oof!—Tooms was killed?" she asked, despite Renie's kick in the shins.

Jane looked puzzled. "Opalooftooms? Is that a person or—"

"Sorry," Judith said. "Leg cramp. The victim was Opal Tooms."

"Oh! Of course! Yes, Mrs. Tooms lived in back of us. We didn't know her well. She worked—divorced mother with two teenagers. Very sad. I didn't realize you were still living here when that happened."

"I wasn't," Judith said, "but I married a police detective after Dan died and my second husband's partner worked the Tooms case. The killer was never found."

"That's so," Jane said, frowning. "We always felt it was some person on drugs who broke in. A random thing. I do recall a very nice young policeman coming to our house a few days after Mrs. Tooms was killed, but there was nothing we could tell him."

Ida tugged at Jane's sleeve. "Are you going to stand here and talk about homicides and drug-crazed perverts or are we going to that fabric shop you brag about? You've been telling me forever that it's better than the one we have at Jantzen Beach in Portland."

Jane's laugh was forced. "Oh, Ida, you can't blame me for wanting to catch up with my favorite librarian. Judith could find any book I ever wanted, no matter how obscure. She was like a library detective."

Ida cast a disparaging glance at Judith. "Well, if she's so smart, maybe she can find out who killed Opalooftooms or whoever. Nice to meet you," she added brusquely, dragging Jane by the arm.

"Gee," Renie said as the women left, "I kind of hope Ida did it."

Judith didn't say anything. To her dismay, she realized that she had no viable suspects. Anybody could have killed Opal, including someone they'd already seen in the Thurlow District.

Chapter 10

Judith removed Woody's case notes from her handbag. "I recall seeing the Bradfords' names on his list from canvassing the neighbors, but I didn't have time to see what Woody wrote about them."

Crissy appeared with their order. "I added some brown rice and our homemade Barbari bread," she said. "It's really good. The owner, Mr. Alipur, makes it himself."

"My," Judith enthused, "I've heard about it. A friend of mine was here on Wednesday and she told me it was out of this world."

"So's my cousin," Renie said under her breath.

Seeing Crissy stare at Renie with a puzzled expression, Judith quickly intervened. "She means my homemade bread is out of this world, too. But it's a French bread I make, nothing at all like this. As Ruby mentioned, this bread has such a golden glow to it. What's the secret?"

"The dough is made of cornmeal," Crissy replied, "and the sauce—kind of a glaze—is made of more cornmeal, baking soda, and water. Really simple."

"So's my cousin," Renie murmured again.

"Yes," Judith responded with a kick at Renie's legs. "I do something like that, except it's a bit . . . different. Were you here Wednesday?"

"Only for lunch," the waitress replied. "We don't do break-fasts."

"Maybe you waited on Ruby," Judith said, relaxing a bit as Renie began attacking the kebabs. "She came in alone, but a man joined her."

Crissy's cheerful expression faltered. "Um . . . is she a blonde?"

"Yes, in her thirties."

"I didn't wait on her," Crissy said. "Julie did. She's not here today. Is your friend . . . okay?"

Judith looked surprised. "Yes, she's fine. Why do you ask?"

"Well . . ." Crissy looked around, as if making sure no one could hear her. "Julie thought your friend was sick," she continued, lowering her voice. "In fact, she acted like she'd been drinking. Slurred speech, wobbly, spilling stuff, disoriented."

Judith evinced confusion. "How odd! Maybe she was upset. It was someone she hadn't seen in a while. I think his name was Jim."

"Jim?" Crissy thought for a moment. "I don't really know, but I've seen him here before. He usually eats by himself and writes in his notebook. We don't have Wi-Fi."

"Oh, of course!" Judith said with a big smile. "Ruby has talked about him. His last name is . . ." She frowned. "I forget."

Crissy hesitated. "Well . . . it's kind of different. Fiddler, maybe, or something to do with music. Your friend would know."

Judith nodded. "Of course. Has he been in since then?"

"I don't know," Crissy said, obviously getting anxious to move on. "I didn't work yesterday or Thursday. Excuse me, I've got an order up."

Judith leaned closer to Renie. "Can't you at least shut up when I'm interviewing someone?"

Renie brushed rice from her olive green sweater. "Sorry, but I had this peculiar idea you'd retired from sleuthing. Yes, I know what you had in mind when we came here, but when you started in on that poor waitress, my brain misfired. Call me crazy, but in the past when we've done this sort of thing, we often end up being almost dead."

"We aren't, though," Judith said indignantly. "Dead, I mean."

"What are the odds that our luck could run out?" Renie asked, looking quite serious.

Judith shrugged. "We aren't getting out of this life alive."

"I mean before our time."

"Okay, so we don't take chances anymore. And speaking of chance, that makes me think of odds, as in betting. I wonder if Uncle Al knows a Fiddler from the racetrack."

Renie rolled her eyes. "I'll pass on making a lame joke about that. Go ahead, ask Uncle Al."

"I will," Judith said. "But first we have to check out the bars."

Renie held her head. "Oh, no! We're going to drink our way through the rest of the afternoon?"

"Of course not. By the way, one of your elbows is in your rice pilaf."

"Oh!" Renie stopped holding her head and examined her elbows. "Damn! I just got this back from the cleaners. It's cashmere."

"Why bother? Your elbow matches your chest. You've still got rice there, too."

Renie made a snarling noise in her throat. "I should bring my tiny hand vacuum with me."

"You should bring a trough." Judith kept quiet for at least a full minute, savoring the kebabs and the bread. "The food here is really very good. I still don't see Mr. Alipur back in the kitchen area."

"You already told me he wasn't helpful," Renie reminded her cousin. "It's three o'clock. How are you going to interview alleged witnesses or suspects or complete strangers who might have once said hello to Opal Tooms and still get home in time to welcome new guests?"

"I have a couple checking in this afternoon and their flight from Chicago doesn't arrive until around six. I've got some frozen appetizers I keep on hand for emergencies like this."

"This is an emergency?"

"You know what I mean." Judith proceeded to polish off her kebab. I wouldn't mind having the recipe for that bread. It's delicious."

"In other words, you have an excuse to call Mr. Alipur at a more convenient time. Like when he's here."

"Well . . . yes, of course."

"I'm done," Renie said, standing up. "I'm going outside to make a phone call." Before Judith could finish chewing a bite of bread, Renie was halfway to the door. Scanning Woody's notes, Judith found the Bradford comments. *Called OT pleasant woman . . . didn't know her well . . . kids played loud music sometimes . . . quiet otherwise . . . noticed male visitor occasionally, not Mr. Tooms . . . didn't recall seeing Mr. T for some time . . . day of murder Mrs. B home waiting for plumber, didn't hear or see anything unusual at OT's house . . . Mr. B volunteering that afternoon at their church.* Judith tucked the notes back in her handbag just before Crissy appeared with the bill.

Judith took out her credit card. "I run a B&B and I'd love to talk to Mr. Alipur about the Barbari bread. Is he here now?"

"He doesn't come in Saturdays," Crissy replied. "The best time to call is when he first arrives during the week, say around ten-thirty."

"Thanks." Judith added a tip and signed off on the card. "You might mention that I'll be giving him a ring Monday."

"Sure," Crissy said. "Have a nice day."

Renie was still outside, leaning against the café window. "When," she asked, "was the last time you made bread?"

"Never," Judith said. "I had to fib. You stiffed me for the bill. Who were you calling?"

"I'll pay next time," Renie said as they headed for the far corner. "I called Uncle Al. I figured I'd save you the trouble. Besides, he got free tickets for Bill and Joe to join him at the University's first conference basketball game. I forgot to tell you that."

"That's great," Judith said. "Has Uncle Al ever heard of someone named Fiddler?"

Renie shook her head. "He knows a guy named Mandolini,

though. Uncle Al played basketball with him. The grandson is part owner of a horse that's running at Santa Anita this weekend in the Breeders Cup."

"That's . . . probably not much help."

"Uncle Al couldn't remember the other two owners," Renie said as they stopped to wait for traffic before crossing the street, "but he did say one of them was a foreign guy who owns a restaurant around here. Oh—the horse's name is Ali's Purchase. Work that out for yourself."

Judith didn't respond until they'd crossed the street and were heading in the direction of O'Reilly's Pub. "I should jump to some weird conclusion, but coincidences *do* exist," she finally said, pushing open the pub's door. "Maybe this stop is a waste of time. This used to be the site of an old dump named Spooner's Schooners. Oh, well—we're here."

"Why?" Renie asked, following Judith inside.

"Because we're going to have a drink. Our old customers may've gravitated to this place." Judith headed for the nearest small table. Much of the bar was filled with men who were watching the Notre Dame football team thrash Tennessee on the big TV at the end of the room. A chubby middle-aged waitress who walked as if her feet hurt approached the cousins.

"Menus?" she asked, smiling faintly.

Renie declined, but asked for a glass of sherry. Judith said she'd have the same. The waitress made her weary way back to the bar's serving area.

"She looks familiar," Judith murmured to Renie. "Subtract twenty years and thirty pounds."

"I don't do math," Renie replied with a sneer. "I'm an *artiste*."

"Then do a visual, Madame Renie-oir."

But her cousin only shrugged. *"Rien."*

"You got zip?" Judith sighed. "Then I must know her from somewhere around here."

"Since she's here *now*, it's likely she was here *then*."

"Be quiet. Here she comes with the sherry." Judith put on her friendliest smile. "Say, don't I know you from the old Meat & Mingle?"

The waitress looked surprised. "You do? Oh, my! I thought I recognized you. Willie and I started this pub back in '98. Didn't you tend bar there? I'm Annie O'Reilly. You're . . . ?"

Judith introduced herself and Renie. "My first husband and I owned the café. I remarried after he died."

"Pleased to meet you," Annie said. "Back then I worked as a cook at Peebles Place. I usually do the cooking here, but our regular waitress has bronchitis."

"What a coincidence!" Judith exclaimed. "You must've known Opal Tooms, the poor woman who was murdered not long after I moved from the Thurlow District."

Annie's plump face darkened. "That was a terrible thing. I don't think the cops ever found out who killed her. Or at least they couldn't prove it." She leaned closer and lowered her voice. "Too bad they never asked me. I had some ideas of my own."

"You did?" Judith responded. "Why didn't you go to the police?"

"Willie told me to keep my mouth shut," Annie replied. "He thought it'd be dangerous in more ways than one, given who I thought it was who done it. I needed to keep working there to save up enough money to start this pub." She suddenly straightened up. "You knew Opal?"

"No," Judith said. "I met her daughter recently when Serena and I were on a trip."

Annie frowned. "I never knew Opal's kids. A son, too, right?"

Judith nodded. "It's not too late to go to the police, you know."

"Yes, it is," Annie asserted. "The person I think did it is long gone."

Renie stared at Annie. "As in dead?"

The waitress shrugged as a roar went up from the Fighting Irish fans. "Might as well be. The funny thing is that the other day a man came in here with a woman who . . ." Her gaze veered to the football fans. "Excuse me. I'd better bring another round for old Notre Dame." She ambled off to the cheering drinkers.

Judith checked her watch. "Time marches on along with the Notre Dame band. Polish off your sherry. Next stop is the race-track."

"The racetrack?" Renie practically shrieked.

"Shhh," Judith warned. "Some people are staring. Yes . . . it's only ten minutes from here. Don't you remember how Dan would often go there to place a bet on a horse that usually came in last?"

"I was *trying* to forget," Renie said. "I figured you'd want to see the Tooms house and maybe your old dump. I mean—"

"We can drive by the Tooms house, but I don't want to see our former so-called home. It's enough off the beaten track that I doubt it's been improved. In fact, it may have fallen down."

"It was leaning that way," Renie said. "Literally. Gosh, all those rats that ran up inside the walls must've been displaced."

Judith shuddered. "Not to mention the hookers that plied their trade on the main thoroughfare in front of the house. You're paying. You fleeced me for lunch."

"Okay." Renie took out a twenty and left it on the table. Catching Annie's eye, she made an okay sign with her thumb and index finger before following Judith out the door. "You do realize they don't have live racing this time of the year at Greenacres, don't you?"

"Of course. But serious track rats go to watch the simul-casts and place bets. Uncle Al does that quite often. You said it was the Breeders Cup. Maybe the trainer on Ruby's list—Jorge Gonzales—will be there."

"He's a suspect?" Renie asked as they made way for a couple pushing twins in an elaborate stroller.

"No," Judith replied. "I think he was Duke Swisher's alibi. Heck, Duke might be there, too. I'd like to see the location of Opal's remodeled house. It's only a couple of blocks from where we parked."

"What did you make of Annie's suspicions about whodunit?"

Judith grimaced. "At first, I thought she was putting us on," she said, smiling at a woman whose tartan jacket matched the coat on the fox terrier she had on a leash, "but her details changed my mind. It sounds as if she was afraid of getting canned. That means someone at Peebles Place, like the manager, Myrna Grissom. Maybe she died."

"Or quit?" Renie suggested.

"Possibly. But what motive would she have for killing Opal?"

"Maybe Opal found out Myrna was juggling the books."

Judith shook her head as they got into the Subaru. "From what little I know of Opal, she wasn't a curious type. I wish Annie had finished what she was about to say when the Fighting Irish fans needed refills."

"As in 'a man and a woman came into a bar'? Isn't that the opening line of a joke?"

Judith frowned. "Maybe the joke's on me for not asking. Now I wonder what it was. Probably nothing important."

It had started to rain and the wind was up, scattering a few remaining leaves from the small trees planted along the sidewalks. As they entered a residential area, Judith noted that the Toomses' address was 4322 on their right. Renie couldn't help but see the big numbers on a pillar near the sidewalk. "It's Twenty-first Century Re-do," she declared. "Lots of glass and boxlike. I hate it."

"Right," Judith said, slowing down, but looking across the street. "I wonder who lives over there."

Renie turned to see an older but well-maintained Craftsman bungalow behind a white picket fence. "Why do you care?"

"Because I just saw a gray-haired woman go in the side door. I'll bet she's lived there for years."

Renie leaned back in the seat. "So what are we selling? Avon? Fuller Brush? Raffle tickets?"

"Jehovah Witnesses," Judith said, pulling over to a parking space a couple of doors down. "Our copies of the *Watchtower* just blew away."

Renie held her head. "Oh God!"

"Don't be a spoilsport! You've heard their spiel. We can do it."

The rain was coming down harder and the wind was still brisk. Judith's jacket didn't have a hood, so she held her purse over her head until they got on the bungalow's porch. She rang the door-bell, but at least two full minutes passed before the gray-haired old lady warily opened the door and skewered the cousins with shrewd dark eyes.

"What is it?" she demanded in a strong, sharp voice.

Judith cleared her throat. "Do you know the world is going to end in five years?"

"I certainly don't," the old lady retorted. "I haven't even looked at the weather report for tomorrow."

"We're Jehovah Witnesses and we know what's going to happen," Judith stated. "It's pretty gruesome, so you ought to be prepared."

"Jehovah is Yaweh to me," the old lady declared. "I'm Jewish and you're ignorant. I'll bet you don't know how Yaweh became Jehovah."

"Gosh," Renie said in a humble voice, "we don't. Can you tell us?"

The old lady looked disgusted. "I could tell you a lot of things, but I don't want to waste my time." She paused, peering more closely at her visitors. "On the other hand, I loathe ignorance in all its forms. Oh," she continued, opening the door wider, "come in out of this rotten weather. I should have moved in with my sister in Miami years ago, but she drives me nuts. I spent a month with her years ago and all she could talk about was what she watched on TV and how many of her friends had face-lifts."

The living room was small but cozy. A brass menorah reposed on the mantel above a tiled fireplace flanked by glassed-in book-cases. Floral drapes hung at the two windows facing the street. "Sit," the old lady said, gesturing at a brown sofa decorated with embroidered throw pillows. "I need a straight chair. Bad back. I'm Ziva Feldstein. You two got names?"

"I'm Judith Flynn and this is my cousin Serena Jones," Judith said, sitting down.

"Judith, eh?" Ziva said, cautiously lowering herself into the ladder-back chair by the hearth. "But you're not Jewish?"

"Actually, the German side of the family was at one point," Judith said. "They got run out of Russia by Catherine the Great."

"Nothing great about her," Ziva asserted. "How'd you get to be Jehovah Witnesses?"

Judith grimaced. "We didn't. We're Catholics."

Ziva looked skeptical. "You changed religions between here and the porch?"

"The Jehovah Witness thing was a ruse," Judith confessed. "We need your help for a friend of mine."

Ziva's eyes narrowed. "I should've guessed you were trying to hit me up for something. How much? I'm not made of money."

Judith shook her head. "No money involved. We only want some information about your former neighbor across the street. My husband is a retired police detective and the Opal Tooms homicide was his partner's first investigation. The case was never solved and now Opal's daughter is trying to find out who killed her mom. Your name wasn't included in the case notes, but you were here when it happened, right?"

"Wrong," Ziva replied, no longer looking wary. "That is, I wasn't here when Opal's body was found. I'd left June seventh, the day after she was killed, to visit my sister in Miami. I was gone for over a month."

"That explains why Woody—he's now Precinct Captain Woodrow Price—didn't interview you," Judith said. "I assume nobody else was living here at the time?"

"Unfortunately, no." Ziva paused, shifting in her chair. "My husband had died in late April. My sister thought it'd be good for me to have a change of scenery, so she invited me to come to Miami to visit. The weather there was fine until it started to get hot by the first of July and Rachel just wouldn't shut up. I came back home. I never did hear anything about poor Opal, but then

I'm not much for gossiping with the neighbors. I leave that to my sister."

"Do you know who lives in that house now?" Judith asked. "I see it's been remodeled."

Ziva grimaced. "Ghastly modern style, if you ask me. It's a young couple with more money than taste. Nice enough, but bland."

"But you knew Opal when she lived there?" Judith inquired.

"In the way you know people you see now and then, but don't have much in common with," Ziva responded. "I never bothered learning to drive, so I took the bus. The end of the line is just two doors down from the Tooms house, so I'd see her sometimes in the yard when I'd go by. She worked odd hours at a nursing home, I think. I'd stop to say hello and we'd talk about gardening—the only thing we did have in common." The old lady paused, shifting in her chair. "You say her daughter wants to find out who killed her? I'd almost forgotten about her. There was a son, too. I think he went into the service. Typical teenagers—no time for older folks. Reuben and I had never had children. Just as well, maybe."

"Children," Renie put in, "are only as bad as you let them be. Are you hinting that Opal's kids were troublemakers?"

"No, no, not really," Ziva said. "Children in general, I guess. The Tooms boy and girl weren't wild—just kind of shiftless. But given that their father was a crook, what would you expect? I was glad when Opal got rid of him. In fact, I heard he ended up in jail. Not surprising. He hung out with some unsavory types. She had a new beau who seemed a notch up, but most women follow a pattern and run to type. It wouldn't have surprised me if her boyfriend had done it."

Judith tried to hide her surprise. "Why do you say that?"

Again, Ziva paused. "Sometimes he showed up with people who looked kind of fishy to me. They had loud parties, too."

"Loud in what way?" Judith asked.

"Music," Ziva said. "Not live music, but they'd turn the sound way up. I'm not deaf, though I wish I had been. In the summer, you could hear it all the way into my backyard. They'd come outside to party sometimes and the men would act as if they were going to get into a fight. But they never did, or at least I never saw it. Just no class and a lot of cussing. The kind of people who spend their spare time in taverns and bars, like an old dump we had around here called The Meat & Mingle."

Judith kept a straight face. "I take it you and your husband never went to that . . . place?"

Ziva shook her head. "Somebody told us the food was decent, but it was a low-life hangout as far as the bar was concerned. Reuben and I didn't drink much. We didn't eat out very often because we kept kosher." She again shifted in the chair, apparently trying to get comfortable. "You know, it's funny how things come back to you. I did see Opal the day she must've died. She was planting dahlias by the porch. Out of pots, no less. Too lazy to start the tubers in March. In fact, when I finally got home, I noticed there was a whole box of primroses wilting near the front porch. She obviously didn't have enough gumption to plant them after she finished the dahlias. I've no patience with people who can't finish a job. I had a doctor's appointment, so I just said hello and kept going to catch the bus."

"What time was that?" Judith asked.

"Around noon. My appointment was for one o'clock. I always see doctors at one. They've just come back from lunch, so I don't have to wait." She leaned forward. "If you ask me," she said, leaning forward, "if you want to find whoever killed Opal, you should try to run down some of that seedy bunch who drank themselves stupid at The Meat & Mingle."

Chapter 11

Judith managed to remain composed. Since she'd introduced herself as Judith Flynn, Ziva wouldn't make the connection with the infamous watering hole. It was Renie, however, who broke the brief silence.

"Gee, Ziva," she said in the ingenuous manner she could adapt when the mood suited her, "you're lucky you never knew any of those low-lifers. That is, I heard this neighborhood used to be rife with that type of person. You seem to have emerged unscathed."

"Oh, I wouldn't say that," Ziva said with a scowl. "Reuben and I had our run-ins with some of those despicable people. Mainly over their ill-behaved children, who had no respect for others or their property. The school bus stops up at the north corner. Those little monsters would take a shortcut through our yard to get home. Reuben and I enjoyed gardening. I still do. Finally we put up that fence to stop them, but some of those bratty teenagers would jump right over it."

Judith surreptitiously glanced at her watch, which informed her it was a quarter to four. Time was starting to run out. "That must've been very annoying," she said, getting to her feet.

"It was," Ziva agreed. "I finally spoke to a parent of one of the girls—Watkins, their name was—and told them if they didn't stop, I'd report them to the school principal. That made an impression."

"Watkins?" Renie echoed as she also got up from the sofa.

Judith had also picked up on the name. "Would that be Marla and Lee Watkins?"

Ziva carefully got out of the chair. "I don't recall. She worked at The Garden of Eden, which is how I knew her. We sometimes bought plants there. They moved a few years after that."

Judith took a couple of steps toward the door. "Out of the area?"

"I'm not sure," Ziva admitted, stretching this way and that. "Marla quit her job. I heard she and her husband bought a house overlooking the Sound. That's expensive property. Maybe they robbed a bank. Or their kids did. Out of sight, out of mind." She shrugged before opening the door for the cousins. "I'm glad you're not Jehovah Witnesses, but in my opinion, your ancestors shouldn't have converted."

"We can't rewrite history," Renie said. "Good thing. My husband likes to eat his lunch off of paper plates. I don't think they're kosher."

On that note, the cousins headed for the Subaru.

"Interesting," Judith remarked after she got behind the wheel. "Strange how certain people's names keep popping up on memory lane."

"Is it?" Renie responded, fastening her seat belt. "It's like any neighborhood—there are all sorts of connections. Heraldsgate Hill is the same way. And if you break the speed limit, we might make it in time for the feature race at Santa Anita."

Judith darted a glance at Renie. "You want me to get arrested for speeding in my old hood? That'd be kind of embarrassing."

"Hey—then you could quiz the arresting officer about some of the other people on your list. Whoever is on patrol probably considers Woody and Joe legends by now."

"These cops aren't in Woody's precinct," Judith pointed out. "In fact, I don't know the captain out here."

"I wonder if Ruby's memory is coming back yet," Renie said as they drove under the freeway. "Did you know any cops when you lived here?"

"Only by sight when they had to bust our customers," Judith said. "The cop who showed up after Dan died was a woman. In fact, she was still there when you and Bill arrived."

"Yes," Renie agreed. "She was young and naive. I overheard you insist your religion forbade autopsies. Imagine that—hearing coz tell a whopper as my foot went through your rotting kitchen floorboard."

"I didn't want anyone to think I'd tried to kill Dan by buying the gallon of grape juice he begged me to get that morning. How'd I know it'd make him blow up? I mean," she added hastily, taking the racetrack turnoff, "I knew it was bad for his diabetes, but I felt sorry for him."

"Of course you did," Renie said, "You're too damned soft-hearted. Hey, pull over by that parking valet. Tell them you're Uncle Al's niece."

Judith shrugged. "Why not? That should get us a free pass inside. Uncle Al helped fund the original track."

The ploy worked. Five minutes later, the cousins were in the clubhouse section, where two dozen TV screens showed the races at various North American tracks. Renie spotted the feed from Santa Anita not far from the betting booths.

"Drinks," she said, leading Judith toward the bar next to the dining area. "I'll get them while you grab us a couple of seats."

Despite the crowd, Judith managed to find two vacant chairs not far from the Santa Anita TV monitor. She opened the racing program she'd picked up at the track entrance and discovered that all of the races were designated as different types of Breeders Cup events. In fact, she noted, similarly styled races had been held the previous day.

Renie appeared with a Scotch rocks for Judith and a CC and 7 UP for herself. "You look puzzled," she remarked, sitting down.

"Did Uncle Al explain what goes on at the Santa Anita track this weekend?" she asked.

"They hold the Breeders Cup," Renie replied, getting her own program out of her purse. "I didn't ask for a history."

"The program says it's a two-day event," Judith explained after taking a sip from her drink. "I haven't found Ali's Purchase yet."

"Keep looking," Renie said, gazing up at the monitor. "We're up to the eighth race. Uncle Al definitely told me the horse was running today."

"The fourth race," Judith said, seeing Ali's Purchase as the third entry on the program. "Juvenile Turf. See for yourself. A field of seven for two-year-olds, five hundred grand purse. And note the trainer."

Renie's eyes widened. "Duke Swisher? He's not exactly in the elite company of Bob Baffert and D. Wayne Lukas. I'll go find the results." She got up and scurried away.

Judith noted that the horse had been bred in California by Ali Baba Stables. The jockey's name was Pedro Feliz, which rang no bells. But, she realized, it had been a while since she'd been to the track.

"This seat taken?" a dark-haired middle-aged man inquired, pointing to Renie's chair.

"Yes. My cousin went to check the results of an earlier race. We got here late." Judith smiled. "Sorry. She'll be right back."

The man put his foot on the chair. "Which race?"

"The fourth," Judith replied.

"The one with the inquiry? That ended up with a disqualification for the horse that crossed the finish line. Some illegal stuff going on in the far turn. The favorite's jockey got unseated."

"Who won?"

"A long shot, Ali's Purchase. I got lucky. You sure your cousin's coming back?"

"Yes," Judith replied. "The winners should be posted on the wall just off the bar?"

"Right," the man said, removing his foot and pulling out the chair, "I might as well sit until she gets here. You come out for the feature?"

Judith fought an urge to turn around and try to spot Renie. "Ah . . . yes, it *is* the big race."

"You pick the winner yet?" the man asked after sitting down and taking a swig from Renie's glass.

"No, not yet. That's my cousin's drink, by the way."

He shrugged again. "So? I'll buy her another one. Don't worry about germs. It's alcohol. That kills 'em. Don't I know you from somewhere?"

Judith forced herself from rolling her eyes at the tired come-on line. "I don't think so," she replied stiltedly. But before asking him to go away, she studied him more closely. His weathered face indicated he was closer to sixty than fifty, so Judith guessed the dark hair was probably dyed. Maybe older, given the sagging skin on his neck. Indeed, there *was* something familiar about him. Curiosity overcame indignation. "Do you live around here?" she asked.

He shook his head. "No. I own a condo downtown. How about you? I know I've seen you someplace." Suddenly he snapped his fingers. "A café . . . Thurlow District . . . The Meat & Mingle?"

Judith gulped. "Yes. We owned it. You were one of our customers?"

The man grimaced. "Hell, no. I was the food inspector. Just retired last year from the city. You owned that place? Really?"

"Yes, and we went broke, but it wasn't because of the food."

"No," he agreed. "The kitchen always got good marks. It was the clientele that was low grade." He put out a hand. "Marv Farrell. Sorry, can't remember your last name."

Judith accepted his handshake. "It was McMonigle, but after Dan died, I remarried. It's Judith Flynn now."

Marv grinned and took another sip of the drink. "I never forget a face. I forgot the place had closed. I'd probably already transferred to another department. Sorry about your losses—the husband and the café, that is."

"Thank you," Judith said. "Speaking of the Thurlow District, did you know that the winning horse in the fourth race is partly owned by someone who has a business there?"

"No, wish I had. My bet was just a hunch. You picked any winners?" He polished off Renie's CC.

"We haven't had time," Judith replied. "As I mentioned, we got here . . ." She stopped, seeing her cousin carrying a giant box of popcorn.

"What the hell?" Renie screeched. "I turn my back, you pick up some guy who takes my seat and drinks my booze? Are you insane?"

"I can explain," Judith said. "You were gone so long that—"

Renie made a dismissive gesture with her free hand. "I smelled popcorn. I'm hungry. There was a line. Maybe I should steal your car and go home. You two seem to be having *fun*. At least I've got popcorn."

Marv shook his head and looked at Judith. "Somebody's crabby."

"She's ornery," Judith retorted. "Move and buy her another drink."

He let out an exaggerated sigh, but stood up, pulling out the chair for Renie. "There you go, little cousin. One CC coming up."

"With 7UP," Renie snarled, plopping down in the chair. "Make it snappy. We haven't got all day." She swiveled to look at Judith as Marv ambled off toward the bar. "What was *that* all about?"

"He's a retired food inspector," Judith replied, not without some embarrassment. "He used to come to The Meat & Mingle."

"No wonder he retired," Renie muttered before shoving a handful of popcorn in her mouth. "Swunnereesuhbibed."

Accustomed to deciphering her cousin's words when she talked with her mouth full, Judith made a face. "He survived just fine. You know Dan's food was always very good."

Renie swallowed before she spoke again. "Too bad Dan wasn't. Okay—so how many suspects from your list does this guy know?"

"I didn't have a chance to ask him," Judith replied indignantly.

"I was preoccupied with what was taking you so long to look up the race results. Never mind—he told me what happened. There was a disqualification, in case you didn't notice while you were overcome with popcorn fumes. I don't suppose you saw anybody wearing a turban?"

"As a matter of fact, I did," Renie said, ignoring a couple of popcorn kernels she'd dropped on her bosom.

Judith leaned forward in her chair. "You did? Where?"

"Coming out of the ladies' room. She was a tall blond goddess."

"Ohhh . . . someday you'll drive *me* to murder!"

"Don't even think about it," Renie said calmly. "I'll rat you out to the cops about that gallon of grape juice. There's no statute of limitations on murder."

Judith leaned back in her chair. "Behave yourself. Here comes your drink."

"CC as ordered," Marv said, setting the drink in front of Renie. "May I sit in your lap?"

"You may not," Renie retorted. "The only one who can sit in my lap is Oscar. And sometimes Clarence, except he sheds."

"I'm guessing Oscar and Clarence are pets," Marv said, bemused.

Judith held up her hands. "Don't pursue this line of inquiry."

"Hmm." Marv stroked his chin. "Kinky, eh? Why do I suddenly feel unwanted? I think I'll go to the private lounge and congratulate the owner of the Juvenile Turf race. I not only had the winning ticket, but I had the trifecta, too. Thank you, ladies. It's been . . . a mixed feed bag of pleasure." He sauntered off to the far end of the dining room.

"Follow him," Judith said. "It just dawned on me that's why we haven't seen Mr. Alipur. He's in the private area."

Renie sighed heavily. "I just got my drink. I've only eaten a fourth of my popcorn. You follow him. Lie your way in or make your pickup guy do the honors for you."

Judith hesitated. "Oh, why not? I can always use Uncle Al's name." She swallowed the last of her Scotch, stood up, and headed in the direction that Marv had gone. By the time she reached the VIP lounge's entrance, he was already inside. Squaring her shoulders, she took a deep breath and opened the polished oak door. A young tuxedoed waiter greeted her with an inquiring expression.

"You're . . . ?" he said tentatively.

"I'm with Marv," Judith said, seeing him talking to a squat, olive-skinned man holding a champagne glass. "He walks too fast."

The waiter nodded. Judith doggedly moved toward Marv, barely taking in the elegant Art Deco surroundings with their sleek yet elegant geometric lines and bold use of color.

"Ah!" he said, turning away from the man with the champagne. "I knew you couldn't resist me."

"I couldn't resist trying to find Mr. Alipur, the part owner of Ali's Purchase," Judith declared with a nod for the other man. "Is he here?"

Marv shook his head. "I suppose he left after his horse won the race." He gestured toward the window that overlooked the track. "There's the trainer, Duke Swisher. Maybe he can give whatever message you've got for Mr. Alipur. Swisher's the one in the brown corduroy jacket."

Judith made a beeline for her prey. She was surprised by the rugged good looks that didn't seem to have deteriorated with what she assumed must be sixty or more years. There was little gray in his fair hair and the lines in his face added more distinction than age. He didn't look much like the riffraff Ziva Feldstein had described. Judith waited for a lull in the conversation he was having with two other men. To her surprise, he spoke first.

"You're . . ." he began . . . and frowned. "Dang—the name escapes me."

"You don't know me," Judith responded. "I'm—"

"No, but you remind me of . . . ah! Al Grover, shrewd handicapper and big sports hero. I've seen him around here for years."

Judith blinked several times. "I remind you of him?" Except for her being tall like Uncle Al and also having dark eyes, no one had ever made the connection by physical resemblance.

Duke nodded. "Yes. One of those family things. Same with people as it is with horses. There's always some giveaway about pedigree." He held out his hand. "Pleased to meet you. Are you a Grover by birth?"

"Uncle Al is my late father's brother. I'm Judith Flynn. I got here too late to bet on Ali's Purchase. How long have you been a trainer?"

Duke shrugged. "I've been around horses all my life, but I didn't become a trainer until about ten years ago. I knew one of the owners of Ali Baba Stables and he talked me into it."

"Mr. Alipur?" Judith inquired.

"He was still in California," Duke said. "It was a local, Lee Watkins. He'd bought his first horse and I'd recently gotten married. I was starting a new life and figured why not? So here I am, puffing up my résumé."

"You've done well," Judith remarked. "Do you still live here?"

"My wife and I spend most of the year in California," Duke replied. "Felicia's from Santa Barbara. I met her when I went down to Palm Desert after going through a rough patch several years before. I needed to get away." His blue eyes shifted to the window, as if he could see into his past. "I lost someone very dear to me." He looked again at Judith. "Sorry about that. Would you like a drink? I wouldn't mind one. May I? It's an honor to meet one of Al Grover's relatives."

"Oh, I probably shouldn't," Judith began. "I left my cousin in the dining room. I just wanted to congratulate you on your win in the fourth race. A friend knows Mr. Alipur. Is either he or Mr. Watkins here?"

"Ali left after the fifth race," Duke said. "He hates leaving anyone else in charge of his restaurant. Lee was here." He craned his neck to search the room. "I don't see him now, though. Let's go over to the bar."

"Who's the third owner?" Judith asked as they made their way through the crowded room.

"I am," he replied. "It's one of only two horses I've ever owned. The other one was a filly."

"Was?" Judith echoed.

Duke nodded, but they'd reached the small bar with its sleek lacquered mahogany paneling. "Two champagnes," he told the mustachioed man in charge. When the drinks were poured, Duke steered Judith to a corner by a glass-fronted trophy case. "She broke down in her first race at Del Mar and had to be destroyed." He raised his glass. "Let me propose a toast to my lost Thorough-bred. Here's to Opal's Eyes."

Judith and Duke clicked glasses. "An interesting name," she remarked after taking a sip of champagne. "For someone in your family?"

Duke's smile was wry. "Almost. We were engaged to be married. Unfortunately, she died suddenly. That's why I headed for California back then. I suppose I was running away. But I ended up meeting Felicia." He shrugged. "Life takes strange twists and turns. I feel like a different person since I met her."

"That's wonderful," Judith said, though her brain was doing all sorts of tricks to backtrack in their conversation. It finally occurred to her that for once, she *could* be candid. She almost surprised herself when she continued. "Oh! This may sound odd, but did you name that filly for Opal Tooms? I know her daughter, Ruby."

Duke's eyes widened. "You're kidding! What a coincidence! Yes. How do you know Ruby?"

"I met her when I was in Little Bavaria last month," Judith replied. "I own a B&B and she's staying there now through the weekend."

Duke lowered his voice. "I haven't seen Ruby since she was a kid. Did she mention I was engaged to her mother?"

Judith could only stick to the truth for so long. "No, but Opal isn't that common a name. I got the impression that foul play might've been involved in Opal's death. Is that true?"

Taking a big sip of champagne, Duke frowned and looked beyond Judith. "Yes. As far as I know, the case was never solved. But I haven't been back to the old neighborhood since I left." He finally turned a flinty gaze on Judith. "I've tried to put the past behind me."

"I'm sorry I brought it up," she said. "I thought that since Mr. Alipur is in partnership with you, he might have talked about the case."

Duke's expression became bland. "No. Why would he? He didn't live in the Thurlow District back then. He probably never heard about it. He's a shrewd businessman, and when I told him the old Lockjaw Tavern was being sold dirt cheap, he jumped at the chance to buy the property. He already envisioned the neighborhood coming up in class. It was a lot less than he would've had to pay for something similar in California."

"I went to The Persian Cat for the first time today," Judith said. "My first husband and I lived in the area a long time ago. I hadn't been back since he died and I moved away. It's certainly changed."

"So I hear," Duke said indifferently as he finished his champagne. "Very nice to meet you. I should head down to the paddock and see if any of the local trainers are hanging out there."

Judith didn't bother finishing her own drink. "Thanks for the bubbly. I'd better track down my cousin."

Duke moved off, pausing briefly to greet a tall, dark-haired man near the door. Judith set her glass down next to a statuette of a woman holding a globe. Taking her time heading to the exit, she saw Duke leave. The other man turned to greet a woman who'd just made her entrance. Judith's step faltered as she saw the man's profile. His nose was hawklike and his chin jutted. She couldn't help but wonder if he was part of Ruby's vision from years ago . . . or her mysterious companion from the Thurlow District.

Or both.

Chapter 12

Judith was tempted to feign some minor distress to get the man's attention, but before she could think of anything, he turned sharply to make his exit—and ran right into Renie.

"Hey!" Renie yelled. "Watch the popcorn, you moron!"

The man murmured an apology, but kept going. Renie was still cussing under her breath as she brushed kernels off of her front.

"Follow that can!" Judith hissed. "I mean, that *man*."

"Why?" Renie asked. "Look at all the popcorn on the floor." She turned to see the man go into a restroom. "You were right the first time. He went into the can."

"Dammit," Judith said under her breath, "I wanted to talk to that guy."

"Jeez!" Renie exclaimed in disgust. "Did you come here to pick up guys or to sleuth? I thought you had to go home before six. It's after five now."

"You're right," Judith said, her shoulders slumping in defeat. "We'd better go. It was probably a nutty idea anyway."

"What was?" Renie asked as they retrieved their jackets in the dining room.

Judith didn't answer right away. "I thought maybe I'd spotted the mystery guy who might've drugged Ruby or could've been from a dream about someone in her past."

Renie stared at Judith as she handed over her cousin's car coat. "That's a lot of maybe, might, and could-have stuff. How many drinks did you have in the VIP lounge?"

"Not even a full glass of champagne," Judith replied, putting on her car coat. "But I had it with Duke Swisher."

"You broke up with What's-his-name already?"

"I lost him along the way," Judith said as they headed for the elevators. "Duke turned out to be very different from what I expected."

"How? Is he really a woman?"

"No. Wait until we get out of here and in the car before I unload."

"Okay." Renie finished the popcorn and tossed the empty box into a nearby receptacle. "I lost two bucks on that last race. I should never bet on a horse with a jockey named Tubby."

"Was he?" Judith asked as they reached the elevators.

Renie pressed the down button. "I don't know. I didn't see the start of the race and he fell off the horse in the backstretch. Or maybe the horse fell down under Tubby's weight. I was still eating popcorn. Hey," she said, pointing to a half-dozen framed pictures of Greenacres' leading trainers. "There's Jorge Gonzales."

Judith peered at the photo. "That's the guy I just saw."

"You want to go look for him in the men's room? Maybe you could con him into buying me a popcorn refill."

The elevator doors opened. "I'd better not. I really have to get home. Damn! I missed my big chance."

"That's what everybody who goes to the track says," Renie noted.

One of the three men who'd also gotten into the elevator laughed. "You're right about that, ladies. Four of my nags came in dead last."

Judith felt the comment was fitting in more ways than one.

Gray clouds had settled in overhead and it was starting to get dark. After the valet brought her Subaru, Judith had to wait for a low-slung silver sports car to move out of the way before she could head for the exit. Once they were in the flow of northbound traffic, she recounted her conversation with Duke Swisher.

"I don't know what to make of him," she admitted in conclusion. "He didn't want to discuss Opal's murder or ask if the case was solved."

"Understandable," Renie said. "He was hit hard by her loss. He's put his past behind him."

"I wonder," Judith murmured as they headed for the freeway on-ramp. "I think he lied about never coming back to the Thurlow District."

"How so?"

"He mentioned that he'd told Mr. Alipur about the Lockjaw Tavern going out of business. Unless I'm confused, I thought that happened only ten years ago. How could Duke know that if he hasn't been here for at least fifteen years?"

"Good point," Renie murmured. "Unless he heard it second-hand."

"Maybe." Judith turned on the windshield wipers as the first splatters of rain fell. "That's not how it sounded." She frowned. "Okay, let's face it—this trip was a bust. Sure, I met Duke and talked to Mrs. Feldstein and Annie O'Reilly, but there wasn't time to track down Lee Watkins or anyone else who could add to the case file. All I got were impressions. I should've stayed retired. I've lost my knack."

"The trail's over fifteen years old," Renie said. "The only way you could learn something helpful would be if Ruby got her memory back. Isn't there such a thing as 'triggers'? You know, like if we took Ruby to The Persian Cat, she might start to recall *something*. It's too bad she didn't want to tag along today."

"No, she didn't. I found that a bit odd. Of course," Judith

went on, maneuvering through freeway traffic that was getting bogged down by the increasingly heavy rain, "this whole visit has been hard on her. It's not as if she's been on vacation. Ruby didn't get away from it all—she walked right into her worst nightmare."

"I wonder if she dreamed what happened," Renie said after a long pause. "That is, she went to The Persian Cat, maybe passed out after a few glasses of wine, and whoever dropped her off was just a Good Samaritan. He—or even she—could've found the purse after Ruby got out of the car and dumped it in the nearest receptacle that just happened to belong to the Dooleys."

As the blurred lights of downtown shimmered before them, Judith considered the possibility. "If this person came from the Thurlow District, then why go up the side street by the Dooley house? It's easy to turn around in the cul-de-sac and head back to the Avenue."

"I see what you mean," Renie agreed, "but when people aren't in their own part of town, they sometimes do dumb things. A stranger wouldn't know that the north–south street doesn't go all the way through. Unless, of course, this mysterious person lives around here."

Judith shuddered. "Don't even think that! Haven't we had enough local loonies in the past few years?"

"It's all this growth," Renie said glumly. "Too many people have moved to the hill, despite the high cost of property. We're just getting a more educated class of loonies."

"Sad but true," Judith concurred as she moved into the exit lane. "It's a good thing I've got some frozen hors d'oeuvres. It's going on six now. By the time I drop you off, I'll only have about fifteen minutes to get ready for the guests' social hour."

"You want me to walk from your house?"

"No. I'd have to listen to you bitch for a week."

"It *is* over a mile. Of course Bill walks at least that far every day."

"Very sensible," Judith remarked. "I wish I could do that."

"I can't. Mostly because I don't want to. I didn't walk at all until I was fifteen months old. I knew I wouldn't like doing it."

"You were born ornery," Judith said, heading for a side street that led to the north part of Heraldsgate Hill.

"Being that way has been good to me," Renie responded in a self-satisfied tone. "You, on the other hand, are too softhearted. Which, now that I think about it, makes me wonder why I let you talk me into this wild-goose chase."

"Because you're more softhearted than you admit."

"Soft-headed, maybe," Renie said as they climbed the steep side hill that led to the Jones residence. "I hope Bill and Oscar had a good time while I was gone. Lots of football on TV today. Bill always has to explain the penalties to Oscar. He doesn't understand phrases such as 'intentional grounding' or—"

"Stop!" Judith cried. "I truly don't want to hear about Oscar. He's a *stuffed animal*."

"Well . . . he's a bit overweight, I'll admit, but—"

"Coz . . ." Judith said in a warning voice. "I mean it. You almost made me miss the turn onto your street."

Renie kept quiet until Judith pulled up in front of the house. "Thanks for the buggy ride, as Grandma Grover used to say."

"You're welcome," Judith murmured. "And thank *you*," she added more loudly.

Five minutes later, she was home. Joe was in the kitchen. "I thought you'd been kidnapped," he said as Judith shook raindrops off of her car coat before hanging it on a peg in the hall. "I just put a couple of those frozen appetizer trays in the oven."

"Oh, thank you!" Judith exclaimed, kissing his cheek. "Frankly, the trip to my old neighborhood wasn't very helpful."

"How come?" Joe inquired, opening the cupboard where the liquor was stored. "Did you go by your old house and get depressed?"

"I don't know if it's still there. It might've fallen down by now. The area has improved since I last saw it." Judith noticed that

Joe had gotten out only two glasses. "Where's Ruby? Or did she already get a drink?"

"She took off this afternoon while I was raking leaves, before the rain started," Joe replied, pouring out the Scotch. "She left a note on the credenza in the hall saying she didn't know what time she'd get back."

Judith took a quick sip of Scotch and headed for the entry hall. A page torn out of a ruled notebook was held in place by a vase containing chrysanthemums from the garden. *Off on an errand,* read the hand-printed message.

Picking up the note, Judith returned to the kitchen. "I wonder how long she's been gone. What time were you outside?"

"Oh—around four or so," Joe replied, leaning against the fridge. "I was back inside around four thirty. It was starting to look like rain." He frowned. "Are you worried about her?"

"Well . . . a little, given her history of going places on her own." Judith took another sip from her drink and shrugged. "I'm going upstairs to change before I greet the guests during the social hour. Don't forget to put the hors d'oeuvres out. They must be almost done."

"I *am* handy around the kitchen," Joe said drily.

"And other places," Judith murmured, kissing his cheek as she went past him to the back stairs.

It didn't take long for Judith to change, though she also paused to comb her hair and reapply some lipstick. Before heading back downstairs, she glanced into the spare bedroom where Ruby had spent the night.

None of her belongings were in sight. Judith went into the small, cozy room to check the other side of the bed and the closet. It looked as if Ruby had cleared out. Or someone had done it for her.

Trying not to hurry down the two flights of stairs to the main floor, Judith felt a surge of panic. Had Ruby really written the message on the credenza? What did her handwriting look like? But unlike the list of witnesses, the note had been printed. Judith's fears rose with every step before arriving breathlessly in the kitchen.

"Joe!" she called out softly, hearing voices in the living room. "Ruby's things are gone."

He looked up from putting some items in the dishwasher. "What?"

"None of her belongings are in the spare bedroom. Did she move back into Room Two?"

Joe shook his head. "It's taken, right?"

"Yes. I thought maybe someone had canceled. What should we do? I'm not sure Ruby wrote that note."

"Damn." Joe was silent for a moment or two. "Do you have her cell number?"

"She doesn't have her cell. Whoever searched her purse stole it along with her journal."

Joe moved toward the phone. "I wonder if I should call Woody. But maybe we're overreacting. Ruby's only been gone for a couple of hours—maybe less than that. I don't know exactly when she left."

Judith sighed. "You're right. But why would she take her luggage if she was only going out for a short time?"

"Beats me. She only had one suitcase, right?"

"Yes. According to Phyliss, she lived out of it. That is, when she got laundry back, Ruby put it in the suitcase. She never hung anything in the closet or used the bureau drawers."

Again, Joe was briefly silent. "I can't call Woody yet. It's too alarmist. I could ask the Rankerses if they saw anybody come and go."

"Wait," Judith said. "They're probably eating dinner. I'd better greet my guests. Oh—did you feed Mother yet?"

Joe glowered at his wife. "I'm not a glutton for punishment.

I had to put up with her telling me what I could do with all the leaves when I was out in the yard. You can guess where she told me to put them. Besides, what *is* dinner? *Where* is dinner?"

"Ooooh . . . I forgot to thaw anything. Forage, okay? I'll take care of Mother after I make nice with the guests."

By the time Judith entered the living room, all of the visitors except the latecomers were engaged in amiable conversation. Having spent so many years welcoming people to Hillside Manor, she could almost do it in her sleep. Which, she realized while smiling and shaking hands, was just about how she was operating on this damp, cool autumn night.

"So glad you could join us . . . Yes, typical for this time of year . . . That's not the ocean you see through the bay window . . . Sorry, I haven't played that piano in years . . . No, you can't take a tour bus from here to the Yukon . . . I'm afraid Arlington National Cemetery isn't within walking distance . . . I can't say I ever really thought about Walla Walla being redundant . . ."

After almost ten minutes of chitchat, Judith headed back to the kitchen, where Joe was standing by the microwave. "I found some of Aunt Deb's chicken-and-spaghetti-casserole recipe you'd frozen," he said. "Open a can of string beans and we'll call it dinner. Okay?"

"Sure." Judith picked up her drink and took a big sip before fetching a can of julienne string beans from the pantry. Before she could head back to the kitchen, Gertrude sailed through the back door in her motorized wheelchair without so much as a glance at her daughter.

"Starving me to death won't work, Lunkhead," she called to Joe. "I've still got two boxes of Granny Goodness Chocolates stashed where the sun don't shine."

"If it isn't my favorite nightmare," Joe said in his mellow voice. "Reminds me of that old song from my youth—'Ain't That a Shame.' How'd it go?" He began to croon in his fairly decent tenor. " 'You made me crow when you said hello . . . You broke my head with a loaf of bread . . . Ain't that a . . .' "

"Pat Boone," Gertrude growled. "But you sound more like his brother, Bab."

"Fats Domino recorded it, too," Judith said, coming up from behind her mother. "Dinner is almost ready. I was running a little behind."

"Nothing little about your behind, Toots," Gertrude rasped.

Judith ignored the comment. "You can eat with us, if you'd like."

"I wouldn't like," the old lady retorted. "I've got my TV programs to watch. Why don't you have a TV in the kitchen like Serena does? That was one of the few smart things she's ever done."

"I gave her that TV for Christmas several years ago," Judith said, opening the can of beans. "She and Bill don't watch it during dinner. They eat in the dinette or the dining room."

Gertrude had pulled up next to the counter. "She watches it while she cooks? No wonder her stuff tastes like swill."

"Renie's a fairly good cook," Judith declared, "as long as she sticks to basics."

Gertrude grunted. "Like bread and water?"

Judith decided to take a shortcut and microwave the beans along with her mother's portion of the chicken and spaghetti. Still preoccupied with Ruby's apparent defection, she wasn't in the mood to listen to Gertrude's harangues.

"Just put it in my lap," the old lady said when the meal came out of the microwave. "I can see myself out. It stopped raining, by the way."

"It did?" Judith said in surprise, realizing that her mother's baggy cardigan wasn't wet. "When did that happen?"

"When your ornery cat wanted to be let out a few minutes ago," Gertrude replied, releasing the wheelchair's brake. "He wanted to find his own dinner. I hope he doesn't want to eat crow tonight. See you in the funny papers." She zipped down the hall and out of the house.

"Ahhh," Joe uttered in relief, and sat down. "The rain may've stopped, but I would never call your mother a ray of sunshine."

"It's her defense mechanism against the world because my father died so young," Judith explained for the umpteenth time, putting the rest of the beans on the stove. She paused to check the oven to see if the chicken dish was heated all the way through. "Mother's always had a sharp tongue and been opinionated, but when my dad was still alive, she was much more cheerful. After that—"

Judith was interrupted by the ringing of the phone. "Maybe that's Ruby," she said, snatching up the receiver. "Hello?"

"Dooley here," Tyler said in a conspiratorial voice. "At four-fourteen this afternoon, Ruby Tooms left your house and got into a dark-colored sedan that turned toward the Avenue after leaving the cul-de-sac. She was carrying two items—probably her purse and some sort of luggage. I would've called sooner, but I had to find my sister's hamster before we ate dinner. One of my brother's hamsters *was* dinner a few years ago."

"Excellent job on your part," Judith said. "The surveillance, I mean. Did you recognize the car's make?"

"Not really," he said with regret. "It was a fairly new-model midsize sedan. If I had to guess, I'd figure it was some kind of Japanese make. I tried to see the license plate through the telescope, but the angle was wrong and it'd just started to rain."

"Could you tell if Ruby seemed reluctant to get in the car?"

"No," Tyler replied. "She hurried down the steps and across the walk. One other thing—I decided to do some homework, but kept my eye on your place. At five-forty, I saw a really flashy sports car pull up and a man got out. I *think* it was silver. Anyway, he went inside. I didn't see him come out, so I figured he was a friend or a guest. But when I looked a few minutes later, the car was gone. I *think*," he continued, "it was a Maserati custom job. I checked images on the computer. That was as close as I could come. But you must know this guy, right?"

"Hold on," Judith said, turning to Joe, who had dished up their dinner and started eating. "Did some guy in a sports car stop here shortly before I got home?"

Joe frowned. "Not that I know of. I was up in the family quarters."

"Do you know if the front door was locked?"

He shrugged. "I didn't check. Maybe Ruby didn't make sure it was locked when she left. Hey, you're the one who doesn't always lock up during the day because too many guests forget their keys."

"Right," Judith agreed under her breath before speaking again to Tyler. "We don't know who the sports car guy is. It could've been somebody checking out the B&B for a potential guest. It happens."

"Then it wouldn't be a mystery," Tyler said, sounding disappointed.

"As a matter of fact," Judith countered, recalling the sleek sports car in the racetrack parking lot, "it might be part of the mystery."

"Wow!" Tyler exclaimed. "How cool is that? What do you mean?"

"I don't know yet. Just keep looking. I mean, when it's not dark."

"Got it. Maybe I can still get my homework finished and play Trivia with some of my sibs. Or cousins. Or—"

"Yes, a lot of Dooleys to sort through," Judith said. "Thanks again. You've been really helpful."

"So," Joe said as Judith finally sat down, "you've got another junior spy from the Dooley brood?"

"Tyler," she replied after chewing some chicken. After a bite of pasta, she related his sightings and the possibility that the second visitor just might have been in the sports car she'd seen at the track.

"That's a stretch," Joe declared, finishing his meal at the same time Judith concluded her recapitulation. "This is Heraldsgate Hill, twenty-first-century edition. Those fancy cars are all over the hill. When was the last time anybody came in unannounced to check out the B&B?"

Judith glared at her husband. "A week ago Friday. A couple

from California stopped in to see if this would be a suitable situation for the husband's parents, who're coming this way after New Year's. I had to show them around while you were taking a nap. Meanwhile, my appetizers got scorched in the oven."

"Oh. Right. Hey—I was tired. I'd just finished a twenty-four-hour surveillance job."

"Of a strip club. No wonder you were worn out."

"A job's a job. Besides, those neon lights hurt my eyes."

Hearing noises in the hallway, Judith stifled a rebuttal. Apparently some of the guests were off on their evening rounds of pleasure.

"It's almost seven," she said, gazing at the schoolhouse clock. "I wish I'd never taken the afternoon off. I didn't learn much of anything. I just missed Lee Watkins and I forgot to ask Duke Swisher about Jorge Gonzales, the trainer Renie literally ran into, but he went into the restroom. If I'd stayed home, I might have some idea of where Ruby is."

"Has it occurred to you that she might have gone out to dinner with somebody she knows?" Joe asked, putting his plate in the dishwasher. "Not every person Ruby runs into is a murder suspect."

"And taken her luggage so she could change clothes en route?"

"You women do some odd things with your wardrobes."

"Not *that* odd." Having lost her appetite, Judith pushed her plate aside. "I'm going to see Arlene and Carl. Maybe they know something we don't. They might've heard about the hit-and-run accident victim's condition. The couple from Chicago won't get here for another hour."

Joe shrugged. "Fine. I'm going to watch some mindless TV as soon as the guests get finished in the living room. Meanwhile, I'll clear up the dinner stuff."

Judith kissed his cheek. "You're wonderful. Really."

His green eyes twinkled. "I'm getting soft with age. I know I can't change you. And except for the occasional killer trying to do you in, I don't want to. I never quite believed it when you swore you were going to retire from sleuthing. As a hobby, it beats knitting me hideous sweaters or making jewelry out of corn kernels like your aunt Ellen in Nebraska."

"Corn's very big there," Judith said, touching his cheek. "You watch some of their football games. Maybe there's one on now."

"Take off so I can watch. I missed most of today's college games."

Judith started for the back door. "*I* know when *I'm* not wanted. But I love you anyway."

"You'd better," Joe said, before resuming his kitchen duties.

Although the rain had stopped, the wind had come up. Judith looked skyward, surprised to see a few stars and at least three airplanes circling to land out at the airport. Maybe her Chicago guests were on one of them. She skirted the hedge to reach the Rankerses' front door.

"Judith!" Arlene cried. "Where have you been? I haven't seen you in . . . hours!"

"Running errands." *Fool's errands,* she thought to herself as she stepped inside and decided not to bother Arlene with an account of her fruitless trip to the Thurlow District. "I was wondering if you've heard anything about Bernard—or Brick—Frosch's condition."

"Not a word," Arlene replied. "Come sit in the living room. Carl's downstairs watching some football game. I don't know why he bothers. They all look the same to me. Pass, run, tackle, fall down, get injured and carried off the field. It's just like watching our kids when they used to play outside—except for the helmets. We should've thought of giving them some. Do sit—but not on Tulip."

"Oh!" Judith had been keeping her eye on Arlene as they entered the living room and hadn't noticed the black-and-white Boston terrier on the sofa. She moved a few feet to avoid the snoozing pooch.

Arlene sat down on the other part of the sectional. "The only thing I can tell you about Bernard Frosch is what Cathy found out today when she went to the house as the rental agent."

Judith was puzzled. "I didn't know Cathy handled that house. Joe's never mentioned it."

Arlene looked askance. "Did I say *she* represented Herself's property? I did not. But Cathy is an agent for rentals as well as being a Realtor. You know that."

"Uh . . . yes, of course." It occurred to Judith that Arlene's subterfuge was almost as disingenuous as her own. "What did Cathy find out?"

"That Herb was at home today, lounging around in his underwear and a very loud plaid bathrobe." Arlene winced. "Of course Cathy couldn't let on that she knew anything about their current situation. Lainie was there doing her nails, so Cathy asked if she was Mrs. Frosch. Lainie said she wasn't. A daughter, perhaps? Lainie just shook her head and went on filing her nails. Antisocial, really. Cathy asked if Mrs. Frosch was home. Mr. Frosch looked quite glum before saying she'd died. Then he belched. Disgusting. That was when Cathy noticed the beer cans by his chair. 'Was it sudden?' my daughter inquired. It was six A.M., Herb said. That struck Cathy as sudden, though of course she knew it already. But she offered condolences. Herb thanked her. Lainie kept on filing her nails."

Arlene had paused for breath. Perhaps, Judith thought, that was why Tulip suddenly woke up and jumped off the sofa. The dog thought his mistress had passed out.

"Did Cathy ask if there was going to be a funeral?" Judith inquired.

"Yes, but they had no plans," Arlene replied. "That's when Lainie finally spoke up, saying how could they even think about a funeral when Brick—that is, Bernie or Bernard or whatever he's called—was barely out of danger from joining his old lady. *Her* words, not mine—or Cathy's."

"Then he's improving?"

Arlene shrugged. "I suppose so. He's at least better than dead."

"Did they say anything else you don't know?"

Arlene caught the gibe in Judith's tone. "Judith! I told you *I* didn't know anything—it all came from Cathy! Shame on you!"

"I couldn't help it. You call *me* a sleuth, but you're no slouch."

"Oh, it's just being neighborly," Arlene said with a wave of her hand. "Besides, with Carl being the block-watch captain, we have to know what's going on around here. I'm thinking about having everybody's mail delivered here first. Just in case, you know, there's a bomb in it or something."

"About now, that's not the worst idea I've heard lately," Judith murmured as Tulip sniffed her shoes. "I do have another question to ask. Did you see Ruby leave late this afternoon?"

Arlene looked stunned. "Ruby left? What do you mean? And how did I miss it? Where did she go?"

"That's the problem. I've no idea. I wasn't home and Joe was taking a nap. She wrote a note saying she'd gone on an errand and would be back soon. That was three hours ago. Tyler Dooley saw her leave with her suitcase. I checked the spare bedroom and it was cleared out."

"Tyler is your new junior spy? How sweet!"

Judith nodded. "He's very good, just like the other Dooley kids. Not long after Ruby went off, he saw an exotic sports car pull up. A man came into the B&B and left a few minutes later. Joe and I have no idea who he was or what he wanted."

"Oh!" Arlene put a hand to her cheek. "Carl did see that car. He remarked on it, saying it was a Mazzerooni or something like that. He was going to ask Joe about it, but he took a nap instead."

"Too bad Joe and Carl take naps at the same time," Judith said. "Maybe we should get them to alternate. Did Carl see the driver?"

"He didn't because it was raining and he'd just let Tulip out for a moment. He did notice that the car had California plates."

Judith grimaced. "I don't suppose he could see the number."

"I didn't ask," Arlene said, looking chagrined. "Shall I do that now?"

"Well . . . I hate to have you bother him when he's watching football."

"It's no bother," Arlene said, getting up and leaving the room with Tulip trotting along after her.

Judith could hear only snatches of the exchange from the hallway on the other side of the living room. When Arlene returned, she was frowning. "At first, Carl said it was twenty-one-ten. That didn't make sense, but then I realized he thought I meant the score of the game. Maybe he's going deaf. He often doesn't hear what I say. The plate didn't have numbers as far as he could tell—just some letters. Being a man, he doesn't recall what they were. A vanity plate, I suppose. People who drive those Mazzeroonis are probably vain and stuck-up."

Judith tried to remember if the car she'd seen at the racetrack had out-of-state plates. She only recalled that it was very sleek and going faster than she was. Renie, however, had a bit of a license-plate fetish. Every time she saw an out-of-state car on the hill, she'd cuss, saying they'd better not move to our too-crowded city. We might *seem* friendly, but we're only polite. Then she'd make an obscene gesture.

"I should go back home," Judith said, standing up. "I've got late arrivals due soon. At least Brick Frosch must be improving. I assume whoever struck him hasn't been apprehended. There's often some front-end damage when a car hits a pedestrian."

Arlene rose from the sofa to walk Judith to the door. "Can't Joe find out from Woody?"

"He can, but without a better description of the car and none of the driver, it'll be hard to track down."

"Hmm." Arlene fingered her chin. "The intersection right by our street . . . so many apartments on the Avenue . . . walking distance to church . . ." Blue eyes widening, she dropped her hand and blurted out, "Bridey O'Leary! You know her—she always sits up front because she's deaf as a post. Over ninety, can't hear the TV or listen to the radio, so all she does is sit by the window. Bridey can still see." Arlene removed her jacket from the hall hat rack. "I'll call on her now. She loves company so I drop in now and then. Of course I have to TALK VERY LOUD."

Judith jumped at the last shouted words. "T-t-that's a good

idea," she said. "Let me know if Bridey saw anything. I only know her by sight."

"And sight is what Bridey still has," Arlene asserted. "You go along. I should tell Carl I'm leaving. I wouldn't want him to think I ran off with a dashing man in a Mazzerooni." She paused, frowning. "Or would I?" She turned around to head for the basement.

Judith stopped by the toolshed to collect her mother's dinner tray. Gertrude was jabbing at the remote and muttering under her breath. "Why isn't Lawrence Welk on Saturday nights anymore?" she demanded.

"Because he's dead?" Judith responded.

Gertrude made a face at her daughter. "So are half the people I still see on TV. Clark Gable, Lana Turner, John Wayne, Joan Crawford, Bing Crosby—one of them pops up every week. Why not Lawrence Welk?"

"That's because he was a bandleader, not a movie star," Judith explained. "I think you can get some of his shows on DVD."

Gertrude looked horrified. "I don't want his show plastered all over my BVDs! In fact, I don't wear BVDs. What's wrong with you tonight? You all thrilled about your gentleman caller this afternoon? Or didn't he ever find you?"

Judith perched on the arm of the small sofa. "What gentleman caller? When was he here?"

"Wouldn't you like to know," Gertrude said with a sniff.

"Yes, I would. Maybe he's a guest. What time was he here?"

Gertrude sighed. "Oh, you have to know everything. It was almost five and it was raining, but I didn't see your car, so I thought I'd go inside to see if supper was ready. You know I like to eat supper at five."

"*You* know I usually don't serve until six. Where was the man?"

"Coming into the kitchen when I came into the hall. He asked if the lady of the house was here. I told him how would I know, I was only her mother. He asked if anyone else was around. I didn't see any sign of Knucklehead or your weird guests, so I told him he'd have to come back later. Seeing as how supper wasn't ready at five, it wouldn't be ready until six. Turned out it was later than that, due to your gallivanting."

"Did he give his name? A card, maybe?"

"*You're* a card. No. Why should he? He didn't come to see me."

"Can you describe him?"

"Tall, dark, and handsome." Gertrude looked smug. "Better-looking than either of your two goofy husbands. But so's a rutabaga."

Judith gritted her teeth before asking another question. "How old?"

"The rutabaga?"

"Mother! Please! This is important. Ruby's gone somewhere and I don't know where she is. I'm worried about her."

"What's that got to do with your gentleman caller?"

"I don't know. That's why I'm asking."

Gertrude's eyes hardened. "He didn't ask about Ruby. Why are you worried about her? It's Saturday night, she's young and good-looking. Why shouldn't she be out on the town? You jealous?"

"No, of course not." Judith stood up and collected Gertrude's tray. "This man didn't say anything else?"

"Not that I can think of. He had manners, I'll say that for him."

"Okay." Judith surrendered. "Maybe he was inquiring about a reservation. I wish he'd left a note or some way to get in touch."

"If he wants to stay at the B&B, he'll call back," Gertrude said in a reasonable tone.

"True." With a firm hold on the tray, Judith leaned down to kiss the top of her mother's head. "Good night. Maybe you can find some old Jack Benny or Bob Hope shows on TV."

"Why would I do that? They're dead, too."

"Then try some vampire programs. They're already dead and they're still walking."

"That's more than I can do," the old lady retorted.

Judith exited the toolshed. The wind was blowing harder, making the almost bare branches of the old cherry tree writhe against the night sky. She jumped when something brushed against her leg. *Sweetums, of course, seeking sanctuary in the toolshed.* But her feet suddenly seemed heavy as she approached the porch. *Too much walking,* she thought, *especially on pavement.* Gripping the handrail, she dragged herself up the steps. As she cast one last look out into the garden, a shadowy form appeared at the far end of the hedge where the garden sloped uphill. Judith froze in place. The shape kept moving toward her.

Chapter 13

Judith!" Carl Rankers called, hurrying to the porch and putting a hand on her arm. "What's wrong?"

"Oh! You startled me! I'm so sorry!"

Carl's usually engaging grin seemed a bit uncertain. "I'd better go inside with you. You seem sort of shaky."

"I am," Judith admitted, letting Carl open the door for her. "I guess I'm just tired. What were you doing outside?"

He chuckled as they went down the hall. "Arlene won't let me smoke inside the house except in the basement. The football game was at the half, so I came upstairs to get a drink. Arlene was worried about the bird feeder at the back of the yard blowing over, so I went out to check. It was fine. But I decided to have a cigarette while I was outside. I saw something white in the hedge. It was closer to your side than ours, so I came out at the other end."

"What was it?" Judith asked, getting her nerves under control.

Carl shrugged. "Some kind of flyers the mailman dropped or somebody left on the porch."

Judith's natural curiosity took over. "Have you got them with you?"

Carl looked puzzled as he reached inside his jacket. "Yeah. I might as well toss them in your recycling, if that's okay. They're kind of damp." He handed over three sheets of dirty, crumpled paper just as Joe came down the back stairs.

Joe ambled into the kitchen. "Oh—hi, Carl. What's up?"

Carl started to answer, but Joe noticed Judith was pale. "Hey—what's wrong? You don't look so good."

"Nothing, really," Judith replied. "I overreacted. I thought we had an intruder, but it was Carl. He was in the hedge."

Joe looked curiously at his neighbor. "Really? Do you always do that at half time?"

"Only when I smoke," Carl replied. "Arlene can't find me there to chew me out."

"Good move," Joe said. "What did you think of the first half?"

Judith turned her back on both men and headed for the recycling bin. She straightened out the three sheets of paper to make sure they weren't of any importance. To her astonishment, they were tip sheets from the racetrack. The Rankerses occasionally went to the races, which ordinarily wouldn't have made her check the dates. But on this stormy night that had followed a seemingly futile afternoon, she saw a tip sheet for the Breeders Cup races and two pages of sports car rally listings.

"Here," she said, breaking in on Joe and Carl's pigskin analysis. "I want Woody to check these for any trace of DNA."

Joe looked puzzled; Carl seemed bemused. "Why?" both men asked at once.

Judith carefully put the pages on the kitchen table. "Because whoever came to the house probably had these with him. The guy in the Maserati visited with my mother."

Joe gazed at the ceiling. "He should either get a medal or be committed. I think you're reaching."

"No, I'm not. I saw that car at the track," Judith asserted, despite her earlier doubts. "Then he shows up here just before I got home. There's got to be some link to Ruby, and thus, to her mother's killer."

Carl patted Joe's arm. "Second half's about to start. Think

I'll leave you two to your discussion. Glad I found some . . . evidence." He sauntered off down the back hall.

Grimacing, Joe finally looked at the soiled sheets of paper. "Okay, they look genuine. Does this mean I have to interrogate your loathsome mother?"

"No," Judith replied. "Let Woody do that. She likes him. He can call her on the phone."

"I should've had Carl do it. She likes him, too."

"True." Judith looked sheepish. "She only dislikes men I marry."

"Okay." Joe seemed resigned. "We're doing this as much for Woody as we are for Ruby."

Judith. "Thanks. I think I heard my latecomers arrive. I have to check them in."

Bob and Doris Schilling were from Toledo, Ohio and had had to change planes in Chicago. The fiftyish couple seemed frazzled, but relieved to have finally reached their destination. They were in town to visit their son and his wife, who lived in a one-bedroom apartment on the top of Heraldsgate Hill. Judith soothed the Schillings with a warm welcome before showing them to Room Four. She'd just come down to the living room, where Joe was now watching the football game.

"Woody told me to say hi," he said, not taking his eyes away from the flat-screen TV Judith had bought him for his August birthday.

Judith sat down in the side chair that was closest to Joe's recliner. "Did he ask if I was making progress?"

"No. He's a veteran cop. He won't ask until you tell him. Woody probably doesn't expect anything to come of all this." Joe suddenly swore. "Another fumble! Can't these clods hold on to the ball?"

Judith decided it wasn't the right time to discuss the cold case with her husband. She got up and was going back to the kitchen when Arlene came in through the back door.

"Bridey is amazing!" she declared. "You should hire her instead of the Dooley kids."

"I don't 'hire' anybody," Judith said. "They volunteer."

"Then volunteer Bridey," Arlene responded. "It's too bad more crime doesn't happen out on the Avenue. She'd be a treasure trove."

"Have a seat," Judith offered, pulling out a chair for herself. "Can I get you some coffee or a soda?"

"Goodness, no," Arlene said, sitting down across from Judith. "It's almost eight-thirty. Carl and I'll be heading upstairs soon to watch TV before we go to bed." She glanced around. "No sign of Ruby?"

Judith shook her head. "Joe just got off the phone with Woody. I don't think he told him about Ruby being gone. I suppose my worrying about her is silly, but still . . ."

Arlene shrugged. "What's the worst thing that could happen to her? She could be kidnapped by white slavers or Somalian pirates. Worse yet, she could be forced to watch C-SPAN for an entire week."

"I suppose," Judith said vaguely. "Well? What did Bridey see?"

"The car, coming up the hill and then gaining speed as Brick was crossing the street. It was a 2002 Acura TL, four-door, dark color. State license plate began with *ROZ* or *POZ* and then three numbers she didn't catch. After hitting Brick, the car went even faster and out of sight."

Judith couldn't help but be incredulous. "This ninety-year-old woman could tell all that in a few seconds?"

Arlene made a face. "Of course she could. She and her late husband owned an automotive repair and restoration shop at the bottom of the hill for over forty years. They were both very knowledgeable about all kinds of cars. Bridey hasn't lost her edge just because she's lost her hearing. You might like to see her miniature car collection. Her spare bedroom is filled with little cars. Trucks, too, and even RVs."

"How is she with people? Did she describe the driver, too?"

"Not in quite as much detail. She likes cars better than she likes people. As she told me, if she were a car, she could go to a

restoration shop like they owned and get new ears put on. Or in."
Arlene paused. "Now, how would they do that? Oh, well. You
know—like your hip replacement. In fact, why can't they replace
ears?"

"I don't know," Judith replied. "The driver? Please?"

"Oh, him." Arlene sighed impatiently. "Probably Caucasian,
maybe dark hair, no glasses, hatless, hairy and rather beefy hands.
Maybe wearing a leather jacket. It looked shiny under the street-
light."

"Not bad," Judith said, impressed. "Very detail-oriented."

"They did that, too."

"What?"

"Detailing. Cars at their shop, of course. What else?"

"Oh. Of course." Judith sighed. "Those first three letters of the
license plate may help along with the car's description. Woody
can check that plate through the system."

Arlene was on her feet. "Would he like to hire Bridey?"

"The police department is short on funds," Judith said, slowly
getting up. She felt stiff as well as tired. "But she's a very keen
observer."

"You'd like her," Arlene said as they headed for the back door.
"Although a visit with her can be exhausting because you have to
speak in SUCH A LOUD VOICE."

Judith gave another start. "Right, right. Thanks, Arlene. I'll
keep you posted."

"Yes, you will." From anyone else, it might've sounded like a
threat.

As soon as her neighbor had left, Judith called Renie. "Do you
recall what the license plate was on that sports car that was ahead
of us leaving the track?"

"What sports car?"

"The silver one. It may've been here just before I got home. By
the way, Ruby's sort of missing."

"Coz, it's going on nine o'clock. Bill and I are watching *Lonesome Dove* for the tenth time, but we like it. I didn't notice much

about the car or the plate. I was still picking corn kernels off my small person."

"Sorry I asked," Judith said. "I know you often notice—"

"Ruby's missing?" Renie suddenly exclaimed. "What do you mean?"

"Just what I told you." She went on to explain about the events that had taken place since returning to Hillside Manor.

"Well," Renie said when her cousin had finished, "that's all really fascinating. But Gus, Call, and Deets have started driving the cattle to Montana. I don't want to miss the part where they get to Ogallala."

Never having seen the miniseries, Judith gazed up at the high ceiling. "Fine. Go watch your damned TV show. Don't worry about me."

"Hey—that's my mother's line!" Renie cried. "I swear you'll turn into her eventually."

"So? You get more like *my* mother every day."

"Weird science. Oh—I'm missing a key scene with Elmira. Bye."

Wearily, Judith disconnected. Maybe she shouldn't worry about Ruby. Having grown up in the area, she undoubtedly still knew some people. The note may have been written before she went out with friends and she'd forgotten to add anything more enlightening.

"I'm going upstairs," Judith announced to Joe. "How long is that game going to last?"

He peered at the screen. "It says nine twenty-two, fourth quarter. I can watch the end of it upstairs if you're in the mood for tackling *me*."

"I am not," Judith declared. "I'm beat. Go ahead and lock up when you're done. I hope Ruby remembered to take her key with her."

"Okay. Whoa! Interception! What a move!"

Trying not to roll her eyes, Judith made her way to the back stairs. The two flights to the family quarters daunted her, but after pausing to take a deep breath, she finally staggered into the master bedroom. Flopping onto the bed to catch her breath, she gazed out the window. The wind was still up, causing the thick shrubbery alongside the house to scrape against the old wooden exterior. Apparently the rain had started after Arlene had gone home. Judith could hear a faint drip from one of the gutters. *Plop-plop, plop, plop-plop* . . . the rhythm soothed her. She was sound asleep by the time Joe came upstairs a half hour later.

Feel better?" he asked when Judith joined him in the kitchen just before seven the next morning.

"You should have woken me up. I don't remember the last time I slept in my clothes. I never heard you come to bed."

Joe shrugged. "I shifted you around on the bed and tucked you in. You sort of mumbled, but that was it."

She kissed his cheek. "Thanks. Who won the game?"

Joe turned sheepish. "I don't know. I fell asleep just before the two-minute warning. If some of the guests hadn't come back a little after ten, I might have ended up sleeping in the recliner."

"Oh, Joe, are we getting old?"

"Sure," he said cheerfully. "That's what people do. I don't know of anybody whoever went in the other direction."

"Did Ruby come back?"

"No idea," Joe said, pouring coffee for both of them.

"I thought you might've checked," Judith murmured. "You knew I was worried."

"*You* didn't check?" he inquired, sitting down at the table.

Judith shook her head. "I was afraid to. Don't you think one of us might've heard her go into the spare room?"

"Not you. A rhinoceros could've roared through the family quarters last night and you'd have slept right through it." He saw the dismal look on his wife's face. "Okay, I'll go up there now and see if she came back."

"Thanks," Judith said meekly.

Five minutes later, Joe was back in the kitchen. "Ruby's still AWOL," he said, his round face reflecting Judith's concern. "Maybe I should call Woody. I might as well ask him if he can take a look at those sheets Carl found, but don't expect anything."

"Don't forget the license plate and the car description," Judith said as she slipped bacon in a skillet. "I gather you've already eaten breakfast."

"Yes. What license plate and car description?"

"Oh! I didn't get a chance to tell you last night." She put a piece of bread in the toaster before giving Joe a quick rundown of Bridey O'Leary's information.

"That's the old lady who sits up front at SOTS?" Joe asked in surprise. "My God, she's better than a trained observer!"

"It's her entertainment," Judith said. "She's very deaf. I assume she can still read, though."

"She sure can see," he remarked. "Okay, I'll call Woody after we get back from Mass. Since he sings in the choir at his Methodist church, he and Sondra usually don't get home until twelve-thirty or so. Want me to make an omelet for your guests?"

Judith gave him her most winsome look. "Would you?"

He squeezed her chin. "Sure. Maybe I'll make two different kinds."

The next hour was spent in preparation for the guests' breakfast. Happily, none of them had dietary restrictions—a question Judith always posed on her registration forms. The first of the current visitors didn't arrive until almost eight-thirty. Apparently the wind and rain had lulled them into a sound sleep, too.

By ten forty-five, two of the couples lingered at the dining room table. Fortunately, they were both staying over until Monday. The departing guests had checked out a few minutes earlier.

Joe, who had been upstairs going over his notes for Woody, arrived in the kitchen as Judith was scraping dirty plates. "Are we on schedule for eleven o'clock?"

"Yes," she said. "I want to finish loading the dishwasher first."

Our Lady, Star of the Sea was only five blocks away at the top of the hill, just off of Heraldsgate Avenue. Before Judith's hip surgery, the Flynns often walked to the church in good weather. But in recent years, the steep climb and the precarious descent was too much for her.

As she was turning the dishwasher on, the phone rang. Judith hurried to the counter to grab the receiver. A male voice inquired if she was the owner of Hillside Manor.

"Yes," she replied. "Are you asking about a reservation?"

"No. I'm asking about a guest named Ruby Tooms. Is she there?"

Judith's grip tightened on the receiver. "No. May I give her a message?"

"No. I'll call back later. When do you expect her?"

"I'm not sure. Do you want to leave your name?"

There was a pause. "Sure," he finally said. "Tell her Jess Sparks called."

Judith tensed. "Did you say *Jess* Sparks?"

"Right. *J-E-S-S.* Thanks." He rang off.

Joe was in the hallway putting on his raincoat. "What was that all about? You look odd."

"A guy named Jess Sparks calling for Ruby," Judith said vaguely, checking the caller ID. "Damn—I answered it so fast the number didn't register."

"Old flame of Ruby's?"

Judith glanced around the kitchen to make sure everything had been turned off. "I doubt it. Remember, the old guy in the nursing home was Hector Sparks. He had a daughter, but no son that I know of. So how is Jess connected to Marla and Lee Watkins?"

"Can we play this game after Mass? I don't have my scorecard handy. Let's go. It's still raining, by the way, so I'll drive your car. It saves wear and tear on my MG. I like it when I can put the top down."

By the time the Flynns got inside the church, Bill and Renie were already there, sitting in front of Carl and Arlene. Both pews were full. Judith and Joe found a place two rows back. After saying her prayers, Judith craned her neck to see Bridey O'Leary in the front row. But too many people blocked her view.

Father Hoyle based his homily on the gospel reading for the day about the five foolish virgins who ran out of oil while awaiting the bridegroom. Joe leaned over to whisper in Judith's ear that finding five virgins of any kind these days was a problem from the get-go. Judith gave him a dirty look and elbowed him in the ribs. But as ever, their pastor's sermon was articulate and thought-provoking—even if Bill remarked after Mass that the reading should be updated so that the virgins ran out of gas. Renie told him that with his chronic bad stomach, at least *he* never ran out of gas. On that note, the Joneses and the Flynns went to their respective cars.

By the time the Flynns got home, the rain had let up, though the wind was still gusting. Judith checked for phone messages, but there were none. She immediately reminded Joe to call Woody. "This is beyond just a night on the town," she asserted.

Joe reluctantly agreed. "I'll call him in about twenty minutes."

"Thanks." Judith smiled. "You have to admit it's worrisome."

"I'd worry more if Ruby hadn't taken her suitcase," Joe said. "If someone is being kidnapped, they don't usually get a chance to pack before they leave."

"What if she was held at gunpoint?"

Joe shook his head and started for the back stairs.

The dishwasher's green light glowed, so Judith unloaded it. Feeling at loose ends, she headed for the front hall to go upstairs and make the beds. Three rooms would be occupied by holdovers and she had only one new reservation—for the single room. Maybe someone would arrive unexpectedly by Monday. It happened occasionally when other B&Bs were already full or someone came to town without a reservation.

She got as far as the credenza. Another note caught her eye. Anxiously, she picked it up and read what looked like hastily scrawled words: *Didn't mean to run out on you, but Ozzie came to town and he and Freddy Mae had an extra bed at their hotel, so am staying*

with them. Thanks for your help. Sorry I caused any trouble. Ozzie says
we should let the past stay in the past. Guess he's right. XXX OOO Ruby.

"Damn!" Judith swore under her breath. She felt like crumpling up the note and tossing it in the recycling bin. She'd have to tell Joe to forget about informing Woody that Ruby was missing. But halfway back to the kitchen, she had qualms. How had Ozzie known where to find Ruby? Why had she left the first note and not a follow-up? And why was she so quick to give up the search for her mother's killer?

Judith sat down at the kitchen table and dialed Renie's number.

"What are you doing?" she asked her cousin.

"Looking at the paper. Why?"

"Have you and Bill got any plans for today?"

"No, just the usual. Bill takes his long walk, then his nap, then we eat dinner. Meanwhile, I'll try to get some work done. Why," Renie went on, sounding wary, "do you ask?"

"Can you spare me a half hour or so? I've got a problem."

"Is it something to do with Joe?"

"No, nothing like that," Judith assured her.

"Then why can't you talk to him?"

"Because . . . well, because he doesn't always humor me when it comes to what he considers my flights of homicidal fancy."

"Oh—Ruby, I suppose. Is she still gone?"

"Yes—in a way."

Renie's sigh could be heard at the other end. "Okay—let me finish the arts and entertainment section and I'll be there."

"Thanks, coz," Judith said humbly.

"Hey—should I bring Oscar? He's having trouble with this Sunday's crossword puzzle."

"Coz . . ."

"Never mind. See you." Renie hung up.

Judith figured she had time to make up at least two of the bedrooms. Usually on Sundays, when Phyliss was praying her way through the Sabbath, Joe helped with preparations. But by the time Judith pitched the soiled linens down the laundry chute and had gone downstairs, he apparently was still in the family quarters. Maybe Woody and Sondra hadn't gotten back from church yet. Renie appeared before Judith could pour herself a cup of coffee.

"Want some?" Judith asked her cousin.

"No thanks," Renie said, sitting at the kitchen table. "I might grab a Pepsi later. Okay, what's got you in a tizzy now?"

Judith showed her cousin the note. "Apparently this was dropped off while we were at church."

"You sure this is her handwriting?" Renie asked.

"The other note was printed. It's hard to compare."

"That's a bit odd, though the other one was short. This is different notepaper, but it could've been written at the hotel."

"So how did her brother know where to find her?"

"She might've called him from here—or somewhere else. I'm guessing she didn't know he was coming to town."

"I'm letting Joe tell Woody she's missing," Judith said. "As far as I'm concerned, she is, note or no note. I'm still uneasy. Do you want to help me start calling the hotels? We can split the list and use our cells."

Renie sat up very straight. "No, I do not want to do that. Do you realize there are over a hundred hotels around here? What if they're staying in one of our suburbs? Have you considered that Ruby used the term 'hotel' loosely and it could be a residence inn or a motel or a flophouse on Skid Row? Are you *insane*?"

Judith felt sheepish. "Well . . . I suppose it *is* like looking for a needle in a haystack. Have you got a better idea?"

"Yes. We take Ruby at her word. Didn't she plan to head back to Little Bavaria tomorrow? She has a job. Why don't you wait until then and call the restaurant where she works."

"You're right," Judith conceded after a pause. "Ruby's an adult and fairly smart. I still wonder why Lainie had Ruby's purse."

"Maybe," Renie suggested, "Ruby dropped it on her way back the night she returned from the Thurlow District."

Judith shook her head. "She was so confused that she went to the Rankerses' house, remember? The rental's on the opposite side of the cul-de-sac. Unlike our house and the Rankerses'—which are the same architectural style—it doesn't face the street."

Renie stood up. "Ruby was dazed. She may've wandered around before she got to the Rankerses' house. Give it up. Ruby has."

The doorbell rang before Judith could respond.

"I'll get it," Renie said, going through the swinging half doors. "Grab me a Pepsi, will you? I'm not leaving here empty."

"Fine," Judith muttered under her breath, rising from the chair and going to the fridge. She was pouring Pepsi into a glass when Renie returned.

"Okay," she said in a somewhat shaken voice. "I'm back in. Your caller is out in the hall. He says he's Jess Sparks, Hector's long-lost son."

Chapter 14

Judith almost dropped the glass of Pepsi. "Here," she said, shoving it at Renie. "You can add your own ice."

Jess Sparks had followed Renie into the kitchen. "Mrs. Flynn," he said, doffing his baseball cap and holding out his hand. "Is Ruby here?"

Judith shook hands, taking the measure of her unexpected guest. He was average height, average looks, and, judging from his rough hands as well as his scuffed work boots, average income. "No," she said, regaining her aplomb. "Ruby left yesterday. How well do you know her?"

"I don't," he said with a crooked smile. "I heard somebody's been looking for her lately. I wanted to know why."

"Let's go into the living room," Judith said. "Would you like something to drink?"

"No, thanks," Jess said. "I just had lunch at the bottom of the hill."

Judith led the way, indicating that Jess should sit on one of the matching sofas. She and Renie sat down opposite him.

"How did you know Ruby was here?" Judith inquired.

Jess had taken off his cap and was rubbing at his auburn hair. "I'm a firefighter. We were called to a house in the cul-de-sac the other day. I've seen pictures of Ruby. I recognized her standing with you and two other women. My battalion chief said they come here fairly often. I switched stations last month, so I didn't know about your . . . background. We didn't stick around because there was nothing we could do for the lady who was hospitalized. I was on duty until Friday and then I crashed, so I wasn't able to check on Ruby until today."

"Why," Judith asked, "do you want to get in touch with her?"

Jess grimaced. "It's a long story. Look," he went on, leaning forward, his brown eyes earnest, "it's a sentimental idea for me. I won't bore you, so if you'll give me her home address, I'd appreciate it."

Judith hesitated. Jess Sparks seemed straightforward. She could easily verify his claim as a firefighter, an occupation she respected for the courage and integrity it often demanded. The station was not only close by, but the Heraldsgate Hill company obviously knew her all too well. In fact, there was something familiar about Jess. Maybe she'd seen him when he'd come to the Frosch rental. "Ruby lives in Little Bavaria," she said, avoiding details. If he was serious, he could do his own digging.

"Okay." He stood up. "Thanks. Sorry to have troubled you. Maybe we'll be coming here again one of these days."

"Yes, that is . . ." Judith struggled to get to her feet. "I mean, I hope it's not for another emergency."

"That's okay," Jess said as the cousins walked him to the door. "I get the impression this is a pretty busy part of the hill."

"Busy . . . yes," Judith agreed. "Be careful out there."

Jess gave her another crooked grin before heading down the porch steps and on to an older Dodge Ram.

As soon as Judith closed the door, Joe appeared in the hallway. "Hi, Renie. You just get here?"

Renie nodded.

Joe pointed at the front door. "You came in this way?"

Renie shook her head.

Joe stared at Judith. "What's wrong? Has she lost her voice?"

"No!" Renie shouted. "But coz here is beginning to make me

feel like Mortimer Snerd without Edgar Bergen." She glared at Judith. "What I really want to say is that I have never seen you wilt so fast when I know damned well you were boiling over with curiosity."

"I didn't feel I could push Jess," Judith replied. "I know where to find him."

"Who's Jess?" Joe asked.

Judith rubbed her forehead. "Supposedly the son of Hector Sparks. I need some Excedrin. I've got a headache coming on."

Renie and Joe followed her out to the kitchen. "I talked to Woody," he said, resting a hand on one of the kitchen chairs. "That license plate will take forever to find. He's a little short on manpower."

Judith didn't respond until she'd swallowed the pills. "I'm a little short on woman power. What did he say about Ruby?"

Joe grimaced. "She hasn't been missing for forty-eight hours. A description of what she was wearing would help."

"I don't know what she was wearing," Judith replied. "Probably black or tan slacks, a dark green all-weather jacket with a hood. She only brought a few things with her."

Joe fingered his chin. "I thought her jacket was blue."

Renie was foraging in a kitchen drawer. "One of every four men is color-blind." She opened a box of pretzels. "Or is it one of five? I forget."

Joe frowned at Renie before turning to Judith. "Whatever happened to lunch?"

"Oh!" Judith cried. "I forgot to feed Mother! And you."

"I'll make sandwiches," Joe volunteered. "You want one, Renie?"

"Wha' ki'?" she asked with her mouth full.

"Walrus hide," Joe replied.

"Good," Renie said after swallowing. "My fave. Actually, I'm going home. Make Aunt Gert's sandwich fast and I'll take it out to her."

Joe was already getting out a loaf of bread. "You got it. I don't need any more criticism from the Grover females."

Five minutes later, Renie was out the door and on her way to the toolshed. Judith remained at the table, looking bleak. "I wish I knew why Ruby suddenly decided she wanted to give up the hunt for her mother's killer." She reached over to the counter where she'd put the note her departed guest had left. "Read this. It bothers me."

Joe perused the note. "It sounds okay to me."

"I don't get it," Judith repeated. "She seemed so determined."

Joe set their lunch plates on the table and sat down across from her. "Ruby's a bit of a flake," he said. "I know the type—so do you. Raised in a family where Dad was a petty thief and Mom struggled to keep the family intact. Growing up was probably a lot harder than Ruby admits, but she probably took the hardship for granted. She comes across a cold case that's been solved because of DNA and gets a wild idea to try to find her mother's killer. Then older brother shows up and tells her she's wasting her time. Maybe Ruby's a little ADD."

"I hope that's what happened," Judith said. "It's plausible."

Joe waited to swallow a bite of chicken sandwich. "Just because Ruby's giving up on the case, it doesn't mean I have to. There's still Woody to consider, which is why I got involved in the first place. By the way, did Ruby show you a picture of her mother?"

"No. I don't think she had one," Judith replied. "Or if she did, she left it in Little Bavaria."

"I'll ask Woody. He probably had at least one photo, but it'd be with the evidence, not in his case file."

The Excedrin was starting to work. Judith smiled wanly. "I'm glad you're still interested. I think I'd have trouble letting this one go."

Joe put his hand on Judith's. "I figured you might. It's not easy to retire, is it?"

Judith's smile brightened. "It depends on who is retiring with you. You're not the retiring type either. Do we really want to buy an RV and move to Arizona like Dan's mother did?"

Joe shook his head. "Not our style. We'd miss the rain. On

the other hand," he went on, the gold flecks dancing in his green eyes, "I could use a little heat. How about retiring to the family quarters?"

"That," Judith replied, "is the kind of heat I like."

On Monday morning, Phyliss showed up just before nine, complaining that her umbrella had blown inside out while she waited for the bus. "The good Lord wasn't watching over me the way He should. This is the second bumbershoot I've lost this fall."

"The wind died down quite a bit," Judith pointed out.

"Not in my neighborhood across the canal. They're building too many big apartments over there. It's like standing in a canyon. Going across the street was worse than crossing the Red Sea. I told Moses he ought to do something about that. Like clean out the drains."

"Moses?" Judith echoed.

"Moses Stivertsen. He waits at the bus stop with me. He works for the city—a godly man. I'm hoping to get him to join my church."

"Is he interested?" Judith asked, trying to be polite.

Phyliss's beady eyes narrowed suspiciously. "In what? Are you suggesting unholy hanky-panky?"

"Of course not. I meant is Moses interested in joining your church?"

Phyliss's narrow shoulders relaxed. "He says he doesn't need a building and a preacher to feel godly. Moses says God is everywhere. I asked him if that was so, then why did my bumbershoot go inside out?"

Judith had long ago stopped trying to answer Phyliss's illogical questions about how God operated on a personal level. "I don't use an umbrella," she finally said. "The question is a moot point for me."

"That's another thing," Phyliss declared, shaking out her black raincoat. "There's a moot at our bus stop who talks with his hands. I can't understand a word he's waving, but Moses can."

"You mean a *mute?*"

"Isn't that what I just said?"

"Right. Sorry. I got another reservation a few minutes ago, so make sure Room Six is ready. Oh—I only did two loads of laundry yesterday and there's more downstairs. The last load is still in the dryer."

"Sounds like you got sidetracked. Oh, well—no rest for the godly." Phyliss headed to the basement.

Joe came downstairs a few minutes later. "I've received an assignment starting this afternoon," he said. "Deep background for somebody the police chief wants to hire for the bomb squad. I got the job through Woody, but I'll have to work on it at headquarters. He does have a couple of photos of Opal Tooms in the evidence room, so I can bring those home tonight."

"Good," Judith said . . . and smiled. "I'm glad you're employed again."

Joe shrugged. "So am I. At least it's not a surveillance job. Those things bore the hell out of me."

The rest of the morning was busy, cleaning up from the guests' breakfast, seeing off the couple that was checking out, and telling the holdovers to enjoy their day. By noon, Judith had Gertrude's lunch ready and was glad to sit down in the toolshed for a brief visit with her mother. For once, Gertrude seemed in a benign mood.

"You forget I'm playing bridge this afternoon at Marcella Maria Lauracella's?" she asked her daughter.

"No, but I forgot she had such a long name," Judith replied.

"*She* forgot that her husband used to own a bakery downtown. So what if he's been dead for twelve years? She can't come up with better snacks than Ding Dungs?"

"You mean Ding Dongs, Mother."

"No, I don't. You ever tasted what Marcella Maria serves?"

"Oh. No, luckily I haven't."

"Frieda Heftmeister's picking up your aunt Deb and me," Gertrude said after chewing a bite of dill pickle. "Frieda's legally blind, so Deb and I have to tell her when to stop and go. Wish Deb would stop yakking long enough to add up the count in her hand when we're partners."

"You know Aunt Deb enjoys visiting," Judith said. "She's a very social person."

"She should save it for social occasions. Bridge isn't one of them."

Judith was well aware of how seriously Gertrude took her cardplaying. When it came to bridge, her mother's mind was as sharp as anyone's this side of Charles Goren. Indeed, she'd outlived Goren, who'd also lived to a ripe old age. But Gertrude seemed likely to outlive most of the people who had been born in the previous century.

Judith patted her mother's shoulder. "Good luck. And have fun."

"Fun? If stomping your opponents is fun, I will. By the way, what happened to that Ruby girl? I haven't seen her since she stopped to say hello Saturday afternoon." The old lady frowned. "Or was it good-bye?"

Judith halted halfway to the door. "When was that?"

"I told you—Saturday afternoon. Come to think of it, I guess it was after four. I was getting hungry for my supper. She had some fella with her, maybe a date. Didn't you say she was gone all night?"

"You forgot to mention that," Judith said. "Who was this guy?"

Gertrude shrugged. "I didn't ask. He stayed outside. Ruby was here for only a minute or so. It was raining and her beau was getting wet."

"Ruby left a note saying her brother was picking her up," Judith explained. "I suppose she's back in Little Bavaria now or will be soon."

"Good for her. Chipper kind of girl." Gertrude took a big bite of her sandwich and waved her daughter off.

Back inside the house, Judith wondered if she should call Ruby in Little Bavaria. During Oktoberfest, she'd had two jobs, but maybe she was now working only the evening shift at Wolf-gang's. At half-past noon, it might be too soon to call. Even in good weather, the road through the mountain pass was tricky and would take three or four hours, especially via bus. Judith decided to wait until at least midafternoon.

Joe left for downtown soon after Judith returned from the toolshed. The next two hours were spent conferring with Phyl-iss, receiving two December reservations, arguing with Phyl-iss, preparing the guests' appetizers, trying to convince Phyliss that Catholics did not worship idols despite the use of statues in churches, and, at three o'clock, getting a request for the single room from a stranded businesswoman whose flight to Fairbanks had been canceled.

Judith finally decided to call Ruby. The phone rang five times before trunking over to a standard voice message saying that the party was unavailable and to please leave a message at the sound of the beep. Judith complied, asking Ruby to phone her as soon as she could. "I have a question for you," she added. "Don't worry—it's not anything upsetting, just my rampant curiosity. Hope all is well with you."

Ten minutes later, the phone rang. Judith saw Ruby's number come up and quickly answered. "Ruby?" she said. "How are you?"

"Excuse me?" a male voice responded. "I must've dialed the wrong number." He disconnected.

Puzzled, Judith wondered if she'd dialed incorrectly. It was possible, given the strain of the past few days. She started to redial, but stopped, realizing she'd probably placed the call to Ruby's cell, which had disappeared. It was the only number listed on Ruby's registration. Judith double-checked to make sure. She'd called Ruby when the cousins were in Little Bavaria, but couldn't remember if it had been the same number as the cell phone. Dialing directory assistance, she asked for Ruby's home number—and was informed it was the same as the cell. Discour-aged, she called Renie and explained her plight.

"You've done work for the phoneco," Judith said. "How do I find out if Ruby has another number?"

"You don't," Renie replied. "She probably doesn't. Wait and call her at Wolfgang's and stop bothering me when I'm working. Just because I've designed a couple of annual reports for the phone company over the years doesn't mean I understand diddly-squat about their operating system. For all I know about technology, they use two tin cans and a string. In fact, I wish they did—then the string might not reach from your house to mine. I'm up against deadline." Renie hung up.

Phyliss came through the kitchen. "I still say they're graven images," she muttered.

Judith didn't bother to resume the argument. Instead, she felt another headache coming on and reached for the Excedrin.

Shortly after four, she decided to call the rental agency that handled Herself's house to see what background they had on the Frosches. She was put on hold for so long that she finally gave up. On a wild impulse, she dialed Herself's number in Panama City. It was seven o'clock in the gulf, so maybe her former nemesis would still be conscious.

"Judith dear!" Herself cried in her throaty, jarring voice. "What a surprise!" A slight pause followed. "Is Joe dead?" she asked in a more somber tone.

"No, he's fine," Judith replied. "We're all fine. I have a question about the people who rented your house. Do you know anything about them?"

"The Frosches?" Herself chuckled, a sound that almost drowned out the tinkle of ice cubes in the background. "Yes, I do. Emma and I go way back."

"Emma? I thought her name was Elma."

"Ah . . . Emma, Elma, Erma . . . I forget. As I said, we go *way* back. I'm not thirty anymore, you know."

Or sixty or seventy, Judith thought. "How did you know her?"

"I met her through my first hubby, Johnny Agra. She lived next door. Such a cute little thing. She wanted to be an actress, but then she got diabetes when she was in her early twenties. That kind of changed her career path, I guess. How is she, by the way?"

It was Judith's turn to pause. "Well . . . she's dead. I'm so sorry," she added hastily. "I didn't realize how well you knew the Frosches."

A choking and gasping sound could be heard over the phone. "Oh! How sad! What happened?"

Judith summed up the diabetic coma and subsequent heart failure. "Then their son, Brick, got hit by a car."

"How sad," Herself repeated. "Poor Ellie. She had a hard life. Somehow—maybe Johnny told me—she divorced her first husband while he was in prison for . . . some kind of crime. Assault, maybe." She hiccuped. "I must admit, I lost track of her for ages, but when she bobbed up again, I just had to help her. By renting to her and Hank."

Judith didn't bother correcting Herself about Herb's first name. Before she could respond, her former nemesis rattled on. "Brick's her stepson. She couldn't have children. How is he? He races cars. That's why they call him Brick. The Brick Yard, Indianapolis, and all that. Oops! I just spilled my . . . juice."

And you're juiced was the thought that crossed Judith's mind. "Sorry to bother you with bad news, Vivian, but I felt you should know about your renters. Just in case their payment's late, you'll know why."

"Why?" Herself sounded bewildered.

"With Mrs. Frosch dying and Brick still in the hospital, Herb might not be very organized when the rent—"

"Oh, Judith, don't fuss over trivial things like that! You take things too hard. I must dash to clean up this mess. If you see Elna, give her my love. Hugs." She hung up.

Joe got home around five-thirty, shortly after the new guests had checked in. Judith immediately told him about calling Herself.

"I thought she knew the Frosches somehow," Joe said when she had finished. "I assume Vivian was sauced."

"What else is new? She couldn't keep Mrs. Frosch's name straight."

Joe shook his head. "I got those pictures of Opal Tooms," he said, handing a manila envelope to Judith. "Good-looking woman. I can see a resemblance to Ruby. You'll notice that one of them was taken when she was a lot younger than Ruby is now. The other is more recent, not long before she was killed. I assumed you didn't want a morgue shot."

"I certainly didn't," Judith murmured, opening the envelope. "Oh, yes," she said, looking at the most recent picture first. "I can see the resemblance between mother and daughter. I wonder if Duke Swisher took this one. Opal looks so happy."

"There's a date on the back—Valentine's Day, the year she was murdered."

Judith turned the photo over and shook her head. "Written in red ink. How bittersweet." She looked again at Opal's smiling face—and then at the background. "This was taken in the race-track's old clubhouse. I recognize the knotty-pine paneling and those trophies."

Joe looked over her shoulder. "You're right. Maybe they just won a biggie. Assuming Swisher took the picture."

Judith studied the second photo, which was a Polaroid. Opal appeared to be very young, perhaps in her teens. The setting looked like a living room with a fireplace in the background. Again, there was a resemblance to Ruby. There was also something else about Opal's semiserious expression that struck a chord with Judith.

"What?" Joe finally said, having poured drinks for both of them.

Judith gave a start. "Huh? Oh—I'm trying to concentrate on

this shot. I wonder if Opal ever hung out at The Meat & Mingle. It's as if I've actually seen her somewhere." She paused, recalling that while she and Renie had been in Little Bavaria, Ruby had said that her father spent many hours in the café's bar. "Jimmy Tooms was a regular, but usually with his equally nefarious buddies. I don't remember seeing a woman with him. But that doesn't mean Opal couldn't have been there."

Joe was again looking over Judith's shoulder. "You might've seen her somewhere else in the neighborhood. She would've been older if she came to the café. Dan didn't open the place until the early 1980s, right?"

Judith nodded. "It only lasted five years before we went broke." She turned to give Joe a wry look. "That's a relative term, of course. We were always broke. That's why I worked two jobs."

Joe put his free hand on his wife's waist. "Every time you talk about those lean years, I feel guilty. There I was, gainfully employed, living with Herself and wondering why she cared more about Jack Daniel's than Joe Flynn. At least I could take some pride in our daughter, Caitlin." His hand fell away. "Damn! I forgot to tell you that she e-mailed this morning to say she'd be here for Christmas."

"Wonderful!" Judith exclaimed. "This will be the first time in ages she hasn't spent the holiday in Florida with her mother."

"Living and working in Switzerland all these years has soured Caitlin on trying to pretend that sand is snow and Christmas cheer isn't found in her mother's bottle of booze."

"It's been over a year since she visited us," Judith said, putting the photos back in the envelope. "Any chance she's found the man of her dreams yet?"

Joe shook his head. "No. The last guy she kind of liked turned out to have two or three ex-wives and a habit of using other people's money to make his own shady investments."

"I didn't think the Swiss let people like that into the country," Judith said after taking a sip of Scotch.

"He was a homegrown product who fled to Belize last month. I guess he didn't trust Swiss banks with his ill-got gain."

Judith glanced at the schoolhouse clock. It was almost six. "Yikes! I better put out the appetizers. Can you check the pork roast for me?"

"Sure," Joe said. "Did you ever get hold of Ruby?"

"No," she replied, dishing up cheese balls, prawns with two kinds of sauce, and a vegetable platter with a cucumber–sour-cream dip. Quickly filling a plate with four kinds of crackers, Judith wondered if she had time to call Ruby before the guests came downstairs to the living room. "I'll see if I can reach her at Wolfgang's in an hour or so. This would be the bar and restaurant's busiest time."

Joe regarded his wife with a serious expression. "Are you afraid to call her because you don't think she's gone back to Little Bavaria?"

Judith didn't answer right away. "No. I'm afraid to call her because I'm scared that she isn't able to go anywhere."

Chapter 15

Shortly after seven-thirty, Tyler Dooley checked in. "You may want to fire me," he said in a doleful voice. "I don't have much to report. The only activity I've seen since I got back from band practice was the young woman coming back to the rental in the Explorer with a Falstaff's grocery bag ten minutes ago. The mid-size sedan—a Kia—is gone, so I figure it belongs to Mr. Frosch and he's off to work at Boring."

Judith agreed. "There's been no obit in the paper yet for Mrs. Frosch, but some people don't submit them because they cost money."

"Right. One of my great-uncles died last year and my great-aunt pitched a fit over what it cost her to list all the survivors. Or was he a second cousin once removed? I can't always keep my family straight."

"I understand," Judith said drily.

"Hey—want me to check with the hospital and pretend I'm Brick or Bernard Frosch's kid brother? I could find out his condition, maybe."

"You can try. Do you have time? It's Norway General."

"Sure. I'm caught up on homework with no action in the cul-de-sac. I'd walk my dog, Barkley, but it's raining too hard."

"Good luck. And keep me posted." Judith rang off.

Before putting the phone back in its cradle, she looked up the number of the local fire station. She believed Jess Sparks, but it never hurt to verify information. She was about to start dialing when Renie came through the back door.

"I just gave Aunt Gert her forty cents' worth," she declared, looking frazzled. "We had Mom for dinner tonight. I mean, we didn't have Mom as the entrée—I invited her over because I'd made my chicken dish with the sour-cream-and-mushroom-soup glop, so I had enough to feed her, too." She paused and frowned. "Feed her two what? Or feed her to whom? I don't know." Renie fell into a chair, running a hand through her disheveled chestnut hair. "I finished the Nordquist concept for the spring catalog. I'm tapped."

"Yes, you are," Judith said, sitting down across from her. "Take a deep breath."

"Of what?" Renie sniffed. "It smells like pig in here. I mean, pork."

"That's what we had for dinner. Why did you give my mother forty cents? Or do you remember?"

"I'm trying to forget." Renie paused again. "Oh—Mom realized she'd shortchanged Aunt Gert on the winner's take at bridge club. She knew your mother would pitch a fit if she realized she was out forty cents. So Mom asked me to give Aunt Gert the money after I dropped her—*my* mom, I mean—off at her apartment. So I did. Drop off Mom and—"

Judith held up a hand. "Stop. I get it. And I know what you're like after you've completed a project. You have to unwind, especially if you're going to drive. Did you run over anybody?"

Renie blinked several times. "I don't think so. There would've been a thump or a thud, right? Besides, there's already been a hit-and-run around here lately."

"True. Would you like some Drambuie?"

"Instead of Pepsi? Oh, why not?" She peered more closely at Judith. "You look like you could use a little pick-me-up, too. What's wrong? You still can't find Ruby?"

Judith stood up and opened the liquor cupboard. "I'm waiting to call Wolfgang's after the dinner rush is over."

"What dinner rush? As I recall, the restaurant's closed on Mondays except during Oktoberfest and December."

Placing two small aperitif glasses on the counter, Judith made a face. "You're right. I assumed Ruby was going back today because she had to work. Unless she still has that other job at the Gray Goose Beer House or has found another one."

Renie nodded absently. "I wonder what happened to that guy she was hanging out with when we first met her."

Judith set the glasses on the table and sat down again. "Burt the Blogger? I didn't ask. They struck me as ships passing in the night."

"I'm afraid there've been a lot of those in Ruby's life," Renie said before sipping her drink. "Mmmm. Good stuff." She licked her lips. "Some of those ships probably just plain sank."

"I feel sorry for Ruby. Say——would you do me a favor?"

Renie's brown eyes were suspicious. "What?"

"I was going to call the fire station here on the hill to make sure Jess Sparks really is a local firefighter."

"With a last name like that, how could he not be?" Renie asked with a wry expression. "Think of the jokes he must hear. Bad ones, of course."

"I didn't consider that," Judith murmured. "Maybe his career was foreordained. Would you mind calling? They know me and I don't need to hear the battalion chief give me a bad time."

"Ohhh . . . what the heck." Renie rummaged in her purse. "I'll call from my cell. If they saw your number, they'd probably start sliding down the pole before you could even say hello."

"Good point." Judith reached around to retrieve the number she'd jotted down on a Post-it note. "Here. I hope he's not on duty tonight. Have you thought up a reason for asking?"

"Yeah. I'll tell whoever answers I'm lusting after Sparks's body because he's so hot. I wonder how many times that line's been used on the poor guy? He *is* kind of cute."

Judith sipped her drink while Renie punched in the numbers on her cell. "Hi," she said, her voice more high-pitched than usual. "Is Jess Sparks there? . . . He's not. Darn. Maybe he's just late. We were supposed to see a movie tonight . . ." She scowled into the phone. "What do you mean, I sound like his mother? . . . Oh . . . he never told me that. Gosh, I don't know him as well as I . . . Hey, it's okay. I'm sworn to secrecy . . . Maybe I should just give up on him. My husband might get jealous. Bye." Renie clicked off the phone and tossed it back in her purse. "Smart ass. Some guys like older women. Of course, that's because they're even older."

Judith was holding her head. "What on earth was that all about? And do you realize they probably noted your cell number?"

Renie grinned. "Ha ha. It's not my cell, it's my son-in-law Odo's. He got the latest model and gave me his old one. I'd like to see even a firefighter tangle with Odo. Anne doesn't call him the Viking for nothing."

"Just answer the question, coz."

"Obviously, Jess Sparks is a firefighter assigned to the Heraldsgate Hill station." Renie paused, as if to let that point sink into her cousin's head. "Not so obviously, whoever answered the phone was in a somewhat frivolous mood. I suppose they get really bored when you don't have a corpse or a fire or some other kind of disaster here in the cul-de-sac."

"*Please,*" Judith begged. "Just tell me what the frivolous firefighter said about Jess."

Renie shoved the overlong bangs out of her eyes. "I could hear the other guys in the background laughing and making some cracks. I couldn't tell what they said, but the one on the phone told me Jess didn't have a mother. Then he added that he didn't mean to say that, it wasn't any of his business, and he should have kept his mouth shut." She held up her hands. "That's it."

"That *is* a little weird," Judith said after taking another sip of her drink. "Why . . . ?" She shook her head. "I don't get it. Unless it's a running gag at the fire station?"

Renie shrugged. "Everybody has a mother, even firefighters."

Judith shot her a sharp look. "Get real. It sounds like maybe it's a sore subject. I still don't know why Jess wanted to get in touch with Ruby in the first place. He referred to his inquiry about her as a 'sentimental idea.' Or was it nostalgic?"

"Either way," Renie said, "it smacks of something from the past. I assume Ruby never mentioned Jess or any firefighter?"

"No. The only connection is Hector Sparks. I figure Jess for late thirties. Probably too old to know Ruby in school. But maybe his father and her mother knew each other."

Renie smirked. "How well did they know each other?"

Judith made a face. "Give me a break. Hector was about ninety and bedridden when Opal knew him." She frowned. "Unless . . ."

"Yes?" Renie had assumed a quizzical expression.

"It *is* possible that Opal and Hector had been acquainted earlier. Maybe that's why Lee and Marla Watkins were so upset about Hector leaving his money to Opal." Judith got up to retrieve the manila envelope with the photos Joe had brought home. "Take a look, especially at the younger version. It bothers me. Why?"

Renie studied the Polaroid for almost a minute. "You got a magnifier handy?"

"Yes," Judith said, opening the drawer by the bulletin board at the end of the counter. "Here."

Renie took her time before speaking. "That's a Lalique figurine and a Wedgwood plate on the fireplace mantel. Do you think those items belonged to the Tooms family?"

"Damn," Judith breathed. "I didn't notice them. I was too focused on Opal. You're right. They could never have afforded items like that. Unless Jimmy Tooms stole them."

"If he had, he would've pawned them, not displayed them in his living room. You have to wonder where this picture was taken."

"It probably wasn't at the Tooms house," Judith said. "But look closely at Opal. What is it about her that bothers me?"

Renie scowled at the photo. "She's young, she's pretty, she isn't wearing a wedding ring. When did Opal and Jimmy tie the knot?"

Judith reflected on Ruby's account of her parents. "They were very young. According to Woody's case notes, Opal was forty-four—or would've been the year that she was killed. She was pregnant when she got married, so Ozzie's midthirties. Opal could be a teenager in that picture. Ruby told me her dad had hocked her mom's engagement ring. Maybe he did the same with the wedding band."

Renie ran her thumb over her own wedding ring, four rows of gold weave from Tiffany's that had cost Bill fifty bucks some forty-odd years ago. Having had a habit of getting engaged to men she didn't want to marry, Renie found engagement rings boring.

"I don't think Opal would've let Jimmy do that," she finally said. "There's not much money in cheap gold bands anyway. I suspect she wasn't married when this shot was taken. Didn't Hector Sparks have grandchildren via Lee and Marla Watkins?"

"Yes," Judith replied. "They were upset about Opal allegedly trying to finagle Hector out of their inheritance. Yet their names weren't on the interview list. Maybe they were too young to be suspects or witnesses."

"If Hector was over ninety when he died, Lee and Marla must have been close to middle age back then," Renie pointed out. "Something's off, as Bill would say. Can you ask Woody about that?"

"I hate to bother him," Judith said. "Of course it *is* his case . . ."

"Then do it," Renie said. "Let me see that later picture again."

Judith handed her cousin the one taken in the old racetrack clubhouse. "Well?" she said after Renie had looked through the magnifying glass again. "Do you see anything unusual?"

"Not really. Wait. She *is* wearing a ring in this one, but her hand's raised, so I can only see her palm. Did Duke give her an engagement ring after she accepted his proposal?"

Leaning forward to look through the magnifier, Judith nodded. "I wonder what happened to it after she was killed."

"Robbery as motive?" Renie suggested.

Judith considered. "Ruby never mentioned what happened to the ring. I've no idea if it was expensive. Duke was working construction back then. I suppose he could've afforded something rather nice. Maybe Ruby kept it or Ozzie gave it to Freddy Mae. If it had gone missing, I assume it'd be in Woody's case notes or Ruby would've mentioned it."

"Maybe Duke took it back," Renie said, before taking a last sip of Drambuie. "I should head home before Bill realizes I'm gone."

Judith checked the time. "It's after eight. He didn't know you left?"

Renie was putting on her jacket. "No. He and Oscar were watching *Lonesome Dove*. Bill was trying to explain why Blue Duck wasn't a likable character. Or a restaurant entrée. Oscar thought it was a cute name. Maybe by now they've——"

"Stop. Please." Judith had also gotten out of her chair. "I mean, go. If you want to, that is."

"I do. See you later." Renie exited via the back door just as the phone rang.

"Wow!" Tyler Dooley said into Judith's ear. "I had to get Mom to pretend she was a doctor to get anything out of those hospital people. It's a good thing she's a sport."

"She is that," Judith agreed, thinking that after raising so many children, grandchildren, and other Dooley offspring, Corinne probably could give a veteran pediatrician a run for his or her money. "What did Dr. Dooley find out?"

"Bernard Frosch has been upgraded from grave to serious condition," Tyler said in a formal voice that suggested he was reading his mother's notes. "If he passes through the night without further complications, he may be moved out of the ICU tomorrow." He paused. "That sounds like he'll live, right?"

"I hope so," Judith responded. "Your mom didn't get to inquire about actual injuries?"

"No. Sophie Marie fell out of her crib again and had to be rescued. She just turned two last week, so she shouldn't still be in a crib, but they ran out of beds. It's a good thing there's a thick rug on the floor."

"That's a shame," Judith said. "You and your mother did a fine job. Any new sightings?"

"No. It's raining so hard I can't see much with the telescope except for the taillights of a car—whoa! Whoever just left the cul-de-sac almost hit a big SUV out on the street."

"That's a . . . close call," Judith said, fairly certain it had been her cousin driving Cammy. "Thanks, Tyler. Don't stay up too late. Especially if you can't see much outside."

As Judith hung up, Joe strolled into the kitchen. "I've been upstairs catching some scores on ESPN. Aren't you going to join me so we can watch a movie or whatever else might be on TV that isn't junk?"

"Renie was here," Judith explained. "She left five minutes ago."

Joe glanced at the photos of Opal on the counter. "Don't tell me you two were sleuthing."

"Sort of." Judith gave Joe her most winsome look. "Would you mind calling Woody and asking him why the Watkins kids weren't on the list of people who were questioned about Opal's murder?"

Joe frowned. "What Watkins kids?"

"Maybe you didn't hear Ruby mention that they were as upset about Hector's estate as Lee and Marla were. It struck me as odd that they weren't interviewed during the investigation. Please?"

"That depends. If they were minors, maybe not, especially if they could account for their time." Joe shrugged. "What the hell. I'll call Woody from upstairs. You coming along?"

Judith smiled. "Give me two minutes. I want to finish tidying up."

After putting Opal's photos back in the manila envelope, loading the aperitif glasses into the dishwasher, and checking the computer for new reservations, Judith started for the back stairs. The doorbell rang before she could get any farther than the pantry.

"Drat," she murmured under her breath, wondering if a guest had forgotten the key. Looking through the peephole, she saw a youngish couple she didn't recognize. "Good evening," Judith said, opening the door. "Have you been sent here by the state B&B association?"

The man pushed back the hood on his green jacket. "No," he said. "I'm Ozzie Tooms, Ruby's brother. This is my wife, Freddy Mae. Mind if we come in?"

Stepping aside, Judith realized there was a resemblance between brother and sister, though it wasn't marked. Ozzie was darker than Ruby, his eyes were hazel, and his face was more angular. Freddy Mae was a petite curly-haired brunette with wide-set blue eyes who seemed to bounce when she walked.

"Nice place," she remarked, her head bobbing as if it were on a spring. "I love these old houses in this part of town."

Judith laughed. "It's very common architecture in the older part of the city. There never were any in this style out in the Thurlow District or the surrounding neighborhoods that grew up later. Why don't we sit in the living room?"

The couple followed Judith from the entry hall, but Ozzie insisted they couldn't stay long. "We have a late flight to San Diego," he said, sitting down with Freddy Mae on one of the matching sofas. "We've been staying at one of those residence inns at the bottom of the hill, so we thought maybe we should stop by to apologize for Ruby."

Judith wasn't sure what Ozzie meant. "You mean for leaving with such short notice?"

Ozzie chuckled. "No. For bothering you about Mom. It's a mania with her. After all these years, what's the point?"

"Closure?" Judith suggested. "Justice? Peace of mind?"

Freddy Mae waved her hands and bounced on the sofa. "It's been like sixteen years. Whoever killed Mrs. Tooms is probably dead, too. Some drifter or crook who came to a bad end, I'll bet." She turned to her husband. "Isn't that right, Ozzie?"

He shrugged. "It sure wasn't anybody we know. Or knew, I mean. Ruby told us you lived out in that area for a while, Mrs. Flynn. You know it was kind of a rough neighborhood back then. Your husband owned The Meat & Mingle, right?"

Judith nodded. "After he died, I moved back here before your mother was killed. Is Ruby back in Little Bavaria?"

"She was headed for the bus depot this morning," Ozzie replied. "I hope she didn't get you too worked up over this whole deal. I think Freddy Mae and I straightened her out about letting go. I mean, what could anybody find out after all this time?"

If Judith hadn't been on guard at first, she was now. "Nothing definitive," she replied casually.

Freddy Mae looked earnest. "No evidence, no clues, no suspects?"

Judith smiled wryly. "Ruby's reason for rethinking the case was based on the lack of DNA evidence available back then. Many cold cases have been solved recently. You can't blame her for giving it a shot."

Ozzie shrugged. "But nothing came of it. The trail was cold." He got up and pulled his wife to her feet. "You must be relieved, Mrs. Flynn. I hope you didn't put much time into this wild-goose chase."

Judith rose from the other sofa. "I like puzzles," she said, gesturing at the jigsaw on a card table by the piano. "Sometimes you stare at the pieces forever and then suddenly realize you've missed the tiniest bit of sky or a subtle change of color. Then it all comes together."

"I don't do puzzles," Freddy Mae said as they walked to the entry hall. She giggled, a faintly jarring sound. "I can't sit still that long."

Ozzie grinned. "That's my girl—always on the go. Guess we'll both be going."

"One thing," Judith said. "I'm curious. What happened to your mother's engagement ring?"

Ozzie picked up Freddy Mae's left hand. "There it is. Why not?" He opened the door and his expression sobered. "I'd stop trying to put missing pieces together if I were you. Good night."

Judith stood in the doorway watching the couple walk to their rental car. And wondered why Ozzie's last words sounded not like advice, but more like a threat.

Chapter 16

How long does it take for you to finish up in the kitchen?" Joe inquired as Judith entered the spare room that also served as their family TV center. "You missed the start of *Star Wars: Episode Three.*" He frowned and hit mute on the remote as Judith came closer. "What's wrong? You look gloomy."

"Not exactly that," Judith said, sitting next to Joe on Grandma and Grandpa Grover's recycled settee. "Ozzie and Freddy Mae Tooms paid me a visit. They don't think much of Ruby's project to find Opal's killer."

"I thought Ruby gave up on it anyway," Joe responded. "Why bother repeating what you already know?"

"I'm wondering now if that was her idea. Ozzie and Freddy Mae don't think Ruby should have taken an interest in the first place."

Joe looked puzzled. "How so?"

Judith recounted the conversation. "Frankly, Ozzie's parting shot upset me. I really got the feeling they didn't want the truth to come out."

Joe turned off the TV. "Refresh my memory. Where was Ozzie when the murder occurred?"

"In the navy. I forget where he was stationed, but it wasn't around here. He had to take an emergency leave to come back to the area."

"That's a solid alibi," Joe conceded. "What about Freddy Mae?"

"Ruby was staying with her and her family because it was senior week," Judith reminded Joe. "Thus, she's in the clear, too. Before you ask me about Freddy Mae's parents, I know almost nothing about them except that they were on the list of people who were interviewed. I assume they're still retired in Arizona."

"Did they work?"

Judith darted Joe a wry expression. "I assume so. They had to retire from something."

"Did Freddy Mae have siblings?"

"I don't know that either," Judith said, beginning to feel frustrated. "Ruby never mentioned any. But she probably keeps in touch with them and they knew she was here."

"How?"

"How what?"

Joe looked impatient. "Ruby lost her cell phone. Did she make calls to Ozzie on our phone? You could have the records checked, including the separate guest line on the second floor. Granted, she might have talked to him before she lost the cell, but when did she decide to stay on here over the weekend? Wasn't that after her cell disappeared?"

Judith glowered at Joe. "I'm beginning to feel like a suspect."

Joe chuckled. "Sorry. Old habits die hard. For all we know, she told Ozzie she was coming to town before she ever left Little Bavaria."

"That," Judith said after a pause, "is probably what happened. I wonder if Ozzie asked for a leave to stop Ruby from digging into the case. Did you call Woody about the Watkins kids?"

Joe nodded. "Two girls, Wendy and Dawn, sixteen and nineteen, respectively. They attended the same high school Ruby did, but Dawn had already graduated and Wendy was two years behind Ruby. They weren't interviewed because they had solid alibis. Dawn had moved out after graduation and taken an apartment near downtown with a girlfriend. She had a job in the stock room of Donner & Blitzen Department Store. Wendy was working after school as a courtesy clerk at that grocery store not far from your old house. You know—the one called Sollie & His Sons. She didn't get off until nine that night."

Judith smiled at the memory. "They had really good meat. They're still around, though I heard they'd moved their location."

Joe nodded. "So the Watkins daughters were old enough to worry about not getting their share of the loot."

"Teenagers can count." Judith leaned against Joe. "Do you think I'm silly to think Ozzie and Freddy Mae were warning me to back off?"

"Well . . . you're perceptive when it comes to people. But that doesn't mean they have anything to hide. Face it, having their mother—and mother-in-law—murdered isn't one of life's cherished memories."

"I can't stop now," Judith confessed.

"Yes, you can," Joe said. "At least until we finish watching *Star Wars*." He put his arm around her and turned up the TV volume.

By Tuesday morning, the rain had stopped. Judith went through her daily routine like a robot. Every time the phone rang, she hoped it was Ruby. But it wasn't. By afternoon, she was at loose ends. She finally called Renie.

"Do you have a lull?" she asked of her cousin.

"Do I?" Renie replied. "Let me look. Maybe I can find it somewhere."

"I'm serious. We need to hit the road."

"Again?" Renie's voice held a touch of anguish.

"What are you doing now that you finished your current project?"

"I'm out in the yard, doing cleanup while it's not raining. I need fresh air." She paused. "What did you have in mind this time?"

"I thought we might go out to Sollie & His Sons. They moved, you know. I'd like to get one of their prime ribs."

Renie's sigh was audible. "Their hamburger always was the

best. They didn't eliminate most of the fat and thus all of the flavor. You drive. Bill's taking the car so he can walk the beach at Shimsham Bay."

"I'll see you in ten minutes."

"Make that fifteen. I look even worse than I usually do and have to change clothes." Renie rang off.

By five after two, Judith pulled up in front of Bill and Renie's house behind a big green city garbage truck that was collecting recycling bins. Renie appeared almost immediately, but motioned to her cousin that she had to put the empty bin back in its place. Just as the truck rumbled across the intersection at the corner, Renie flopped down inside Judith's Subaru.

"Good timing," she murmured, fastening her seat belt. "If the wind picks up, the empty bins end up halfway down this steep hill. Bill wants some of Sollie's sausage. He remembered how much he liked it. Now tell me why we're really going there."

"Sollie's was always an excellent gathering place for neighborhood gossip," Judith explained, turning around to head back up the hill. "Yes, they've moved, but only a few blocks east. Before we get there, let me tell you about my visitors from last night."

By the time she concluded her encounter with Ozzie and Freddy Mae, the cousins were coming out of the tunnel onto the viaduct. Toward the west, she glimpsed the sun trying to peek above the mountains. Farther north, ominous dark clouds were slowly moving in over the bay. It was the second week of November. When it came to weather, almost anything could happen in Judith's part of the world, even a minor heat wave. She recalled that when she was in second grade the temperature had hit the midseventies in November.

Renie seemed to be watching a white-and-green state ferry easing into the downtown terminal's dock. But when she spoke, it was on a different subject. "Ever think we should take up another hobby besides chasing killers?"

"I tried to retire," Judith replied with a frown. "Then Ruby showed up. At least it's an old case. Nobody I know has been murdered lately."

"Don't brag," Renie said. "I don't like Ozzie's attitude. Or his wife's. I don't even think I'd like them if I met them."

"You won't," Judith declared. "They flew to San Diego last night."

"You should check on Freddy Mae's parents. If she and Ozzie are protecting anybody, they're the obvious suspects. Arizona, did you say?"

"Yes," Judith said, managing to make all the traffic lights on the straight stretch of street that went past the Boring Aerospace Company's headquarters. "I wonder how long the Frosches have been in this area. The rental agreement shows that their previous address was right around here, not far from Boring Field."

"I don't see why that matters, but if it does, I've got some contacts there from doing design projects for them over the years. Their top PR guy, Caspar Milksop, probably retired ten, fifteen years ago, but I also dealt with some of his underlings."

Judith shot her cousin a quick look. "Was that his real name?"

"It wasn't. But it was his real personality. I never could figure out how that guy got into PR in the first place."

Instead of using the turnoff that went directly to the Thurlow District, Judith kept to the route that would take them a few miles north of the airport. "I called to get their new address. It's the same old sign and the same old phone number, but it's on the right-hand side and should only be another three or four miles from here."

"Got it," Renie said. After a brief silence, she spoke again. "Lainie? Who is she, really?"

"Brick's girlfriend? That's all I know about her. She's not friendly. I *would* like to check birth records to see if Jess Sparks is Hector's son."

Renie hauled out her cell. "I wonder if I could do that on my new whiz-bang-everything-but-washes-windows phone."

"Don't bother," Judith said. "Joe can find that out. They may charge a fee to look up records these days."

Renie, however, was making an attempt to find the county's vital statistics site. "Damn! Why am I coming up with a fish market?"

"Skip it. Keep your eyes to your right so we don't go by Sollie's."

Only a minute passed before Renie spotted the familiar sign. Judith pulled into the parking lot, which was almost full. Unlike the lot at the previous site, this one wasn't gravel, but freshly paved.

"I wonder if Sollie is still alive," Judith murmured before they entered the store. "He was getting up there by the time I moved home."

"Let's not find his body in the meat locker, okay?" Renie shot back.

The two butchers behind the busy counter weren't Sollie, but Judith recognized them. And the nearest one recognized her. "Mrs. McMonigle," he exclaimed. "Long time no see. I'll be right with you."

"Long time to wait," Renie muttered. "There are at least six people ahead of us. Is it illegal to shout 'hungry' in a crowded butcher shop?"

"It is for you," Judith said, also keeping her voice down. "I'd have to make Joe arrest you. The one who spoke to me is Pete. The other one is Paul." She looked around to the checkout stands. "I don't see the third brother, Pat."

Renie shrugged. Judith edged up to the counter to look at the rib roasts. Prices had certainly gone up since her last visit, but they weren't outrageous. Nobody seemed to be complaining, apparently satisfied that they were getting their money's worth. Both Pete and Paul worked efficiently and the customers were dispersed in a fairly short time.

Pete, who was a husky, dark-haired six-footer, beamed at Judith. "We kept wondering what happened to you after Mr. McMonigle died and you moved away. It's great to see you. I wish Papa could be here, but he passed on five years ago the day after

Thanksgiving. Sort of fitting, in its way. He left everybody full and satisfied."

"He was a wonderful person," Judith said. "I'm so glad you and your brothers are carrying on the tradition. Where's Pat, by the way?"

Pete gestured to the rear of the store. "In the office. He's the oldest, so he runs the place. How can I help you?"

Judith noticed that only a couple of other customers were now waiting to be served. "I want one of your prime ribs for starters," she said, grabbing Renie's arm and hauling her closer. "My cousin Serena would like to buy some items, too. By the way, I'm Mrs. Flynn now. She's Mrs. Jones."

Renie's smile was a bit thin. "I've been that for a long time. And no, it's not an alias."

Pete chuckled obligingly. "We've got lamb chops on special."

"I'll take six," Renie said. "Bill Jones—yes, his real name— loves lamb chops."

"The same for me," Judith put in. "In fact, make that eight. My mother lives with us. Sort of," she added under her breath.

Pete looked surprised. "Really? She must be . . . old."

"She's eternal," Judith replied—but she smiled. "By the way, do you know Lee and Marla Watkins?"

Pete counted out the chops before responding. "Sure. They come in here a lot. I mean, they came to the old shop, of course, and I think they've been here once or twice since we reopened. They've been good customers for the past dozen years."

Judith did a quick calculation. Maybe Lee and Marla couldn't afford to shop at Sollie's until they inherited Hector's estate. "I ran into Hector Sparks's son recently. He's a firefighter in my Heraldsgate Hill neighborhood."

Pete wrapped Renie's chops and put them on the counter. "Hector Sparks? I can't place him. Did he know Papa?"

"I've no idea," Judith admitted. "Hector is Marla Watkins's father."

"Oh." Pete finished weighing and wrapping the chops for Judith. "I never knew her maiden name."

"That reminds me," Judith said as if suddenly thinking of it, "do you remember Lee and Marla's daughter Wendy? She worked for your father years ago as a courtesy clerk."

Pete laughed. "Wild Wendy? You bet. She was hired before I met her parents. Papa came close to firing her about six times before she quit. She was a real piece of work."

"How so?" Judith inquired.

Pete looked around to make sure no one was eavesdropping. "I shouldn't have said anything about her, but she was probably the worst employee we ever had, even for a teenager. Papa was usually right on when it came to reading people, but Wendy was such a cute kid and she could sweet-talk her way out of just about anything. She'd carry out a load of groceries for a customer and not come back right away. Pat found her once by the loading area with a customer—an older married man—and they were . . ." He lifted his thick dark eyebrows. "Let's say we wouldn't have been surprised if she'd become a hooker."

"How do you know she didn't?" Judith asked.

"We heard a couple of years later she ran off with some guy and got married." Pete shrugged. "Heck, maybe she got herself straightened out. I never felt right about asking her parents about her. It might have been embarrassing. Anything else you need?"

"Yes," Judith replied, moving toward the beef display. "That second prime rib looks like the right size. Did you know the other sister, Dawn? She was the older girl."

Pete paused with his hand on the roast. "No. Maybe," he continued, removing the meat and putting it on the scale, "that's just as well if she was anything like her sister."

"I'd also like two pounds of your hamburger," Judith said. "My cousin wants some, too." She turned to Renie. "How much?"

Renie put her hand around her throat and looked goggle-eyed. "Gosh, I can talk! Somebody please call Lourdes! It's a miracle!"

"Just tell Pete about the hamburger," Judith said, trying not to sound annoyed.

"Three pounds," Renie stated in an overloud voice. "And while you're at it, Pete, I also want a pound of the regular pork sausage, the biggest prime rib you've got in the case, and two rib-eye steaks, bone in. Now I'll be quiet and let coz jabber her head off."

Pete grinned at Judith. "Your cousin's quite a card, huh?"

"In a way," she murmured. "Not exactly the joker, though. I also want a pound of the spicy sausage and three T-bones. Oh, three pork chops, too. And some pig hocks for a boiled sauerkraut dinner."

Paul, who had been serving someone in the seafood section, paused to greet Judith, who introduced Renie. "We thought you'd forgotten about us," he said.

"Not a chance," Judith assured him. "But I've owned a B&B for several years and it keeps me busy. I was afraid you'd forgotten me."

"Not a chance," Paul said. "Papa always told us to put names with faces, put faces with names. But we get so many customers who don't come in on a regular basis, but are from another part of town. I'd better tend to some of them now. Good to see you."

Pete had their orders ready. He smiled a bit guiltily as he showed the cousins their bills. "I know you're getting quality," he said. "Prices have risen since you lived out this way, Mrs. Mc . . . *Flynn,* I mean."

Judith smiled back. "We knew what we were in for. It's worth it. We'll try to come back more often."

Pete saluted as the cousins headed for the door.

"What really gets me," Renie said after they got into the car, "is that I've been to their store without you and they don't remember me at all. I feel like a shadow when I hang with you. And before you say anything about me probably making a scene when I've been at Sollie & His Sons, forget it. Other places, yes. But never there."

"Are you done?" Judith inquired, pulling out of the parking lot.

"Yeah. I think so. Did you glean anything besides a lot of meat?"

"Not anything startling, though I wonder what happened to Wild Wendy Watkins."

"Not any wilder than you just making a right instead of a left turn out of the parking lot," Renie said. "Why are we not going home? Our meat might spoil."

"In forty-six-degree weather? We're heading back to the Thurlow District—or paradise, also known as The Garden of Eden."

"I should've guessed," Renie murmured, leaning back in her seat. "Oh, well—maybe I can get some mums."

"Don't," Judith warned. "If you buy anything, get bulbs. They can't ruin those if they come from a reputable bulb farm."

"Let me think," Renie said, a hand to her head. "Many years ago, Marla Watkins worked there. We're going to learn where Marla and—"

"—Lee live now," Judith chimed in, "so we can pay them a call."

"Do we have to be Jehovah Witnesses again?" Renie asked in a plaintive tone.

"No. We'll think of something else. Give me time."

"Just for once, couldn't we barge in and say we suspect them of murdering Opal Tooms?"

"But we don't," Judith responded. "They both have solid alibis." She took a deep breath. "Or do they?"

"What do you mean?"

"I'm not sure yet. The problem with alibis is that even law enforcement people tend to take them as ironclad if they sound credible and there's someone to substantiate where the person was when the crime took place."

Renie was thoughtful for a few moments. "Yes. I see your point. But what about Ozzie's alibi? He wasn't in town."

"We don't know that for sure," Judith replied, taking the turn to the south end of the Thurlow District. "Ruby never told me where he was stationed—just that he was in the navy. He could have been somewhere close by. Admittedly, Woody probably checked on that, but it's not in his notes. Even assuming Ozzie was out of the area, that doesn't mean he couldn't have arranged to have someone else kill Opal."

"His own mother?" Renie shook her head. "My kids may want to kill me now and then, but I don't think they'd actually do it."

"I don't mean that I think Ozzie was the killer," Judith asserted. "That's just an example of alibis that may be misleading."

"It usually goes to motive," Renie remarked. "I suppose you've considered it could have been a random act of violence."

"Yes. But it was during the day or at least probably not after dark. It happened in the living room, which means Opal must've let her killer in. That indicates she probably knew him—or her. There was no sign of a struggle. I assume she was taken by surprise. Woody thought so, too."

"Poor woman," Renie murmured. "Hey—where are we? I don't recognize anything around here."

"Neither do I," Judith admitted. "In fact, The Garden of Eden should be almost straight ahead on our left. Maybe it's not there any . . . oh, good grief! It's gone upscale, too!"

Both cousins stared at the vine-covered arbor entrance to what looked like an acre of hothouses and open-air nursery stock. "Darn," Judith said under her breath as she pulled into the big parking lot, "if this place is under new ownership, they may not know the Watkins duo."

"Why not? Where else would they go to landscape their mini-mansion?"

Judith pulled her aging Subaru in between a Lexus SUV and a Range Rover. "Everything around here has grown so much in the past few years," she grumbled. "I feel as if I'm in another part of the country."

"That thought has crossed a lot of people's minds," Renie said, unfastening her seat belt. "And that's what they've done—moved here."

The cousins walked under the arbor along cobblestones flanked with winter pansies and bright chrysanthemums. "I'll bet their prices have gone way up, too," Judith murmured. "Look." She pointed to a trio of yellow, purple, and pink primroses in a terra-cotta planter. "Twenty-five bucks. I can buy three primroses at Falstaff's for five dollars and use an old loaf pan to get the same effect."

"Are we sleuthing or comparative shopping?" Renie asked in a strained voice. "Maybe you should have retired and fixated on your garden. It'd be a lot safer in the long run."

Judith sighed. "You're right. Sort of." She nodded toward the customer-service area. "I don't see anybody I recognize."

"Good. Then if I make a scene here, you won't care."

Ignoring Renie, Judith went up to the counter and caught the attention of a silver-haired, middle-aged woman who asked if she could provide assistance.

"Yes," Judith replied, fumbling in her purse before taking out a rumpled slip of paper. "I was supposed to meet some friends here almost an hour ago and I got lost. Now I discovered I took down the wrong phone number for them. Do you know Marla and Lee Watkins?"

"Oh, yes," the woman replied with a big smile. "They're regular customers. Would you like me to call them for you?"

"No," Judith said, aware that Renie was trying to look at the paper she held in her hand. "I know they don't live far from here. The address will be fine. Did you see them earlier by any chance? I was supposed to meet them in the tree section."

"No," the woman replied, checking her computer. "I only got back from lunch about fifteen minutes ago." She paused to write down the address. "Here. It's easy to find once you get onto Deauville Avenue Southwest. Good luck."

Judith offered her thanks and turned around to head for the exit. "First I have to find Deauville Avenue," she said in annoyance as soon as they were outside. "Can your amazing phone do that?"

"Probably," Renie replied. "Wish I knew how to use it. I was sort of hoping the clerk would ask to see your Bartleby's shopping list with the bunion pads and flea powder for your mother."

"The flea powder is for Sweetums," Judith retorted, "which you know damned well."

Renie smirked before getting into the car. "Sorry. My mistake."

"Maybe," Judith said when they were both inside, "if I can figure out how to find an address on your phone."

"How about this? You head for the Sound and find a north–south street that spells out *D-E-A-U-V-I-L-L-E*?"

Judith started to say something snappish, but refrained. "That's not really a bad idea. It's a view property, as I recall."

The cousins headed due west, where the pale November sun was now fully visible above the snowcapped mountains across the Sound. After they stopped for a red light in the Thurlow District, they drove less than a mile before Renie spotted Deauville Avenue Southwest. "The house numbers get higher, so take a left," she said.

Within two blocks, they spotted the house. Or at least a jutting boxlike building that seemed to be all glass to the north and probably to the west. The five-digit address on a steel post looked as if it was made of glow-in-the-dark glass.

"I'd say the Watkins had no taste," Renie said as they pulled up on the verge of the uncurbed street, "but they do. And it's all bad. Maybe someday the city or the county will finish the roadwork around here. They can't keep pace with all the newcomers."

A stiff breeze had come up while the cousins made the short drive to the Watkins residence. Carefully going up a half-dozen curving steps to the austere front porch, Judith shivered slightly.

"I'm cold and this house is cold," she declared. "I don't like this boxy style with all the huge windows and often no drapes—just blinds."

"You're right," Renie agreed. "It's artless, with no character. I've seen some of them on the hill the last couple of years. Ugly, too. I don't see much indication that their landscaping is all that great either."

The chime played "The Trolley Song." Judith smiled. "Lee was a bus driver. Or they like old musicals. I haven't heard that one in ages."

After a lengthy pause, the door was opened by a frumpy, gray-haired woman wearing a flowered apron. "What do you want?" she demanded gruffly.

"We're from *Modern Manse* magazine," Judith replied. "Your home was suggested as a feature for our May issue, Mrs. Watkins."

The woman sneered. "It's not *my* home and I'm not Mrs. Watkins. I'm Mrs. Grissom. Come in. I'll see if Mrs. Watkins is busy."

The entry hall felt like a tunnel. Except for a large potted fern, it was bare and long with a sheet of glass at the far end, apparently looking out to the western view. Mrs. Grissom had exited through a sliding door that was painted gray to match the walls.

"Could we have some imagination here?" Renie finally said in an anguished voice. "Could they have used the money they saved on the architect to hire an interior decorator?"

"I wonder," Judith mused, "how much money there was in Hector's estate. I have no idea how he earned it either."

Renie shot Judith a sharp glance. "You might've warned me we were magazine writers. Are you sure we aren't selling subscriptions?"

"Does it matter? We got in the door." Judith grabbed Renie's arm and spoke in a whisper. "Mrs. Grissom! I just remembered why the name was familiar. She's the one who ran the nursing home where Opal worked. She must be the Watkins's maid or . . . what?"

"In-house blackmailer?" Renie suggested. "I thought she looked familiar, but she's even homelier than I remember."

Before Judith could say anything, the sliding door reopened. A woman who was probably close to sixty, but trying to look forty, offered the cousins a smile that didn't quite make it to her glacial blue eyes.

"I'm Marla Watkins," she said, but didn't offer her hand. "You're . . . ?" The cold eyes with their taupe-covered lids veered from Judith to Renie and back again.

"Judy Grover," Judith replied. "This is my assistant, Renée D'Oscar."

Renie waved halfheartedly.

If the response struck Marla as strange, she didn't show it. "Won't you come into the solarium?" she said, leading the way with a swish of her gaudy, floral silk lounging pajamas. Near the end of the hall, she opened another sliding door on their left. "You'll enjoy the view. My husband and I spend hours in here."

If ever a room didn't look lived in, it was the solarium. Four cube-shaped gray chairs were set around a glass table on steel legs. A black metal sculpture resembling Phyliss's umbrella turned inside out stood in one corner between two huge windows, one looking south and the other to the Sound and the mountains. The rear wall displayed a fabric hanging that depicted what resembled a manhole cover. The only item that suggested anybody ever used the room was a telescope on a tripod. It was, Judith thought, more attractive than the sculpture.

"This really is a . . . view," she said after they sat down in the cubes. "How long have you lived here?"

Marla ran a hand through her highlighted brown hair. "Almost twelve years. We had it built to our specifications. How did you find out about us and our house?"

"Referrals," Judith responded. "We have people all over North America looking for unusual modern homes. Did you hire an architect?"

Marla shook her head. "We knew what we wanted. My father owned a construction company, but sold it when he retired in his seventies. The people who took over the business treated us very well. In fact, Mr. Morris asked Lee—my husband—to become a consultant."

Judith concealed her surprise. "Would that be Frank Morris?"

"No. It's Ed Morris, though I think he has a brother named Frank."

"This may seem like an intrusive question, but it's something our readers always want to know," Judith said, sounding apologetic. "Given that this is prime property, how much did the entire project cost?"

"Just under three million," Marla replied. "We were very fortunate. My late father left us a comfortable nest egg. Lee and I were both able to retire. Of course, he keeps his hand in with the construction company. I'm busy with my crafts. Though I don't feel like it, I'm a grandmother twice over." She simpered, her glossy mauve lips curved ever so slightly.

"How nice," Judith said. "Are the grandchildren around here?"

"You mean in the house?" Marla looked faintly alarmed. "No. Dawn and Perry, my daughter and son-in-law, live over on the Eastside. But that's close enough. We see them every month or two, usually at their home."

"Oh," Judith said. "I thought Mrs. Grissom might be your nanny."

Marla laughed in a rather jarring manner. "Heavens, no! We raised two girls of our own. Isn't that enough?"

Judith didn't respond to what she decided was a rhetorical comment. "Does your other daughter live nearby?"

"She moved out of state." Marla's face had turned stony. "Do you think you'll feature our home in your magazine?" she asked after an awkward pause.

"It's very tempting," Judith conceded, getting to her feet.

Marla also stood up. "Did you want to look at the rest of the house?" she inquired. "Frankly, it's not at its best. We've just started preparing for the holidays."

"I understand," Judith said, noticing out of the corner of her eye that Renie appeared to have gone to sleep. Moving closer to the cube where her cousin was sitting, she gripped her shoulder. "We'll be on our way now," she announced a trifle too loudly.

Marla leaned toward Judith. "Doesn't your assistant speak?"

"She speaks only French," Judith replied as Renie shook herself and got up from the cube.

Marla looked puzzled. "I thought you said your magazine was only for North America."

"That's true," Judith replied. "Renée handles the French-Canadian edition. She came along to see how I conduct an interview. She's very good at nuance."

"Oh, of course." Marla led the way down the hall. When they reached the door, she asked if Judith had a business card.

"We don't use them," Judith said. "They're so old-school. As soon as we leave, I'll zap all the information to the publisher and you'll receive an e-mail confirming our visit. That should come to you within twenty-four hours. Thank you so much for your cooperation."

"My pleasure," Marla said in what almost passed for enthusiasm. But she closed the door immediately behind the cousins.

"You went to sleep!" Judith cried softly as they went down the steps. "Or did you?"

"I thought it'd be more fun to count up all the lies you told. Better than counting sheep. No wonder I nodded off." She stopped at the bottom of the stairs. "Uh-oh. Here's Mr. Watkins in a Cadillac Escalade."

Judith watched as he pulled into the driveway—and stopped. Lee got out and walked over to the cousins. If Marla was a bit blowsy, her mate was nondescript, an average-size middle-aged man wearing a down vest and a baseball cap. The lines in his plain face indicated he'd traveled some rough roads besides the ones he'd covered as a bus driver.

"You want to see me?" he asked in an abrupt manner.

"No," Judith replied, wondering why he looked vaguely familiar. "We came to see your wife."

"What about?"

"Your house," Judith said, edging toward the Subaru. "It's quite fascinating. We may use it in our magazine."

"Magazine?" Lee frowned. "What magazine? Hey—I know you from someplace. Let me think . . ."

Judith opened the car door and got in. Renie followed her lead on the passenger side. Lee started to wave his hands as he came closer to the Subaru. But before he could get to Judith's window, she reversed and made a quick U-turn in the middle of the street.

"Meat & Mingle customer, huh?" Renie said as they took the second corner almost on two wheels.

Judith nodded. "I recognized him as soon as he recognized me. I don't remember Marla, though. In fact," she went on, looking through the rearview mirror to make sure Lee wasn't following them, "I'm trying to recall who he used to hang out with." She paused and sucked in her breath. "My God—it was Jimmy Tooms!"

Chapter 17

What's next?" Renie asked as they drove north through the Thurlow District.

"Home," Judith replied. "It's after four. Guests will be arriving soon. Besides, I think we learned some things today."

"We did?"

"First, why did Myrna Grissom quit her job managing Peebles Place? Retirement and nursing homes pay their managers quite well. You may not have been too far off the mark when you mentioned blackmail. Hush money might be more like it."

Renie stared at Judith. "You mean Marla and Lee offed Hector?"

"More along the lines of rushing the old guy to his heavenly reward. Nothing overt—just telling Myrna to avoid extreme measures to keep Hector alive. Being in his nineties, nobody would request an autopsy. If he was in pain, it might be the merciful thing to do. We should find out when he died."

Renie nodded thoughtfully. "It couldn't have been too long after Opal was killed. I'd guess within a year or two, given when they began planning the house. But it does make Annie O'Reilly's suspicions seem more credible. She was afraid to finger her boss."

Judith nodded. "It might also explain why Annie made it sound as if Myrna had fallen out of sight. She either conspired or knew too much, if in fact, Hector was hurried off to heaven. With their windfall, Lee and Marla could afford to give her a big raise."

"And," Renie pointed out, "they can keep an eye on her. Is Myrna now your number one suspect or are the Watkinses moving up on the list despite their alibis?"

"I'm not sure." Judith stopped at a red light not far from where she'd once toiled at The Meat & Mingle. "Lee knew Jimmy Tooms. If Jimmy hadn't been in jail, I'd wonder if the Watkinses hired him. For enough money, he might've been willing to knock off his ex. No love lost there, I assume. But that's impossible. However, Myrna suddenly goes up on the suspect list. Woody didn't note any alibi for her because he had no reason to suspect her."

"She was probably at work until five or six that day," Renie said. "Does time of death extend beyond five?"

"No. Five is the latest according to the M.E. Myrna should've been at work that afternoon, but that doesn't mean she couldn't have taken off. Peebles is probably only a five- or ten-minute drive from Opal's house." Judith picked up speed as they took the main thoroughfare to downtown. "The most curious thing about our visit is the house."

"In what other way than it's ghastly?"

Judith grimaced. "Maybe I'm crazy, but I think it's a sham. Yes, it's big and it's pretentious and it's ugly, but I don't think there's much to it."

"There's certainly not much *in* it," Renie said.

"Exactly. I wonder if a lot of that space is empty, which makes me think that maybe Lee and Marla are broke. Did they blow all their money on the house itself? Or is somebody blackmailing them? I don't mean Myrna—she may be paid to keep her mouth shut, but if she got too demanding, they could deal with her somehow."

"Hold it," Renie said. "Isn't Lee a part owner of a horse? You have to have money to get involved in Thoroughbred racing."

Judith glanced at Renie. "He got in, but can he get out?"

"Huh?" Renie made a face. "I'm baffled. What are you implying?"

"I'm not sure," Judith admitted, noting that the dark clouds now obscured the mountains to the west. "This case is so complicated. And yet I feel that like most murders, it should be rather simple. Man shoots wife in a fit of jealous rage. Two drunks get into a brawl and one of them offs the other one. Robber shoots store owner during a holdup. But this is different. If Woody couldn't solve it, how can I?"

"Because you're FASTO?"

"I don't feel very fast," Judith replied as they entered the tunnel at the end of the viaduct. "I feel as if I'm in one of these, but there's no light at the end of it."

Renie didn't respond until they were out of the tunnel and almost to the Heraldsgate Hill exit. "Did you and Woody ever reconstruct the crime scene? I ask because if there's one thing I'm good at, it's visuals."

"We didn't go into details, but everything was in his case notes," Judith replied, before slowing down to take the right-hand turn.

"That's my point," Renie said. "It was his first homicide. Even Woody might overlook small things that could help. I'd talk to him again if I were you."

"Maybe I will, but I hate to bother him." Judith slowed down even further to wind around under the bridge that went over the ship canal. "I'll try to call Ruby tonight at work, too."

"The missing link," Renie murmured.

Pausing at the six-way stop, Judith glanced at Renie. "Don't say that. I keep thinking that maybe Ruby *is* missing. And that's my worst nightmare."

When Judith arrived home a little after four-thirty, Phyliss was just leaving. "More rain's coming," she said, digging around in her coat pocket. "If I see the animals gathering two by two, I'll know we're in for it. I need a new bumbershoot." She held up a rain bonnet. "These things don't do much good in a deluge."

"You'll be fine," Judith assured her. "Judging from the clouds, the rain won't start until after you get home."

Phyliss's thick gray eyebrows came together. "You don't know the ways of the Lord. Those clouds could be bringing fire and brimstone, just like the Lord did with Sodom and Gomorrah."

"Make up your mind, Phyliss," Judith said, trying to be kind. "If it's fire and brimstone first, the deluge will put it out. See you tomorrow."

"It could even be clouds of locusts," Phyliss muttered before making her exit.

Judith checked phone messages first. There was a call for a mid-January reservation, a message from Auntie Vance saying that she and Uncle Vince were coming to town over the weekend, and the last one was somebody peddling carpet-cleaning services. Finding the listing for Peebles Place, Judith dialed the number and asked for the manager. She was put through to Emily Stromberg who answered in a brisk manner.

Judith had her latest not-so-small fib at the ready, giving her name to match what came up on her caller ID as J. G. Flynn. "Ms. Stromberg, this is Jennifer Flynn. I'm an attorney handling the estate of Hector Sparks, one of your former patients. We recently discovered a codicil to his will with a bequest to one of your employees. I know the delay is inexcusable, but these things happen. I refer to Erma Schram."

"I've been with Peebles less than two years," Emily replied. "The name isn't familiar. You should contact my predecessor, Margaret Glenn. She's working for the state in the Department of Social and Health Services. Would you like her number?"

"I'd appreciate it," Judith said, almost as brisk as Emily.

"Just a moment." There was a pause on the line. "Here it is. This is direct." Emily slowly and distinctly read off the number in the state capital. "I'm sure she'll be of more help. However, if you need to contact me again, feel free to do so."

Judith thanked her latest dupe and dialed Margaret. A recorded message came on the line. Maintaining her bogus identity, Judith rattled off her credentials and voiced her hope for an early response.

She'd barely hung up when the first of the guests arrived—a mother and daughter from Augusta, Maine. The next hour was taken up with more guest check-ins and the preparation of hors d'oeuvres. Joe arrived home at 5:40, looking grim.

"Traffic's a bitch," he complained, hanging up his jacket in the back hall. "I left headquarters at five. It took me almost half an hour just to get out of downtown."

"Next time leave earlier," Judith said as Joe gave her a quick kiss. "You're not on the clock."

"Maybe not," Joe conceded, "but the guy I'm checking out worked in Honolulu for several years so I had to wait for my contact there to get back from lunch because of the two-hour time difference." He paused to make drinks. "Anything happen around here besides Phyliss trying to show you the error of your sinful ways?"

"Well . . . Renie and I took a little trip this afternoon."

Joe's expression was ironic. "No kidding," he said, handing Judith her Scotch. "Dare I guess you went south?"

"We did," Judith admitted, proceeding to relate their experiences as she dished up the appetizers. "I'm not sure," she said in conclusion, "that we got any questions answered, but the trip certainly raised a lot of new ones."

"I like the part about the house," Joe said. "When will you ask me to find a pliant building inspector from the city to check out the place?"

"That's a good idea, but I'm not sure I want to put the wind up yet as far as the Watkinses are concerned. Though," she continued, slicing potatoes, "it might work as part of the gig about being a scout for *Modern Manse* magazine. Let me think about it."

"You do that while I change," Joe said, setting his glass on the counter. "You want me to take those appetizers out to the guests? I hear some of them heading for the living room."

"Please." She reached out to put her hand on Joe's sleeve.

"Thanks for not getting upset about my involvement in the Opal Tooms case."

Joe shrugged. "I'd like to see it resolved for Woody's sake."

"Say," Judith said, "would you mind calling him later to ask when Hector Sparks died? And ask if he can remember anything at the crime scene that might not be in his case file."

Joe looked vaguely pained. "Woody has always been thorough."

"I know, but even the most methodical person can overlook things that seem irrelevant."

"Okay, but I'll wait until Woody has time to decompress. It's in his interests, I suppose."

Joe carried the tray out to the living room. Judith turned up the heat on the frying pan for the fried potatoes and got out a heavier skillet for the steaks she'd bought at Sollic's. She was cutting some of the thicker ends off of asparagus when Gertrude sailed down the hall.

"Is my midnight supper ready yet? Where've you been, kiddo? I'm almost passed out from starvation."

"I bought special steaks," Judith said. "Dinner will be ready in about ten minutes. Do you think you can survive that long or did you run out of Granny Goodness Chocolates this afternoon?"

"Wouldn't you like to know?" Gertrude huffed, bringing her wheelchair up next to the stove. "Asparagus, huh?"

"Yes. Tomorrow night I'll make a boiled dinner with sauerkraut and nefle. I bought pig hocks, too."

Gertrude perked up. "Well. That's more like it. You've been gallivanting. Don't tell me about it. You must've been with my idiot niece. Deb called four times to say she couldn't get hold of Serena. She needs more Tums. She's down to her last three rolls. Deb, I mean, not Serena."

"Aunt Deb's a worrywart," Judith remarked, filling a kettle with water to steam the asparagus. "She likes to keep Renie hopping."

"It's good for Serena," the old lady declared. "Otherwise, she'd just sit around the house and make doodles she calls traffic designs. What's wrong with the ones that say 'stop' and 'yield'? They look fine to me. Who needs a bunch of squiggly stuff when they're driving?"

"You know Renie does *graphic* designs," Judith said, hearing the chatter of her guests in the living room. "Can you wait here until your dinner is done? I should greet my guests."

"You watch dinner while I greet your guests," Gertrude responded.

Before Judith could turn down the heat on the skillet, the old lady revved up her wheelchair and headed out of the kitchen. *Why not?* Judith thought. Her mother could pour on the charm when she was in the mood. It would be pleasant, she mused, if the old girl could do it on a more regular basis.

The phone rang as Judith was turning the steaks. Irked, she hurried to take the call before it went to voice mail.

"Ms. Flynn?" the pleasant voice said. "This is Margaret Glenn from DSHS. I was in a very long meeting this afternoon and only now got around to your request about Hector Sparks's heir who worked at Peebles Place. Is this a convenient time?"

"Of course," Judith lied, assuming her lawyerlike persona. "Thank you for being so prompt."

"I'm working from memory," Margaret said apologetically, "but I remember Erma Schram fairly well. She was hired as an aide, then later worked as a cook. She'd been divorced, but remarried and quit to move out of state with her new husband. Her employment at Peebles was to see her through until the decree was final. She also had some health problems. I don't have a forwarding address, but if memory serves, her second husband and his children lived in Idaho. Is that any help?"

Judith said it was—and thanked her for being so cooperative.

Her next task was to contact the restaurant at Wolfgang's in Little Bavaria. A deep male voice with a faint German accent took her call. Judith asked if she could speak to one of their servers, Ruby Tooms.

"Ruby does not work here anymore," the man replied. "Try her elsewhere." He hung up.

Judith peeked into the living room. It was empty, so Joe must have gone up to the family quarters. Frustrated, she hesitated briefly before calling Renie. It was seven-thirty. Bill Jones's moratorium on answering phone calls during the dinner hour had expired thirty minutes earlier.

Renie picked up on the third ring. "Do you miss me already?" she asked with unusual warmth.

"No. Why do you ask?"

"It's Nazi night on TV. I am *so* fed up with Hitler. Sometimes I wish he *had* escaped and was living in Jersey so I could sink one of my Manolo heels into his half-witted skull."

"As a matter of fact," Judith said, "I'm calling about a German."

"Hitler? Or my Manolos? Blahnik isn't German, he's Spanish. You can't borrow the shoes. Your feet are too big. Get your own. By the way, Uncle Al called about some basketball tickets for Bill and Joe. By chance, he was at the track today and ran into Jorge Gonzales. I'd mentioned him to Uncle Al when I called him outside of The Persian Cat."

"And?" Judith inquired as she sat down at the kitchen table.

"Gonzales—Uncle Al describes him as a real character, which means he's a good guy—started young as a jockey, but kept growing and became a trainer. I mention that because he encouraged Duke Swisher to help mend his broken heart by getting into the training business. Jorge alibied Duke, though he admitted he was a little vague about the time frame, being otherwise occupied that day. However, he knew Opal."

"You mean from seeing her with Duke at the track?"

"Yes," Renie replied. "He only met her a few times, but thought she was nice, if a bit flighty. On one occasion Opal was feeling sorry for herself because she had to leave the track early to work the evening shift. She didn't like that because she claimed there was another aide on that shift who was out to get her."

"Did Jorge have a name?"

"No," Renie responded. "He told Uncle Al it was a woman who was going through a divorce. Opal already had been divorced, and thought the other dame—quoting old-fashioned Uncle Al here—should be more sympathetic and not so mean."

Judith ran a hand through her shoulder-length hair. "That might be someone we sort of know—or knew. Let me tell you what I just found out about Erma Schram."

When she wound up her account of the phone call with Margaret Glenn, Judith finally remembered what she'd called Renie about in the first place at Wolfgang's. "Ruby's no longer working at Wolfgang's. The man told me to try elsewhere."

"Where *is* elsewhere?"

"I don't know," Judith retorted.

"If she's elsewhere, that probably means she isn't dead."

"I hope so, but I'm still worried."

"You know people in Little Bavaria. Put one of them on the case."

"Good idea. I'll do that tomorrow. Is Goebbels still bellowing?"

"No. That was Bill, bellowing at Himmler. Give yourself a break," Renie advised. "Pack it in for the night and relax. You sound tired."

"I am," Judith admitted. "Talk to you tomorrow." She rang off. Through the kitchen she could hear rain falling on the Rankerses' hedge, a familiar, yet soothing sound. The wind seemed to have died down and the only other noise from outside was a drip from a downspout Joe kept forgetting to fix. It seemed to hypnotize Judith, who felt she was falling asleep at the table. Five minutes later, she was heading for the family quarters, when Joe came out of the door on the second floor.

"Hey—I was just coming down. I talked to Woody. Are you on the way up or checking the guest rooms?"

"Up," Judith said. "I'm beat."

Joe took her hand. "Come on. I'll haul you upstairs. Maybe

you'd rather wait until tomorrow to hear what Woody had to say."

Judith saved her breath until they reached the combination sitting room and office. "No. If it's a list of items he thought he might not have officially noted, it shouldn't take long. I can let whatever they are roll around in my brain before I go to sleep."

"Okay." Joe picked up a computer printout from his desk and sat down on the settee next to Judith. "First off, Bernard—aka Brick—Frosch has no criminal record. Beaker Schram was in prison at the time of the murder, but he and Jimmy Tooms were in different facilities. Schram was serving a twenty-year stretch for attempted vehicular homicide." Joe's green eyes glittered. "He tried to run down his estranged wife after she got off of a bus in the Thurlow District, missed her, but seriously injured a couple of innocent bystanders."

Judith's jaw dropped. "My God!" she cried. "Maybe he tried to do the same thing with Brick."

"I wondered. Woody will check him out. Beaker got out a couple of years early for good behavior. Guess they didn't let him drive while he was in the slammer."

"But why would he . . . ?" Judith tried to revive her tired brain. "Never mind. Revenge on Herb for taking Erma—or Elma— away from him. He probably lurked about in the neighborhood, but the elder Frosch was at work and poor Brick was the default victim."

"Makes sense in the way people with no sense operate," Joe agreed, taking a sheet of paper out of the computer printer tray. "Without his case file at hand, Woody included some of the crime scene items that he noted at the time. By the way, Hector died January third, 1989."

Judith nodded, offering her husband a tired smile. "Thanks. And thank Woody for me."

"Will do." Joe handed her the two pages of items.

Strap used to strangle vic

Empty vase on floor (knocked over by Mrs. Crabbe?)

Unopened package that had been left on front porch

People and US magazines

Daily Star tabloid (May 27th edition)

Furnishings (undisturbed): sofa, side chair, recliner, end table, one floor lamp, one table lamp, footstool

Fireplace—no sign of recent burning

Mantel with photos of son, daughter, Opal (vic) with fiancé Darrell (Duke) Swisher, 3 figurines, 2 scented candles

Garden gloves (used) on coffee table

Dirt on carpet and residue on vic's shoes

Kitchen wastebasket containing old tabloid newspapers, aluminum foil, race card from previous weekend, six losing tote tickets (checked), ice cream bar wrapper, crumpled tissues (checked), empty egg carton, 2 receipts from Mel's Market, 1 from PayView Drug Store, 2 from Garden of Eden Nursery

Garbage can under kitchen sink recently emptied; outside garbage can also empty (pickup day in the neighborhood; can had been moved away from curb, indicating vic had probably retrieved it around 1 p.m.—estimated time of collection in neighborhood

No sign of robbery in vic's bedroom; costume jewelry seemingly undisturbed; small box containing engagement ring on dresser (given to her by Swisher); photo of son in navy uniform on dresser

No sign of drugs other than over-the-counter; no pot or other illegal items

"That's much more detailed," Judith said, still studying the list. "The only thing that leaps to mind is why the engagement ring was in its box. Maybe she didn't want to flash it around at work. Ruby indicated that Peebles wasn't exactly a high-class establishment."

"Maybe she broke up with Swisher," Joe suggested.

Judith grew thoughtful. "The picture of Opal and Duke was on the mantel. If the engagement was off and she'd removed the ring, I would think she'd also ditch the picture. That's what women do."

Joe grimaced. "Did you ditch my photo when I ran off with Vivian?"

"I never had a photo of you. I don't remember either of us ever taking pictures of anything."

"Just as well," Joe said with a roguish grin. "They might not have gotten by the censors at the photo shop."

"Joe!" But Judith laughed. "We did have fun, didn't we?"

Joe fingered her chin and kissed her. "We still do. It just takes longer for us to recover after we have it."

Later that night, as the rain splattered against the bedroom window and the last leaves from the old cherry tree fluttered to earth, Judith chided herself for not following up on Ruby. Checking her contacts in Little Bavaria would be her morning priority once the guests were fed.

I can't take on as much as I used to, she told herself, nestling down under the covers. *Ruby is a bit of a flake. Maybe I'm on a wild-goose chase.* She closed her eyes and drifted off to sleep. Dreams took her back to the snow-covered mountain town where a boxlike house of glass hung above the river and a dozen men in lederhosen tore up losing race tickets in the high school parking lot while a dachshund played the accordion—off-key.

Chapter 18

A little after ten the next morning, Judith decided against calling Suzie Stafford, the owner of the pancake house in Little Bavaria. She'd still be hustling breakfasts. Father Dash wouldn't show up in town until Saturday for the evening Mass at St. Hubert's and Ruby wasn't a member of his flock. She decided her best option was Jessi Stromeyer-Bosch at Sadie's Stories, the local bookshop.

Jessi was elated to hear from Judith. "I never got a chance to talk to you about your scary adventures with a killer," she said in her pleasant voice. "You were a big topic of conversation in town for days."

"I suppose things got a bit dull when Oktoberfest was over," Judith remarked diffidently. "I'm sure my role was exaggerated. I'm trying to get hold of someone my cousin and I met while we were in town. Do you know Ruby Tooms? She was a waitress at the Gray Goose Beer House and Wolfgang's Gast Haus."

"I've probably seen her," Jessi replied, "but I can't say I really know her. Barry and I had dinner at Wolfgang's Friday," she added, referring to her boyfriend, who was also Suzie's son.

"Ruby wasn't there that night," Judith explained. "She was here at my B&B. She lost her cell phone while she was in town and I can't get hold of her. When I called Wolfgang's they said she didn't work there anymore. I didn't check the Gray Goose, as I got the impression she only worked there during the town's big events."

"That's likely," Jessi agreed. "Jobs in a tourist town are very seasonal. Do you know where she lives?"

Judith searched her memory. "Not exactly. She might be in your phonebook. I do know that it wasn't far from Wolfgang's and near the railroad tracks."

Jessi laughed. "In a town this small, everything is near Wolfgang's and by the railroad tracks. Maybe Barry has some ideas. He's staying in town until after the first of the year before going back to his studies in Europe. I expect him to drop by later." She lowered her voice. "I've got a customer. I'd better go. Bookshops need every penny they can get these days. Take care and say hello to your cousin. Your number's on my caller ID." Jessi rang off.

Judith checked on her guests in the dining room. Only the mother and daughter from Maine were still eating. Their plans for the day included visiting relatives who lived across the Sound. They'd stay on at Hillside Manor until the following day, when they'd take the train to British Columbia.

Joe left around eight for police headquarters; Phyliss arrived with a new bumbershoot. A miracle, she insisted. Someone had left theirs on the bus that morning because the rain had stopped shortly after sunrise. The Lord had been good to her again, she declared, though she wished the umbrella wasn't plaid. Judith wished Phyliss would shut up. Or attend a church that didn't see God sitting at the controls of a heavenly computer commanding every earthly occurrence, but only getting credit for the good stuff.

Renie called shortly after eleven as the last of the guests departed for the day. "What are your plans? I'm freed up for the moment. I'm waiting for those dunderheads at the city's lighting department to figure out what they want for their new bill inserts. I suggested that in my case, they stop sending me a bill, but they demurred."

"No kidding," Judith said. "I'm mulling. Can you come over after lunch to take a look at Woody's list of the things he didn't include in his original notes? I was so tired last night that I may've missed something."

"Sure. Shall I dress for public viewing or wear my regular clothes?"

"Given that you look like a bag lady in your regular moth-eaten pants and worn-out sweatshirts, why not at least put on something respectable? And clean. Remnants of root-beer floats do not become you."

"Hunh. You sure are fussy. Okay—see you around one."

Judith decided to get an early start boiling the pig hocks for the sauerkraut dinner. She so informed her mother when she took lunch out to the toolshed a little after twelve. Gertrude seemed pleased.

"Nothing like old-fashioned food," she asserted. "Some of those fancy dishes you throw together are unidentifiable. Who wants beef covered in piecrust? And why is there cheese under a chicken breast that has some shriveled-up thing on top that might be bacon, but isn't. That's not real food—it's like one of those mysteries you try to figure out."

"I usually only make those recipes for company," Judith said. "My guests always seem to like what I serve."

"Even when you blow up your oven trying to cook them?"

"Never mind. That was partly your fault. By the way, Renie and I may go someplace this afternoon."

"I won't ask where," Gertrude replied, after biting into her salami sandwich. "I have a date."

"With who?"

"Carl. He's coming over to play cribbage with me. Now, there's a man who makes me wish I were twenty years younger. Or would it be more like forty? He knows how to treat a lady—unlike Lunkhead."

"I doubt Arlene will let you borrow him for anything more than an afternoon of cribbage. Have fun with Carl, Mother."

Judith headed back to the house. Renie showed up an hour later.

"How do I look?" she asked, twirling around in the kitchen.

"Much improved," Judith replied, taking in her cousin's forest-green slacks, black cowl-necked cashmere sweater, and black high-heeled boots. "You're clean, too. How come you got the car? Is Bill staying home this afternoon?"

"It's not raining, so he decided he'd walk up to the top of the hill and browse the bakery. Where's that list Woody gave you?"

Judith removed the two pages from the manila envelope she'd put them in earlier that morning. "I haven't gone over it since last night, so maybe I should take another look after you finish."

"Okay." Renie began to read through the items, but before going to the second page, she held out a hand. "Pepsi, please. I need fuel."

Judith produced a cold can of Pepsi from the fridge. "See anything interesting yet?"

"Wait until I'm done." Renie paused to swig down some soda. Judith waited patiently across the table. Finally her cousin looked up. "The losing tote tickets. People usually tear them up at the track. It's almost a reflex action. Nobody likes to hang on to a loser. Why did Opal do that?"

Judith thought for a moment. "If the tickets were for the last race or two, they may've left early and didn't know who won until they heard it on the radio or saw it in the paper. I recall doing that once or twice."

"True. Unfortunately, Woody doesn't say what race they were for. Think of another reason."

"Offhand, I can't."

"What if they'd won? Especially if they won big? They wouldn't care about losing tickets." Renie leaned forward. "I keep my tickets in my wallet until a race is over. If they're losers, I toss them. But if I won big, I might not bother. I'd be too excited."

"I understand," Judith said, frowning. "But I still don't get it."

Renie grimaced. "I'm not sure I do either, but it seems odd."

Judith thought for a few moments. "Let's say she and Duke did win big that day. I'm assuming she went to the track with him. Opal somehow strikes me as a person who would get very excited. Other people around her would know she won. Maybe she collected the winnings and took them home, but didn't put the cash in the bank. If so, we have robbery as a motive for murder. Woody wouldn't look for money he never knew existed."

"It's a theory," Renie said. "Come to think of it, wouldn't Opal have told Ruby about a big win?"

"Ruby was spending most of her time at Freddy Mae's when she wasn't in school," Judith reminded Renie. "Maybe Opal didn't have a chance to tell her." She sighed. "Let's move on. Anything else?"

"I don't think so," Renie said, after giving the list another look. "I'm wondering what isn't on this list that should be. No daily newspaper, but even back then not everybody was a regular subscriber." She leaned back in the chair, arms folded. "We're missing something."

Judith started to shake her head, but stopped. "The light bill."

Renie sat up straight. "Oh! The shutoff notice? But didn't Ruby say the bill got paid?"

"That's what I mean. Ruby never knew who paid it. Being a kid back then, she didn't try to find out."

"Swisher, maybe?" Renie suggested.

"He'd be the most likely." Judith was silent for a moment. "Did you say you were about to start a project for the lighting department?"

"Right. I've done work for them before. This is actually a fairly small job, though it's the kind that can bring out the nitpickers."

"Would they have billing statements from fifteen years ago?"

"They might." Renie frowned. "My contact in that department is fairly new. A woman . . . Janice . . . Santelli. I haven't worked with that group for a long time. Shall I call her?"

Judith hesitated. "Oh, why not? Ruby might want to solve that little mystery. That is, if she's still around to care about such things."

"Don't be so grim," Renie chided, digging into her purse for her cell. "Ruby may be job-hunting. I can dial the billing bunch from memory."

Judith resumed looking at Woody's list while Renie was connected with Ms. Santelli. Caught up in focusing on the items, she didn't zero in on her cousin's make-nice conversation until the mention of a familiar name grabbed her attention.

" . . . before you took over Marv Farrell's job," Renie said. "It's been a while. Take your time. Thanks so much for humoring me."

"Did you say Marv Farrell?" Judith asked as Renie put the cell back in her purse.

"I did. So what?"

"That's the name of the guy you accused me of picking up at the track, you idiot! Or are there two of them?"

"You never introduced me," Renie shot back. "How'd I know what his name was?"

"But it sounds as if you worked with him at the city's lighting department," Judith persisted.

"I did, a few years ago, but everything was over the phone. I never actually met the guy. You know how I hate meetings."

Judith held her head. "You're right. But I would've thought one of you might've recognized the other's voice."

"From business phone conversations? I assure you, I adopt a different persona when I'm working. Probably Marv did the same thing. And phones can distort voices to some degree."

"Marv knew those horse-racing people," Judith said. "So how does he figure in as far as this case is concerned? I remember now that he mentioned being transferred to another department after being a food inspector, but he didn't say which one." She shook her head in frustration and got up to pour herself a glass of water. "Instead of becoming clearer, this blasted case keeps getting murkier."

" 'Through a glass darkly,' " Renie murmured as Judith sat down to take a sip of water.

"I don't need quotations," Judith said. "I need help."

"I am helping. I'm talking about your glass. I think you just swallowed a bug."

"Awwrrgg!" Judith cried, staring at the almost full glass. "You're right. I mean you're wrong. I didn't swallow it, but there's something in the bottom." She got up and emptied the glass. "It's not a bug. It's just a speck that must have come off something in the dishwasher." She rinsed out the glass and poured more water. Before she could sit down again, Renie's cell rang.

"Hi, Janice," she said. "That was quick." She went silent, listening intently—and finally fretting her lower lip with her teeth. "Well. That's kind of odd, isn't it? . . . I see . . . Yes, it's good PR. Thanks, Janice. I appreciate your time and trouble. Let me know when you make up your mind about the insert project." Renie disconnected. "Opal's bill was marked 'paid in full' and initialed by one of their linemen who later became head of the billing section—Marv Farrell."

I wonder," Judith mused after the shock had worn off, "how Opal paid off that bill."

Renie looked somber. "With her body—or her life?"

Judith didn't respond right away. "Motive?" she finally asked.

It was Renie's turn to mull. "No sign of a struggle. I don't recall any indication about Opal having had intercourse recently."

"It was in Woody's case notes. She had, but given that she was engaged, that's not surprising. And Ruby was at Freddy Mae's house most of that week, so there'd be privacy for Opal and Duke. Not that I think Opal was overly fussy about such niceties. I'm not saying she'd flaunt her amorous activities, but . . . you know what I mean."

"Right. She'd close the bedroom door and try not to cry out too loud with ecstasy."

"Did Janice mention a date on the payment of the light bill?"

"Yes, but she cautioned that you had to allow up to four or five days between payment and posting. It was within the time frame, but barely, being posted the Monday after Opal's death."

Again, the cousins grew pensive. Judith tried to imagine how Opal would have reacted to a virtual stranger coming into her house. On her guard? Maybe. But if the person had a viable reason, she'd take him—or her—at face value. What apparently was on Renie's mind was another Pepsi. She'd gotten up to retrieve a second can from the fridge.

"The UPS delivery," she said after sitting down. "The package with the dress. Was it on the porch?"

"Yes. But that doesn't mean it hadn't been inside the house first."

"You mean if the delivery guy was the killer and he put it back out there after he did the deadly deed?"

"Right." Judith sat up straight and stretched. "We're going in circles. It's after two. Let's go question some people so we can become even more confused."

"Okay," Renie said. "I was beginning to think I got gussied up for nothing. But I'm taking my Pepsi with me. Who are we grilling this time?"

"We'll start close to home," Judith said, taking her jacket off the peg in hall. "We're calling on the Frosches."

"Hey," Renie cried, "they know me as the flower lady!"

"They won't recognize you. You're all cleaned up."

Renie looked skeptical, but kept her mouth shut for once. She even abandoned her Pepsi. The cousins went out the front way and crossed the cul-de-sac to the rental. After a long wait, Lainie opened the door.

"Yeah?" she said, looking wary.

"I'm Mrs. Flynn—you know. From Hillside Manor." Judith gestured toward her house. "This is my cousin, Mrs. Jones. We were wondering how Brick was getting along."

"He's still a mess, but he'll live," Lainie replied.

"That's encouraging," Judith said. "I spoke with Vivian, your landlady. Uh . . . would you mind if we came in for just a moment?"

Lainie looked as if she did mind, but after a long pause she stepped aside. "Go ahead. Herb's in the can. He's getting ready for work."

Judith glanced around the living room, which looked as if no one had done any housecleaning recently. The two easy chairs were covered with magazines and dirty TV-dinner trays. The sofa appeared to be where Lainie kept some of her clothes and cosmetics. She made no effort to clear away any of the clutter.

"What about Mrs. What's-her-name?" she asked.

"She wanted to know when Mrs. Frosch's funeral would be held," Judith said. "Vivian knew Mrs. Frosch from years ago. She'd like to send some kind of memorial."

"Herb decided not to have a funeral," Lainie said. "He's not religious. They cost too much. He had his wife cremated. Maybe he'll keep her ashes around for a while." She shrugged. "Whatev'. All I want is to go home. Brick and I only came over here for him to check out a race car that was for sale. Turns out he never got a chance to see it."

Judith put on her most sympathetic expression. "That's a shame. Will he be able to race again when he recovers from his accident?"

"It's not like it's any more dangerous than walking across the street. Not that Brick is going to win any big races. He's lost his edge. He might have to get a real job." Lainie made a disgusted face. "I didn't think I was hooking up with a loser. Serves me right for dissing Dirk McQueen. Oh, what the hell—my own fault. Bad judgment." She shrugged.

Judith was momentarily speechless. Renie spoke up, if only to prove she could talk. "You know who hit him?"

"No," Lainie replied. "Brick never got a look at him." She punched her fist into her palm. "It was like *blam!* He didn't come to until the next afternoon. A kid, maybe, going too fast and too scared to stop."

"Possibly," Judith allowed. "It must be especially hard on Brick to lose his mother while he's laid up in the hospital."

"Elma was his stepmom," Lainie said. "They never got along too good. His dad's okay." She glanced into the hallway. "Jeez, what's Herb doing in the can? Drowning himself? That sounds right about now with this bunch."

"We should leave," Judith said. "If you need anything, just——"

"I need a lot of things," Lainie broke in. "But you can't do any of 'em for me. Thanks anyway. See ya." She turned and headed for the hall, apparently to see if Herb was underwater.

"She's a piece of work," Judith said when they got outside. "Let's move on out. We'll take your car for a change. It's blocking the driveway."

"Fine," Renie said as they got into the Camry. "But I'd like to know where we're going. Directions will help me get there."

"Head downtown to Uncle Al's former café on Fourth Avenue. The owners keep up with the sporting world. I want to check their archives or pick their brains for a big win when Opal might've gotten lucky. I know the approximate date. Who knows? We might hear some gossip about the current racing crowd."

"Got it," Renie said, pulling out of the cul-de-sac. "I could use a snack about now."

"Go for it. What did you make of Lainie?"

Renie turned onto Heraldsgate Avenue, but slowed down as the traffic light at the bottom of the hill turned from amber to red. "She's a self-serving twit with not enough class to qualify as a gold digger. She'd be lucky to find an agate."

"You've nailed her," Judith remarked. "I wonder if Brick was really hit by accident."

Just before the light changed, Renie darted Judith a quick glance. "And if it wasn't, then you think . . . ?"

"Lainie's the one who hit him."

Chapter 19

Downtown parking during the day was at a premium. After circling around the immediate area where the Sporting Chance Café was located, Renie finally dropped off Judith and said she'd park in a garage about a block away.

Getting out in front of their uncle's former eatery and back-room betting establishment, Judith noticed that whoever now owned the place had done some refurbishing. The plain wooden door had been replaced with a Victorian-era oval of etched glass set in dark oak. Inside, the marble counter remained, though the dozen stools sported new green covers. The booths had also been reupholstered and the white globe ceiling lights were gone. Art Nouveau canopy shades hung in their place.

The café was fairly busy for midafternoon. Judith slid into an empty booth not far from the door. A young server with a black bow tie and long sideburns came over to ask if she was ready to order. Judith told him she was waiting for someone and was in no rush.

Five minutes passed and Renie hadn't shown up yet. Maybe the garage had been full. It wouldn't be uncommon during a work-day. Having studied the menu, she was putting it aside when she heard a familiar voice and looked up to see Marv Farrell leaning on the back of the booth.

"We meet again," he said. "It must be fate."

"Have a seat," Judith said, trying to hide her surprise. "But beware. My cousin is coming. Don't steal her food or drink this time."

"I've already eaten," Marv said. "I'm just hanging around for the race results."

"Funny you should mention . . ." She stopped as her cousin appeared.

"Good grief!" Renie exclaimed. "You didn't tell me you were rendezvousing with your secret lover from the track. Move over," she said to Marv. "And keep any other moves to yourself. It turns out we know each other. How's life after the billing section at the lighting department?"

"Good," he replied, looking puzzled. "How do I know you?"

"I'm Serena Jones, graphic designer. We only talked on the phone way back when."

Marv laughed. "I'll be damned. I always pictured you as a willowy blonde with blue eyes that could cut glass. You're a brown-haired squirt."

"I'm in disguise," Renie retorted. "Give me a menu or I'll have to hurt you."

Marv complied. "Why do I feel this meeting isn't accidental?"

"But it is," Judith said. "Our uncle used to own this place."

Marv frowned. "Al Grover? I remember him. Helluva guy."

"He still is," Renie said. "I want a hamburger and fries. I can make something I don't like for Bill tonight and then I'll have an elaborate snack before I go to bed."

The server returned. Renie gave him her order, adding a vanilla malt. Judith asked for chips and salsa. Marv mulled for a moment, finally saying he'd indulge himself with a slice of blueberry pie and a refill on the empty coffee mug he'd left at the fountain.

"Chips and salsa?" Renie said after the server had left. "That's a lame snack, if you ask me. And you're only drinking water?"

"I'm fine," Judith said, sounding irked. "I like chips and salsa." The truth was that it was the first item she'd glimpsed on the starter menu. Her brain was primarily engaged in thinking of ways to elicit information from Marv about his days as a lighting repairman in the Thurlow District.

It was Renie, however, who broke the brief silence. "Hey, Marv," she began, "is it true that after being a food inspector, you had to hit the streets—or should I say the wires?—to keep everybody out of the dark?"

Marv chuckled. "I sure did, but only for a couple of weeks to—as they put it—'get a feel for life in the field.' I wore a hard hat, but I never had to climb any poles, thank God."

Renie wrinkled her pug nose. "So what did you do? Watch other people climb poles and yell, 'Look out! Here comes a woodpecker!'?"

Marv didn't answer until the server had brought their beverages. "I checked on complaints, handled shutoff notices, did some safety inspections, whatever I could do and still stay on the ground."

The food arrived. Judith saw an opening of her own in Marv's recital of his experience in the field. "Wasn't delivering shutoff notices as dangerous as being up on a pole?"

He shook his head. "I probably didn't have more than a dozen. You just hang them on a doorknob and walk away. The customer's already gotten a notice in the mail. The hand-delivered ones state the exact date power will be shut off with a twenty-four-hour warning. More, if it's a Friday."

As far as Judith could tell, Marv was perfectly at ease. She decided to press the issue. "Did you ever have to deal with anyone face-to-face?"

Marv frowned slightly as he took a sip of coffee. "No. The closest I came was some old guy who was out in his yard. But it turned out he didn't live there. He was looking for his missing cat."

Renie scowled at Marv. "Are you sure he wasn't a burglar?"

"On a walker?" Marv shook his head. "I tried to help him find the cat. No luck."

Judith was getting desperate. The chips and salsa were making her thirsty. She'd already downed over half of her water. "Say," she said, as if taken by surprise, "do you remember a family from my old neighborhood named Tooms?"

"Tombs?" Marv said. "As in graves?"

"No." Judith spelled the name. "Meat & Mingle patrons." It was only half a fib.

Marv's face darkened. "Yes. I do. Wasn't the owner killed right after I finished working in the neighborhood?"

"That's right. I'd moved away by then, but I heard about it later." *Much later,* she thought. *Not a fib, just an exaggeration.*

"I think," Marv said slowly, "she was one of the customers I had to leave a notice for. I'd forgotten all about that. It must have been at least fifteen years ago."

"What do you do when that happens?" Judith asked. "Collect from the estate?"

"Sometimes." Marv's color had returned to normal. "Usually, that's not necessary. Survivors pay the bills, though it can take a while. Now that I think about it, somebody stepped up to pay the Toomses' bill. A relative, maybe. It's somewhat easier nowadays with online billing." He took another drink from his coffee mug. "Time for me to head home. My condo's only about eight blocks from here. It's good exercise." He stood up, got out his wallet, and tossed a five-dollar bill on the table. "For the pie. We've got to stop meeting like this." He winked—and was gone.

"I'm losing my touch," Judith murmured. "That was a bust."

Renie frowned. "Could he be innocent?"

Judith gazed up at the high ceiling. "Of what? I'm not even sure now what I thought he was guilty of. Maybe Duke Swisher paid the light bill."

Renie didn't speak until she'd eaten her last french fry. "We don't know exactly when Marv worked in the neighborhood. Does it matter?"

"I don't know what matters anymore," Judith admitted. "I

thought I could read people fairly well. Granted, Marv seemed just a tad shaken by my mention of the Tooms name, but maybe it was the memory of having had some sort of contact with Opal about the time she was killed."

"It could creep a person out," Renie said, before taking a sip from her malt. She frowned. "This is very good, but some of the malt's stuck." She blew lustily into the straw, splattering drops on the table. "Damn," she muttered, using her fingers to wipe up the mess. "At least I missed my cashmere sweater." She licked the residue off her fingers. "Don't look at me like that," she admonished Judith. "Nobody's watching."

"Missing," Judith said, as if she hadn't heard her cousin. "That's what's missing from Woody's file." She pointed to the spot Renie had just wiped clean. "Fingerprints."

Renie's eyes widened. "You're right. Apparently the killer didn't leave any. You're thinking premeditated?"

"Yes, possibly. Who'd carry around or wear gloves on a pleasant day in June?"

"Are we back to a guy on a pole?"

"I don't know. Unless . . ." Judith shook her head. "I have to refocus. Are you finished?"

"Almost," Renie replied, then polished off her malt. "Now what?"

"We check the boys in the back," Judith said, catching the eye of their server. "I wonder who runs the operation these days. In fact, I wonder what kind of ruse they use to keep it quasi-legal."

"The recent investigation of the police department obviously didn't shut it down or Joe would've told you," Renie remarked, taking out her Visa card as their server arrived. "For both," she told him. "My treat."

The server smiled and moved off to the register. "You didn't need to do that. I'll pay for parking."

"Yes, you will. It's twenty bucks for an hour during the day unless you have a monthly rate. I got off cheap."

"You're cunning, I'll say that for you," Judith said, getting out of the booth. "I'll head for the back room and meet you there. I'm still not walking quite as fast as I should today."

Renie arrived at the unmarked knotty-pine door almost at the same time Judith did. It was locked. The cousins both noticed a peephole almost hidden in one of the knots.

"Who's there?" an echoing deep voice inquired.

Judith saw some tiny circles that must be the speaker just below the peephole. "Al Grover's nieces, Judith and Serena."

There was a pause. Then the door swung open. "It's me, Swede Lundquist," the tall, broad-shouldered man with the snowy-white hair said. He held out a beefy hand. "How are you two scamps doing? I haven't seen you in ten, fifteen years."

"At least that long," Judith said, smiling up at Uncle Al's old chum from their basketball-playing days. "Don't tell me you finally retired from being a longshoreman."

"Just last year," Swede replied. "But I couldn't just sit around, so your uncle saw to it that I had something to do." He made a sweeping gesture at the large, paneled room where a couple of dozen people—all men—sat in comfortable chairs watching TV screens showing various sporting events and making notes on laptops, iPads, and old-fashioned paper tablets. "We privatized. You're now members." He reached into a beer stein and took out two small bronze pins with gold lettering that spelled out WIN. "I'll defer your dues for now. Or did you pay for some grub here?"

"I did," Renie said. "Can we grandmother her in? She actually has grandchildren. I, alas, do not. Yet."

"Sure. Al wouldn't have it any other way. How is he? I haven't seen him for at least a month."

"As far as we know, he's fine," Judith said. "Auntie Vance and Uncle Vince are coming down from the island over the weekend, so we'll probably have a family gathering."

Swede nodded. "I remember Vince when he drove a truck. Does he still go to sleep at the wheel?"

"Oh, sure," Renie replied, "but Auntie Vance stabs him with a fork and he wakes up."

"She's a character," Swede declared. "Got a real mouth on her. Great gal. Okay—so why are you here?" He looked at Judith. "You wouldn't be involved in one of your mysterious adventures, would you?"

"I would," Judith said. "*We* would, I mean. Renie's a big help. For starters, do you have archives from the old racetrack?"

"Sure. Got it all on the computer now, back to the early days in the thirties. I almost know how to run the damned thing. I can even turn it on. Come on into what I call my office. It's where I take my naps. Not as young as I used to be."

Swede's office was small, cluttered, and faintly redolent of cigar smoke. He lowered his husky frame into the old-fashioned swivel chair behind the oak desk. "Got dates for what you need to find out?"

Judith gave him the three weekend days she thought that Opal and Duke might have been at the track. "I'm looking for big winners," she said, "which would probably mean Saturday or Sunday."

Swede nodded once. "Got it. Early in the season, so could be some upsets. Not many big-stakes races then. And, as you know, no betting on any races but the local track."

Judith nodded. "That came along after the new course was built."

"Dang!" Swede exclaimed. "They don't make these keys big enough for my paws. Hold on. At least I got the right year."

Judith gazed at the walls, which were covered with all sorts of sports memorabilia including some from Swede's own ball-playing days.

"There's Uncle Al," Renie said, after joining her cousin in the stroll down memory lane. "Imagine—being a center back then at only six four."

"Got it," Swede announced. "Only one long shot that weekend, ninth race on Sunday. Went off in the feature at twenty to one. A five-buck bet would get you over a hunsky."

"That's it?" Judith said in disappointment.

Swede shrugged. "Depends on the amount wagered. Just do the math if you think somebody bet the house."

"True," Judith allowed, wondering if Opal—or Duke—had wagered more than a fairly conservative amount. "What was the horse's name?"

Swede looked at the screen. "Two-year-olds and up, winner was a local chestnut gelding trained by Jorge Gonzales, ridden by Omar Alvarez, horse was Duke's Dream. Is that any help?"

"It might be," Judith said, smiling. "That reminds me—do you know a trainer named Duke Swisher?"

"I've seen him around." Swede stared off into space for a moment. "Fairly successful, though he came late to the game. I think he spends part of the year in California." His blue eyes twinkled. "Hold it. Is there some connection between Swisher and Duke's Dream?"

"I think he may've bet on that horse in the race you just looked up," Judith said. "He's also got a stake in Ali Baba Stables. The other owners are Lee Watkins and a Mr. Alipur, who owns The Persian Cat in the Thurlow District, my old neighborhood."

Swede chuckled. "Oh, yeah. Mr. Alipur. Now, there's a slippery character. I don't know anything about Watkins, but Alipur ran book out of his joints in California. That's why he moved up here."

"But he's stayed clean since then?" Renie asked.

Swede shrugged. "Can a leopard change its spots?" He frowned. "Maybe snow leopards can. But not cats like Alipur."

"Interesting," Judith murmured. "We'd better leave you in peace, Swede. Thanks for the information. And the membership. We just might come by more often."

Swede got to his feet. "You do that. Next time the grub's on me. And tell your uncle to get his butt down here PDQ." He leaned across the desk to shake hands with the cousins. "Take it easy," he said. "And stay out of trouble. Odds are that if you look for it, you'll find it."

Back out on the street, Renie offered to get the car to save her cousin the three-block trek. After starting to insist she could manage it just fine, Judith gave in. It was the pavement that bothered her more than the actual walking. Besides, the weather was holding and she enjoyed watching the passing parade of downtowners.

When Renie showed up almost ten minutes later, she was cussing her head off. "All this damned traffic! Where do these people come from? Five minutes to go three blocks? That's galling!" She sped up though the traffic light was already amber and raced across the intersection, startling some pedestrians who had dared to take a step off the curb. "See what I mean? Nobody knows how to walk, let alone drive."

"Coz," Judith said, gritting her teeth as Renie pulled out into oncoming traffic around a car that was trying to pick off a vacant parking spot, "someday you're going to get arrested."

"Good. Then I can sit in a nice cell and work on my graphic designs in peace. Except," she went on, glaring at a young man who looked as if he might be thinking about jaywalking, "even our jails are too crowded. Half the people who move here must be criminals."

"Like Mr. Alipur?" Judith said in a mild tone.

"Huh? Yeah—like him."

The tactic worked. Renie seemed to calm down. The absence of opposition usually cooled her quick temper.

"I wonder," Judith continued, "if Ruby asked too many questions at The Persian Cat."

"I didn't know she asked any," Renie said in her normal voice.

"I don't know either, because she couldn't remember what happened after she got there."

"True," Renie agreed. "But what would she ask about that might alarm Mr. Alipur?"

"I have no idea." Judith sighed. "I should do some asking of my own—namely about why there was no mention of fingerprints in Woody's report. It's so obvious an omission that I assume the killer wore gloves. But it still seems strange. Again, I feel as if I'm missing something."

"I've missed quite a few cars in the past five minutes," Renie said. "Thank goodness we're almost to Heraldsgate Hill. Cammy's like a horse—she knows when she's heading for home."

Judith checked her watch. "It's a good thing we are. It's almost four. I wonder if Jessi has called back from the bookshop."

"Jessi? I didn't know you talked to her."

"I forgot to mention it. I asked if she could find out anything about Ruby. Barry's still around, so maybe they can track her down."

Renie had started up the Counterbalance. "Oh, great! I'm behind two buses. How many buses do we need on this hill? The city is talking about consolidating the four routes. The one on our side of the hill has never made much sense the way it zigzags all over the place until it starts the descent toward downtown. The only good thing is that the end of the line is just two blocks from our house. Not that I ever take the bus, but Bill does sometimes."

"I can't recall the last time I took a bus," Judith said as they waited for one of the two trolleys to pull out from a stop midway up the hill. "I suppose I could bus it to Falstaff's, but then I'd have to lug heavy bags of . . ." She went silent.

"What?" Renie finally said, before making the left turn off the Counterbalance.

"I just realized what *I'm* missing," Judith said. "Now, why didn't I think of that before?"

Despite Renie's badgering, she refused to give voice to her sudden insight.

"You know that when I get one of these weird ideas about a case, I have to mull before I tell anybody, even you. I want to be darned sure I'm not making a fool of myself."

"I've seen you do that often—and vice versa," Renie countered.

"But never when it comes to murder. That's different. I can't afford to be wrong." Judith opened the car door. "I may be crazy. Let me sort through a few things and then I'll tell all."

Renie surrendered. "Okay. You still owe me for parking."

Judith turned around before stepping onto the pavement. "If I'm right, Joe and I will take you and Bill to dinner—anyplace you choose."

"How about Paris?"

"Get real. See you later." Judith headed for the house.

The first thing she did was check phone messages. So far, Jessi hadn't called back. Phyliss apparently was still finishing the laundry in the basement. Judith could hear her singing float up the stairs in an off-key rendition of "Gladly the Cross I'd Bear." Upon one memorable occasion, Gertrude had listened to Phyliss butchering the hymn and said she thought her religion must be pretty dumb if they worshiped a cross-eyed bear. Phyliss hadn't taken kindly to the comment.

Feeling antsy—and not being able to endure the cleaning woman's attack on "The Old Rugged Cross"—Judith went into the living room and picked up the phone on the cherrywood table. She felt presumptuous about dialing Woody's direct number, but did it anyway.

She had mixed feelings when he picked up on the first ring. "Oh, hi, Woody," she said, sounding surprised, as if she hadn't realized *she'd* called *him*. "I hate to bother you, but I have a question that may sound stupid. It only occurred to me after going over your case file and it occurred to me there was no mention of—"

"Fingerprints," Woody said, chuckling in his rich baritone. "I wondered why you hadn't asked, but assumed Joe told you."

"Joe?" Judith said, feeling dopier by the second.

"Yes, but maybe he thought it was obvious. There weren't any, except for the victim's. If we'd had DNA back then, it might have solved the case. But of course that came along later."

Judith thought for a moment. "Did you keep Opal's gloves?"

"The ones she used for gardening? Yes. They're still locked up in the evidence room."

"You mean she had other gloves?"

"She may have, but we didn't go through all of her personal belongings. Nothing was disturbed anywhere else in the house and there were no traces of dirt past the living room, so it's possible that even Opal didn't go beyond there either. Reconstructing her movements before she was killed, it appeared that she'd come inside, sat down on the sofa or in one of the chairs, and was reading a magazine when the killer arrived. She'd put in quite a few plants and it was a fairly warm day."

"That's my point," Judith said. "Who'd be wearing gloves?"

"Wearing or carrying?" Woody responded. "Yes, that suggests the murder was premeditated. Time of death is tricky because it got much warmer as the day moved along."

"Oh!" Judith exclaimed. "I keep forgetting to tell you that Renie and I talked to a neighbor you didn't interview, Ziva Feldstein, who lives across the street from the Tooms house. She left town shortly after the murder occurred, but she saw Opal working in her garden around noon. Mrs. Feldstein spoke to her only in greeting because she was hurrying to catch the bus."

"That does move time of death up a bit," Woody conceded. "I gather you didn't get the impression this neighbor might be a suspect?"

"No, though she didn't think much of the company Opal kept." Judith paused, hoping that Woody wouldn't scoff at what she intended to say next. "I think the killer wore Opal's gloves."

"Yes, that's possible," Woody conceded. "But what does it prove?"

"Nothing, really. Except that if the killer is ever found and you still have Opal's gloves, you might be able to nail him. Or her. DNA, I mean."

"That's also possible," Woody said drily. "But first we have to find him—or her."

After she'd rung off from talking to Woody, she felt foolish, despite his assurances that he still believed in her logical and uncanny ability to sort through even the most baffling of homicide cases.

"Down in the dumps, huh?" Phyliss said, putting on her raincoat. "Feel like the Lord doesn't love you? Could be true, given the way you people worship pictures of some gal jumping up and down on a snake."

"The Blessed Mother isn't 'some gal' and she's *standing* on the serpent that represents Satan and evil," Judith asserted with less than her usual vigor. "Even you know better than that, Phyliss. It's symbolic."

"I know what I see with my own two eyes," Phyliss muttered. "Maybe you've got the epazootik. Isn't that what your mother calls it?"

"It's sort of a family saying," Judith said. "My grandmother used that term to describe any illness that hadn't been diagnosed."

"Hunh." Phyliss started for the door. "Then with all my troubles, I must have about twenty epazootiks. See you tomorrow." She went on her way in a flutter of black all-weather fabric and pious self-righteousness.

Judith checked in the arriving guests—two couples, one from Juneau and the other from Kansas City, Kansas. She'd keep the appetizers simple: a platter of prawns, vegetables, tiny sausages, two kinds of dip, and an assortment of crackers. By the time Joe came home just after five-thirty, she was peeling potatoes for the boiled dinner.

"You look worn out," he said, after kissing her hello.

"I'm frustrated," she admitted. "I think I'm getting somewhere with this case and then I think I'm nuts." She put her hands on his shoulders. "Were you serious about that pliant inspector for the Watkins house?"

Joe frowned. "Well . . . not really, but if it'd help Woody . . . and you . . ."

Judith smiled. "It might. You can tell whoever it is that the visit comes as a request from *Modern Manse* magazine."

"That almost sounds real," he murmured. "Hey—why can't I be the inspector? That'd save me begging a favor."

"I . . . why not? But you're working."

"I'm on my own time and I'm making progress. I could do it tomorrow afternoon. I wonder if Bill would like to go along? There's a new sporting goods place south of the Thurlow District that we've been thinking of checking out."

"Good idea. Bill's a trained actor. He'd be perfect."

"I keep forgetting that," Joe said, getting the Scotch down from the cupboard. "Just as well he gave up a career in theater to become a psychologist. He got all the drama he needs living with Renie."

"He provides enough of his own," Judith said. "Let him take the lead. You might start acting like a cop."

Even before taking a sip of her drink, Judith began to feel better. She was further buoyed by Gertrude's pleasure over the sauerkraut and boiled pig hock dinner, though she noted that Judith couldn't make nefle like Grandma Grover did.

"Nobody can," Judith said, "unless it's Auntie Vance."

"She comes close," Gertrude allowed.

"How'd you do at cribbage with Carl?"

"I beat the socks off of him," the old lady replied. "He's good, but I outpegged him six games out of nine."

"Good for you," Judith said, and on that note she went back into the house just as the phone rang.

"Hi, Judith," Jessi said. "Barry and I found out where Ruby lives, so we went over there after I closed the shop, but she wasn't home. The place was dark. Maybe she got another job."

Judith's rebooted spirits plunged. "If you hear anything, would you let me know? By the way, when we first met her she was hanging out with some guy named Burt. He's a blogger. Do you know him?"

"I don't think so," Jessi replied. "Maybe he was in town only for Oktoberfest."

"Very likely," Judith agreed. "Thanks for checking on Ruby. I realize you don't know her well, but what's your impression of her?"

"Just from seeing her on the job, she strikes me as kind of tough, but I sense it's a put-on to hide bad things that've happened to her."

"You're right about that. Someday I'll tell you her story."

"I hope it has a happy ending," Jessi said.

"So do I."

But Judith's worst fear was that the ending might have already come for Ruby.

Chapter 20

The phone rang just after Judith finished cleaning up from dinner.

"Dooley reporting in, Chief," Tyler said in a conspiratorial tone. "Silver sports car I saw earlier, possibly a Maserati, just pulled into the cul-de-sac by the Frosch house. Man got out, waited for someone to let him in, and went inside. Couldn't see who opened the door."

"It had to be Brick's girlfriend, Lainie," Judith said. "Herb Frosch is at work. I don't suppose you have to walk your dog. You could check out the make for sure and get the license number."

"I already took Barkley out before dinner, but I can do it again. To heck with Algebra Two. I'm on the case." Tyler rang off.

Judith stood in the kitchen, wondering if she dared peek outside from the parlor. It was dark and the view was impaired. But it was time to put out the Pilgrim and Indian figures Aunt Ellen had sent from Beatrice, Nebraska. She'd used corncobs for bodies, corn husks for clothes, corn tassels for hair, and corn kernels for eyes. Aunt Ellen had also made a Thanksgiving wreath out of sixteen-millimeter film strips that wasn't as appealing.

Joe had already headed up to the family quarters, apparently to talk to Bill about their roles as building inspectors. It took Judith at least five minutes to get the decorations from the basement.

By the time she went out to the porch, the sports car was still parked by the Frosch rental. Tyler was entering the cul-de-sac with Barkley, but stopped when he saw her. She moved her hands in a shooing gesture, indicating he should keep going.

By the time she'd arranged the figures near the door and hung the wreath, Tyler was approaching Hillside Manor. "Cute stuff, Mrs. Flynn," he said in a voice a trifle too loud. "How come those Pilgrims and Indians look blind?"

"The dots my aunt painted on the corn-kernel eyes wore off the first year I had them," Judith explained, speaking in a natural tone. "I consider the result symbolic. Both Pilgrims and Indians are blind to the fact that they belong to different races. A portent of things to come." She lowered her voice. "You got the license plate?"

Approaching the steps, Tyler nodded and also spoke quietly. "*M-C-Q-S-P-Y*. Maserati Spyder, first ones came out in '01. Not a race car. Serious wheels, though."

Judith zeroed in on the license plate. "*M-C-Q-S-P-Y?* I get the 'SPY' for Spyder, but . . ." Movement in the direction of the Frosch house caught her eye. "Come up on the porch, Tyler. Don't look around. I think somebody's coming out of the rental."

Tyler climbed the steps at a normal pace with Barkley at his side. Judith edged to her right, by the planter box and behind the large rhododendron that grew next to the porch.

"They can't see us, but we can see them," she whispered.

"I don't see anybody," Tyler whispered back. "The door's still open."

"Here comes the man," Judith said. "He's carrying a suitcase."

"And here comes the woman I saw in the Explorer. She's got a bunch of stuff."

"She sure does." Judith watched Lainie head to the Maserati while the man closed the door. "Lainie's leaving. I mean, really leaving." She stopped speaking, seeing the couple get into the car and pull out of the cul-de-sac.

"That license plate—I wonder if the 'MCQ' stands for Dirk

McQueen. I spoke to Lainie this afternoon and she mentioned his name. I gathered he's another race car driver she'd turned down in favor of Brick."

"Hmm," Tyler murmured. "Could that be a motive for running down Brick?"

"It wasn't a sports model that hit him. In fact, there's a much better suspect who drives a Nissan very like a witness's description of the car. He'll probably get collared very soon."

"Who is it?" Tyler asked excitedly.

"Wait until the arrest is made," Judith replied. "He's an old foe of the Frosches. Hey—do you want to come in?"

Tyler grimaced. "I better not. Barkley likes to chew stuff he's never seen before." He glanced down at the dog, who was looking up at his master with fond eyes and a wagging tail. "Any point in me staying at my post by the telescope tonight?"

"Maybe not as far as Lainie and McQueen are concerned," Judith said. "But who knows what else could happen around here. I wonder how Herb will feel about Lainie defecting."

"Mr. Frosch? Maybe he's glad to see her go."

Judith considered Tyler's words. "Yes. Maybe he told her to get out. Herb ought to know her a lot better than I do."

After Tyler left, Judith went out to talk to Gertrude. "Mother," she began quite seriously, sitting on the sofa's arm, "think back to the tall, dark, and handsome caller you talked to the other day. I know you told me what he said, but is there anything you might've left out?"

Gertrude narrowed her eyes at Judith. "You think I've got Alzie's?"

"No. But you insist you're deaf. And"—Judith softened her tone and smiled at her mother—"you also tend to be flippant when you tell me things. Think back to what the guy told you. Maybe I'll find more pig hocks in the next couple of days."

Gertrude gave her daughter a gimlet eye, but grinned. "You're not always so dumb, kiddo. Okay, for pig hocks, I'll try to remember. To tell the truth, I'm not sure what I told you in the first place. He didn't say all that much, in fact. Refresh my non-Alzie's memory."

It took Judith a moment to resurrect the conversation. "You already told me he didn't ask about Ruby, right?"

Gertrude nodded. "I didn't mention her either. No reason to."

"He wanted the lady of the house, not Mrs. Flynn or the B&B owner?"

Her mother nodded again. "No name. Just . . ." She frowned. "It wasn't exactly the lady of the house. It was the landlady."

"Oh!" Judith slipped off the sofa arm. "That makes sense now!"

"I don't suppose you'll tell me why," Gertrude chided.

"Yes, I will." She quickly explained about the sports car's return and Lainie's going off in it with her belongings. "The driver may not have been at the track when Renie and I were there. Silver sports cars aren't that unusual in this city. I think McQueen showed up that day to find Lainie, but didn't know exactly where she was. He may've had Joe's address as the rental contact and thought the landlady lived here. That explains his question. At some point in the last few days, he must have gotten in touch with Lainie or vice versa. And now they've taken off."

Gertrude frowned. "So what's it got to do with Ruby?"

"Maybe nothing, but when Mrs. Frosch was taken to the hospital, Ruby said she recognized someone. I figured it was the son, Brick Frosch. I was wrong."

"Wouldn't be the first time," Gertrude said. "Don't get your tail in a knot over it. You married two of your mistakes."

"Mother . . . please, stop," Judith said, getting off of the sofa arm. "Just when I was thinking what an old darling you really are."

"I don't want you getting used to that idea and me going all mushy on you like your aunt Deb does with Serena. Makes me want to puke."

Judith leaned down to kiss her mother's cheek. "Don't worry. I don't expect miracles."

"Neither do I," Gertrude retorted. "But I do expect more pig hocks."

Back in the house, Judith plotted her next move. The plan that evolved in her mind made her feel not just devious, but almost evil. She grabbed a paper-towel roll, a box of matches, and the phone. Moving purposefully to the front door, she went outside, removed Aunt Ellen's wreath, and set it on the porch. Then she called 911 and reported a fire.

Judith waited until she heard the sirens before putting the paper towels and the wreath on top of the rhododendron bush, but making sure they weren't too close to the porch. Lighting the paper, she rushed back inside to drop the matches in the elephant-foot umbrella stand. By the time the fire engine roared into sight, the flames had consumed at least half the paper. And, of course, the sirens had already attracted the Rankerses and the Porters.

"You're on fire!" Arlene cried. "Stop, rock, and roll!"

Judith moved into full view. "It's 'stop, drop, and—' " She broke off as the firefighters came racing toward the house, hose at the ready.

"Lordy!" Rochelle Porter exclaimed, hands pressed to her face. "Are we hexed? What will happen around here next?"

"Aren't we due for something *good*?" her husband, Gabe, replied. "There *is* a law of averages. Unless you're Job, I suppose."

As the hose went into action, Judith realized she'd better get out of the way and shut the front door. She barely made it before she heard a burst of water hit solid wood.

"What the hell's going on?" Joe demanded, hurrying down the stairs. "Is it a heart attack or a fire?"

"A fire," Judith said, forced to raise her voice to be heard over the high-powered hose. "Don't worry, it's not serious."

Joe stepped down into the entry hall. "Serious? Are you nuts?

It sounds like whatever's happening is right outside the house."

"It is. I'll handle it. Go ahead and watch TV."

Joe's face turned very red. "You *are* nuts! Tell me what's going on before I pitch a five-star fit!"

"Okay, okay! You never liked Aunt Ellen's Thanksgiving wreath anyway."

"Aunt Ellen's . . ." Joe seemed to deflate, shoulders slumping. "Right, it's hideous. *Was* hideous?"

Judith nodded. "I decided to get rid of it."

Joe ran his hand over his head just as the hose went quiet. "Okay. I'm beginning to figure out what's going on. Yes, there's some basketball on that I might enjoy. In fact, I'd enjoy watching a test pattern if they still had it on TV. I'll now leave you to your latest weird yet misguided scheme." He turned around and went back upstairs.

Judith cautiously opened the front door. The Ericsons, the Bhatts, the Steins, and some of the Dooleys—including Tyler— had shown up, but they'd all moved away from the house. Judith wondered if the firefighters were going to call for crowd control. The porch was awash, though the inevitable slant of most structures in Earthquake Country allowed the water to slowly but surely run down the steps onto the pavement.

Ignoring the smoking mess atop the big rhododendron, Judith scanned the firefighters for her prey. Sure enough, Jess Sparks was standing some ten feet away, making sure the hose didn't get caught in the low-growing plants around the rhododendron. As she realized he was about to walk away, Judith called his name. He turned around and mounted the stairs.

"You okay, Mrs. Flynn?" he asked.

"Yes, I'm fine," she replied, though not with her usual aplomb. "You'll need some kind of statement from me, right?"

"Yes, if you have any idea of how the fire started. But the battalion chief should be the one to talk to you."

Judith folded her hands, as if in prayer. "Please. I know you. I don't know your chief. I've had such a scare. Do you mind if I speak to you instead? Inside, of course. I have to sit down. I'm kind of shaky."

"Well . . . let me go ask," Jess said. He moved quickly down the steps.

"Judith!" Naomi Stein called. "Can any of us help?"

"No," Judith responded. "I have to talk to one of the firefighters. But thanks. The fire apparently didn't do much damage."

"Okay," Naomi said. "Let us know if you need anything."

"I will," Judith replied as Jess came back onto the porch.

"I can't get to the chief," he told her, "so I guess it's okay for me to take over. One of your neighbors has practically got him nailed to the engine."

Judith glanced at the onlookers, who were beginning to disperse. She saw Carl, but not Arlene. "It's probably the block watch captain's wife. She's very . . . involved. Let's go inside."

Judith allowed Jess to go first. Glancing at the Pilgrims and the Indians, she thought that the figures looked as if they'd lived long enough to survive the Johnstown Flood. But barely. *Oh, well,* she thought, *corn can withstand a little rain. They'll dry out.* She figured the battalion chief might be in worse shape by the time Arlene got through with him.

Judith offered Jess a seat in the parlor. "What do you need to know?" she asked, sitting in a matching chair.

"Have you any idea of how the fire started?"

"A prank, I suppose. Kids these days." She shook her head. "I assume there wasn't much damage?"

"Not that I could see," Jess replied. "That big bush was only scorched. It's a good thing we've had so much rain. We couldn't really tell what it was that got burned, though."

"It's hard to say," Judith said. *In more ways than one,* she thought to herself. Not everybody had a holiday wreath made out of filmstrips. Or so she hoped.

"Maybe trash kids picked up someplace," Jess suggested. "Just be glad it wasn't heavy-duty fireworks."

"My, yes!" Judith exclaimed, feigning relief. "Say," she said as if the thought had just occurred to her, "did you ever get in touch with Ruby?"

"No. I tried to, but I couldn't track her down in Little Bavaria." He frowned. "Are you sure she's still there?"

"Not really," Judith replied, sitting up very straight and shedding her air of distress. "I think something may have happened to her. Why don't you tell me the reason you wanted to meet her."

Jess removed his firefighter's hat and put it in his lap. "It's personal. How well do you know her?"

"Fairly well," Judith replied. "Granted, I only met her last month in Little Bavaria, but she stayed here for several days last week. I do know a lot about her past, though."

Jess studied Judith for a few moments before he spoke again. "I wanted to tell her something. In fact, it's something she doesn't know about her past." He cleared his throat and turned his gaze to the stone fireplace. "Ruby and I had different fathers, but the same mother. I wanted to find out if she had any idea about who killed our mother. She was Ruby's mother—and mine. My father, Hector Sparks, and Opal Tooms were lovers."

Judith realized she should have guessed. It explained so much, including the photo of Opal in a house with expensive decor, in Ruby's recognizing someone when the firefighters arrived at the Frosch rental, in her own reaction when she met Jess that there was something familiar about him. The resemblance between him and Ruby was slight, but it was there.

"Have you met Ruby?" Judith asked.

"No, but I've seen a picture. My father was in his sixties when I was born." Jess smiled wryly. "He was still pretty frisky, I guess. He didn't want to raise another kid. His legitimate daughter, Marla, was in high school about the time I was born. Her mother had died a couple of years before that. My father gave me his name and put money aside for my education, but Marla never knew about me—or my mother. I was raised by my uncle, Harold Sparks, and his wife, Patricia, over in a small town in the southeastern part of the state. They couldn't have kids. Aunt Patty died of leukemia when I was twelve and Uncle Harold got hit by a truck right after I finished high school. I wanted to try city life, so I moved to Oregon, later came up here and became a firefighter." He made a face. "Sorry. I didn't mean to tell you the story of my life. I should get back to work before the chief comes looking for me." He stood up and put his hat back on. "Are you okay now?"

Judith also got to her feet. "Yes. But one thing . . . when you came here before, you referred to wanting to get in touch with Ruby as 'a sentimental idea.' Was that the only reason?"

Jess looked embarrassed. "Well . . . no. My father was eccentric in some ways. In addition to providing for my education, he'd put money into a trust for me and for Opal Tooms. My share won't come to me until twenty years after his death. He thought young people couldn't handle money wisely. He stated in the trust that both money and people needed to mature." Jess laughed softly as they walked to the front door.

"Did Opal get her share?" Judith asked, knowing that her death had occurred before Hector's.

"I learned just recently that Opal was killed before my father passed away. Her money should've gone to her heirs. It didn't. I found out that Opal's son was in the navy, but not stationed around here. I decided to try to find Ruby first. I found out about the trust a couple of years ago because there was a stipulation that when I reached thirty-five, I should be advised I had money coming when I hit forty. A cushion against midlife crisis, maybe." He shrugged. "Another one of my father's quirks. I've tried to find Ruby ever since. All I had was a high school picture of her, but I recognized her the other day. I'm good with faces."

"You certainly are," Judith said, opening the door. "I'm surprised you didn't hire a private investigator to find her."

"Oh, but I did," Jess replied, standing on the threshold. "That's how I knew she was somewhere in the vicinity. Good night, Mrs.

Flynn. And a word of advice: don't ever play with matches."

Judith merely smiled.

Turn off the TV," Judith ordered Joe. "We have to talk."

Joe looked away from whatever Discovery Channel program he'd been watching. "Why? Is our marriage in trouble because you tried to burn down the house? I'm not holding that against you. It's better than having you face off with homicidal maniacs."

"I mean it," Judith said, collapsing next to him on the settee.

Joe muted the sound. "Just when I was about to find out the secret of the universe. Okay. What now?"

"Who, among your PI colleagues, tracks down missing heirs?"

Joe looked puzzled. "Anybody who wants to take on the assignment. I've never been asked to do that. Hell, I don't hang out with my fellow private eyes much. Why do you ask?"

Judith regaled him with Jess's story. "I wasn't sure he was telling the truth at first," she said in conclusion, "but it makes some kind of wacky sense, given what I can figure out about Hector Sparks."

Joe looked thoughtful. "I've heard of stranger things with rich people disposing of their estates. Hector's idea beats leaving his money to a pet ferret. It even makes sense about young people blowing a windfall."

"I agree," Judith said. "It also might explain why Ruby kept seeing the guy with the hooked nose and jutting chin. Maybe he was the PI. But would he be the one who drugged her and stole her purse?"

Joe touched Judith's cheek. "I've spoiled you with my utter integrity and high standards. There are some sleazebags in my profession, just as with doctors, lawyers, and maybe Indian chiefs. In fact, that one on the porch with the corn-kernel eyes looks suspicious to me. You can't look him in the eye because he doesn't have any."

"Skip that," Judith said. "Do you know any sleazebag PIs?"

Joe leaned back on the settee and stretched out his legs. "Not really. Woody might, but what's the point? The guy's doing his job and he earned his money. Nailing him could get his license suspended—if he has one—but what's any of that got to do with who killed Opal?"

"I've no idea," Judith admitted. "But I'd like to know why Opal's heirs never got their money. Maybe Hector's lawyers were sleazebags, too. Or dilatory, at best. I remember Aunt Deb talking about the attorney she worked for as a legal secretary and how he'd take forever to settle an estate, and sometimes so many years went by that the heirs had died."

"It can happen, I suppose," Joe said. "You see that sort of thing in the legal notices they run in the newspapers. But I still think you've gotten distracted. Focus on the murder itself. Your forte is in the details. You have some unusual gift for going beyond motive, evidence, opportunity—all the usual things we normal detectives consider."

Judith frowned. "Maybe you're right. I've gone offtrack."

"You'll get back on board," Joe assured her. "Dare I ask if the fire did any damage?"

"Only to the rhododendron. It needed pruning anyway."

Joe nodded. "Okay. Let's get serious here and find out what's going on in one of our parallel universes." He turned the sound back on. Judith snuggled up next to him and tried to keep her mind off of what was happening in her own little world of more mundane, but equally mysterious murder.

Chapter 21

Judith slept like a log that night. She remembered no dreams and woke up Thursday morning feeling refreshed. The B&B was booked through the weekend. Until early January, Hillside Manor would turn a solid profit. The weeks after that would be lean until St. Valentine's Day. Then would come the long, often dry, haul into spring. But she was used to the seasonal ebb and flow of guests. Despite the hard work and uncertainties of her chosen field, running her own business gave her a sense of pride.

"You should be ashamed of yourself," Phyliss declared upon her arrival. "Why don't you have that beautiful Thanksgiving wreath up on the front porch? And what happened to that big rhododendron out there? It looks as if somebody torched it. Is that one of your semipagan religious rituals?"

"I had a little accident," Judith replied, not wanting to go into details or let the cleaning woman spoil her buoyant mood. "Make sure you check on all the guest rooms. They'll be full tonight."

Phyliss harrumphed, but headed upstairs. Judith went into the dining room to make sure that the half-dozen people who were currently eating breakfast had everything they needed. The couple from Juneau raved over the waffles. The pair from Kansas City asked for powdered sugar. They didn't care for syrup on their French toast.

Joe called from police headquarters to tell Judith that Woody had sent him the original mug shots of Beaker—real name Lawrence—Schram so she could make sure it was the same guy she'd seen at the Frosch house.

"Add at least fifteen years," Joe advised. "I just faxed the pix. I'll hold while you take a look."

Judith tapped her foot while waiting for the delivery into the printer tray. She gasped before removing them. "Good grief! I never got to see much of his face, but this guy has a hooked nose and jutting chin!"

"I suppose," Joe said drily, "that's why he's called Beaker."

"That's not the point," Judith said excitedly. "He must be the man Ruby recognized from . . . somewhere."

"Hunh. You could be right. Any way to check it?"

"Well . . . maybe."

"You work on that," Joe said. "I've got to call Bill."

Judith dialed The Persian Cat. A recording told her to phone back during business hours. Frustrated, she sat at the kitchen table. The café didn't open for at least another hour. Crissy, The Persian Cat waitress, hadn't mentioned anything remarkable about the man who had been with Ruby. In fact, he hadn't sounded much like Beaker Schram. Judith found that odd.

"Hallelujah!" Phyliss cried from hallway, making Judith jump. "When I took the last load out of the dryer, one of those green washcloths was missing to that new set. I looked all over and I couldn't find it, so I asked the Lord to show me the way, and sure enough, there it was, in my other hand. When one door closes, another door opens, as they say."

"Good for you, Phyliss," Judith said halfheartedly.

"Amen," Phyliss declared, before going upstairs.

But for once, Judith realized Phyliss was right. There was one door that had only been half opened. She looked up the number of O'Reilly's Pub, hoping its owners were already on the job. To her relief, Annie answered on the third ring.

After reintroducing herself, Judith got to the point. "I'm trying to track down someone who may've been in your pub a week ago Wednesday afternoon." She described Ruby, adding that she might have been with an older man.

"Oh, yes," Annie replied. "They came in together, but she didn't look very happy about it. I wondered—given the age difference—if he was her dad. But they sat in a booth for a long time, drinking beer and eating snacks. She left first, and very unsteady she was, though I'm sure she hadn't had more than a couple of drinks. He paid their tab and left not long after that. Oh! There was one other thing . . . she didn't have a purse, at least not when she left. I suppose that's why he paid."

"Thanks, Annie," Judith said triumphantly. "You've made my day."

Annie chuckled. "I wish I could do that for everybody."

As soon as Judith hung up, the phone rang again. "Got to make this quick." Joe explained that Bill was taking the bus downtown around two and they'd drive to the Watkins house in their guise as building inspectors. After that they wanted to go to the new sporting goods store. If there was any big news, he'd call Judith. If there was some new winter fishing gear at the store, they both might be late for dinner.

"They're idiots," Renie declared when she phoned a few minutes later. "They'll pay big bucks for a bunch of flashy lures and high-tech reels, but still get skunked. What's the point?"

"Let them have their fun while I tell you about Beaker Schram."

Renie was aghast. "Why would he do such a thing to Ruby?"

"He somehow tracked her down, maybe via her cell," Judith replied. "He probably wanted to know if Opal had gotten Hector's money. If she hadn't, maybe Erma had, and he felt she owed him. The Frosches haven't been in the rental long enough to be in the phone book. Face it, the guy's a head case."

"He must be if he drugged poor Ruby. No wonder he stole her purse. It's a miracle he didn't take her cash, too."

"He's self-destructive," Judith asserted. "Beaker may be one of those guys who likes prison better than the 'real world.' Say," she said as yet another idea struck her, "why can't we show up at the Watkins place in our role as *Modern Manse* magazine staffers?"

"Because our husbands would kill us," Renie retorted. "This is their finest hour. We can't spoil their fun."

"How could we spoil it? Come on, coz, be a sport. They might get a kick out of it. It'd be a couples thing."

"The only kick we'd get is in our rear ends when we went sailing out the front door," Renie said. "You got any better ideas? I still have some free time. I haven't heard back from Ms. Santelli. I'm bored."

Judith thought for a moment or two. "What I'd like to do is call Jess Sparks to see if his PI could look for Ruby in Little Bavaria. But he should think of that himself. Besides, Jess was on duty last night when he came here to put out the fire, so he may be off—"

"What are you talking about?" Renie interrupted.

Judith realized she hadn't told her cousin about the previous evening's events. "Never mind. Get presentable and be here around one. I'll fill you in after I hatch a plan. I have to make Mother's lunch."

"Fine. See you in an hour." Renie rang off.

Judith hustled for the next sixty minutes, fixing Gertrude's meal, making a sandwich for herself, taking two new reservations, seeing that Phyliss knew what else needed to be done around the house, and realizing she should go to the grocery store, but that would have to wait.

Renie arrived at five after one, wearing a fitted brown faux alligator jacket, taupe slacks, knee-high leather boots, a trailing beige chiffon scarf, and a fawn-colored snap-brim hat.

"Good grief!" Judith exclaimed. "You look . . . overdone."

"But I'm presentable. It's Hermès."

"It looks more like Hisses," Judith said. "But it's certainly . . . something." She glanced down at her own navy tailored slacks and red sweater over a white blouse. "I feel very plain, if patriotic."

"Hey, 'America the Beautiful'—you do all the talking when we're on this gig. At least I can make a visual statement. I even borrowed one of Bill's snap-brim caps. Jaunty, huh? Let's hit it. We'll take Cammy. You can tell me all as we head out for wherever we're going. Start with how your rhododendron out front got fried."

After they'd settled into the car, Judith told Renie to head back to the Thurlow District, an order that her cousin grudgingly obeyed. By the time they'd reached the now-familiar turnoff, Judith had concluded recounting the previous evening's events— including the flora flambé by the porch.

Renie seemed bemused. "I kind of like your gimmick to get Jess Sparks to your house. But wouldn't it have been easier and even less dangerous to talk to him on the phone?"

"I couldn't take that chance," Judith said. "He might've been called to duty at any moment. Besides, I like to study people when I chat with them. Body language and facial expressions are crucial."

"True," Renie allowed. "I can't say I'm sorry you sacrificed Aunt Ellen's wreath. That was right up there with the Christmas tree ornaments she made out of pig's feet. Now where are we headed?" she inquired as they turned onto the Thurlow District's main street.

"The Persian Cat," Judith said. "I want another look. I'd like to know if Mr. Alipur is really running some sort of illegal operation behind the kitchen. Maybe you could fake a peanut allergy."

"Again? I had to do that in Little Bavaria. Give me a different job. Besides, did the clientele look like the sporting type?"

"Of course not. They seemed very genteel. A perfect cover."

"Okay." Renie slowed down as they came within a block of the café. "Somebody's pulling out. Maybe I can nab that spot."

To Judith's horror, Renie made a U-turn against oncoming traffic and almost plowed into a light standard when she went up on the curb. "Damn," she muttered. "I wish I had depth perception like other people. I could've sworn that pole was a couple of yards away."

Judith had a hand on her breast. "Honestly, someday you're going to get us killed!"

"That's your job, not mine," Renie said. "Oops! Looks like we're too late. The Persian Cat has flown the coop. Or fled the cathouse."

Judith turned to stare at the "Closed" sign on the door. "I'll be darned," she murmured. "Maybe Swede was right."

"Are we going to bust in anyway?"

Judith considered the idea. "No. It's probably impossible. There could be somebody still inside." She rolled down the window for a better look. "Everything's in place and tidy. It doesn't appear that the café was abandoned in haste. If the cops shut the operation down, they usually post an official notice. Maybe they haven't had time to do that. Or Mr. Alipur got advance warning."

"Now what?" Renie asked.

"Head for the former Tooms house. I want to study the neighborhood more closely."

"Are we calling on Ziva again? This time I'd like to be a Camp Fire Girl. An *old* Camp Fire Girl, of course."

"No. I think we've gotten everything out of Ziva that she knows. I'm more interested in demographics."

Renie pulled out into traffic, forcing a FedEx van to come to a screeching stop. "Gosh," she said, "I hope that's not one of the drivers who delivers to our house. I like those guys."

"Wrong route," Judith remarked absently. She pointed to the windshield. "Follow that bus."

"Okay. Why not? I don't see any cabs. I guess you're not ready to tell me what your recent insight is, right?"

"Not quite. I'm still mulling. Jess's revelations threw me off my pace last night."

The bus turned the corner three blocks away from The Persian Cat. After making one stop and going another four blocks, it stopped again. Two teenagers got off.

"Pull over," Judith said.

"Pull over what?"

"Just do it."

Renie managed to reach the curb without incident. "Now what?"

"We wait." Judith noticed the greenery of a pocket park by the bus stop. "Interesting," she murmured.

"What? All I see is a bus. Oh—the driver's getting off. This must be the end of the line."

"In more ways than one," Judith said. "Skip driving by the former Tooms house. We're going to catch up with the intrepid building inspectors."

Renie sighed. "I should have known. We're about to face off with the most dangerous adversaries of all time. Our husbands."

Judith checked her watch. "It's only a few minutes after two. They won't have arrived yet. Our timing is perfect." She dug into her purse to get her cell and dialed Woody's direct number. The call was transferred to a receptionist. Judith asked to have the precinct captain contact her as soon as he was available.

Renie scowled at Judith. "We need Woody? Now I'm getting nervous. At least he'll be armed. I don't think this jacket is bulletproof."

It took five minutes to reach the Watkins house. On this gray November afternoon, the stark structure clinging to the edge of the hill looked forbidding, reminding Judith of a giant bird about to pounce on its unwary prey.

Renie pulled up on the verge and gazed at Judith. "Are you sure this is a good idea?"

"It's the only idea," Judith declared. "See those packing crates in the driveway? I have a strange feeling that Marla and Lee are about to take off. It just dawned on me that the rest of the house wasn't empty because it had never been furnished, but because it's been cleaned out."

"Maybe they've already left," Renie said.

"We're about to find out," Judith replied as she got out of the car.

The cousins trudged up to the door. Renie pressed the bell.

The cheerful, nostalgic "Trolley Song" didn't fit its austere setting.

Again, Myrna Grissom took her time coming to the door. "Oh," she said glumly, "you're back. I suppose you want to see Mrs. Watkins."

"Yes," Judith said. "Is Mr. Watkins here? We only met him briefly on the way out the other day."

"He's here somewhere," Myrna said tersely. "I'll get the missus."

"Remember," Judith whispered to Renie, "you're French."

"Good thing I'm wearing Hermès," Renie whispered back.

Marla Watkins appeared in a flowing purple-and-black caftan. Despite her artful makeup, she looked tired. "Well!" she said with forced enthusiasm. "Does this mean we're going to be featured in *Modern Manx?*"

"*Manse,*" Judith corrected gently. "It's very promising. The final decision will be made Monday. You'll be available, I trust?"

"Of course," Marla responded. "Would you care to sit? The view from the solarium is a bit gloomy today, though."

"We were hoping Mr. Watkins could join us." She turned to Renie. "Isn't that right, Renée?"

"*Oui,*" Renie said.

"I think," Marla said, "Mrs. Grissom has gone to fetch him. He's downstairs in the saloon. We entertain there. It's fitted out like a ship. The water view, you know."

"It sounds elegant," Judith said as her cell rang. "Oh, excuse me. You and Renée go on ahead. I'll be right there."

"*Enchantée,*" Renie said. "*Merci.*" She followed Marla down the hall.

Judith hurriedly picked up the call. "Woody? This is Judith. I have to make this quick. Now, here's what I'd like you to do . . ."

It took her no more than a minute to give her instructions. Woody wasted no time with questions. Judith had just rung off when she saw Lee Watkins. He'd opened one of the sliding panels out of her line of sight while she'd been talking to Woody.

"What was that all about?" he demanded, his eyes narrowed.

"My editor," she replied. "He's in town and wants to see the house."

"Okay," Lee said. "Why don't I fix drinks for you and your helper."

"That's not necessary," Judith said. "We won't be staying long."

"It might take longer than you think." He smiled, but there was no amusement in his eyes. "Go on to the solarium. I'll join you there."

"Thanks," Judith said.

Lee disappeared through another sliding panel. Judith walked purposefully down the hall. Before joining Renie and Marla, she checked her watch. It was seventeen minutes after two. Not enough time yet for Joe and Bill to get from downtown to the Watkins house.

Marla was trying to make conversation with Renie, whose only rejoinders seemed to consist of *"Mais non," "Mais oui,"* and *"J'ai faim,"* which, Judith thought, meant "I'm hungry."

"There you are," Marla said, sounding relieved. "Renée and I were having a little chat."

"Où est le chat?" Renie asked, looking around the room.

"I think," Judith said as she sat down in one of the cubes, "she's asking where your cat is."

"We don't have a cat," Marla replied. "We don't care for pets."

"They can be a bother," Judith said. "By chance, I saw a smaller remodeled home similar in architecture to your house near the end of the bus line. Do you know if the same contractors built it?"

Marla looked puzzled. "I don't know the house."

"Never mind," Judith responded. "I wondered if there were more in this area like yours. The previous owner is a distant cousin, but I've fallen out of touch with her. You might know her—Opal Tooms."

Marla's face paled under her makeup. "I never heard of her," she replied after a brief pause.

Judith grimaced. "Are you sure? The Thurlow District seems like a close-knit community. How long have you lived here?"

"Forever," Marla asserted, rearranging the caftan's folds and assuming a casual air. "The name rings no bells."

Lee entered the room bearing a tray with four tall frosted glasses etched with the initial *W*. He set one glass down by the empty cube, handed another to Marla, and proffered the other two to the cousins.

"Drink up," he said, seating himself between Judith and his wife. "It's my special Bacardi and orange juice recipe. I call it my Knockout Punch." He laughed rather coarsely.

"Sounds intriguing," Judith remarked, pretending to take a sip and hoping that Renie would follow her lead. "Mmm, that has real bite."

"Yes," Marla said. "It's hard to resist."

Judith turned to Lee. "Your wife and I were just talking about Opal Tooms. Surely you remember her. Marla doesn't."

Unlike his wife, except for a blink of his chilly dark eyes, Lee seemed unmoved by the name. "Can't say as I do. Why do you ask?"

"She's a distant cousin," Judith said. "She worked at Peebles Place. One of our uncles was there before he passed away. That was years ago. I'd come out to visit him shortly before he left us." She paused to stare at Lee. "That's why you looked familiar! I saw both of you visiting an elderly man in the room next to Uncle Gordo. What a coincidence!"

Marla's face was expressionless. "I don't remember you."

Lee looked grim. "I do. Drink up, ladies. Yeah, I thought I'd seen you before, but it wasn't at the nursing home. You and your old man owned that Meat & Mingle joint. What kind of stunt are you trying to pull, Mrs. McMulligan?"

"I'm not and never have been Mrs. McMulligan," Judith declared, wondering where Joe and Bill were. She didn't dare glance at her watch, but knew it must be after two-thirty. "You must be confused."

Lee shook his head. "Oh, no. I heard you on the phone out in the hall. I don't know who you were talking to, but it sure as hell wasn't about magazines. Hurry up, polish off those drinks." He glowered at Renie. "Myrna remembers you, too, Madame Runty or whoever. You're not French, you're some kind of designer. Down the drinks and get out."

Renie gasped and slumped in her cube. The glass tumbled to the floor, spilling its contents in every direction.

"Renée!" Judith cried. "She's had one of her fits! Call 911!"

"Nice try," Lee said. "I guess you won't be leaving after all. Finish your drink, Mrs. McMulligan. Or do you need some encouragement?"

Judith set her drink on the glass coffee table. "Not until I know Renée is still alive. I can't lean over to check on her. I might dislocate my artificial hip." She turned to Marla. "Would you see if she's alive?"

Marla laughed. "It doesn't matter. You're both dead meat. I don't know who or why you're here, but you smell like cops to me. And you sure as hell know too damned—"

The doorbell sang "The Trolley Song." All heads except Renie's turned. Judith gripped the heavy glass coffee table with all her might and turned it over, pinioning Marla and Lee's legs against their cubes. They both screamed and swore in pain.

Renie scrambled up off the floor just as Myrna appeared with a man Judith didn't immediately recognize. The housekeeper opened her mouth to speak, but no words came out. Both Watkinses were trying to push away the coffee table, but the spilled punch had made the floor very slippery. As the man turned to look at Marla, Judith realized he was Beaker Schram.

"Okay," he said, taking a gun out from under his denim jacket and pointing it at Myrna's head, "where's my share of Hector's loot?"

Lee turned very red in the face. "Who the hell are *you*?"

"Never mind," Beaker growled. "You owe me. Which one is Marla?"

Lee gestured at Judith. "She is."

Beaker looked faintly puzzled. "You sure of that?"

Judith stood up, but was afraid to move for fear of falling. "I can prove I'm not if you'll let me get my purse."

Beaker scowled. "No tricks. Just pony up."

A terrified Myrna pointed to Marla. "She's Hector's daughter."

"You ungrateful bitch!" Marla shrieked, wincing from pain. She managed to point a shaky finger at Beaker. "I don't know who you are, but you're not getting any money."

Beaker looked briefly conflicted. "Fine. Then I'll just start shooting people. That way nobody gets anything but dead." He shoved Myrna farther into the room. "This," he went on, "is going to get messy."

A shot rang out. Judith sucked in her breath. Renie gasped. Myrna screamed. Lee swore. Marla groaned. Beaker fell to the floor.

The first person to speak was Bill. "As a city building inspector," he announced in his theatrically trained voice, "I believe there are some inherent hazards in this house. Either that or those two goofy-looking women have turned the table on the owners. Furthermore, one of them has trashed my cap."

Beaker was writhing in agony, gripping his left thigh. Joe put his Smith & Wesson M&P revolver back into his shoulder holster. Woody appeared immediately with backup. He busted Lawrence "Beaker" Schram for attempted assault with a deadly weapon. Marla and Lee Watkins, along with Myrna Grissom, were charged with conspiracy to commit murder. An ambulance arrived to take Beaker away, but he—along with the others—were first read their rights. After the perps were removed from the premises, Woody finally had a chance to speak to Judith out in the hall.

"I don't mean to question your judgment in any way," he said rather deferentially, "but which Watkins actually strangled Opal Tooms? You didn't tell me over the phone."

"Lee," Judith replied. "The end of the line for his bus route is just around the corner and a couple of doors down. Maybe you can get his DNA off of those gardening gloves. I don't know why Opal let him in, but maybe she knew him from taking the bus."

"Okay," Woody said, "but I won't charge him with the homicide yet. We've got enough to hold all of them for now. I don't know how to thank you for doing this. You put yourself and Serena in grave danger."

"We're used to it," Judith replied, though she was feeling a delayed reaction to the traumatic experience. "I think I want to go home now."

"Do that," Woody said. "I'll be in touch."

Joe, along with Bill and Renie, had come into the hall. "We're out of here, partner," he said, saluting Woody. "Your guys need some room to process the crime scene. Besides, I'm upset. I got to shoot Beaker, but I didn't have a chance to deliver my lines."

Woody chuckled as the two couples headed for the door. Renie was bitching about her jacket getting doused with her drink; Bill was griping about his damaged snap-brim cap.

"If Myrna's smart," Judith said as they went down to their respective cars, "she'll rat out Marla and Lee. Imagine—all that conspiring for a meal ticket."

"Meal!" Renie cried. "I really am hungry. It's too bad The Persian Cat has been shut down."

"What do you mean?" Joe asked.

"Illegal gambling," Judith said. "Don't you remember? I told you what Uncle Al's old pal Swede had to say about Mr. Alipur."

Joe laughed. "I heard you. I checked him out this morning through vice. He's clean. At least in this state."

"Then," Judith inquired, "why is the café closed?"

"Alipur's a Muslim," Joe replied. "It's Eid al-Fitr, one of their big religious deals. I read about it in the paper the other day."

"Oh." Judith got into the MG. "I guess Renie and I jumped to conclusions. By the way, what took you so long getting here? I was beginning to panic."

"The bridge was up," Joe said, starting the classic sports car.

"I should have thought of that," Judith murmured. She looked at Joe. "I was beginning to think time was up for Renie and me. I knew it'd take Woody longer to arrive."

Joe shot Judith a sidelong glance. "You were never in much danger. Woody sent backup from the local precinct. They parked out of sight, then went around to the west side of the house a few yards down the hill where no one inside could see them."

"I wish I'd known that," Judith murmured.

"No, you don't," Joe said. "That would've taken the fun out of it."

Judith didn't comment.

Even before they got home, Judith called Renie on her cell, inviting the Joneses to dinner. Her cousin protested, saying she thought the B&B was full up and it'd be an imposition. Judith, however, persevered.

After the Flynns got home around three-thirty, Judith admitted she was suddenly overcome with fatigue. Joe told her he'd take over with the guests and make dinner. With a tired smile and a grateful kiss, she headed up to the family quarters to take a nap.

Just after five-thirty, Joe came into the bedroom to wake her up. "Sorry, but Woody has to talk to you. Don't get upset, but I think you blew this case."

"What?" Judith croaked, still fogged with sleep.

"It's okay," Joe assured her. "He's on the line. I'm going back downstairs to finish the appetizers."

Judith fumbled for the phone on the nightstand. "What's wrong?" she asked, still feeling drowsy.

"Well . . . let's say you were half right," Woody said. "It wasn't Lee who killed Opal. It was Marla."

"Oh, no!" Judith shrieked, suddenly alert.

"Lee wasn't on that bus route the day Opal was killed," Woody explained. "He took over for a sick driver. I didn't believe him at first, but when Marla insisted she didn't remember that, I got suspicious. Sure enough, they got into it and Lee ratted her out. No love match there, at least not anymore. Lee knew Opal. He hung out sometimes with Jimmy Tooms—you'll get a kick out of this—at The Meat & Mingle. Jimmy was often too drunk to drive home, so Lee would give him a ride. He got to know Opal and had a thing for her. Nothing came of it, but Marla got jealous, which strengthened her motive to kill Opal. According to her confession, Marla was working at The Garden of Eden that day and made an unrecorded delivery to the Tooms house."

"Wait," Judith interrupted when Woody paused for breath. "You mean the nursery receipts were from two different days?"

"No. Opal must've bought the dahlias that morning at the nursery. Maybe that's what set Marla off, so she showed up with the primroses later. I vaguely recall a box of flowers in the yard, but I didn't think anything about them. The devil's in the details, I guess."

"That's where I screwed up, too," Judith said in disgust. "Ziva Feldstein mentioned seeing those primroses on her way back from the bus. I flunked."

"No, you didn't. You still found the killer."

"Yes, but . . . oh, never mind. I'm just glad it's over. But I'm still worried about Opal's daughter. Can you put out an APB on her?"

"I can," Woody said, "but we usually wait ten days. Are you sure she's really missing?"

"I can't be completely sure, but . . . okay, I guess we might as well hold off. Maybe I can try to reach her brother." Judith still felt tired. "Say—was the house empty?"

"Bare as a bone. They were heading for Grand Cayman. We don't know why, but it may involve some unethical legal doings. We have to talk to some lawyers. The Watkinses have gone through quite a bit of their money, especially lately."

"I had so many suspects," Judith lamented. "The UPS delivery person, a lighting department guy, the bus driver—and I blew it."

"The case is solved, Judith. I couldn't do it in over fifteen years. You did it in less than fifteen days. I owe you."

"No, you don't," she said. "You and Sondra are friends. That's what friends do. There's no payback in friendship. We're all in this together."

"So we are. And isn't that the best way to be?"

Judith came downstairs a little after six. The guests were in the living room, Gertrude had her "supper" in the toolshed, Joe was in the kitchen, and the Joneses were on their way to Hillside Manor.

"Woody brought you up to speed, right?" Judith said as she picked up the drink Joe had made for her.

"Right." He looked up from the salad he was making and grinned. "Nobody bats a thousand."

"I know, but . . ." The front doorbell rang. "That can't be Renie and Bill," Judith said. "They come in the back door. I'll get it. You're busy."

Glancing into the living room, she saw that her guests seemed to be enjoying themselves. She'd greet them after taking care of her unknown caller. Maybe it was Jess Sparks, making sure she hadn't set fire to the Pilgrims and Indians. Judith opened the door—and felt weak in the knees.

"Ruby!" she cried, oblivious to the young woman's male companion. "You're safe!"

Ruby threw her arms around Judith. "I'm not only safe, I'm married! Is it okay to come in?"

"Of course!" Judith stepped aside just as Joe entered the hall.

"The prodigal guest has returned," he said. As the dark-haired man followed Ruby inside, Joe asked if he should set two more places.

"Ohhh . . ." Ruby seemed uncertain. "What do you think, Win?"

He shrugged. "I'll check the conditions on the pass. It could be dangerous driving to Little Bavaria if it ices up later on. I left my cell in the car." He headed back outside.

"Come into the parlor, Ruby," Judith urged, taking her by the arm.

Joe wagged a finger at their allegedly missing guest. "You had Judith in a tizzy. Did I hear you say you got married?"

"Yes! Last Monday. I never made it out of town. We honeymooned at the Cascade Hotel. It was heaven!"

"Good for you," Joe said. "The Joneses should be coming along through the back door. I'll check on dinner." He headed for the kitchen.

Judith and Ruby sat down in the matching chairs. "How did you meet—Win, did you say?"

Ruby nodded. "Winston Flugelhorn. He was working as a private detective, just like Joe. In fact, that's how we met. Would you believe he's been following me ever since I got here?"

"Actually, I would," Judith said, thinking of the PI Jess Sparks had hired, the handkerchief in the laundry with the initial *F,* Crissy the waitress who stated that the man with Ruby had a name like a musical instrument, and that Ruby no longer worked at Wolfgang's, but hadn't been in town since she left Hillside Manor. It made sense, in a weird way.

The whole story tumbled out. "I'm still fuzzy about what happened in the Thurlow District, but Win filled me in. I was headed for O'Reilly's Pub because it was another of my dad's hangouts when it was Spooner's Schooners. Do you remember Burt the blogger?"

Judith nodded. Ruby smiled. "Kind of a dud, but he called me a week before I came here. He'd decided to do a series on ex-cons and rehabilitation. Burt knew my dad had been in prison, but later died, so he asked if I knew any other people who'd done time. The only one I could think of offhand was the guy who'd been married to Erma Schram. So who should I run into in front of the pub? Beaker Schram! I'm still fuzzy about this, but I guess Burt contacted him. Beaker had recently gotten out of jail and was trying to track down people who he thought had inherited money from Hector Sparks."

"That's true," Judith said, and was about to explain what had happened to Beaker, but Ruby kept talking.

"I'd told Burt I was coming into town and staying at your B&B." Ruby grimaced. "Maybe I was desperate. I figured Burt was better than nothing, especially if he sold his blogs as a magazine series. Anyway, I guess Burt told Beaker I was in town. He—Burt—showed him a picture he'd taken of me during Oktoberfest. Beaker recognized me when I got off the bus a few doors down from O'Reilly's. He stopped me on the street and we went into the pub. Everything after that is a blur."

"But you left the pub and went to The Persian Cat," Judith pointed out. "You were with Win by then, right?"

Ruby smiled. "So he tells me. He didn't come inside the pub, but he saw me leave and noticed I didn't have my purse. Win watched me go into The Persian Cat, but waited to see if Beaker was coming out of the pub. When he did, Win accused him of stealing my purse. Beaker argued, but Win threatened to call the cops, so he handed over the purse and took off. Win didn't realize I'd had my journal in it, but the money and credit cards were still there. Not that I remembered any of that. Win came into The Persian Cat, realizing I'd been drugged. He wanted to take me to the ER, but I wouldn't let him. I mean, I didn't know him, but he seemed nice and . . . he finally brought me to your place."

Judith was puzzled. "But you ended up at the wrong house."

Ruby looked chagrined. "I passed out before I got to the B&B. By the hedge or your garage, maybe? No clue. Somewhere along the way I dropped my purse. I don't know how I ended up at the Rankerses' house."

"What happened to your cell?"

Ruby giggled. "Win kept it so he could make sure he wouldn't lose me. He had to wind up his PI gig before he could ask me out. Saturday he called there when you and Joe weren't around to ask if I could meet him for dinner and . . . well, you know. Before I left, Ozzie phoned, asking me to meet him at the residence inn where they were staying. I had Win stop by and wait in the car so I could pop in to explain I had a big date. Ozzie got ticked off and started lecturing me. I left." She grimaced. "I didn't want you to worry about me, so I dropped off the note saying I was with Ozzie and Freddy Mae. I didn't want you to think I was a floozy. So Win explained everything and he was so sweet and so kind and so . . . really *incompetent* as a detective. I mean, he was only doing it as research for his next novel." Ruby suddenly sobered. "He's very successful, but doesn't write under his real name. Flugel-horn doesn't fit thriller novels very well. He writes as . . ." She leaned closer to whisper his nom de plume.

Judith's jaw dropped. "You're kidding! I've read two or three of his books. He's not only a best-selling author, but an excellent writer."

"Please don't tell anybody," Ruby begged. "Not even Joe. Win's a very private guy. He never, ever makes public appearances. Readers terrify him. Can you believe he's never been married?"

"I can believe anything right now," Judith admitted. "Did Win manage to finish his PI assignment?"

"Yes, but he hasn't reported back to his client yet. I've no idea who hired him, because it's confidential. I didn't bug him about it because we were so . . . preoccupied. And room service was to die for."

Judith refrained from saying that she thought Ruby had died for something else. "Did you ever make up with your brother?"

"Win had called him, but he was back in San Diego. He's such an old woman sometimes. It's being in the military, I guess. Anyway, he was worried that I was trying to snoop around about Mom's murder. I told him I'd given it up—I was in love. That *really* pissed him off!" She giggled some more. "Besides," she went on, "solving an old case is hopeless, even with DNA. Oh—here comes Win. What'd you find out, lover boy?"

"Snow in the forecast," he said. "We'd better get going. Sorry, Mrs. . . . Flynn? Thanks for taking care of my little lamb chop."

Judith and Ruby both stood up. Win put his arm around his bride and leaned down to kiss her. He had a strong chin and an aquiline nose. The man of Ruby's dreams was now a reality, but, Judith realized, more eagle than vulture. "If you ever come this way," she said, "don't forget about Hillside Manor. It's not the Cascade, though."

Win smiled. "We're off to Rome next week. Maybe coming back?"

"You bet," Ruby said. "This place feels kind of like home." She blew a kiss to Judith as they went down the stairs.

Renie practically flew into the hall. "Where are they?"

"Off to Little Bavaria," Judith replied, still reeling from the visit.

"Damn! I missed seeing them. What did Ruby think when you told her you'd solved her mother's murder?"

"I didn't tell her," Judith said as they headed back to the kitchen, where Joe had prepared their drinks. "I'll wait until Ruby and Win have their first big fight."

"Something's off," Bill asserted.

Joe frowned as he handed Judith her Scotch. "I wonder if this guy knows about Ruby's future inheritance. Maybe he married her for the money."

"No," Judith said, before taking a large swallow of Scotch. "You're both wrong. He has his own money."

"Wow," Renie all but whispered. "I can't believe it. A happy ending for Ruby? It's almost too good to be true. On the other hand, sometimes life does sort of even out. I don't suppose you told her about her half brother, Jess?"

"I didn't have time to tell her much. She came and left like an autumn breeze." Judith paused, hearing the newlyweds' car drive away. "Ruby deserves to be happy. There's no point in rehashing all this tonight. After a stop in Little Bavaria, they're off to Rome." She raised her glass. "To Mr. and Mrs. Flugelhorn. Ruby has gone with the Win."